survived by

ebonee monique

Survived By
A novel by Ebonee Monique

Copyright © Ebonee Monique, 2026
ISBN-13: 979-8-234-05779-2

Roanoke & Kin, LLC.
P.O. Box: 390531
Snellville, GA 30039

RoanokeAndKin.com

Marvin: My superhero. I love you.

Elle: This is for you. I love you more more than infinity x infinity. There's nothing you can't do. Nothing you can't be. Go do it.

To my family: I am because of you. Thank you for the prayers, sacrifice, support and love.

prelude

Have you ever aimlessly searched a crowd of faces? Investigating green, blue, and brown eyes for some sort of familiarity? Maybe you've studied the physical attributes and hairstyles of someone, hoping that a make-over could have altered the looks of the person you're searching for. My eyes darted from wide noses, small noses, big hands, little hands, freckles and moles – all while trying to find an ounce of reason to believe that this person could be the one to end my search. But it never ends. For some reason, the heart has a tendency to embrace the truth long after the mind has.

Do you know what it feels like to stand in a room full of people and only be able to run one name, one voice, and one face through your mind? It's beyond the point of obsessive, and just below pathetic; and yet, the search for closure has no shame. It's like running around a group of people with your zipper down, exposing everything below the belt. And while you want to zip up your pants and cower in a corner out of sight, your hands are frozen, your eyes are set, and your mouth can't utter the words that your heart is dying to say,

"Help me!" It's like walking in a never ending circle with a blindfold over your eyes, restricting your vision, your heart, restricting your emotions and your soul, restricting your growth. The on-going cycle of finding a sense of peace, while standing in the dark, can be pretty amusing to the unassuming. Close your eyes and imagine the never-ending circle you're in, and think about what you would do to get out.

This is my daily routine. Welcome to my world.

Before you start thinking I'm an overly-dramatic obsessed person, let me take you to a time when I was far from the person I slowly became.

chapter one

Dear Diary,

I wish I could say that today was out of the ordinary, but it wasn't. I woke up and found Pop asleep with the remote in one hand, and a cold beer in the other. I swear he works too hard, and for no reason at all. I've told him over and over that I make enough money to take care of him; and yet he still works day in and day out driving The Marta. As selfish as it sounds, it just looks bad to have my father, of all people, driving a city bus while I make the money I do. But it's what he needs to do for himself, I guess.

The contractors haven't been by in two

days, and I think I'm officially through with their services. Every day I go back and forth about whether it was a good idea to completely redo the house I grew up in. Pop said he didn't want to move out of Bankhead, and that the best gift I could give to him was to remodel the house, and raise the property value in the neighborhood. Isn't it like my father to think about all of Bankhead instead of just himself? I have to say, though, I like knowing that I'm giving back and still staying in the house that has given me so many memories. Kenya asked me the other day if I was considering buying a spot closer to the radio station, but I told her I'm going to stay in Bankhead until I can't anymore! Her exact words were, "If it was me, I would be kissing Bankhead goodbye and Buckhead hello!" I love my girl, but she doesn't have any idea how much this neighborhood means to me. I can't just up and leave; I can understand Pop not wanting to either. Not only would we be walking away from our beautiful house, but we would be walking away from mom; I just can't do that.

I'm going in early to work this afternoon to record some commercials for Lenny. Brendan and I were supposed to meet for breakfast this morning, but he said he had a couple of errands to run for the shop. I used to see him every night, but lately it's like I barely get a glimpse of him. Hopefully that will change soon. Our anniversary, and my birthday, are both coming up and I can't say I'm looking forward to the latter. I'll be twenty-seven years old, and I'm just now realizing I'm not a spring chicken anymore! But the station and a couple of my promoter friends are throwing me a birthday bash, so I guess I should be happy about that, right? Someone is banging on the front door. Gotta go!

Lauren Washington

———

There I stood in my Morris Brown t-shirt, dingy sweat pants, and floral house shoes, with my hair standing on top of my head and my hands on my hips. It always amazes me that the moment a woman decides to let herself relax – be it a facial, pedicure, hairstyle experimentation, or the dreaded monthly waxing – someone is bound to show up and catch her looking like Herman the

Munster. Today, it seems, was my chance to flaunt my just-rolled-out-of-bed-breath-banging-like-Bruce-lee look.

"Yeah," I said, trying to lace my voice with plenty of attitude to let the short White guy in front of me know I meant business.

Glen Towers had been signed to remodel my house, and yet, he had been absent for two days.

"L-Lauren, hey ma'am," Glen said nervously.

I stood my ground and leaned my head back with a look of confusion on my face.

"Glen, it's been two days since y'all came by here, and now you show up at 8:00 in the morning ready to work?" I shot back.

Dropping his head, Glen stood back and stuffed his hands in his tight, dirty Levi jeans. He was wearing a plaid shirt with a Nike ball-cap that allowed his dirty blond hair to peek out slightly. He looked as though he hadn't taken a bath in days, and he reeked of alcohol. From what I discovered, his wife left him five years earlier, and it seemed as though his life was on the fast track to destruction.

Kenya was amazed that I had even hired Glen to work on my house.

"I just don't understand why you'd let a drunk, like Glen, work on something so special to you," she said in disbelief.

There were two reasons why I had agreed to let Glen get the job. Number one: my father.

"He needs it, Sugar Baby," Pop said, yawning one evening over dinner.

Pop knew which words would pull at my heart strings. The nickname, Sugar Baby, had been something he and my mother had called me when I was growing up. According to him, kisses from me tasted sweeter than any Sugar Daddy he had ever eaten; and since I was his baby, he quickly threw the nickname my way.

"Just give him a chance," he said, winking his eyes at me.

While I love my father, I wasn't completely sold off of the "he needs it" spiel; which leads to the second reason why Glen got the job, despite his alcoholism and questionable background.

Simply put, he is the best contractor in all of Atlanta. Drunk or not, no one else in the city could touch Glen's years of experience. That being said, Glen signed on to complete the work on my house within nine months. It's now six months into the job, and I can't see the end being anywhere near.

"I-I understand Lauren, and I apologize. I've just been busy with a couple of other jobs, that's all," Glen said, not making eye contact with me.

I rolled my eyes and stepped back, allowing him into the partially-completed house.

Ladders, dust, tools, and complete disarray were all I could see as we walked into the house and looked around. I fanned my hands around as some of the sawdust flew in my face, agitating me.

"Look, Glen...I'm paying you close to half-a-million dollars to remodel this house. Now, if this is too much for you and your guys to handle, we can always..." I started, knowing I didn't want to finish the sentence.

I wanted Glen to get his money, and even more importantly, I wanted my house completely revamped. Waving his grimy hands in the air, Glen cut me off with a sheepish grin.

"I promise, Lauren. Trust me. We'll have this completed in time," Glen said, glancing around the mess and debris in the room.

"Okay," I said, crossing my arms across my chest. I didn't want to be a bitch, but this *was* a lot of money I *was* investing in this house, and it had to be tight.

I strolled into the kitchen and mixed up some eggs, bacon and grits for me and Pop, and I quickly devoured my portion. I glanced around the room as the workers piled in the door and began hammering and sawing throughout the house; I was content.

Maybe a stern talking to was all Glen needed, I thought as I headed to my room to shower and change.

I quickly jumped in and out of the shower, threw on my t-shirt, jeans, and designer flip-flops, and stood in front of the mirror contemplating how to do my wild hair.

My jet black tresses, which hit the middle of my back, were a gift and curse. On one hand it came in handy by making any hairstyle I could ever fathom a possibility without a weave. But, on the flip side, when it got hot in Atlanta, I wanted to parade around like Sinead O'Connor with nothing but my scalp to catch the cool breeze.

As I stared at myself in the mirror, while letting the curling iron heat up, I smirked.

"I look just like mom," I whispered to myself as I turned my head and checked out the side profile.

My mom's name was Kori Bordeaux-Washington. From what I could remember, she was the best mother ever. She worked as an officer for the Atlanta Police Department. Pop tells me she was a tough woman too. When she was pregnant with me, she worked a desk job, for safety reasons; but two months after my birth, she was back on the streets of Atlanta tracking down criminals.

Now, as the pages on the calendars turn and my face and body matures, I seem to miss her.

Even though she died when I was nine, I still wake up to the sound of her voice.

I wasn't like the rest of the girls in the neighborhood who had their mothers by their sides. I didn't have anyone's clothes to play dress up in, I didn't have anyone to help me get ready for my high school prom or tell me about menstrual cycles, and I didn't have anyone to talk to me about men; but I think I made it out of my adolescence okay.

For as long as I can remember, even before mom died, Pop made sure he had a firm grasp on my life.

As I curled the ends of my thick hair, I made sure to smooth my edges down. My hair had always been thick, yet manageable and long , just like mom's. My butter-pecan skin glistened from my moisturizer; and while I normally wouldn't bother with makeup, I was feeling good that day and opted for a little mascara, eye shadow, and lip gloss.

I smoothed my shirt, which stopped just above my belly button, and checked myself out in the floor-length mirror in the bathroom before gathering my things to leave.

I kissed Pop on the head before jetting out of the house and into my brand new silver Volkswagen. I had opted not to get a Mercedes or Range Rover like everyone told me I should have, because I wanted to stay as grounded as possible.

What's the use of staying in the 'hood' if I'm not putting my money to good use?

So, with that said, my home remodeling project started, and I quickly forgot about the heated luxurious leather seats that my dream Range Rover had. I turned the volume up with one hand as I searched my junky purse for my sunglasses.

It was a beautiful day outside. The sun was beaming down without too much heat, the breeze was blowing effortlessly, making the trees sway from side to side, and little kids were out playing in the streets with their bicycles and jump ropes.

"Hey Mystique!" They yelled out to me, referring to my on-air name. I waved back with a huge smile on my face; it felt good to be recognized because it hadn't always been that way.

During my college years, I had taken an internship at V104 in Atlanta; and within two years, I got a weekend spot hosting a slow jam show. At first I was confused about what I would call myself; I even considered "LW" "Lauren Wash" and "L Boogie," but Brendan told me he liked the name Mystique. He said it reminded him of me because of my mysterious side. And just like that, Mystique was born.

Making the jump over from the well-known V104 to the newly revamped 104.5 "The Buzz," was a transition; but I dealt with it, and I quickly became the most listened to DJ in all of Atlanta during the 7:00 p.m. to 11:00 p.m. slot.

I was amazed at how much money could be made in radio. In a huge market like Atlanta, the sky is literally the limit. But I got into radio as a way to deal with my mother's death, not to make money. It gave me an opportunity to shut off Lauren Washington's problems and act as Mystique – the woman of confidence, beauty, and fearlessness.

As I drove down the crowded interstate, I glanced over and saw a woman staring at me. In a split second she was motioning for me to roll down my window.

"Are you Mystique from 104.5?" The thirty-something-year-old woman said as she shoved her glasses on top of her head to get a better glimpse at me.

Smiling widely, I nodded my head. "Yes, I am." I felt kind of guilty about liking the attention.

The woman began clapping her hands and screeching.

"My daughter just loves you," the woman said as the car behind her began honking. We were in bumper-to-bumper traffic, and now wasn't the time for socializing.

"Tell her to call the station," I yelled. "I'll get her a Buzz gift pack!"

I praised the car gods as my lane began moving, leaving the ecstatic mother of one of my fans in the dust. It wasn't that I didn't want to mingle, but the day was so beautiful I wanted to take it all in with no interruptions.

It was a rarity for me to be up so early in the morning, even though I knew the monster traffic that lay ahead of me. I guess you could call it denial. Every time I thought the traffic gods were shining a light on me, I ended up with my hands on top of my head, a fistful of hair, curse words spewing from my mouth, and a poor excuse for a driver in front of me. But this was Atlanta, and as much as I gripe about it on and off air, I love it here.

As soon as I exited I exhaled, knowing the worst was behind me. I barreled into the parking lot of the radio station and sighed heavily as I saw the car of Lenny Shaw, the program director for 104.5 "The Buzz," in my assigned parking spot.

"Dammit, Lenny," I said as I parked in another spot, and headed toward the glass building…bypassing a teenager who looked like he was trying to hustle his way in.

"Lady, they ain't letting no one in," the brown-skinned, cute kid said.

"Oh really?" I said, putting a hand on my hip.

"Yeah…they told me it would be another hour or two before I could even drop my single off," he said, smacking his teeth as he looked up at the tall building.

I tried my best not to smile as I reached for my badge and swiped it across the electronic entry way.

"Thanks honey," I said, turning to find his mouth wide open. "But I'm good."

I loved when people second-guessed me.

When I started my job at 104.5, people told me I wouldn't last longer than a month; here I was, five years and millions of dollars later. The person I had replaced when I started had been an aging White man who was a bigot. He had bigot fans, bigot co-hosts, and a bigot program director. The only thing that remained after I started on air was the bigot Program Director, Lenny; I could deal with that. After the station switched formats from Talk Radio to Urban R&B/Hip-Hop/Talk, I slid right in and never looked back.

"Y-yooo, ma!" The cute kid stuttered as he slung his foot in front of the door and tried his best to keep it open. I looked down at his foot and shot him a look that let him know to quickly move it.

"My bad," the kid said, moving backwards. "I'm Dee."

I crossed my arms and listened as he rapidly went through a seemingly scripted introduction.

"I got this rap group and…and…we're called Rhymesters. We've got this new joint that I think you'd like. We're from Atlanta, and we work really, really hard; we're just trying to come up," Dee said, sparking my curiosity. I was always interested in helping fresh talent out of Atlanta. He looked as though he couldn't have been more than fifteen years old.

"What's the name of the song?" I asked.

"Um…y-y-yeah it's called…i-i-it's called "Rhyme it out" a-a-a-annd it's h-h-hot." Dee said getting so excited he was stuttering over every other word.

I smirked as I saw the CD dangling from Dee's skinny fingers. Grabbing it from him, I looked the simple CD over and shook my head.

"How old are you anyway? Shouldn't you be in school?" I said, sounding more like a mother than I'm sure he wanted.

Dee crossed his arms and quickly dropped his head. "I'm thirteen and these streets is my school," Dee said, sounding confident in his improper reply.

I shook my head and wished I could tell him to get his narrow behind in school. But I understood his frustrations and desperation for success. While some teenagers in Atlanta depended on their parents' million-dollar salaries and big names, people in my 'hood' knew about struggles and hustles from day one. There were no parents with big dollars to help out, or big names to lean on. If you wanted to shine, you had to hustle to make it happen; otherwise, you were just someone on the sideline watching it happen.

"The streets aren't always going to be there for you," I said as I turned and started to walk away.

"Do you think you could get Mystique to play it on-air tonight?" Dee asked sincerely.

I chuckled with my back to him and spun around with a straight face. "I *am* Mystique, Dee."

"O-oooh," Dee stuttered as he finally looked me in my eyes as if he had seen a ghost.

"I'll listen to this. Make sure you tune in; maybe it'll get picked for the local spotlight," I said, turning to walk away. As the doors closed, I glanced at the disk in my hand, and made a mental note to *actually* give the CD a listen.

Walking into the radio station, my mind went back to my stolen parking spot.

"Lenny, do you know you parked in my spot *again*?" I asked, rolling my eyes while passing his junky desk.

Lenny Shaw was one of the most well-known men in radio; with over forty years as a disc jockey, thirty years of that as Program director of the ever-growing 104.5. Known for his ignorant racial jokes, distinctive voice, and hilarious dry humor...Lenny was one of the few people I could say I disliked.

"I didn't figure you would actually be on time," Lenny said without looking up from his computer. He was an old man with troll-like features. Wrinkly skin, huge nose, complete with massive nose hair, smoker's breath, and eyebrows that had taken on a life of their own.

I sucked my teeth as I made a joke in my head about Lenny's bald spot. *That's exactly why your ass is bald,* I snickered as I tossed my purse on top of my desk.

Lenny and I hadn't always irked each other. When I started working there, we would walk on egg shells around each other. We were working closely, after all, and to make the situation uncomfortable wouldn't be smart. But our clash was inevitable; a joke turned into a smart comment, which turned into the silent treatment, and finally created the environment we call work.

"Why wouldn't I be on time, Lenny? You asked me to be here at 11:00 and I'm here," I said, turning my computer screen on and moving the mouse around a few times.

"Whatever," Lenny said under his breath.

I started my daily routine of searching for entertainment, and local and national news to try to incorporate into my show. As I reached across my desk for a highlighter, I knocked over a picture of me and Brendan. I loved that man.

Growing up, I had never been one of those girls who was waiting on "Prince Charming" to come and rescue me; but when I found Brendan, I all of a sudden felt free. A slight glance from him would ignite butterflies in my stomach while my heart fluttered with excitement. My best friend Jasmine, who is married with twin girls, told me the butterflies, giggling, and PDA would die down over time; but I just couldn't see it happening with us; we were different.

Women ask the question all the time, "When do you know he's *The One*?" I've known that Brendan was *The One* from the moment our hands met. It was a feeling I hadn't yet had - even at the age of nineteen - when we met.

My man, Brendan Deondre Lewis, is everything I could've ever dreamed of. Born in New Jersey; he, his mother and older brother - Ms. Pat, and Terrence - relocated to Atlanta when he was nine. He is a professional; the owner of a very successful barbershop and beauty salon named "Cutterz," a romantic, an intelligent, and he can be a roughneck.

When you have a man who has the eyes of Boris Kudjoe, the skin of Morris Chestnut, the body of Shemar Moore, with the smooth thug appeal of Jay-Z, what else would you expect me to do but feel butterflies about him?

I reminisced as I stared at the picture of me and Brendan cheesing widely in front of a Ferris wheel, sporting matching jeans sets from Old Navy. Brendan and I have been dating eight years this coming Friday. I know, I know. My friends say it all the time…"Damn! When are y'all getting married?" It's not that I don't want to be Mrs. Brendan Lewis, it's just I'm not trying to rush Brendan into anything *he's* not ready for. I know he loves me, and it's beyond what a ring can say. I also know neither one of us is going anywhere. We started dating a day after I turned nineteen; he was twenty-one and still fine as hell. Regardless of the circumstances of how we met, it turned out to be one of the best days of my life. I remember it like it was yesterday.

To commemorate the ten-year anniversary of my mother's death, the Atlanta Police Department named a street after her, not far from our house, in recognition of all her years of service to the department. To show their support, it seemed like all of Atlanta came out. The streets of Bankhead were packed, and I was having a hard time concentrating on anything in particular. I glanced over my shoulders and saw hundreds of people smiling and waving in my direction. It was the type of attention I didn't want. As they replaced the old street name with Kori Washington Way, my heart sank. I gripped Pop's hand as I saw a tear roll down his cheek. We both had done a good job of desensitizing our emotions when it came to mom, but I was no longer a nine-year-old little girl; I was the woman of my house and I had learned to pick up where my mother had left off. I glanced into the crowd and saw friends from school, neighbors, and even some people I had never met before; and in the blink of an eye, Brendan appeared right behind me with a tissue.

"Here you go," he said slowly as he handed me the napkin. I hadn't even realized that I had been crying.

"Thanks," I said nervously, taking the napkin from the handsome stranger.

Nothing else needed to be said between the two of us. As he stood directly behind me and Pop, I felt a sense of security I hadn't felt since the day I found out my mom died. After the ceremony, Pop eagerly invited everyone over to the house for a fish fry; just like Mom would've liked. As I strolled down my familiar street, with Jasmine silently walking beside me, I finally spilled the beans.

"Did you see that boy who was behind me while they were changing the street sign, Jas?" I said, kicking a rock as kids ran past us.

Jasmine Wilkes has been my best friend since pre-k and she knows me better than I do. In comparison to Jasmine I was chopped liver, or so I thought. Jasmine had skin the color of coffee beans, and long curly hair which she always slicked back in a tight bun. Her body, from the time we were children until right before she had her own babies, was banging. Her 36D breasts were attention grabbers, while her ass, hips, and flat stomach were the envy of every girl on the block.

Additionally, she had the face of a supermodel, and the mouth of a sailor; guys flocked to her like a magnet.

"You mean Brendan?" Jasmine said, looking up from the ground. I could tell something was bothering her that day as well. I shrugged, hoping she would continue.

"I guess."

Jasmine smiled and bumped me with her big hips before continuing.

"You like him? He's fine, girl! And he's twenty-one!" she said, getting excited as she jumped up and down. "Y'all would be so damn cute together!" I rolled my eyes in embarrassment.

"Shut up Jas, damn." I said, pulling her shirt toward my house. People were dancing, talking, drinking, playing dominoes, and laughing loudly as I made my way toward the front door.

It was funny how fried fish, liquor, music, and friends brought about good times like nothing else.

"Hey Sugar Baby! You and Jasmine come over here and get some fish," Pop said from behind the deep fryer he was working.

"I will," I said as I pushed past a crowd of people and headed toward my bedroom.

Jasmine shut my door behind her and plopped on my bed. I sat at the foot of the bed, leaned back and exhaled.

"What's wrong, Lauren?" Jasmine asked me as she flipped the television on and started skimming through channels.

I shook my head knowing damn well what was on my mind.

"I just…I guess today made me realize how much I miss mom," I said, not taking my eyes off the television screen.

Jasmine sat silently on the bed for a few minutes before she joined me at the foot of the bed. Jasmine tried her best to comfort me.

"It's okay girl," she said, wrapping her arms around my shoulders and pulling me into her.

I laid my head on Jasmine's shoulder and thought about my mom. "She would've just turned forty, Jas," I said, sounding defeated.

Jasmine listened in closely, and soon we were both crying rivers of tears. If there was anyone in the world who could have understood the pain of losing a parent, it was Jasmine. Her father, Marcos, had been gunned down when we were seven. It happened on the very street that my mother had died on, and had, in turn, been re-named after her. It was sadness that had initially bonded us, and love that kept us friends.

Jasmine was my support system; and while Pop tried his best to be there for me, I knew he was hurting too much from his own void.

A knock at my door startled both of us as we separated from our hug.

"Yeah," Jasmine said, wiping her tears.

"Jazzy, it's me," a deep voice said through the wooden door.

Before I had a chance to get up from the floor, Jasmine had

swung the door open and was embracing her high school sweetheart, now her husband, Lance.

Lance and Jasmine were destined for each other. He was the soft-spoken, romantic one, and she was the loud, spontaneous one. In each way they balanced each other out.

"Are you okay?" Lance said, looking over at me as Jasmine clutched his side.

I liked Lance, and despite the fact that my best friend was now spending all of her time with him, I knew he was a good guy.

"I'm okay, Lance," I said, sitting on the bed with my legs crossed.

The three of us sat in that room and watched episode after episode of *Def Comedy Jam*. It was just the therapy Jasmine and I needed.

Jasmine sat cradled in Lance's lap as he flipped open his mobile phone.

"Hey, man," he said as he played with Jasmine's hair.

"Okay, yeah. We're upstairs in Lauren's room," he said before hanging the phone up and returning his attention to the television.

Jasmine and I must have looked as if Lance were crazy, because he slowly turned to us and shrugged.

"What? It's my homeboy; he came with me and I kind of did leave him downstairs," Lance said matter-of-factly.

"He better not be a thief or a thug, Lance," I said, stretching my legs and heading to the restroom.

Jasmine and Lance laughed, but I was serious. There were very few people I trusted in this world besides Jasmine and Pop; and I hoped Lance knew that although I was quiet, I would kick his ass if anything of mine was missing on the count of his "homeboy."

When I got back in the room, there sat Brendan looking more handsome than I had remembered from the ceremony.

"Hey," he said, standing up and walking toward me to

shake my hand. The butterflies had returned. I've been waiting for them to leave since then.

"Jazzy, I've got to get my mom from work so we need to be out," Lance said, winking his eye to Brendan who dropped his head.

"Brendan, you'll be straight; right?" Lance asked.

Brendan nodded awkwardly.

I watched as Jasmine gathered her things and followed closely behind Lance, stopping only to hug me.

"Girl, I told you he's fine," she whispered in a giggly school girl voice.

I watched as Jasmine and Lance exited and I was left with Brendan, the consolation prize.

"I-I'm Brendan," he said, leaning against one of my walls.

I nodded my head, trying to figure out if I wanted this man in my face.

"Lauren," I said smiling.

The two of us stayed silent for over fifteen minutes as *Def Comedy Jam* continued airing.

"Do you want to sit down?" I asked finally.

"Thought you'd never ask," he said, laughing and exposing his deep dimples while he walked toward my bed.

As the credits began to roll for *Def Comedy Jam*, Brendan reached over and grabbed my hand.

"I'm sorry about your mom. I-I saw that they were having a memorial service for her; I remember it being in the news when I was younger. I had to come out and pay my respects," he said as my heart jumped into my throat.

I could barely move, let alone speak, as Brendan continued.

"You are so beautiful," he repeated, looking deep into my eyes.

"Thank you," I finally said as I cleared my throat.

Brendan and I sat on the bed and ran our mouths for almost two hours as we talked about the things we wanted out of life, things we liked/disliked, and everything in between.

"So you're a barber at Tight Cutz?" I asked, listening closely. Everything that came out of Brendan's mouth was interesting to me.

"Well, for now. I mean, one day I'm going to own my own barbershop, and it'll be the biggest thing Atlanta has ever seen," he said, speaking convincingly.

I had never been around someone, other than car salesmen, who could sell their dreams so well. But I believed every single, solitary word that came out of Brendan's mouth, and I hoped that I would be there to see his dreams come true.

I looked out of the window and saw Pop still deep frying fish.

"Your dad is a good man, Lauren," Brendan said, joining me at the window and placing his hand on my waist. I can remember his touch that first time as if it were yesterday.

I could feel myself beginning to throb in places I never had before. My body was responding to his contact in an unknown way. The hairs on my neck lifted slowly as my hands clammed up. I wanted to know what it felt like to make love to him; our connection was that instantaneous.

"Do they know what happened to your mom or who did it?" Brendan said, destroying my mood.

I shook my head. That had always been a sensitive spot with me; but, for some reason, I felt liberated in sharing my story with Brendan.

"One night while mom was working late, she stopped a stolen car and they opened fire on her. They shot her ten times, and no one saw anything. Then, to make matters worse, they ran her body over with their car," I said quickly.

I didn't want to hear the words coming out of my mouth, and I didn't want to visualize my mother in her coffin.

"I know just about as much as the public does. As much as I appreciate the APD doing what they've done to keep my mom's name alive, I feel like they haven't done shit to find who k…killed her."

It was the first time I had said the word killed since my mother's death.

My mother had been *killed*.

As I opened my mouth to say more, tears came pouring from my eyes with no control from me. I had tried too long to suppress the overwhelming feeling of loneliness that had been inside of me for years. I wanted to snap my fingers and make my curiosity, pain, and tears go away, but as I was finding out now – as I sat trying to contain the spill over of tears and emotion – snapping fingers wasn't going to do it. I felt the back of my throat tighten up as I finally allowed the emotions to take over me.

My mother had been killed.

Sitting on the ground, I covered my face with my hands as they shook ferociously. It wasn't that I didn't know my mother was dead, but to admit to myself that someone else had played a part in her not being there stung me to the core.

"Are you okay?" Brendan asked, kneeling down to my level.

"Yeah. I'm okay," I lied as I tried wiping the never-ending tears from my eyes. Brendan, however, saw straight through me.

"No, you're not. Come here," he said, sitting next to me and embracing me in his arms.

He caught one of my tears with his fingers and wiped it off on his Enyce shirt.

"Talk to me," he said.

"For as long as I can remember, I've convinced myself that my mom died of cancer, or a stroke, or high blood pressure…" I said, sighing.

"Knowing that there is someone out there with so much hate in their heart that they would take away a mother from a child, and a wife from a husband, it…it's kind of sickening," I said loudly.

The only other person, besides Brendan, that I spoke freely about my mother's death to had been Jasmine.

"I'm here," Brendan whispered into my ear as he hugged me tightly.

And there began my relationship with the best thing that ever happened to me. As I stared off into space, Lenny walked up and slightly kicked my desk.

"Do you think I could get you to cut a commercial like we're paying you to do?" he said sarcastically.

Normally I would have snapped his head off; but today was a good day, and I was reminiscing about my baby.

"Lenny, I'll do the commercial just for *yooou*!" I smiled as I blew him a playful kiss.

I cut the commercial, prepped for my show, and then headed out to grab a bite to eat at Wendy's.

"Hey baby!" Brendan said loudly into the phone. I could tell he was probably at the shop by the music that was blasting in the background. I told him on several occasions that the shop seemed more like a nightclub than it did a barbershop; but it *was* the hottest barbershop and salon in town, so what did I know?

"Hey sweetie," I said as I pulled into the drive-thru and placed my order. I paid for my food and headed back to the station while running down my day with Brendan.

"You know what? I was thinking about the first time we met at mom's memorial service," I said while eating my frosty in the parking lot of the station. My show was beginning in thirty minutes, but I knew I needed to hear Brendan's voice just like he needed to hear mine.

"Oh yeah?" he said, sounding surprised by my memory.

"Ummm hmmmm," I smiled, wishing he was there so I could kiss his juicy lips. "That *was* a good day, huh?" Brendan asked.

"The *best* day ever!" I squealed.

"Baby, I've got to go. We've got a staff meeting in like five," Brendan said very abruptly as I heard a woman's voice next to him.

"Okay. I love you," I said, wishing I could get closer to him.

Some days it seemed like Brendan was right next to me, feeling the same way I felt, and wanting the same things I wanted; other days it felt like I was closer to a stranger than to him. My heart ached at those moments.

"I love you too," Brendan said before hanging up.

I got my headphones, CD case and mini-disks ready for my show, and sat at my desk waiting on Patrice Jonesy, the drive-time diva, to finish her show when my phone rang.

"Hey girl!" Jasmine said on the other end.

"Hey boo," I replied, smacking my teeth playfully.

Jasmine was still my best friend and still a beauty. She was also a wife, mother, and owner of her own publishing company. Homegirl was definitely doing big things. After having twins just two years earlier, Jasmine's once banging body was just banged out. With over fifty pounds of added weight, she was miserable, but hid it well.

"I know you're about to go on-air, but I wanted to tell you what Lance heard!" she laughed.

"What girl?" I asked, knowing it had something to do with Brendan.

"I heard for your birthday and/or anniversary that Brendan has dropped big bucks on some exclusive diamonds," she said in a hushed tone.

I wanted to jump up and down and scream, but with Patrice in the same room I had to compose myself. I cleared my throat and giggled excessively as I thought about Brendan proposing to me.

"Did you hear me say diamonds, girl?" Jasmine asked me again to make sure she had said the right words.

"I heard you!" I shrieked with excitement as I got in the sound-proof studio by myself.

It wouldn't surprise me if Brendan spent too much money on me. I'm used to it. He drives the hottest Escalade truck, dresses fly and is the barber for some of the city's most elite movers and shakers. In a nutshell, my man had the means to spoil me and was never shy about showing it off.

"I've gotta go, girl. I'll call you tonight," I said as I checked the time and plugged my headphones in tightly.

The countdown began, and as my intro played, I took my position in the black swivel chair. As I hit the *MIC ON* button on the board, I became *Mystique*. I was no longer Lauren Washington worrying about my problems at home, with my boyfriend, or upcoming celebrations. I was *Mystique*, the chick with enough confidence for all of Atlanta. For four straight hours, I could kick back, relax, and do what I do best.

The beat smoothed out and I found my way back into the ears of all ATL-iens for another day.

"Hey, hey y'all…it's your girl Mystique…"

chapter two

Dear Diary,

There's something about summers in Atlanta that are nostalgic. I think back to days when I would sit on the front porch with Jasmine eating tomatoes with salt, and listening to Ghost Town DJs while the breeze barely made its way toward us. Pop would be at work, and we would feel like we were grown women holding the fort down. Ha! I had a pretty good show last night; nothing out of the norm. I met a cute little boy outside of the station yesterday and he gave me his CD to listen to; it wasn't bad at all. I think I may play it next week or so. Glen is moving slowly, but he's getting things squared away. I still can't even walk into the living room without tripping over some piece of equipment. I want all of this to be done ASAP so I can enjoy it. Tomorrow is my birthday! I'm finally getting excited too. Today Jasmine, Kenya, and I are going out to look for dresses for my birthday bash at Compound tomorrow night. I rarely get a night off from work; but since it's my birthday and I'm going to be getting ready for the biggest party the "A" has ever seen, I think I deserve it (Don't I sound vain?)! Anyway, my girls have today planned out to the T. We're going out for brunch this morning, shopping for dresses afterwards, manicures and pedicures after that, and off for a massage! I'm working tonight, so I'll head straight from the massage parlor and after my show is over guess where I'm going...to Kenya's house for a girls-only pre-birthday sleepover. Don't I have the best girlfriends ever? So, I'm pretty excited about my day/night. And with all the commotion surrounding my birthday party, I can't forget about my anniversary. Brendan says he has something planned for me tomorrow afternoon. Goodness, look at the time! I've got to get ready for my day of beauty!

Lauren Washington

———

"Did you tell her?" Jasmine asked me as she stuffed her face with a piece of waffle.

Our favorite chicken and waffles spot in Stone Mountain was, without a doubt, our go-to. It was where we went to unwind, celebrate, and simply feed our faces with great food. The down-home cooking, matched with the beautiful sounds, smells, and people made the perfect atmosphere for our tight circle. The syrupy-smooth sounds of R&B music poured from the speakers as we allowed the familiar scents or cornbread and red velvet cake to fill our nostrils.

"Tell me what?" Kenya asked, slightly annoyed by the fact that she had been left out of yet another secret.

I shrugged as I reached for my orange juice.

"It's not a big deal, and we don't even know if it's true," I said, returning my glance to Jasmine who sucked her teeth. I had to remind my friend that even though Lance and Brendan had once been tight friends – who had by now drifted apart – his information hadn't always been 100% accurate.

"So, tell me then," Kenya snapped as she tossed her jet-black hair over her shoulders.

Kenya Green had been my best friend since my freshman year of college. Although we were completely different, she was the type of friend any woman would die to have. She was a natural protector, so she did everything in her power to make sure everyone around her was cared for.

Like me and Jasmine, Kenya was naturally pretty, with natural hair that stopped just below her shoulders. Her slanted eyes, full lips, hourglass figure, and creative style were what made her stand out from the three of us. While I thought both Jasmine and I were beautiful, there was some-thing about Kenya that made men stop dead in their tracks. Although Kenya had an amazing body, that wasn't the reason people took notice of her. She was original, outspoken, beauti-ful, and successful…and homegirl knew it.

Working as a stylist for celebrities, Kenya was less estab-lished than Jasmine, but that didn't mean she was anywhere near broke. My girl raked in big dough styling all the up-and-coming R&B groups, rappers, and even me. She had flair about her when it came to styling. Her tastes meshed perfectly with the trends.

"Lance heard that Brendan was *supposedly* buying me some big, expensive diamonds for either my birthday or our anniversary," I said, making sure to emphasize the word *"supposedly."*

Kenya raised her eyebrows and shook her head while a smile slowly grew on her face. I could tell she was thinking about Lance's information track record, but she hid it well as Jasmine stared over at her.

"That's great, Lauren," she said sort-of nonchalantly as she patted my hand softly.

"Great? Kenya, don't you realize that this time tomorrow she could be engaged to the man of her dreams?" Jasmine said, looking over toward me and Kenya.

As hardcore as everyone thought Jasmine was, she always got excited when the prospect of one of us getting married and joining the "Black Wives Club" came up.

Kenya shrugged her shoulders and giggled to herself.

"What's so damn funny, Kenya?" Jasmine said, trying not to snicker. She knew how she got when weddings and marriage talk came up, so she could only imagine what Kenya was thinking.

"Bridezilla returns and it looks like she's counting down until she can get a side-kick to join her," Kenya said, finally laughing loudly as she shaped her fingers like claws and poked at Jasmine's arm.

All of us laughed as we finished our food and had small talk amongst ourselves.

"So, who can you give me dirt on today?" I said, nudging Kenya's side as she laughed.

Her eyebrows rose as she wiped her mouth and prepared to share some exciting news with me.

"Oh…one of my clients told me that NFL-er Michael Seldon is supposed to be screwing his teammate, Rob Trent's, wife. They say it's getting pretty hot and heavy," Kenya said matter-of-factly.

I smacked my teeth and crossed my arms.

"That's all you got? Shoot…I could've looked that information up myself on all those gossip blogs! You're supposed to drop all the insider secrets to your best friend," I said, hoping she had more or better information.

Even though I worked in the entertainment industry, Kenya was the one who could slip in and out of conversations with artists, managers, publicists—whoever—without anybody realizing she was gathering information. She had this smooth, undercover way of picking up the kind of celebrity gossip people weren't sharing publicly yet. Then she'd bring it straight to me, and I'd turn her exclusives into headline moments on my show.

"Dag, girl! I didn't even get a chance to get it all out, "Kenya said, playfully rolling her eyes.

"I was going to say that one of my sources told me that Rob found out about his wife's 'entanglement' and went ballistic. I'm talking about breaking headlights, stalking Michael, and even trying to fight him at a club," Kenya said slowly as I ate the information up.

"What?!" Jasmine and I said in unison. My audience worshiped Michael Seldon, and they would devour the information as soon as I reported it.

"Yup. And someone told me she could even be pregnant too," Kenya said, adding the cherry to the top of the already decadent dessert.

I made a mental note to jot the information down as soon as I got close to a piece of paper. To avoid all liabilities, I made sure to turn the news piece into a blind item. Blind items give away all the information and clues, but require the listener to make their own guess as to who it is.

"See, that's why I say 'keep your friends close and your enemies closer,'" Jasmine said disgustedly.

She and Lance had their share of problems earlier in their seven-year marriage, but since the birth of the twins, they seemed to be doing better.

Still, if either of us were honest, Jasmine and Lance were part of the reason Kenya and I were hesitant to ever become brides. A year into their marriage, Jasmine cheated on Lance and attempted to leave him, but she eventually decided to stay and work things out. It seemed that Jasmine was staying out of obligation rather than out of love. Lance had put up with a lot of her crap and she felt required to love him as much as he'd loved her in the hard times. Their relationship was a strange one to folks looking in from the outside. They operated as a loving family with beautiful twin girls and a tight bond, but I knew that when they were alone at home, away from the eyes of friends and family members, it was a totally different story. When I would look into my best friend's eyes, I could see the unhappiness settling in.

I sat in silence as I finished my waffle, and I listened to Kenya and Jasmine trade stories about celebrities who had cheated on their spouses. Jasmine seemed oblivious to the fact that she was a reformed cheater. Kenya rolled her eyes and directed her attention back to me.

"Anyway, girl…what are you and Brendan doing for the big eight-year anniversary?" she said as she sat back in her chair and exhaled. The butterflies I always felt when Brendan's name was mentioned flew around in my tummy rapidly.

"He says he has a surprise for me tomorrow; he's taking me to lunch."

"Do you think he could be pro-...?" Jasmine asked, sitting forward.

Kenya rolled her eyes again and giggled at the animation Jasmine was giving.

"Dag, Jas."

"What?" she asked.

I watched my two best friends playfully bicker about whether or not Brendan was going to propose. It would all be perfect if he did, but I decided not to get my hopes up.

After we paid for our food and left, we headed straight to my favorite designer boutique. It's a fabulous upscale store that I frequent as much as possible.

"Hey Lauren!" Adrienne, the manager, said from behind a tall stack of slacks she was carrying.

"Hey there,"

I ran my fingers over an empire-waisted dress. It was black and white and had cute little yellow daisies all over it.

"This is cute, huh?" I said, turning to Jasmine who looked as if she were about to pass out after looking over the $350.00 price tag.

"No! Lauren, take a look at these pieces," Kenya said, appearing with three dresses in her hands.

It always amazed me how long it took me to find one horribly ugly outfit I liked, and how quickly it took Kenya to find a banging outfit. In the time it took me to find something mediocre and forgetful, my girl would have accessories, shoes and even the perfect lip shade and perfume picked out.

I held one of the dresses up to my body and smiled in the nearby mirror. It was gold and strapless; it was definitely a slim-fitting dress that would show any and everything I had eaten. You know the kind of dress that requires a Jell-O only diet the day before you slipped it on. It was going to be sexy, but I was definitely going to have a painted on look. I was all for trying out new trends, and I trusted Kenya, but I wasn't so sure about this one.

"Just trust me," she said, shooing me into the dressing room.

I slipped into the dress and turned around in the dressing room; eyeing my body with satisfaction. The dress seemed to fit perfectly – from the A-line bottom which hugged my hips, to the strapless top which cupped my breasts. A darling little bow tied across the chest giving it the perfection I was looking for.

"Let me see!" Jasmine said loudly as I pulled the curtain back and awaited their responses.

Jasmine covered her mouth while Kenya stood back like her job had been done.

"I told you it was hot!" she said, holding her finger up and disappearing around the corner. "Let me get something else!"

"That looks amazing on your Lauren!" Adrienne said as she approached Jasmine and I with her hands on her hips.

"Thanks."

"You know this is from the summer line, and we *just* got it in the other day." Adrienne said, winking her eye as she took her place back behind the cash register.

"Lauren, this is definitely the one, right?" Jasmine asked as she smoothed down the bottom part of the dress.

I smiled widely at the mirror thinking of what Brendan would say when he saw me dressed up at the party. I couldn't wait to see the look of pleasure and approval on his face.

"Yeah. This is it," I said, twirling around.

"Here…these shoes go perfectly with the dress," Kenya said, holding up a pair of stilettos that matched the fabric of my dream dress with a splash of teal added in.

Just that quickly I had found my look for the party; everything was falling into place.

We spent the rest of our day shopping, talking and wondering why being a Black woman felt like an endless, thankless job. It was within our inconsistent sisterhood circle outings that we realized the sacredness of what we'd built brick-by-brick in our friendship. The place we could go to be loved, held accountable and even checked or protected when the rest of the world was fighting so hard to keep us vulnerable. It was days like this, walking around in midtown Atlanta, that I realized how blessed I was to have built my own circle of sisters. Thankfully, our plans ended earlier than planned, and I had a chance to go home and sit with Pop.

"Hey Sugar Baby, how's it hanging?" Pop asked me as I kissed him on his forehead and joined him on the living room couch.

"Everything is everything," I replied as I watched Judge Joe Brown scream at someone on television.

"Where's the Glen?" I said, glancing around the quiet house.

There was no one hammering, no one sawing, and no one working. I was starting to feel my blood boil. Pop twisted his lips, letting me know I wasn't going to like the answer.

"He, uh…he got sick today and had to leave early," Pop said, looking at me out of the corner of his eye.

"Pop, this is nuts. Next week I'm going to start looking for another contractor because I can't keep hoping that Glen is going to get the work done."

"Sugar Baby, let me talk to him one last time, and after that…it's all your decision," Pop said, setting the remote down and looking at me in my eyes.

"Pop, there have been one too many opportunities for Glen. I'll draw up a letter for him and let him know he's being released," I said, shaking my head.

After exhaling, my father turned back to the television and turned it up as Judge Joe Brown was just about to throw the gavel at someone.

"It's your decision," he said softly.

Leaning my head back on the couch, I checked the time. I had an hour to nap before I had to get up for work.

I closed my eyes, and within seconds, I was in the deepest sleep I had been in for a while. I didn't want to deal with Pop, Glen, or even the pressures of a possible engagement. For that second, on that oversized couch, I wanted to rest.

When I finally opened one of my eyes, I noticed I was in my bedroom stretched out on my bed.

Stretching my hands upward, I leaned back against the headboard and yawned. I had only been asleep for about thirty minutes and still had time to spare.

As I started making the transition from getting out of bed to my closet, I jumped when my bedroom door swung open.

"Hey baby," Brendan said, smiling his beautifully-perfect smile in my direction. I hadn't seen my man in two days; and now that I did, my hair was standing on top of my head. *Perfect, how fitting.*

"Hey," I said, trying to smooth down the hairs that were out of place.

Brendan stepped back and laughed with his hands across his chest. I eyed him suspiciously before rushing out the door toward the restroom.

"Lauren, you act like I've never seen you with your crazy hair and funky breath," Brendan laughed knocking on the bathroom door.

When I emerged from the restroom with my hair pulled into a tight bun and my breath much fresher, I stood in front of Brendan blinking my eyes.

"Now...what were you saying about seeing my crazy hair?" I said, standing on my tip-toes and wrapping my arms around his neck.

His arms slipped on my waist as he slowly kissed my waiting lips. If this were all I had as a birthday and anniversary present, I would be more than pleased.

"What are you doing here?" I asked as we finished kissing and headed to my bedroom.

"Do I need a reason to stop by your house?" he asked seriously before relaxing his eyebrows.

I ignored his response and leaned back into his chest as I looked up at the ceiling.

"How was work today?" I asked, stroking his chocolate hands. *I love this man. God knows I do.*

"It was straight. You know the same old same old. Cut a few heads, supervise the staff." He said, shrugging his shoulders as I sat in his lap.

"What about you? What did you do today?" he asked, looking me over with a grin on his

I told him about my dress and even offered to try it on for him.

"Let me see it tomorrow night. I want to see your fine ass all made-up," he smirked as he slightly moved me so he could get up from the bed.

I glanced at the clock. If I wanted to make it for my show, I needed to leave in fifteen minutes.

"Want me to drive you to work tonight?" Brendan asked, walking toward my dresser and clearing his throat.

I shook my head as I reached in my closet for a new shirt to toss on. I knew I would only be on the radio, but I was always prepared in case someone stopped me. I didn't want them to walk away saying, *"That was Mystique?? Really!? She looks worse than I thought."*

"I'm spending the night over Kenya's house tonight. It's like a pre-birthday slumber party," I said enthusiastically as I took one shirt off and replaced it with another one.

Brendan scrunched his face in disgust and started laughing.

"Aren't y'all a little old to be having slumber parties?" he said, straightening out his white t-shirt and jeans.

I rolled my eyes. Brendan never really understood the

bond I had with Kenya and Jasmine. Growing up an only child, I had always craved that built-in closeness other people had with their siblings. So when life handed me the chance to have not one but two women who felt like sisters, I held on tight. Yes, I loved ending my day curled up under Brendan's arm, but the comfort my girls gave me hit a different part of my heart—one he couldn't quite grasp, no matter how many times I tried to explain it.

"Don't hate because you wish I was having a slumber party with you!" I said, sauntering over to him.

He watched my hips move from side to side and licked his lips.

If we had more time, we would have been starting our anniversary early; but I had work and he knew it.

"Just don't start anything you can't finish," he said, placing his hands on my hips as I kissed his soft lips gently.

I wanted Brendan to give his all to me; and I wanted him to know that regardless of anything, I wasn't leaving his side.

"I love you," I said, pulling back and staring into his dark brown eyes. His response came much slower as he looked at my entire face, searching for something to say before closing his eyes.

"I love you too," he said pitifully.

"What's wrong, baby?" I asked, confused by his hesitation to respond to our normal "I love you's."

He shook his head and stepped back from me while taking a deep breath.

"Come on, you need to be leaving. You know the traffic is going to be insane," he said, tugging on my hand as we walked down the stairs.

Although I wanted to shake the feeling that he wasn't telling me something, I couldn't. I knew Brendan like the back of my hand, and I knew when he was holding back.

Maybe Jasmine had been right; maybe he was planning on proposing and was getting nervous about it. Maybe the shop was getting hectic; or maybe he was having problems with his difficult mother. There were a million and one reasons that Brendan could be distracted; I just hoped he would snap out of it.

I jumped into my car and rolled the window down as I watched him stroll to his truck.

"I love you, baby," I said as I pulled up beside him.

He dropped his head and chuckled.

"Girl, get on out of here; call me in the morning so I can tell you where we're going for lunch."

I blew him a kiss and headed off toward the building that transformed me into a person with no real problems.

———

"WAKE YOUR ASS UP!" Jasmine screamed as I cracked one eye open and stared at her and Kenya holding a huge cake in their hands.

I had only been asleep for about fifteen minutes and they had decided it was time to officially celebrate my birthday. I was all for a celebration...but why did it have to be so damned late?

"Oh my goodness," I said, rolling over on my back.

My girls gathered around me and finally sat the cake, with a picture of me on it, in front of my lap.

"Happy Birthday, diva!" Kenya screamed as she pulled a gigantic gift bag from behind her tiny frame. Jasmine's eyes lit up as she pulled out her smaller bag. After they butchered the "Happy Birthday" song, they sat in front of me quietly.

"Aren't you going to open your presents?" Jasmine said politely as she scooted her bag in front of Kenya's, wanting me to open hers first.

"You are such a brat, Jas," Kenya laughed, pulling her bag toward her.

I would be lying if I said I wasn't over-the-moon about

getting gifts from my girls. Their taste was unreal—impeccable, effortless, the kind of style you can't teach—and somehow they always managed to spoil me just right.

"Okay…Jas, yours goes first, I guess," I said reaching inside the black and red bag; as I fished around in the tissue paper, I pulled out a narrow white envelope. I tore it open, and as my eyes adjusted to the certificate like paper, Jasmine blurted it out.

"It's a trip for two to Jamaica!" she screamed at the top of her lungs.

"Jazzy. Oh my…why did you…for me?" I said, almost out of breath out of her gesture.

Normally, Jasmine got me a gift certificate for one of my favorite boutiques and called it a day; this was far more extravagant than any of us expected.

"This must've cost a fortune, Jas! I can't let you spend this kind of money on me, and…" I said as I started putting the information back into the envelope.

"This is from me, Lance, and the girls. It's been a great year for the company and I've got the money to spend on those I love," she said grinning as she nudged me.

I wrapped my arms around my childhood best friend and tried not to cry. Jasmine loved me; and even if she hadn't purchased the elaborate vacation, I knew it.

"Thank you, sis."

Kenya stood back with her hands on her hips and a devilish grin on her face.

"Open mine, Lauren," Kenya said, pushing the monstrous bag in front of me. I could only imagine what it could be; with Kenya…there was no telling. The teal and silver metallic bag was the biggest gift bag I had ever seen in my life.

I took a deep breath, stuck my hand in and felt around.

I squealed as I held up the baby doll dress I had been eyeing the day before in the boutique.

"Oh my gosh! Kenya!" I said as I pulled the dress out and held it up to my chest.

As I fished around in the bag a little more, I found two more dresses, a pair of jeans, some shorts, shirts, and a fabulous pair of heels at the bottom. I was completely floored.

"Where did you…how did you?" I stuttered as I eyed the beautiful items.

"I've just been picking pieces up since last year. Every time I saw something that reminded me of you, I bought it. It's been a good year for me too," she winked as we embraced.

"You guys don't know how much this means to me," I said as I wiped my eyes.

My girls had really outdone themselves this time. I stood there trying to gather myself, blinking back tears that had no intention of staying put. Growing up, I had never known what it felt like to have someone who just *knew* you and who paid attention to the little things, who filed away the offhand comment you made about a dress in a boutique window and turned it into something you'd remember for the rest of your life. I had never had a sister to do that. No one to notice. No one to remember. For most of my life, love had felt like something I had to ask for, something I had to explain and justify and spell out carefully so it wouldn't be misunderstood.

But *this* was different.

This was the kind of love that didn't need instructions. Kenya hadn't asked what I wanted. Jasmine hadn't waited for a list. They had simply watched me and they had shown up. Fully. Completely. Without being asked.

This was sisterhood; not the blood kind, but the chosen kind, which I was beginning to think might be even more powerful.

I looked at both of them, their faces bright and waiting, and I felt something settle inside me like it had finally found the place it belonged.

"Let's eat some of this cake," Jasmine said hungrily while walking toward the kitchen for forks and plates.

I yawned as I stuffed everything back in their bags. I couldn't wait to tell Brendan everything the girls had gotten me. I knew he would be thrilled about the trip to Jamaica. Having the gift-giving logistics out of the way, Kenya, Jas, and I sat, laughed, and talked about the usual: men, fashion, celebrities, and love.

"Will you be disappointed if he doesn't ask you to marry him today?" Kenya said, licking icing off of her hand.

I shrugged my shoulders and tried to think of the best answer possible.

"I want to marry that man, y'all. I really do. But I don't want him to feel pressured into anything. I don't want us to rush into something just for the sake of getting married. Right now, we're good; Lord knows marriage has lost its value nowadays anyway. People get married but rarely do they want to *stay* married," I said, looking over at Kenya.

Jasmine sat quietly listening to me, probably feeling like I was talking directly to her. I could see the wheels moving in her head as she thought of something to say.

"Has he gotten better at opening up to you?" Jasmine asked curiously without looking me in my eyes. She knew I didn't tell anyone, not even Kenya, about Brendan not being able to fully open up to me. It was something I shared exclusively with her, and now she was breaking our code of silence and spilling the beans.

I paused to collect myself without getting angry, and I noticed that Kenya was listening in closely.

"I know there are things in Brendan's past that I don't understand, and probably some things I never will. I have to respect the fact that if he tells me he doesn't want to talk about it, he doesn't want to talk about it," I said, snapping at Jasmine.

Kenya noticed the friction between me and Jas and sat

back against a wall watching. It was very rare that Jasmine and I fought, but when we did…the fireworks came out.

"I'm just saying you've been with this man for almost eight years now, and you still don't know about his past?" Jasmine said, throwing the attitude right back at me.

"Sounds suspect to me," she added, rolling her eyes.

I threw my hands up and pushed back from the couch, heat rising in my chest as I stormed into the kitchen. As I passed Jasmine, I sucked my teeth loud enough for her to hear and muttered under my breath, "At least I want to be with my man, and I know he wants to be with me too."

That did it.

Jasmine shot up so fast her chair scraped across the floor. Her fists were balled tight at her sides, shoulders squared like she was ready to swing. The fury in her eyes hit me before her words did, and for a split second, I felt the air shift to thick, electric and dangerous.

I knew I had crossed a line. But so had she, and I wasn't about to shrink back.

"Lauren," she snapped, stepping toward me, "if you think you're so much better than me, why don't you write a damn book telling me how easy marriage is, huh? Who are you, Ms. Perfect?"

She kept coming, inch by inch, until she was right in my face, breathing hard, daring me to say one more thing.

And I almost did. I had been in plenty of fights during my life, and Jasmine Wilkes didn't scare me in the least. I knew her scare tactics, I knew how she intimidated people and, most of all, I knew she would never hit me.

"Jasmine, what you need to do is back up off of me and calm the hell down," I said nonchalantly. I wanted to scream, *"Step back or it's on!"*

"No. I want you to tell me who the hell you think you are to say I don't want my husband or he doesn't want me. I *want* him; so know that, a'ight? And trust that he loves me. You worry about *your* boyfriend of eight years, and why he isn't yet convinced that you're *the one*; how about that?"

That comment took me over the edge. Jasmine screamed as I shoved her shoulder. Kenya jumped up between the two of us and blocked any fists from being thrown.

"Lauren, sit down over there," she said pointing to her black futon.

"And Jas sit down over here," Kenya said, taking her to a kitchen barstool across the room. Jasmine snatched her arm away from Kenya and rolled her eyes.

"I'm out of here," she said, grabbing her purse and bolting out of the door with tears streaming down her face. Laying my head back on the futon as Kenya chased after Jasmine, I closed my eyes.

My birthday was already starting off on the wrong foot, and a knot in my stomach told me it wasn't about to get any better.

———

WHEN I GOT HOME that morning, Pop had actually cooked me a decent breakfast. My favorite. Salmon croquettes, biscuits, scrambled eggs, thick lumpy grits and a side of freshly squeezed orange juice. The kitchen made my stomach smile in the most obnoxious and necessary way possible.

"Happy Birthday, Sugar Baby!" Pop sang as he held a cupcake in his hand and covered the burning candle. I blew out my candle and eyed my breakfast closely before diving into it. I slowly picked over the plate that Pop made for me, and pondered telling him what was going on between me and Jasmine. Before I could bring it up, Pop had pulled out a jewelry box and sat it in front of me.

The box sat on the table in front of me, small and unassuming, wrapped in the kind of stillness that made the rest of the room fall away. I don't know how long I stood there with my hands hovering over it – long enough for the noise around me to blur into background, long enough for my heart to start doing something funny in my chest.

When I finally lifted the lid, the breath left my body all at once.

There, nestled against a bed of ivory silk, was the necklace.

Her necklace.

The stones were the same impossible shade of turquoise I had memorized as a little girl; that particular blue-green that existed nowhere else in the world except pressed against my mother's collarbone on Sunday mornings or Saturday evenings. The silver setting caught the light and threw it back at me, intricate and familiar, every curve and detail exactly as I remembered. Someone had loved it back to life. The tarnish was gone. The small chip on the center stone — the one I used to trace with my fingertip when she let me hold it — had been smoothed away, delicate and whole again.

My hand trembled as I reached in and lifted it.

I was six years old again, standing on my tiptoes at her dresser, watching her fasten it around her neck in the mirror.

"When I grow up," I used to tell her, "I want one just like yours."

She would smile at my reflection — she had such a slow, patient smile — and say, "Baby, one day."

I hadn't known then that *one day* would look like this.

"Pop..." I said as I lifted the necklace and held it up to my neckline trying to fasten it. Tears rolled down my cheeks. I thanked him as he wrapped his arms around me.

"It's what your mother would've wanted, Sugar Baby," Pop said, fighting back his own tears.

After Pop had fastened the necklace, we sat at the table holding hands. I gazed into my father's aging face and grinned. Even though his pain, hurt, and years of stress had taken a toll on him, Pop still maintained himself. With his hair in a neatly picked salt and pepper afro, and a mustache that covered his upper lip, my father looked nothing at all like me, with the exception of his button nose, which I had inherited.

I let my fingers drift across the necklace, tracing its familiar shape as memories of my mother wrapped themselves around me like a fog I could never quite step out of. Eighteen years had passed, yet the ache of losing her still sat in my chest. The police had done everything they could, or at least everything they were willing to do. And Pop...he wanted answers just as badly as I did, but I could see the fear in his eyes whenever the subject came up. He wasn't just afraid of what we might find, he was afraid of what it might break inside him.

So the weight fell on me.

Standing there, holding the necklace she once wore, I felt her presence so strongly it almost stole my breath. It was as if she were right beside me, her hand on my back the way she used to when I was little, whispering that it was okay to keep going, okay to fight for the truth, okay to finally let myself live.

And for the first time in a long time, I believed her.

"Pop, I know you told me that you don't really know much about mom's mur...death, but I think it's time I start looking into it."

Pop listened without speaking. His eyes seemed like they were blinking in slow motion as I continued.

"I've been thinking for some time about hiring a private detective. You know...someone who can investigate even further than the police have. One of my co-workers is married to the best P.I. in Atlanta and..."

"Lauren, if you are ready to start looking into it that's fine. I'm not going to fight you on it." Pop said as he turned away from me. There was an uncomfortable seriousness in his voice.

"Just know that regardless of what you find out, nothing can change the past. But if this is what you need to do for closure…then do it."

I nodded my head quickly and reached over and kissed my father's cheek. For years we had fought over hiring someone to find out what happened to mom, but Pop always objected.

"It's just going to stir up emotions in the both of us that neither of us needs to revisit." That's what he told me when I turned twenty-one and begged him to let me look into mom's death. I yearned to know who, what, when, where and most importantly…why someone had killed my mother.

"Thank you, Pop." I was relieved that I didn't have to fight him on it. I had already made my mind up and was determined to follow through with getting to the truth, but it was a relief that Pop was on my side.

I couldn't stop thinking about the necklace, so I let it slip slowly between my fingers, the cool metal grounding me as my mind drifted back in time. I closed my eyes and suddenly I was eight years old again, perched on the edge of my parents' bed on a Saturday night for our unofficial "date night ritual."

That was when I got to see my mother in all her beauty.

She would stand in front of the mirror, letting her long hair fall from its clip, dark waves tumbling over her shoulders before she curled a few pieces to frame her face. She never needed much makeup, just a touch of gloss, a hint of blush. Her skin already glowed on its own. Then she would step into a long, flowing dress that swished around her legs, slipping on heels that made her look like she was floating instead of walking.

And right before she called Pop in to tell him she was ready, she would tilt her head and spray a soft mist of *Obsession* across her collarbone. The scent would drift through the room, warm and sweet, wrapping around me like a hug.

I would sit there in my *Care Bears* T-shirt and shorts, pigtails sticking out every which way, giggling at how effortlessly stunning my mother was. She would catch my eye in the mirror and wink at me, like we shared a secret no one else knew.

Then came the final touch: the turquoise and silver necklace. She would fasten it around her neck, and somehow it made her look even more radiant, like the piece had been crafted just for her.

Now that same necklace rested against my skin, and holding it brought her back to me in a way nothing else could.

"One day this will be yours," she had told me as she turned around and winked her eye at me before joining me on the bed. I stood up and wrapped my small child arms around her neck.

"You're so pretty mama." That was how it always ended before she would dance off for her date with Pop.

It all seemed like yesterday; and while I had my memories, the only tangible thing I had to prove her existence was her necklace and some photos.

"Sugar Baby," Pop said, waving his hands in front of my daydreaming eyes.

"Yeah?" I asked, getting slightly annoyed by his pestering.

"I asked you what Brendan was doing for your birthday," Pop said, picking up an empty plate and heading over toward the sink before turning back to me. I smiled, forgetting about my drama with Jasmine and my overwhelming feelings about mom.

"He's taking me to lunch this afternoon; he's planning to give me my gift."

"Sounds…interesting," Pop said, turning back to the sink.

"What's that supposed to mean, Pop?" I said, glancing at the clock before throwing my hands up.

"You know what? I don't have time to figure it out; we'll

talk tonight or something," I said, rushing over and kissing Pop's cheek before dashing out of the kitchen toward my bedroom.

I giggled as I pulled out the dress Kenya gave me for my birthday. It was perfect for a brunch with my baby, I thought as I turned on the shower and laid out my accessories. I checked myself in the mirror as I tugged on a stray hair on the side of my head. It was clearly another hot day in Atlanta, and even at 10:00 A.M., my hair would frizz up as soon as the humidity hit it. I slicked down my perfectly proportioned bun and turned to the side to catch my profile. I smoothed a little bit of bronzer and lotion on my smooth legs and arms while my toes peeked out from the designer sandals. The dress was perfect. It wasn't too tight; yet it was still close enough to my body that it accentuated my shape.

Grabbing my clutch, I rushed down the stairs and past Pop.

"See you later, Pop!" I screamed as I slammed the door behind me.

It was my birthday, and despite the excitement with Jasmine earlier that morning, I was already over it and hoped she was too. After reaching my car, I looked at the antenna with a grin on my face.

Tied with a white ribbon was a red rose with a note attached:

> Meet me at the restaurant where we
> had our first date.
>   ~Brendan

I smiled. My baby was full of surprises. Even though I wasn't a huge fan of red roses, any type of romantic gesture from Brendan was enough to light up my day. Pulling out of the driveway, I picked up my Blackberry and dialed Jasmine's number. Just like I suspected, she didn't answer. It was like a common routine for me and Jasmine when we argued. We would yell, she would run out, I would call hours later, she would not answer my calls, and eventually one of us would break and call the other and we would make up. I listened to her voice message and thought about what I was going to say.

"Jas, it's me. Call me when you get a chance. We need to talk about what happened this morning and…just call me."

Then I tried to call Kenya. I was sure she had been in touch with Jasmine, and that she would tell me exactly how my best friend was feeling.

"Hey birthday girl!" Kenya squealed excitedly answering her cell.

I laughed at my friend's animation.

"Hey," I snickered.

Kenya knows me entirely too well, because before I could even get the question out, she was blabbing the information I needed to hear.

"I was just on the phone with Jasmine."

"And…" I said, wanting more information.

"And what? You know the child is sensitive; and you know the truth stung a little bit, I guess," Kenya said, sighing before continuing. "But you know you were wrong for trying to call her out like that."

"And she wasn't wrong for doing the same to me?" I shot back, upset that *my* friend, the one I had introduced to Jasmine, was now taking her side.

"Wait…wait. I didn't say anything about her not being wrong. I just think the two of you need to talk things out. You both said some things I *know* you didn't mean."

As much as I wanted to object to what Kenya was saying, I knew she was right and she knew I knew she was right.

"I tried calling her, but she didn't answer. I left a message," I said, letting Kenya know I had attempted to right my wrong. We continued our small talk, and just as the conversation was getting good, I reached IHOP.

"I've gotta go, girl. I'm at the restaurant," I said trying to rush my friend off as my eyes locked with Brendan's.

"I still can't believe this boy is taking you to cheap ass IHOP!" Kenya laughed loudly as I quickly wrapped her up.

"Whatever girl!" I said laughing, "I'll talk to you later!"

I flipped down the visor and checked my hair, teeth, and makeup. If IHOP hadn't been so near and dear to me in regards to my relationship with Brendan, I might have felt the same way as Kenya. It wasn't at all expensive, it was fattening, and most of all it was…IHOP. But it was the spot where we had solidified our relationship and gone on our first date, and it would always be the best memory of us in our earliest stages.

"Hey baby," I said, approaching my man with a huge grin on my face.

He looked damn good! He was wearing loose jeans with a crisp white t-shirt, and his hair was freshly cut. His athletic body seemed as though it was calling my name, so I hugged him. I couldn't help holding him for a second longer than normal. I inhaled his Burberry cologne and was instantly ready to take this party back to the house.

"Hey gorgeous," he said as he kissed me on the lips.

"We've got your table ready over here," a flamboyant gay man said as he sashayed toward an open booth. The two of us sat across from each other as Brendan's hands shook uneasily while he gripped the menu.

"Happy Birthday, baby," Brendan finally said before taking a sip of water. "And Happy Anniversary!" he added.

"Thank you, baby!" I smiled. "And Happy Anniversary to you too!"

"How was your slumber party last night?" Brendan asked, leaning back into the booth and focusing his attention on me. The way his brown eyes pierced my body was unexplainable.

"It was good. Jas and I had a fight," I said, rolling my eyes. I didn't feel like reliving the fight or the moment. I wanted to enjoy the time I had with my boyfriend.

"About what?" Brendan said, sounding surprised.

I cleared my throat, unsure if I should explain to him that he and Lance had been at the root of our argument.

"It was something stupid, really," I said, looking over the menu before switching subjects.

"But she did come through with a bomb ass gift, baby!" I said, pulling the envelope from my purse and sitting it in front of him.

"A trip to Jamaica?" Brendan said, sounding uninterested.

"Yeah. Can you believe that? We haven't taken a vacation in so long. I think it's about time; don't you?" I said, talking quickly as thoughts of Brendan, me, and the beach danced in my head.

"I probably won't be able to go, though," Brendan said, sliding the envelope back to me slowly.

My face wrinkled up as the waitress came and took our orders; I returned my fiery glance in Brendan's direction.

"What do you mean you can't go? This thing doesn't expire for another five years."

Brendan shrugged his shoulders.

"With the business and all, I'm lucky that I can even be here at breakfast with you," he said, looking around the restaurant.

I huffed loudly and sucked my teeth. I didn't want to argue, but I could feel my blood boiling.

"Whatever, Brendan. When it's you going to Las Vegas or something with your boys, you *make* time, right?" I said with an attitude.

"Yeah, but that was before..." Brendan said, cutting himself off.

"Before what?" I inquired, crossing my arms. Nothing he was saying was making any kind of sense.

"Nothing," he said, looking at me deeply in my eyes.

Something in my soul told me to hug him, kiss him, and hold him until he felt better; but his barrier wasn't allowing me to do that. I was getting angry about it, too, and all I could hear was Jasmine saying that my man wouldn't open up to me.

"I would like to say I understand, but I don't. I never do," I said as the waitress brought our drinks and scurried away.

"I'm not trying to argue with you today, Lauren. It's your birthday!" Brendan said, returning to his usual vibrant, funny, outgoing self. His mega-watt smile made me forget about any harsh feelings I was having. I was back to being putty in his hands.

"Fine, but we're going to talk about this later," I said, raising an eyebrow as he rubbed my hand gently.

We ate, laughed, and joked just like old times; and for a second I forgot about the gift. Had Jasmine and Lance been right and Brendan was going to propose? He *was* nervous, fidgety, and sweating like crazy.

I excused myself from the table and headed to the restroom. After I had done the usual hair and makeup check, I walked back toward my seat and I ran right smack dab into a small body.

"E-e-eeeeexuse me," the voice said as he bent down to pick up his baseball cap which had flown off his head.

"I'm sorry, honey," I said, reaching forward to make sure the person was okay.

"M-mmmyssssstique?" The stuttering voice inquired.

His face looked familiar. But I met so many people on a daily basis that I was at a loss.

"Do I know you?" I asked, stepping backwards as I watched the adorably cute kid hold his hat behind his back as a gesture of courtesy.

"I met yoo-uuuu the other dddday," he said, closing his eyes as he struggled to get the words out. I eyed his features a little closer and finally got it. It was Dee, the young teenager that I had met outside the radio station.

"Oh! That's right…it's Dee isn't it?" I asked just to make sure.

"Yup. Y-ooouuu got it!" he said, smiling widely.

"I listened to your CD, and it's actually pretty good. I'm going to talk to the Program Director, Lenny, about having you on. Sound good?" I said making it all up in my head.

I hadn't meant to invite Dee to the studio, but with the kid standing in front of me, I wanted to give him some type of news.

"W-wwwoorrd? That's dope," Dee said, pumping his fist in the air excitedly.

I grinned as I peeked around an animated Dee and saw Brendan starting to look anxious. I held up one finger to Brendan and turned my attention back to Dee.

"Yeah. I'll check into it with him and I'll hit you back with his verdict. Your number's on the CD right?" I asked.

"Yeah."

"Okay cool. You take care, okay?" I said as I patted his shoulder and proceeded to pass him by.

"Mystique?" he said, turning to face me.

I lifted my head up so I could hear his voice clearly.

"I'm going to start going back to school on Monday; I'm registered and all," he said proudly.

I beamed and nodded my head. Maybe my influence was a little stronger than I thought.

"That's wassup! You keep that up and you'll be a hot rapper *and* a smart business man," I said, winking my eye and heading back toward Brendan who was on his cell phone.

"Here's your gift," Brendan said with the phone still glued to his ear. I sat motionless as I waited on him to finish his conversation.

"Yo. Let me call you right back," he said.

I looked over the gift and quietly contemplated what

could be behind the wrapping. My heart wanted it to finally be an engagement ring, but I knew otherwise. I knew that Brendan loved me; but I also knew we both had issues to comb though before making the ultimate commitment.

"You know I love you, right?" Brendan said as he stumbled over his words.

I nodded my head and finally looked into his eyes. They seemed so lonely and so eager for new light that I was moved to run my fingers across his face. To feel the smoothness of his baby face, while taking in the beauty he exuded, was breathtaking in itself.

"And I love you too," I said while finally opening the gift.

Brendan looked as if he was about to grab his things and leave as I slowly tore through the metallic wrapping paper slowly.

"I hope you like it," he said, sitting straight up in his seat.

As I got through the mounds and mounds of wrapping paper my eyes landed on the most beautiful piece of jewelry I had ever seen. It was a ring; it was *the* ring and it was *my* ring.

The ring sat cushioned in red velvet and was big…no it was huge. The gold band was 24K, while the diamond in the center had to have been about five karats. It wasn't my taste, but it was still beautiful.

"It's…it's…" I said, lifting the ring out of the box and examining it closely. Brendan held one finger up to my mouth and shushed me.

"I know I'm not always easy to deal with, but I love you and you've been there for me more than anyone else has ever been. I don't know where I would be if I wasn't with you right now," Brendan said while staring into my eyes, which were filled with tears.

"I've grown into a better man because of you; and I thank you, baby," he said.

I got up from the booth and joined him on the other side. I

tried to hold back the river of tears waiting to jump from my eyes.

"So this ring is for…" I asked, not understanding where the *"Will you marry me?,"* drop on one knee, heartfelt, over-the-top proposal was. I had waited for years and years to be proposed to…and I *knew* he wasn't about to simply toss a box at me, in IHOP, and expect me to propose to myself. Brendan cleared his throat loudly and bit his bottom lip.

"It's not an engagement ring; but it is a promise ring."

I pulled back from our embrace and dropped my mouth. I hadn't heard the words "promise ring" since I had been in the seventh grade. I didn't understand, either. I had given Brendan eight years of my life, my virginity, my love, my trust, and my heart…*but he still wasn't ready?* As much as I had tried to convince myself that I didn't care whether or not he proposed… I did. I wanted him to *want* to be my husband as much as I wanted to be his wife. *Did he not crave my kisses in the morning the way I craved his? Didn't he yearn for the moments when we would intertwine our bodies when love making?* I knew I did.

"A promise ring?" I repeated, my voice thinner than I wanted it to be. I tried to steady my breathing, tried to keep my face neutral, but inside I was cursing Jasmine for planting that proposal fantasy in my head. She'd had me picturing candlelight, a velvet box, the whole damn fairytale.

Brendan reached for my hand, his eyes soft, almost pleading.

"Listen to me. Please don't be mad. I love you, Lauren; no ring or vows can define that."

I nodded, because that's what my body knew how to do; but the moment I slid back into my seat on the opposite side, everything inside me went loud. My ears were hearing him, but my face was burning, my palms slick with sweat. My body was reacting to a truth my mind refused to swallow. I had actually believed wholeheartedly that Brendan was about to make me his wife. Even though his emotional walls had been telling me otherwise for months, I still let myself dream. Still let myself hope.

They say love makes you do stupid things while looking even dumber. That was me; sitting there, trying not to crumble under the weight of my own denial.

I stared at him, expressionless, as he kept talking, his voice drifting in and out like background noise.

"I've got to get everything straight with the business," he said, exhaling hard.

"And my mom and brother… they need me financially right now. It's just the timing…"

Brendan always carried the world on his shoulders, and God knows I wanted to help him carry some of it. But he never let me. Not really.

"I understand," I whispered, though my eyes were darting around the room, searching for something…anything, to anchor me. The clinking glasses, the dim lights, the soft music…it all felt too romantically ironic for what was actually happening.

I was supposed to be celebrating a future with the man I loved. Instead, I was trying to swallow the truth that he wasn't ready for me. Brendan could sense I was clamming up. He simply pulled out his wallet and slapped $30 on the table.

"You ready?" he asked, sounding annoyed.

I played with my food as I shook my head, no. He wasn't getting out of talking to me that easily.

"I've got another surprise for you," he said, standing up and leaving me at the table. "Come on."

I knew I should have still been mad, but deep down, I couldn't be. I followed behind Brendan and exited the restaurant. As soon as the blistering sun hit my pecan skin, I was ready to find the nearest air conditioner and stick my head in front of it.

"Get in," he said as he unlocked his Escalade truck.

I slid into the leather seats and buckled my seatbelt tightly; ready for wherever Brendan was taking me. The sounds of Jill Scott filled the car and I was soon humming along.

We rode quietly in the car before Brendan turned to me and placed his hand on top of mine.

"You know I love you; why are you tripping over a ring?" he asked as he drove onto the interstate and into traffic. I shrugged. I didn't have an answer. I knew I wanted to be married, but I also knew that both parties needed to want it.

I exhaled through my nose and folded my arms across my chest, not in anger exactly, but in the way you do when you're trying to hold yourself together. When I finally looked at him, my jaw was tight, my eyes glassy with something caught halfway between hurt and exhaustion.

"Do you know how long I've wanted to call myself Mrs. Brendan Lewis?"

I let that sit there between us for a moment, unanswered, like it had been sitting inside me for years.

"And each year it just seems like we're getting further and further from it."

My voice didn't break. I had practiced this too many times in my own head for it to break. But my chin trembled just slightly, just enough, and I pressed my lips together and looked away, because some things are too honest to say while looking someone directly in the eye.

Brendan blew out air and stared straight ahead as he gathered his words.

"I love you. Men propose and get married every day, knowing they aren't ready to take that step. Shit, look at Jasmine and Lance. All that matters is I love you." His words were not in alignment with what I wanted to hear.

"But it's something *I* want; I'm not trying to pressure you to get it. If you don't want to ever get married…" I began again.

"I never said that; stop putting words in my mouth," he shot back angrily.

The thing with Brendan was his attitude flared up at the most inopportune times; today just wasn't the day for me.

I folded my arms and sat in silence. Before I knew it, we were pulling up to the The Peachtree Plaza Hotel. Although I had been all around Atlanta, I had never been to this hotel.

Brendan glanced over at me and smiled.

"I know you're still mad, but bear with me."

I tried to keep my *I'm mad, don't talk to me* look to myself as I stared out the window.

"Sir…madam…can I take your bags?" the bellboy said as he came to the car quickly.

"They're in the trunk," Brendan said, not looking at me.

"Bags?" I said with a slight smile on my face. "I've got my party tonight."

Brendan ignored me and hopped out of the car and slapped some money into the bellboy's hand.

"I've already got our key, so you can just take them up to the Governor's Suite," he said, coming around to my side of the car to help me out. He handed his keys over to the valet and got the ticket.

"Brendan, what's going on here you've got to…"

"Hush and just come with me," he said, grabbing my hand tightly as we followed behind the bellboy who was gripping two pieces of luggage and a tall garment bag.

The elevator ride up felt like anticipation made physical. Brendan stood beside me with that quiet, satisfied smile he only wore when he knew something I didn't. I opened my mouth twice to ask questions and thought better of it both times. Whatever this was, he had planned it carefully. The least I could do was let him have his moment.

When the bellboy pushed open the door to the suite, I stopped walking.

The room unfolded before me like something out of a magazine spread I had dog-eared and forgotten about, convinced that places like this only existed for *other* people. Floor to ceiling windows stretched across the far wall, and beyond them, Atlanta glittered in every direction. I could see the radio station tower blinking in the distance, the broad shoulders of the Georgia Dome, the CNN building lit up against the darkening sky, and further out, the Georgia Aquarium sitting squat and luminous like something dreamed up. The city looked different from up here. Softer, somehow. Like it was putting on its best for us.

I stepped further inside, almost forgetting to breathe.

The suite was dressed in tan and cream, every surface deliberate and unhurried, with an understated luxury pouring from every corner. Fresh flowers sat on the console table near the window. The lighting was low and warm, giving me hope that this was the beginning of a good night.

I sat down on the bed mostly because my legs suggested it before my brain did. The hotel's famous mattress received me like it had been waiting; layers of cloud-soft linen rising up around me as I sank into it, and I let out a breath I felt like I had been holding all day.

Across the room, Brendan moved slow and easy, fixing our drinks at the bar cart. He glanced over his shoulder at me with that smile again, the private one, and something in my chest went soft and warm.

He carried both glasses over, kicked off the second shoe, and settled in beside me.

"You trying to get me drunk?" I asked, winking my eye.

Brendan had an effect on me that didn't require any alcohol. I was a permanent drunk when it came to him.

"Not at all," he grinned while taking a sip.

It was noon, and I was ready for the birthday and anniversary present I had been waiting on: Brendan and I making love. I was also ready to give him a gift that I was sure he wasn't expecting; but would hopefully be happy about.

"Why did you bring me here?" I asked.

"I wanted to be alone with you. We needed a change of scenery; so I thought your birthday and our anniversary deserved the best," he chuckled.

My head lay on Brendan's shoulder and I closed my eyes as he rubbed my thigh. His hands went higher and higher, and before I knew it, I was straddling him fervently. I couldn't kiss him hard enough, and my body wouldn't move quickly enough. I wanted all of him right then and there, but he had other plans.

"Go take a bath," he said, patting my ass.

I sat up and pouted.

"But baaaaby…" I whined wanting him inside me.

"Go!" he said sternly.

I listened.

As soon as I stepped inside the bathroom, my eyes lit up. Rose petals followed my footsteps throughout the marble flooring; as I got closer to their ending, I saw that there was already a bath drawn for me with rose petals also floating in the sudsy water.

I gasped and turned to call Brendan, but was met with his hands on my waist.

"I told you I love you, girl!"

I wrapped my arms around his neck and pulled him into me. I kissed his soft, juicy, pink lips ferociously as if it were the last time we would be together.

"Unzip me," I said, letting go of him and pointing to the zipper at the back of my dress.

By this time, Brendan was fully ready for our duo bath. But first, I thought, I needed to give him his gift. I stepped out of the dress and quickly turned back to face Brendan. I let the dress drop to the floor and stood in only my tan bra and matching panties. Brendan got in the warm water and watched my strip show from the tub.

"Damn baby," he managed to say as I saw his hand begin playing with himself.

I stepped out of my panties and undid my bra seductively as music from the bathroom radio played in the background. I couldn't even make out the song, but all I knew was that my baby was getting turned on, and that was turning me on. My body slowly gyrated to the beat.

"Come in here," Brendan said. He was so incredibly sexy and manly…I didn't know how to keep my hands off him.

"Wait. Before I do, I need to give you your present," I said, walking toward the edge of the tub and bending down to kiss him deeply.

I bit my top lip and turned around so my back was facing Brendan's face. It took him a minute, but when he finally saw it he jumped out of the tub in disbelief. Water and suds splashed all around us as he scrambled to put his hands on my waist.

"Oh shit. Baby…I love you, you know that right?" he said as he rubbed his hand on top of the tattoo with his initials – BDL – that sat near the middle of my shoulder blade. I had gotten the simple tattoo a month earlier and somehow had managed to keep it from everyone, including Jasmine and Kenya.

I looked over my shoulder and smiled as I saw Brendan's emotional reaction. He ran his fingertips up and down the tattoo over and over, as if to make sure it was really real.

"I can't believe you did this," he said with a smile.

I typically wasn't into tattoos. I hated pain, I was always thinking *what if?* and I had always been against them; they were much—too eternal. But when it came to showing Brendan just how serious I was about *us*, I was willing to do anything. Maybe this would be the nudge he needed, I thought.

We finally made our way into the tub and gave each other an anniversary present neither of us would ever forget.

After back breaking, frizzy hair making, sheet wetting, unbelievable sex, I was worn out and ready to start thinking about my party. The bash was hours away and getting ready hadn't even crossed my mind.

"Kenya called," I said while scrolling through my missed calls. Surprisingly, Jasmine hadn't called. I looked over at Brendan, who had just jumped out of the shower. As he went through his bags for a fresh white t-shirt and jeans, I watched. I gripped the covers up to my chest and yawned.

Brendan looked over at me and winked.

"Tired?" he asked as he chuckled. "I got that effect on you."

"Whatever." I laughed, knowing he was right.

"By the way, what did you get from Kenya and your father for your birthday?" Brendan said, making small talk as he dried off.

"Well, Kenya got me a new wardrobe. The dress I wore today…that was all her!" I was excited about all the new clothes I had received. Brendan nodded his head as he looked at the television and listened to me.

"And Pop…well, he gave me mom's old turquoise necklace."

"Oh really? That's cool; you've wanted one like it for a minute, right?"

"Yeah. I couldn't believe he was actually letting me have *her* necklace. That made it the best birthday ever!"

Brendan laughed and went back into the bathroom and shut the door while I continued talking loud enough for him to hear.

"And guess what? Pop gave me the go ahead to hire a P.I. to look into what really happened with mom's death," I said, laying my head against the pillow.

"As long as I've been asking him to let me look into it, he finally decided that I'm ready, I guess. I think he's scared I'm going to get so consumed in trying to find out the truth that it'll take over my life or something."

Brendan returned to the room silently and looked at me for a second before speaking.

"Are you sure you're ready for this? I mean…it's been eighteen years since her death; the police have been on this for so long that…"

I stopped him mid-sentence, the same way I had stopped Kenya and Jasmine when they tried to discourage me from looking into mom's murder.

"I'm sure. This *is* my mother; if I can't make the move to find out who did this and why, then I feel like I'm doing her a disservice," I sighed. I was tired of everyone trying to put off my attempts.

"I hear you. I'm just saying…what if you don't find *anything,* or…worse," he asked as he lathered lotion on his legs and arms. I knew he cared for me and was extremely protective, but he needed to trust my judgment.

"If I find nothing then at least I'll know I looked."

Brendan took a deep breath and turned around with a forced smile.

"If it'll make you happy, I'm with you on it." he said as he started tickling my feet.

He jumped up from the bed with lots of energy and began looking around the room for his bag.

"Where are you going?"

"I've got to get back to the shop, baby," he replied as he stepped into his boxers and retreated to the bathroom.

"So, are you going to drop me back by IHOP so I can get my car?" I yelled from the bed.

"Nope. I've got everything here for you. I'll have a car pick you up at the hotel for the party tonight," he said, coming closer to the bedroom with a sly grin on his face.

"But what about my dress?"

"It's hanging in the closet."

"My shoes?"

"Right here."

"I've got to have my makeup, Brendan."

I appreciated the gesture, but he was throwing me out of my element, and I wasn't sure I liked it. Brendan's eyes watched my composure change as I double checked what he was telling me, and headed to the closet to make sure my dress and shoes were there.

"Don't you trust me?" he finally asked as he adjusted his platinum chain that hung to the middle of his t-shirt. Fully dressed...my man was still a sight to see.

"I trust you," I said as I headed back to bed.

Brendan's phone vibrated. He scurried off into the bathroom to answer it. It was the fifth time since we had been in the hotel that he got a call, and I could only imagine who had been calling so consistently. I peeked into the bathroom a few times to see him cradling the phone and scribbling something on a piece of paper. When he heard me at the door, he quickly folded the paper up and stuffed it into a bag next to him.

"What are you writing?" I asked curiously.

He shrugged and gave me a half smile.

"Just things I might need to say one day." He sighed.

"Baby...I've got to go," he said as he bent down and pecked my forehead and then my lips. I didn't want him to pull away; I wanted to continue to lick, suck, and devour his lips.

"Don't go," I pleaded.

"You know I don't have a choice. I've got a business to run," he said, standing over me with his hand resting on the shoulder where his initials lay tattooed on my body.

I already knew that Kenya, Jasmine, and my father would flip about the tattoo, but the satisfaction on Brendan's face was more than enough to make me disregard their impending reactions.

"I know. I just wish you *could* stay. You're going to be there tonight, right?" I said pathetically as I stared up into the eyes that controlled my every move.

"I'll be there," he said, patting my head.

Just as he started to grab his things, I jumped up from the bed and blocked the door. The bed sheet trailed behind me as I gripped it close to my naked body.

"What about my car?" I inquired again.

Brendan placed his hands on my stomach and pushed his tongue into my mouth forcefully. I loved when he took charge that way and showed off the thug side of him.

"I told you…I've got everything under control, right? I know you need your car; I know you need your girls," he said, pecking my lips one last time and pushing past me so he could open the door.

"What are you talking about?" I said with one hand on my hip.

I could see exactly what he was talking about. Kenya stood silent on the other side of the door with a devilish grin on her face.

"Kenya!" I screamed. "What are you doing here?"

Brendan smiled and slipped past the two of us. I looked down at myself and felt around at the top of my head and my messy hair; I knew my best friend knew what had gone on in the hotel room.

"I'll see you tonight, baby," Brendan said, rushing down the hallway toward the elevator. Kenya pulled in her suitcase on wheels, her makeup and hair kit, and began shouting.

"Your man outdid himself this time! Let me see that ring!" Kenya said, dropping her bags and rushing over to me.

"It's not what you th-…"

"Daaaamn! I knew he was balling, but this is next level type of jewelry, girl!"

Kenya said, pulling me down on the bed. I wanted to explain to my friend that it wasn't an engagement ring, but instead, a promise toward an engagement. The more I thought about it, the easier the angry emotions came.

"Kenya…chill out. Okay?" I said, yanking my hand away and walking into the bathroom to get my clothes off the floor. I threw on some sweats and returned to find Kenya in the mini bar mixing together some concoction.

"Where is Jas?" I asked with both of my hands on my hips. It had been our plan that we would all get ready for my party together; yet one-third of our crew was missing.

I heard Kenya suck her teeth and saw her shoulders shrug.

"I'm tired of being in the middle of y'all's mess," she said, emerging from the mini bar with a glass of dark liquor and ice.

"Want some?" Kenya asked, raising the glass.

I shook my head and looked at the clock. It was about 5:00 P.M. and I had a couple of hours to kill, so I decided to make the best of the time I had with Kenya. I looked at my best friend as she watched the news. She was wearing her hair in a huge, curly, Diana Ross looking style, and looked fabulous enough to pull it off. Her cigarette jeans and vintage Coca-Cola t-shirt and jean vest was an example of her unique style, which I envied.

"Kenya…" I said, playing with my promise ring.

"Yeah?" she said slowly, tearing her eyes from the screen.

"It's not an engagement ring. It's a promise ring," I said softly.

Kenya's eyes grew large, and upon seeing my reaction, they quickly returned to their normal size.

"Well…that's not too bad, is it?" Kenya said, stroking my frizzy mane.

I knew she was just trying to make me feel better and that's what was making me upset. I just wanted her to tell me exactly what she was thinking.

"Kenya, be real with me, girl. I don't need you to always

agree with me." I said bitterly. This was one of those moments when I needed Jasmine's outspoken opinion and advice.

With Kenya, I damn near had to pry things out of her; but when I did get it out, it was out.

"Okay. Look...the two of you have been together eight years and he gives you a promise ring? I mean...what other promises do you need? What is Brendan so scared of?" Kenya asked, raising an eyebrow.

I knew one of the things he was nervous about: divorce. He had only been three years old when his mother and father separated, leaving his mother a single parent and struggling. Brendan had told me that he barely knew his father, and didn't have the desire to know him after what he had done to his mother.

"I'll never understand how a man can just up and *leave* his family," he told me once over dinner earlier in our relationship. The anger in his eyes as he stared over my shoulder at nothing in particular haunted me for days. I respected his past, but at what point was he going to let go and begin to fully live his life with me?

"I think the thing with his father, and the fact that he has problems opening up...I know it's a very good excuse...but life goes on, and he either has a choice to move on or remain stagnant. So are you going to give him an ultimatum?" she asked me seriously.

I didn't want to be that person. You know...the girlfriend who can't deal, function, or live without her man proposing. But the more I waited, the more I started feeling like it would never happen.

"I don't know; probably not," I said, sighing and lying back on the headboard of the bed.

Kenya shrugged her shoulders and stood up from the bed.

"I'll be back. I think I left my purse in the car," she said, leaving the room and letting the door slam.

I took my fingers and ran them over my new necklace and

smiled. *What would mom have done?* She probably would have told me to get over myself and the hold Brendan had on me, and just tell him what I really wanted from him. My fingers traced the necklace's familiar shape and quickly left and ended up on my shoulder blade, where the tattoo sat.

The look of approval in Brendan's eyes when I had showed him the tattoo had been enough for me. Our bond was unbreakable. I knew it was permanent, but so was our love and relationship.

I took a deep breath and exhaled.

As I curled underneath the covers, I closed my eyes. I needed the rest.

I envisioned Brendan in bed with me and I finally felt content. At times, it was the only way I could sleep at night. He was my everything.

And life as I knew it would soon become all about my everything.

chapter three

Dear Diary,

Tonight is the night. Can you believe it? It's my birthday and I'm sitting here in the this fancy hotel with Kenya getting ready for my birthday party at Compound. Brendan and I had the best time together, and I have to admit all of his surprises were really thoughtful and unexpected. I finally showed him my tattoo, and I thought he would never stop saying how much he loved it. I'm not sure what's going on with him, though. It's almost as if he tells me one thing, and acts completely differently. I know he loves me...I know that much; but it's hard to fully agree that he knows what love really is. Anyway, Kenya is here with me and as much as I appreciate her surprising me and helping me get ready, I miss Jas. I tried calling her again, but she's playing around and I can't keep chasing behind her. I'm going to enjoy my day and my party and deal with Jasmine tomorrow; if she chooses not to come, oh well. I'm going to start looking for another contractor on Monday. That's yet another thing I have to worry about. Oh well, at least I have one night off from the station to rest, relax, and enjoy myself. Kenya is getting ready to start on my hair and makeup for the party, and she's starting to get impatient. Ha! Hopefully when I write tomorrow I'll have nothing but good memories to jot down!

Lauren Washington

"I have a hot curling iron and a bad hand; do you really think it's a good idea to keep me waiting?" Kenya joked as I put my diary down and sat in the chair.

I was lucky to have Kenya as a friend; not only because she was completely loyal, but also because she could style me, make me up, and then do my hair. In high school, Kenya received her cosmetology license thinking that was what she would be doing with her life; but after finding fashion, she put hairdressing on the back burner.

"Sorry, girl," I laughed, sitting Indian style in the chair.

Kenya ran her fingers through my thick hair and sighed.

"What do you write about in those journals? I swear that you're always writing in that damn diary," Kenya remarked as she reached in her bag for some moisturizer for my hair.

I shrugged. I was public about a lot of things, but my diary was for me and me only. My therapist and Pop had gotten me hooked on writing down my feelings as a way of dealing with mom's death. So for eighteen years, I've been a journal-loving, diary-keeping, secret-having, fool; and I love it that way.

"Just what's on my mind," I said, focusing my attention on the television.

Kenya knew when to leave something alone and when to nudge me for more information.

"I see," she said, picking up a thick comb.

I rarely got my hair done, but when I did, it was always soothing. Some people considered pedicures, manicures, or facials to be the ultimate relaxation time, but not me. For me, there was nothing like sitting relaxed in a chair as my hair-dresser pulled, yanked, straightened, fried, dyed, and styled my hair; that was *my* soothing outlet.

"What kind of style were you thinking?" Kenya said as she continued combing out the kinks.

I shrugged as I always did when I got my hair done by her.

"I saw this really cute hairstyle on Rhianna that I think would look hot on you," Kenya said with a smile on her face. I trusted my girl's taste and knew she wouldn't screw me over.

"Okay, work your magic then," I said as I closed my eyes and prepared for her to do her usual straightening, bumping, curling, and spritzing routine.

"You know…you should think about cutting your hair. I bet you could rock a Halle Berry look," she said, stopping mid-way.

I raised one eyebrow and turned to look at Kenya's to see if she was serious.

Cut my hair? She had to be crazy. For as long as I could remember, my hair was my pride and joy. It hung well below my shoulders, just below the middle of my back. It was just like mom used to wear hers, and was exactly what Brendan loved.

So cutting it was definitely out of the question.

"I don't mean like Halle Berry short; I meant just take a little off the top for some bangs and maybe layer it," she said, picking up a strand of my hair and then glancing down at me.

I must have been looking at her like she was speaking Russian, because as soon as the suggestion left her mouth, she was already calling the dogs off.

"Okay, okay...you don't want to cut your hair. I got it," she laughed while sectioning off a piece of hair.

I smirked and returned to my serene place. The heat on the back of my neck felt so warm and comforting I dozed off into a light sleep.

"Okay, let me clean you off," Kenya said, pushing my shoulders after what seemed like the shortest nap of all time.

I had been asleep for close to twenty minutes as Kenya straightened my hair to mimic the Rhianna like hairdo. I checked the clock and saw it was almost 9:30 P.M. and I realized that people were probably starting to arrive at the club. It hit me then...my birthday party; the one I had hyped up to all of Atlanta for the past three months was finally here!

Jasmine still wasn't there. I'll be honest...I really thought I would wake up from my catnap with Jasmine sitting on the edge of the bed, ready for the party. But I checked my phone. No Jasmine. I checked the room. No Jasmine.

"Has Jas called you?" I asked as I looked at my bone-straight hair in the mirror. Kenya began applying her makeup and shook her head.

"Nope."

I dropped my shoulders. As selfish as it seemed, all I wanted was for Jasmine to get over her petty anger and attitude and at least show up for my birthday party. Kenya glanced over at me and saw my disappointment and tilted her head sympathetically.

"One monkey don't stop no show, girl!" Kenya smiled as she turned up the music in the bathroom. Almost immediately, she was sprinting into the living area and had turned up the radio too.

Beyonce blasted from the speakers, and soon we were both out of breath from dancing around like we were video girls.

After Kenya and I had done our Beyonce walks, she finished her makeup and then did mine. We slipped into our dresses, then she finished bumping the ends of my hair. I was feeling good, and the three shots of tequila had me feeling as though this was *the* night I had been waiting for.

"I think I'm going to say something to him, girl," I rattled on as Kenya slightly curled one piece of her hair.

"Who?"

"Brendan. The man of my *dreams*," I laughed to myself.

I wasn't drunk, but I could feel myself going to a place that was funny and free. Kenya held the curling iron away from my face and stepped in front of me, with one hand on her hip.

"You're going to say what?"

"I dunno…maybe *I'll* ask him to marry me," I said.

Kenya's eyes shot open widely, and we stared at each other for a minute, trying to figure each other out.

"Lauren…you can't…you can't ask him," she said, kneeling down in front of me.

I didn't want to hear it. I just wanted to listen to the music, dance, and have fun; but Kenya was persistent.

"Ever since I met you, you've been talking about the special way you want to be proposed to; let Brendan be the man and do that," she said, rubbing my shoulder and standing back up to finish my hair.

We sat in silence as the music continued blaring throughout the bathroom. Within moments, my hair was finished and I was up and ready to go.

Kenya was wearing an eighties-inspired, skintight, mini dress with a wide belt. Her curly hair was pushed to one side, and her makeup was flawless. We both looked like the video girls we had pretended we were earlier.

"You ready?" I asked Kenya as I hung up the phone with the car service downstairs. It was a quarter till 11:00, and I was more than anxious to get to my party and see my baby's reaction to my look.

"Give me two seconds!" Kenya screamed.

I stared at myself in the mirror and smirked. My hair had been flat ironed bone straight, bumped under at the ends, and parted right down the middle. It was just what I liked – classy classy but simple.

"Do you have any lotion?" Kenya asked, scrambling toward me with her makeup bag in her hand.

"Check my suitcase," I said, shrugging. "And bring some," I yelled as I sat on the bed.

We put lotion on and stood up to leave.

"Hold on, get my shoulders," I said, forgetting all about my tattoo.

"Your ashy ass shoulders need…" Kenya said, stopping when her eyes met the tattoo with

Brendan's initials on it.

"Lauren, what the…" she said, almost screaming at me.

"Kenya, it was an annivers…" I started before she cut me off.

"This is outrageous. Are you serious?! You got Brendan's name tattooed on you? Why?" she said, sounding more hurt than anything. She rushed to my back and began rubbing the tattoo in an attempt to take it off.

"I want him with me forever," I said, knowing I sounded stupid.

Kenya stood silent for what seemed like five minutes before she threw her hands up in the air and rubbed my shoulders with the lotion.

"I just can't fucking believe you," she said angrily.

For the life of me, I couldn't remember the last time she had cursed at me, let alone been angry with me. But this wasn't the way I wanted the night to go, so I tried my best to fix the situation.

"Kenya, don't be mad. I'm not asking you to agree with it, and I'm not asking you to do the same thing. All I'm asking is for you to support me – your best friend." I felt the tears working their way to the surface.

Kenya covered her mouth and sucked her teeth.

"Fine, Lauren. Fine," she said as she brushed past me.

We stood silent waiting for the elevator to come, and I looked over at her for a sign that everything was okay. She glanced back at me and shook her head.

"I can't believe you, Lauren. You said that he can't commit to "forever" right now, so why would you?" Kenya asked as the elevator door opened.

I hadn't thought about it like that, but what was done was done…and I didn't need her questioning what I did.

"If we're going to argue about this all night, let me know now. I don't need this at my party, Kenya," I said, gripping my purse to my stomach.

I just wanted to go back to the fun we were having in the bathroom, but it seemed Kenya was nowhere near letting it go.

"This is crazy," she whispered as we got off the elevator and made our way to the Lincoln Town car waiting for us.

I was stressed, and my sweaty palms and throbbing head were clearly a result of it.

Kenya looked out the left window as I sat looking straight.

V104 was blasting from the stereo, so I quickly turned the dial to my station.

Jay-Boski, the station's hip-hop DJ, was taking his first mic break of the night, and was sounding crunk as ever.

"...Y'all got to check my girl Mystique's birthday party out! It's going down at Compound, and from what I hear, it's already packed wall to wall. My homie Crystal Bright is down there now and she's checking in, letting us know what's really good down there. Crystal?" Jay said as his raspy voice cracked.

Crystal Bright was an intern that had transitioned into a weekend on-air personality, and she seemed pretty ambitious. Some days, I could hear her practicing her mic breaks, and I could have sworn she was trying to sound like me. Brendan told me I was being paranoid; but in this business you can't afford *not* to watch your back.

"Yeah, Jay! I'm down here at Compound and let me tell you just how crowded it is out here! If you're not down here, then you're nowhere! Everybody and they mama is kicking it up in here, showing love for our own Mystique as she celebrates her birthday! Happy birthday, baby girl! So get on down here now, if you can! This is your girl Crystal Bright with the all new Buzz 104.5!"

I smiled to myself as I thought about all my friends and colleagues who had promised me they would come out and show support. I turned my head to look at Kenya, and she was staring at me with a silly grin on her face.

"Girl, they said I wonder if T.I. is in there!" I said excitedly, hoping the tension had vanished. Kenya rolled her eyes and started grinning widely.

"I still don't think what you did was a good idea, but it's your life, Lauren...and you're going to live it," she said, raising one eyebrow.

I understood where Kenya was coming from, and I

completely felt her need to be protective over me, but she was right – this was my life and my decision.

"Look, we're about to get into the hottest club in town – for the hottest birthday party around, *AND* we look fabulous! It doesn't get much better than that. Let's have a good time and worry about all the other stuff tomorrow," Kenya said, finally returning to her giddy self.

As the town car pulled up to the club, I checked my Blackberry one last time, but still no word from Jasmine. The line into the club was so long I couldn't even tell where it stopped. Music was thumping from the outside speakers as people crowded around the entrance. Lights glared from every direction, and as the car slowed down, I finally started getting nervous.

"This is bananas!" Kenya said, looking out of the tinted window.

I was in awe of everything that was going on. *Was this really all for me?* I saw skinny girls with their stomachs showing, big girls with their makeup done flawlessly, and men who had, obviously, just left the barbershop with their fresh fades. Before I had a chance to vocalize what I was thinking, the door on my side swung open.

"Mystique!" I heard a girl yell from the line. Soon everyone was staring directly at me and Kenya as we made our way onto the red carpet and into the club. I had been surprised to see some local media there as well. Kenya and I posed for a couple of pictures. My dress was perfect for the occasion, and I would swear a couple of people whispered, *"Where'd she get that dress?"* That made Kenya's night.

The inside of the club looked like something out of a music video, and I couldn't take my eyes off all the people who were having a good time. Plenty of people stopped me to take pictures and chat. Some even bought me a drink or two. I felt the love throughout the entire club. As much as I felt the adoration, I also felt a strange churning in my pit that told me that tonight wasn't going to go as smoothly as I had hoped.

Kenya and I locked arms and made our way into the V.I.P. section as the sounds of ATL classics blasted from the huge speakers, making everyone in the club get on their feet and dance.

I was thrilled to see all of my celebrity friends in the spot. T.I. and Tiny played it cool in a corner, while Venus and Serena danced with a couple of their male friends. I thought I saw Trina, Gabrielle Union, and Sanaa Lathan in the club too; but with everything that was going on I couldn't be sure. The champagne, liquor, music, and fun were flowing around V.I.P. like no one would believe, and after I had had a chance to settle in, I was finally feeling at ease. I stared out over the crowd of people who were partying and grinned.

Kenya sat down next to me and handed me a drink.

"Thanks," I said as I slowly sipped the drink.

Even though I was off work, I was fully aware that I was still on public display and had an image to protect. I wasn't getting drunk, but I was definitely going to enjoy myself.

"Have you seen Brendan?" I asked Kenya as I scanned the room.

She shook her head and looked over her shoulder at Lorenzo Black who was looking sexy as ever. Lorenzo was one of the hottest up-and-coming actors in Black Hollywood. With five movies under his belt from the previous year alone, he was said to have raked in millions with even more projects on deck. He was fine, too; but in a boyish kind of way.

He had big brown eyes. His skin was reminiscent of fresh hot chocolate, while his neatly-kept locs stopped at his shoul-ders. He was an Atlanta native with deep roots in the community, and I had to say, I was impressed by who he appeared to be. If I wasn't head over heels in love with Bren-dan, I might have thought about giving him a second look. But word on the street was that he was also a notorious playboy, and had been seen around town with just about every Black actress in Hollywood.

"Why don't you just go up to him? He's standing by himself," I said, elbowing my friend's side. She shrugged her shoulders before returning a glare.

"Girl, please. I am not thinking about Lorenzo Black," Kenya said, trying to play down the sexual fantasies I knew were dancing through her head.

It wasn't that she couldn't pull Lorenzo, but I think she was scared of all the extra attention that came with being a celebrity's girl. That's why she always made sure to date "regular" guys. Kenya was so intent on being the only one to have her man's attention that she figured she would do better with a banker or teacher than an actor or rapper.

"You want me to introduce you?" I kidded, knowing Kenya would object. "I know his peoples."

"Whatever," she said as she sipped her drink.

I kept my eye on the entrance in hopes that Jasmine or Brendan would soon come in.

"Do you want another drink?" Kenya yelled over the music as I leaned in to get a better listen.

"Yeah. You could get me a..." I started before I was interrupted.

"Happy Birthday, Ms. Mystique!" Lorenzo yelled over the music as he leaned in for a loose hug.

"Thanks honey!" I said as I smiled and stole a quick glimpse of his perfect skin.

Before I could ask him what he was working on, if he was enjoying the party, or who he had come with...Lorenzo had turned his attention toward Kenya.

"Hello there. I saw you from across the room and I just wanted to introduce myself. I'm Lorenzo Black," he said, looking at Kenya from her legs all the way to her slanted eyes.

I could've screamed at the irony of the situation; but instead, I excused myself as Lorenzo got comfortable on the couch next her. Kenya's eyes seemed to sparkle when she and Lorenzo talked, and surprisingly, he seemed really in tune to her as well.

I mingled with a couple of people at the bar before I turned around and saw Brendan enter the room.

Whoever I was talking to was now zoned out. My body was there, but my mind and heart were with my man. He looked more handsome than any guy I had seen in the club. He was wearing a pair of pressed jeans and a crisp button-down. He was also sporting a pair of mirror-tint sunglasses and had a fresh haircut.

My man is so fine, I thought as I sat my cup down on the bar.

Brendan couldn't see me from where I was, but my eyes never left him. Just as I started getting closer to him, I noticed a woman very close to his side. She wore a texturized short-do, was really small, and a little pudgy. If I didn't know that *I* was Brendan's girlfriend...I would have thought *she* was. I couldn't tell if her hand was intertwined with his, or if my eyes were playing tricks on me. He leaned down to her and she whispered something seductively into his ear; he smiled widely and began laughing. I hadn't seen a laugh like that in such a long time from him, so I stopped in my tracks.

Something wasn't right, and I knew it. She was wearing a cheap looking halter-top and a pair of jeans that seemed like they were spray painted on. I watched as Brendan's arm lightly touched the woman's waist. I felt as if someone were hitting me in the chest with a sledgehammer. Not just a regular sledgehammer, mind you...but a sledge hammer with nails glued on the base. My feet seemed to be cemented into the ground, because I couldn't move. It was as if I was being tortured.

Brendan wouldn't do this; not at my birthday party.

After much effort, I began to march past all my guests and

toward my boyfriend. The woman saw me and backed away from Brendan quickly.

"I'll be back," I heard her say as she swiftly left Brendan's side.

I couldn't tell if Brendan was shocked to see me, or if there was relief plastered all over his face.

"What's going on?" I asked him to reassure me that I had been seeing things.

"Hey baby," Brendan said, leaning down to kiss me on the cheek. I backed away and blocked his kiss with my hand.

"Brendan, who is she?" I said, pointing to the woman who was at the bar watching us.

"She's a friend," he said shortly.

Obviously she had been a friend; I wasn't that stupid. I knew she hadn't magically appeared on his arm and at my party. I wanted to know *who* she was, and why they seemed to be all over each other. I crossed my arms and looked at Brendan intensely.

"I'm still allowed to have friends, right?" he said sarcastically with a bright smile.

My mind was racing a thousand miles a minute. I felt like I couldn't breathe. This couldn't be happening to me. Brendan couldn't be cheating *could he?* I'm not sure if it was the Patron, or the drinks I had had in the club, but I was feeling a little brave. *How dare Brendan roll up in my party with a "friend" I had never met, let alone invited to my party?*

"I want her out of here! I don't know her, and she's not welcome," I said harshly.

Brendan watched me with a look in his eyes that I had never seen before. He looked like he wanted to hug me, but he also looked like he was ready to cry. I could tell he knew he hurt me with his nonchalant attitude and disrespectful actions.

"So, what…you just want me to leave too?" he shot back.

"I said I want *her* out of here. If you think that means *you* too…then fine…leave!" I shouted angrily.

I had tried my best to hide how I was feeling, but Brendan was making it harder than normal.

"Come here," he said, pulling my arm as we made our way into a spacious, empty handicapped bathroom.

I could still hear the music thumping and people talking outside the door, but my attention was on Brendan who had, by now, removed his glasses and was kneeling in front of me as I sat on the toilet.

"She's just a friend. You said you trusted me," he said, reminding me of our conversation earlier. I put my head in my hands and sighed.

"I'm not crazy; I know what I saw. If I was to walk into a club with a 'friend' of mine all on me like that, you would lose it," I said, snapping at him.

Brendan exhaled as he tried to calm me down; but the alcohol in me wouldn't let him get away that easily.

"I'm sorry," he said softly.

"You promised that you would always be real with me and tell me what's going on," I said, pulling myself together.

Brendan pulled me up from the toilet and pulled me into his body. I felt at home.

"If you want me to get rid of her, I will…" he said in my ear.

I thought about it long and hard. I wanted the situation to be done with. If she was a "friend," as he claimed, I didn't want to cause any further friction between us over her.

"Just keep her hands off you and vice versa," I said, sighing.

Brendan had a hold on me, and no matter how many times I told myself we needed to work on things, it never happened.

"Thank you," he said, kissing my forehead.

We exited the bathroom and took a seat at a couch close to Kenya and Lorenzo, who were still conversing.

We snuggled on the couch together, forgetting our earlier argument, while people danced around us. I was having the time of my life and was glad my baby was able to be with me.

"So, you're not wearing your ring," Brendan said, picking up my hand to find that it was bare of his promise ring.

I swallowed a huge lump in my throat and took a deep breath.

"I was going to talk to you about that..." I started as I searched his eyes.

"Talk about what?"

I knew what I wanted to say, but I didn't know how to say it without seeming needy, dependent, or nagging; however, it was going to go, it needed to happen.

"I didn't wear the ring tonight because I wanted to figure out where we're actually headed."

"Uh huh..." Brendan said slowly as I continued.

"I don't want to be your girlfriend forever. One day I would like to think I could be your wife," I said while Brendan moved his hand away from my shoulder.

It was clear that his body language was changing; I needed to reel him back in.

"You know I love you, and well...we've been together for eight years, and if we're going to do it...I want to know so I'm not just hanging on."

I saw Brendan's jaw clinch up as I stared at him for a response.

"Say something," I said in his ear as the music seemed to get louder.

"What do you want me to say?" he asked, looking around the room.

It was as tense as it could be in a room full of people bumping and grinding. I watched as people headed out of the club; and soon, standing in front of us, was the woman Brendan had come into the club with.

"Brendan, I need to get home," she said softly. I could tell she was intimidated by me, and as I rolled my eyes, she backed up.

Kenya came behind us and stood beside me.

"Is everything straight?" she asked, looking the woman up and down.

This was why I knew she was my ride or die; she always had my back.

"We're cool," Brendan said, turning toward the exit with the girl behind him. *He wasn't leaving me, and he wasn't leaving with her*, I thought. Not that easy!

"Wait a minute!" I yelled at Brendan as I reached for his arm.

"Lauren, we'll talk tomorrow."

"No. Listen to me, Brendan. I love you. I'm not trying to pressure you into anything. I just wanted you to know how I felt," I whispered so only he and I could hear.

The club was just about to close, and as people bumped into us, I kept my focus on my boyfriend. Something was happening between us, and I couldn't put my finger on it. It was like he was purposely trying to get me upset or push me away.

"I'm not ready to marry you. And you know what...I might not ever be," Brendan said nonchalantly.

I felt my eyes stinging before I felt the tears. Before I knew it, I was gasping for air.

You know that moment people talk about when their life flashes before their eyes in a split second? That's what was happening to me in the club. I saw flashes of Brendan and me together, planning our lives, and even making love.

Where was all this coming from? Earlier that day he had said we were so tight that we were already married in his mind. Now this?

"What are you talking about?" I asked, trying to catch the tears as they continued to flow.

"I think we need a break. Can we talk about this tomorrow?" Brendan said, still not making eye contact with me – like I was a meeting he could reschedule.

That was when Kenya moved.

She had been standing close enough to hear every word, and I knew it because I saw the moment it landed on her face. The easy smile she had been wearing all night disappeared and something else took its place. She straightened up slowly, deciding how much of herself to let out.

"Excuse me?" Kenya said, stepping forward so that she was no longer beside me, but slightly in front of me. Her voice was controlled, which was somehow more alarming than if she had raised it.

"Did you just tell her you might *never* be ready, and then ask her to talk about it tomorrow? Tonight? After she just poured her heart out to you?"

"Kenya." I touched her arm. She didn't move.

"No, Lauren." She held one finger up without taking her eyes off Brendan.

"I have sat here and watched you love this man with everything you have, and I am not about to stand here quiet while he does this." She turned back to Brendan, her voice dropping low and even.

"You do not get to say something like that to her and then just check out! That is not how this works."

Brendan shifted his weight and opened his mouth.

"I am not finished," Kenya said simply.

She turned to me then, and her whole face changed. The sharpness softened; and she reached out and cupped my face in both her hands.

"Stop catching those tears," she said quietly. "You hear me? You stop that right now! You did not do anything wrong."

I nodded; even though I didn't fully believe her yet.

She pulled me into her and held on, one hand firm against the back of my head, and I felt her exhale slowly against my shoulder. Over her shoulder I could see Brendan standing there, jaw tight, looking like a man who had not expected any of this to cost him quite so much.

"A b-break? What's that supposed to do? Why are we breaking?" I said angrily.

Brendan struggled for something to say, and finally bit his lip and looked at the ground.

"I just need to clear my head, that's all."

I didn't know what was going on, or what Brendan was trying to do, but my heart was aching as I stood still. My legs felt like they were about to give out, but somehow my mouth found a way to say,

"Fine."

Brendan leaned in to hug me and I felt his strong masculine hands wrap around my waist; and as he inhaled my scent, I did the same. I pulled back from him and looked over at the mystery woman who was silently watching us. I placed my lips to Brendan's and I slowly swirled my tongue inside his mouth. My hands found their way to his back and as I ran my fingers up and down his body, I felt his bottom lip quiver before he pulled away abruptly.

"I love you," he said to me as Kenya pulled me away. Kenya stopped walking.

I felt her hand tighten around mine and I already knew what was coming. She turned around slowly, looked at Brendan, then at the woman beside him, then back at Brendan. She took her time about it.

"You love her?" Kenya repeated, her voice flat and precise.

"You love her, and that is who you chose to be standing next to tonight?" It wasn't a question. She let it hang there in the air between all of them – ugly and obvious.

The woman shifted. Brendan said nothing.

"That's what I thought," Kenya said.

She turned back around and put her arm firmly around my shoulders, tucking me into her side like she was shielding me from weather. I could not speak. I could not look away from him either; even as Kenya guided me forward, even as the distance between us grew. I kept my eyes on him until the crowd swallowed him whole and there was nothing left to look at.

The town car was waiting at the curb. Kenya opened the door, helped me in, and slid in beside me without a word. She pulled the door shut, and the noise of the night cut off all at once, leaving the two of us in the quiet hum of the car pulling away from the curb.

That was when something in me gave way.

The sob came from somewhere deep and private. It tore out of me before I could catch it, and I fell forward into Kenya's chest. She caught me without flinching, one arm wrapping around my back, the other hand pressing gently against the back of my head, holding me like she had done it a thousand times before.

"I know, baby," she said quietly into my hair. "I know."

She didn't tell me it was going to be okay. She didn't say he wasn't worth it or that I deserved better…not yet. She just held me steady in the back of that town car while Atlanta slid past the windows and let me fall apart for as long as I needed to.

That was enough. That was everything.

Aside from the day of my mother's funeral, I had never cried so hard in my life. Just when my tears started to cease, I would remember the love making, the future, and the tattoo…and the waterworks started all over again. *Had I played myself without even noticing it?*

Thoughts of Brendan ran through my mind as I got under the covers with Kenya at the hotel.

How could Brendan and I take a break? He was all I knew, and all I wanted to know; and yet, he wanted a break from me.

And just like the old cliché says, *"If I knew then what I know now…"* I might have walked away with my sanity right there.

chapter four

Dear Diary,

Well, I'm sitting here trying to convince myself that it's time to get up, shower, and head into work. I told myself I was going to go in early and tackle a couple of things, but I'm moving so slowly. Last night was a mixture of emotions. I had the time of my life at the party, but the unexpected definitely happened. Brendan and I are officially on a "break." I don't know the clear definitions of a break, and I don't even know why we're taking the break, but it's where we are. But I can't front, though...I looked damn good last night. I got up extra early this morning, checked out of the hotel, headed to Kenya's house, and jogged. I never exercise until I'm mad about something. I'm trying to tell myself this is temporary, and that we'll pull through this...but I just don't know. Brendan was acting stranger than I've ever seen. It was almost like he was purposely trying to push me away from him; and as easy as that would be, I'm not going anywhere. I'm trying not to trip out completely, and I figure keeping myself busy is the best way to do that. Kenya gave me the number to her cousin who is a contractor, and I think I'll give him a call to schedule an estimate. And the Jasmine situation? Well, as you can see, I've got so many other things to stress about. Kenya thought that I might have pressed Brendan too hard, but I don't know. He seemed like he was itching to find anything to argue about, and the promise ring was the easiest way out. Hopefully we'll talk soon and iron this out because I can't imagine my life without him.

Well, I need to get home.

Lauren Washington

———

I was irritated and completely aggravated when I arrived at my house. Not only had the drama from the night before stuck with me, but my car was acting up. I took a shower and cleaned up the kitchen before sitting at the table and pulling out the piece of paper that Kenya had given me with her cousin's number on it.

While I fully trusted Kenya, this was a huge job and I needed to make sure her cousin could handle what I needed done.

"May I speak with, um…?" I said, looking at the paper, "Trey?"

"This is him."

"Oh, hey. My name's Lauren Washington and your cousin Kenya gave me your number. She said that you were a contractor that might be able to help me out with some renovations I'm doing in my house."

Trey paused for a second before chuckling.

"You wouldn't be from Bankhead, would you?" he asked, still laughing.

"Yes, but do I know you?" I said shortly. I wasn't in the mood for jokes or even laughing. This was business, and he was already working my nerves.

"This is Travon Grables. I went to elementary school with you. My family calls me Trey, though," he said.

I tried to rack my mind about a Travon that I knew in elementary school, but I knew I would never remember him. With mom's death, everything in my childhood seemed like a constant blur.

"I'm not sure I remember you."

"Well, well, well. I guess some things haven't changed, now have they?" Trey joked with me.

"I guess so," I said dryly. I didn't know who this guy thought he was, but I wasn't feeling his jokes.

"So how have you been? I haven't seen you since I moved out of Bankhead," Trey asked kindly.

I was sure this guy meant well, but his kindness was falling on deaf ears.

"I've been fine. Look…do you think you would be able to come over to give me an estimate and let me know if you can handle the job?" I said, cutting the personal talk out.

"Sure. You're still in the same house, right?" Trey asked.

"Yeah. I'll be here until 2:00 P.M., so if you can come by today, that would be great."

"I'll be there in twenty," Trey said.

I hung up more irritated than I was before I had dialed Trey's number. After I finished cleaning up my room, I kicked my feet up and turned on the television and allowed it to watch me. I wasn't in the mood to do anything, and I was just pissed. I was mad at Brendan for changing everything he had promised. I was angry with the mystery woman for being with my man. And I was angry at Trey for making me angrier. Looking at my cell phone, I hesitated before dialing Brendan's number. I didn't know what I was going to say, nor did I know what to expect, but I decided it was worth the effort to find out.

"Hey…this is Brendan, leave a message and I'll hit you back when I can. One!"

I didn't leave a message, but I knew that he would know I called. Before I had a chance to second guess not leaving a message, there was a knock at the door and I jumped.

Standing before me was Travon "Trey" Grables, my elementary school crush. Why hadn't I been able to remember him earlier? Trey stood about 6 '4" and had silky butterscotch skin, jet black eyes, and a smile that would melt any woman's heart, not to mention, perfectly cut hair. He wasn't a "pretty boy", but he was definitely not hard on the eyes. He was sporting glasses, a polo shirt and khaki slacks. He looked good; really, really good. For a split second I felt giddy; like I was back in elementary school running the playground with him. As soon as he spoke my reminiscing was done.

"Skeeter!" Trey said as he reached in and wrapped his strong arms around me.

I thought I had escaped my elementary school nickname, which came from a day on the playground when Trey snuck up behind me on the monkey bars and literally scared the piss out of me. From then on, Trey and everyone in my class stuck me with the name "Skeeter." Lucky for me, Trey was the only one who kept the name up until middle school when he moved away.

"Trey?" I was still surprised that he was Kenya's cousin.

"I swear it's been what forever. You've grown up, Skeeter!" he said, closing the door behind him as I cringed at the nickname he just wouldn't let go.

"Yeah, well, it's been forever, like you said."

I liked him so much when we were growing up, and he never paid me any attention other than calling me "Skeeter" and making fun of me.

Elementary and middle school likes were so fascinating. Fascinating in a way that had me normalizing memorizing his schedule. The kind of like that led me to know he had Mrs. Patterson third period before I even had a reason to know. The kind of like that had me picking out my outfits the night before, pressing my edges down with my mama's Pink lotion and a silk scarf, hoping that *this* would be the day he actually *saw* me. Not Skeeter. Not the girl he scared off the monkey bars. *Me* — Lauren, who had read every book on that classroom shelf, who could double dutch without missing a beat, who everybody's mama called "such a sweet girl." I had a whole world inside me that I was just waiting for him to ask about. He never did. He'd look right through me like I was a window, only glancing my way long enough to get a laugh at my expense. And the worst part? I'd laughed too. Every single time. Giggled right along with everybody else so he wouldn't know how much it stung, so nobody would know I had folded myself small just to survive liking someone who didn't know I was worth seeing.

"So, what are you doing with yourself nowadays, Skeeter?" Trey asked, looking around the living room where we stood.

"Look, "Skeeter" was a long time ago, so why don't you just call me Lauren?" I motioned for him to follow me into the dining room.

Ladders, paint, and tools lay around aimlessly as Trey let out a whistle.

"So who did you trust this with because they have messed you up!" he said with his hands on his head.

"Gee thanks," I said with plenty of attitude in my voice.

Trey wasn't paying me any attention as he roamed, room to room, looking at the things Glenn had left either unfinished or damaged. I was kind of embarrassed. I had been expecting some overweight old guy; and yet, I had someone who I used to draw hearts on my folder for. I watched in silence as Trey eyed the workmanship of Glenn, hoping he would be able to give me a good deal. My eyes followed his body closely and then I remembered Brendan.

"Skeeter..."

"I *said* call me Lauren, Trey," I chimed.

Trey chuckled to himself and found a seat at the dining room table, then he pointed to a chair next to him.

"So, you never told me what you've been up to," Trey said, sounding genuinely interested in what I had to say. I cleared my throat and smirked.

"I'm working at 104.5 The Buzz, re-doing the house, and just trying to live," I said, breathing a sigh of relief.

Trey raised his eyebrows, impressed by what I was telling him.

"I never really listen to the radio; it's too much crap on there," he said, exposing his perfect teeth.

"Yeah. I can see why you would say that. Now about the house..."

"I didn't know you were friends with my little cousin; ain't it a small world? Who would have thought I would ever run back into Skeeter?"

I tried to keep my composure as the comedic Trey continued with his personal interrogation.

"Whatever happened to...what was her name? I think it was Jasmine or Gina."

I smiled for a second until I remembered I was still feuding with my best friend.

"It's Jasmine...and she's still around. She got married, had twins, and owns her own publishing company," I said, impressed by my best friend's successes.

"Really? Do you remember when the two of you got in trouble for stealing tater tots from the lunchroom?" he laughed loudly. I couldn't help but to snicker, thinking about the trouble that Jasmine always seemed to get me in.

"I remember that mess," I laughed, pushing my hair behind my ears.

"And do you remember when Mr. Maloney fell during the pep rally..."

"And he lost his toupee?" we both said at the same time as we shared a laugh.

Trey sat back in the chair and nodded his head.

"There's the old Skeet...I mean Lauren."

I needed the laugh, and I needed the walk down memory lane with Trey.

"What about you? What have you been up to?" I asked, putting my hands underneath my chin in an effort to hide my patience, which was running low.

"Well, you know I moved away right before high school, shortly after graduating high school, I got married, and then I started my own construction company. I just moved back to Atlanta about six months ago, so...let's just say you're lucky to have these hands in your presence," he said laughing.

For a second I imagined what my life would have been like if I would have been the wife in Trey's life.

"So, how's married life?" I asked.

"It *was* good until she decided she didn't want to be married anymore," he laughed softly as he clasped his hands together.

He glanced down before I realized what he was looking at.

"I should be asking you the same question," he said, nodding toward my hand. I followed his eyes and felt my stomach drop.

The ring. I had put it on that morning without even thinking because my mind hadn't caught up with my heart. Brendan and I were on a break. He had stood in that club and told me he might *never* be ready, and then disappeared into the night with another woman on his arm while Kenya held me together in the back of a town car. I had cried myself empty over that man. And yet somehow, in the quiet of getting dressed this morning, my fingers had found that ring and slipped it on like it still belonged there.

I hadn't even noticed it until he called it out.

I closed my hand slowly and dropped it to my side, heat rising to my face.

"I...it's not a...I'm not married," I said, mortified that an explanation would have to be given at all. What I did not say, what I could not say to a stranger in the middle of a conversation like this one, was that taking it off had felt like giving up on something I was not ready to give up on yet. That morning it was easier to just let it sit on my finger and pretend that everything was still intact.

"Now I heard that platform shoes are out...but I didn't know wearing gigantic, non-commitment rings were in," Trey joked in his normal goofy manner.

"My boyfriend gave it to me, but it's not an engagement ring," I said, ending the conversation.

Trey had always been a funny guy with plenty to say and joke about; sometimes I liked it, and other times it seemed aimed directly at me; especially right after mom's death. I couldn't shake the feeling that he was always picking on me.

"How long have you been with this joker?" Trey inquired.

"Eight years, today."

"And he hasn't made you the Mrs. yet?"

I bit my bottom lip and shook my head before changing the subject. "Trey, what am I looking at in terms of costs for fixing up my house?"

"I guess playtime is over, huh, Ms. Washington?" Trey laughed, pulling out an estimate sheet.

He started jotting down a couple of numbers and pulled out a calculator.

"Do you want something to drink?" I asked, getting up from the table and walking into the kitchen.

"Jack Daniels straight up, if you got it," he laughed without looking up from the table.

I returned to the table, with my grape juice, to find Trey's estimate in front of my chair and Trey gone.

"Trey?" I yelled while picking up the paper.

"Here I am," he said, reappearing from the dining room area.

"Did you have a chance to look it over?"

I glanced down at the paper and just about lost my marbles. His estimate was for one-fourth of the amount Glen was charging me.

"So, are we in business?" he asked, raising an eyebrow.

I was speechless. I knew it would cost more money to correct the problems Glenn and his crew had made, so why was Trey's estimate so low?

"I don't think you added in everything, Trey."

"Let me see that," Trey said, wrinkling his eyebrows and grabbing the estimate from me.

I knew he had overlooked something. *How could it be so low?* Not that I was fighting the amount, but I just wanted to make sure I wasn't getting over on Trey.

"There. That should take care of it," he said, marking something on the paper and handing it back to me.

I looked over the paper and started laughing loudly. Trey had written in one stipulation to him working for me.

Ms. Washington must let me call her Skeeter whenever I please.

"Trey, this cost is…are you sure?" I asked after my laughing fit.

"You're my peoples…and honestly, it'd be my pleasure to renovate this house," he said smiling.

"You don't know how much this means to me."

Trey rubbed his face and looked around the house.

"So, when should my guys show up? I was thinking we could start on Monday, if that's good with you," he said, picking up a picture of me with my parents.

"Monday sounds good," I said, signing the estimate and handing it back to him.

"Alright, well here's my card. You have my numbers. If you need anything or have any questions, call me," he smiled as he opened the door.

I pulled his arm and gave him a big bear hug.

"Thanks! You really saved me months of stress!" I laughed as I hugged him tightly.

Trey seemed to be blushing as he hugged me back.

"I guess this makes ghosting my client worthwhile," he said laughing.

"Come again?" I asked, standing outside of the door as my hair blew in the afternoon wind.

"It was nothing. I just had a lunch meeting with a client, but that can always wait until later. This was much more important," Trey said as he stood in front of his Ford F-150.

"I appreciate it."

I watched as Trey got in his truck and proceeded to back down the driveway. He slowed, rolling his window down.

"Next time I want my Jack Daniels, Skeeter!"

I shooed him off and dashed into the house just as my cell phone began to ring.

"Hello?"

"Hey baby, it's Brendan. Can you talk?"

"Yeah. I can talk."

"I want to apologize to you for last night. I was wrong for disrespecting you at your own party; I was even more wrong for flipping out on you," he said quickly as if he was rushing to meet a deadline.

"And I'm sorry for everything too. The party wasn't the time or place to start talking about marriage or our relationship," I said, curling up on the couch.

I silently thanked God for bringing Brendan around.

"You know I would never do anything to hurt you, Lauren," he said, sounding like he was getting ready to cry.

"I know, baby…I know." I said, wishing I was there to wipe each tear that was probably falling from his eyes.

"It's just…I'm realizing now that there's shit about me that I'm not happy with, but you've always looked past those things and loved me unconditionally."

I was surprised to hear Brendan talking like that because he rarely ever did.

"And I always will," I said, beginning to cry myself. Maybe this was the breakthrough we needed.

"Promise me that," he said, sighing. "Promise me you'll always love me."

"I'll always love you, baby!"

He sounded like he was wiping his nose and catching his breath at the same time.

"So, what have you done today?" he asked me as he cleared his throat.

I could have inquired about the mystery woman at the club, but I figured it would be better to leave well enough alone.

I ran down my morning, being reunited with Trey, and hiring him to finish the house. It felt good to talk to Brendan again. It seemed like we were talking for the first time; my heart finally felt at ease.

"After your shift, I was wondering if you could meet me at my house for dinner," Brendan said softly.

"I would be delighted," I said, checking my watch.

"I'm going to meet with this private investigator in a half hour, so I need to throw some clothes on and do something with my hair," I said sweetly.

Brendan inhaled and started laughing.

"So, you're really going through with it this time, huh?" he asked.

"Yeah, can you believe it? After all these years of me swearing I was going to do it...I'm actually pushing forward."

"Well, let me let you go. I'll see you tonight," he said.

We hung up and I stood in my living room feeling renewed. My house was in order, and my boyfriend was finally getting back on track. The last piece of stress in my life was my feud with

Jasmine, and that had to change quickly. As I headed toward my bedroom, I dialed Jasmine's number.

"Damn," I said as the voicemail came on.

Jasmine couldn't stay mad at me long. Now the ball was in her court. I was done trying. I jumped into a pair of jeans, a nice gray V-neck shirt and a pair of my black pumps. I slicked my hair back into a ponytail and threw on some lipgloss.

I gathered all the paperwork from the shoebox Pop kept on mom's death, and I headed out the door.

As I pulled up to the station, I saw that Lenny had once again parked his raggedy car in my spot; but today I wasn't tripping. I didn't care about the stupid parking spot; all I wanted was to get inside and meet with the private investigator.

I stepped out of the elevator and was greeted by the secretary and a couple of the interns.

"Lauren, you've got company in the conference room," Abigail, the secretary, said as she pointed to the room down the hallway. I was running about five minutes behind, and I hoped it wouldn't be held against me.

"Hello. I'm Lauren Washington. I'm *so* sorry I'm late," I said, extending my hand to the older Hispanic man who sat at the head of the conference table.

"Ralph Martez. Nice to meet you Ms. Washington. I have to say my kids are huge fans," he replied, cracking a smile.

He was a short man, standing about 5'4", with a huge gut that stuck out over his belt. His hair was peppered, and I saw that he walked with a slight limp as he headed toward me.

I let out a slight breath of relief.

"Tell them I said thank you so much for listening!" I said, taking my seat and gesturing for him to do the same.

"Let's get to work, then," Ralph said, putting on a pair of reading glasses.

My smile faded as Ralph combed through the information before him. Articles, police reports, pictures, and even Pop's recollection of the night were read over by Ralph slowly.

"I remember this case, it's been what? Twenty years?" he asked, taking off the glasses and looking at me.

"Eighteen actually. Do you think there's anything you can do?" I asked, clasping my hands together.

I was nervous; real nervous, and my hands would only give that away unless I controlled them.

"I can definitely do my best. I can't promise I'll find anything, but it's definitely worth a shot. Let me look over these documents and start asking some questions. I'll get back with you in, let's say, a week or two?" Ralph asked, raising one eyebrow.

"Sounds good."

I showed Ralph the way out, then made my way to my desk. For some reason, my good mood was slowly trickling down. Thinking about Ralph coming back with information on mom's death was a lot to deal with, but it's what I wanted. Regardless of what I was feeling, I had to strap on my grown woman shoes and handle whatever came my way.

"Well, I didn't think we would see you for another couple of hours," Lenny said sarcastically as he typed away at his computer.

I ignored his comment and sat at my desk and began my research. I was anxious, but I wasn't sure why. It was like I was waiting on the unknown to happen, and my soul couldn't sit still until it arrived.

"This is Lauren," I said as my office phone rang.

"Hey girl, it's me," Kenya said in her cheery tone.

"Hey."

"So, I heard you and Trey hooked up," she said.

"What do you mean 'hooked up?'" I asked, getting defensive. I wasn't sure what Trey had told her, but I was about to set the record straight.

"I mean he's coming by your house on Monday to start working on the house, right? What did you think I was talking about?"

I rolled my eyes at my paranoia.

"I don't know, girl. I'm tripping. I didn't know you and Trey were cousins; we grew up together," I said cradling the phone with my shoulder as I typed up my entertainment news.

"Yeah, his uncle married my aunt a couple of years ago," Kenya said matter-of-factly.

"Well, thanks for the contact. Have you heard from Jas today?" I asked, changing the subject again.

"Yeah. She called and asked how the party went. I told her she needed to call you."

"Hmph," I grunted, wishing Jasmine would just put her pride aside and call me.

"She's coming around, though, just give her time."

Before I could respond, Lenny was standing in front of me with his hands on his hips.

"Kenya, I gotta go. I'll call you when I get off," I said, looking up at Lenny.

"I don't pay you to stay on the phone chatting it up with your homies," he said, rolling his eyes and tossing a newspaper in front of me.

"You don't pay me at all, the station does; and what's this?" I said, picking up the paper for a better look.

I covered my mouth with my hand and gasped. I was on the front page of the local section. There I was, in my party dress from the night before, looking like I was in a heated argument with Brendan and the mysterious woman.

The headline said: *"Local DJ ends party with a bang!"*

"This isn't exactly the coverage the station was looking for," Lenny said, walking back to his chair and plopping down.

I tossed the paper in the garbage and massaged my temples. I knew exactly the message this was sending, and I was furious that someone had caught me in a weak moment.

The only thing I could do was to downplay it when I went on-air. I would play it to my advantage because I am the everyday woman – someone who every listener can relate to.

I finished a couple more documents and grabbed my things in preparation for the show. As I plugged in my headphones, I felt weird. I forced a smile and took my first mic break:

"What up all my ATL-iens?! It's your girl Mystique...the most talked about DJ in all of Atlanta; don't believe me? Check out your local section of the Atlanta Journal Constitution. Oh…they're trying to catch me riding dirty, y'all!" I said, laughing into the microphone.

"We're going to talk about this drama a little later, y'all… but right now, I've got brand new music from my boy Ludacris. Check it out. It's The Buzz 104.5!"

That night, I had a good show. A really good show. The kind where everything clicks into place from the first break and you leave the booth feeling like yourself again.

I opened with an energy set that had the phone lines lighting up before the second track faded out. When the rumors about the paper came up, as I knew they would, I addressed them the way I had learned to address everything on air. Calmly, directly, and then I kept it moving. I was not about to let somebody else's narrative hijack two hours of my night. I had music to play.

I debuted three new joints that I had been sitting on for a few weeks, records I had a really good feeling about. The phones confirmed what I already suspected. The listeners trusted my ear, and tonight they were riding with me.

I talked about the party, gave the highlights without giving everything away, and let the callers fill in the rest the way they always did.

But the moment I had been quietly looking forward to all day came near the end of the show, during my "Pump It or Dump It" segment. That was the portion where I premiered unreleased material and let the listeners be the jury. No context, no cosign, just the music standing on its own. If the phones blew up, it got the pump. If the lines stayed quiet, it got the dump. Simple as that.

I leaned into the mic and kept my introduction short.

"Alright, y'all. I've got something special for you tonight. This right here is the brand new single from The Rhymsters."

I hit play and leaned back in my chair.

By the time the hook dropped, every line in the studio was blinking.

Not to my surprise, everyone loved it and wanted more. My producer was waving at me through the glass with both hands, mouthing something I didn't need to hear to understand. The listeners were calling it a hit before the record even finished.

I smiled to myself as I faded it out and went to break. I hoped Dee was listening.

I headed out to my car and jumped in. I was finally about to see my man, and I couldn't wait for dinner and make-up sex. I also couldn't wait to see the look of pleasure in his eyes as I undressed, pressed my body against his, and purred lightly in his ear. I imagined his hands grabbing my waist and bringing me into him as he had done so many times before.

I giggled to myself as I thought of the things we would do that night. I got on the interstate and headed toward Brendan's condo, which was across town. I loved going to his spot; it was sophisticated, clean, and a definite step up from his humble beginnings. Just as I prepared to turn off on his exit, my phone began buzzing.

"Hey b-baby," Brendan stuttered; sounding as if he had too much to drink.

"Hey honey, I'm almost there. Do you want me to stop and get anything?" I asked, looking over my shoulder at the cars in the next lane.

"No. B-but we've got a change of plans. I need to go to the shop for something, so I'll just meet you at the IHOP where we had our first date," Brendan stuttered.

"Are you sure? I can wait for you at the condo if you need me to," I offered up.

After all, the IHOP he was talking about was at least twenty minutes away.

"No, I'll meet you there; I might be running late so just sit tight," he said sternly.

"Okay. I'll just order for you," I said sweetly.

Brendan hesitated before responding. "Yeah. Do that."

"Okay, I'll see you there."

"I love you, Lauren."

I smiled. It was weird how many butterflies I got after hearing Brendan say those words. A silly grin was plastered on my face as I responded the only way I knew how.

"I love you more," I said.

As I pulled into IHOP, I thought I had spotted Brendan's car, but was wrong. I sat in our normal booth and ordered the French toast and eggs for myself, and ordered Brendan the vegetable omelet. I checked my phone after thirty minutes, and still hadn't heard from him.

"Will the other party be joining you?" the waitress asked as she refilled my coffee.

"Yeah. He's just running a little late," I said smiling.

My emotions went from anxious, to worry, to anger, and back to worry. I had dialed Brendan's number repeatedly. When it hit the one hour mark, I paid for the food and headed out the door.

"How the hell are you going to stand me up, Brendan?!" I screamed into the voicemail as I drove to my house.

"You better have a helluva excuse!"

Pop was in the den, half-slouched in his favorite chair with the TV humming in the background. I poked my head in long enough to tell him that Trey was officially the new contractor. He nodded, eyes still glued to the screen, and that was that.

I headed upstairs, stripping out of my clothes and pulling on my pajamas with the kind of exhaustion that settles in your bones. I wasn't about to sit around waiting for Brendan to call and apologize. If he wanted to talk and if he wanted me, he was going to have to put in the effort this time.

I slid under the covers, laid my head on the pillow, and forced my eyes shut. Sleep didn't come easy, and it definitely wasn't peaceful, but my body demanded it.

The calm before the storm.

Before I had a chance to write in my journal, Pop woke me up by blasting Al Green. He normally did this on Sundays, but today I wasn't in the "Love and Happiness" mood. Besides the fact that Brendan had stood me up and Jasmine and I were still at odds, I had a splitting headache.

"What do you know about this, Sugar Baby?" Pop said, dancing around the kitchen joyously. He was dressed in a pair of dark-colored shorts with bleach spots all over, a white-turned-pink shirt, and a pair of reading glasses. Sundays in our household had always been about breakfast, church, and then dinner.

Even in our darkest hours, Pop made sure we both stayed anchored in church. New Corinth Missionary Baptist had been our family's church since before I was born. Walking through those doors felt like being wrapped in something older than grief. The smell hit you first: cedar wood polish and somebody's good perfume mixed with the faint sweetness of communion grape juice that never quite left the air, no matter what Sunday it was. The carpet was that deep burgundy that every Black church seemed to share, and the pews were cushioned in maroon velvet, worn soft in the middle from decades of mothers and grandmothers settling their good skirts against them.

The mothers of the church sat up front in their pill hats and white gloves, fans from the funeral home moving slow and steady in their hands like they had all the time in the world. Their stockings never ran. Their shoes always matched their bags. They nodded at you over their glasses, which knowingly meant *I see you, baby* and *you better act right* all at once. The choir stand was always packed — robes pressed, voices stacked — and when the organ dropped and the whole room rose together, you could feel it in your sternum. Not just hear it. *Feel* it. Like something inside you was being wrung out and handed back clean.

I might not have gone every Sunday, but I made sure I

was in the back pew of the church at least once a month. Slipping in just after devotional, sliding into that velvet cushion, letting the sound of it wash over me. I didn't always have words for what I needed. But the church always seemed to know anyway.

I snapped out of my sour mood and joined my father's crazy dancing, when the house phone rang. I wiped away a bit of sweat from my top lip and fell into one of the chairs near the kitchen table.

"Al Green's house of music!" I heard Pop say into the phone playfully. I loved Sundays because it allowed us the chance to relax just like the old days.

"Hold on. I can't hear you!" Pop said, running to the stereo and turning it down. I picked up a grape and popped it in my mouth as I watched Pop's face go blank.

"Yes, she's here," he said, taking the phone slowly from his face. He covered the mouth of the phone with his hand and whispered something to me.

"It's the police. I don't understand what they're saying," he said, passing the cordless phone to me.

As soon as he said that, my stomach began to flop. *What in the world had I done that warranted a call from the police?*

"This is Lauren," I said nervously.

"Ms. Washington, this is Detective Matthews with the Atlanta Police Department. I need you to come down to the police station immediately."

"Can you tell me what this is all about?" I asked as sweat built up on my forehead. My hands were shaking and I couldn't make them stop. I searched my mind for the good things the police called for, and I kept drawing blanks.

The last time we had received a call at our house from the police, it was to tell us that mom had been killed. The flashback was more than I could handle.

"We'd like to tell you about this in person," the officer said.

"Sir, if you don't mind, I need to know what you need me at the station for," I said. "Just tell me," I pleaded.

The officer put me on hold and came back to the phone seconds later.

"Ma'am, I didn't want to be the one to tell you this, and especially not over the phone, but we found a Mr. Brendan Lewis last night outside of his condo," the officer said slowly.

"Found him? What do you mean?" I wanted him to explain.

"Ms. Washington, he was found dead last night," he said, pausing. "It looks like it was suicide."

In that moment, it seemed like time stopped and I had stepped outside of my body. I looked at Pop for some type of help as I felt my knees wobbling. I felt the tears filling my eyes while I gripped the phone tighter. I couldn't breathe. My head began to swim, and before I knew it, I was screaming into the phone hysterically.

"Let me talk to your fucking boss! It's not right to make up lies like that!" I yelled before Pop came and snatched the phone from me.

He talked to the officer while I stood silently looking off into space. *This must have been some kind of mistake. How could Brendan be dead?* I had just spoken to him hours earlier.

I hadn't realized it but my entire body was shaking, and Pop was slowly walking toward me. The look on his face said it all.

I grabbed Pop by the shoulders and yanked his body harshly.

"No! No! Pop...no!" I said as I fell to the ground. Pop tumbled with me, and we sat there and sobbed.

As hard as I tried, I couldn't see, hear, or feel anything as we rode down to the police station. It was a familiar ride for me; it was the same path and speed we had taken when the police called us to say that mom had died; it was the route I took to work every day, and it was even the path I took to Brendan's house.

Sure Brendan had been stressed at work, but nothing could have prepared me for the thought of him committing suicide. He had everything: plenty of money in the bank, a hot business, a loving girlfriend, and an envied car and home.

My heart sank when the police officer escorted me into the cold, white and sterile interrogation room. I turned to Pop and begged him to come with me. I knew he wasn't strong enough for it, but I needed him; I didn't have anyone else to turn to.

Officer Matthews sat with me as my puffy, red eyes looked up at him for clarification. His ashy hands reached across the table as he passed a note that was scribbled out in Brendan's handwriting. All it said was,

> I'm sorry. I can't take it. Everyone is better off. It'll all make sense. Call my girl Lauren Washington 404-444-5777.
>
> Brendan

I scanned the note over and over, and before long, I couldn't see anything except my tears. Officer Matthews talked generally about what the next steps would be, and as much as I wanted to tell myself that it was true…my heart wouldn't accept the truth.

"I need to see him," I said as I interrupted Officer Matthews's conversation with Pop.

After taking a big gulp, Officer Matthews left the room, leaving Pop and I sitting at the black table. I gripped his hand tightly, and looked at him for some sort of explanation.

"Ms. Washington, I can't authorize you seeing the crime

scene pictures, but I can give you this," he said before passing something in my direction.

"This was on Mr. Lewis at the time we found him," he said, handing me the Rolex watch that Brendan never took off.

I held the metal watch in my hand tightly and stroked the face of it. If what they were saying was true, this watch was all I had left of my boyfriend. Just like with my mother, all I had to symbolize his existence was a piece of jewelry.

I screamed loudly into the air as Pop held me tightly. He knew what I had been trying to challenge was true – Brendan was dead.

My everything was gone; and life, as I knew it, would be no more.

chapter five

Dear Diary,

Brendan is dead. It's taken me seven hours and two "happy" pills to say that. When I got the call, I thought it was some sort of bad joke; but it wasn't. Brendan is dead and he killed himself. How is this happening? Why is this happening? I haven't been able to do anything since I got home. All I can do is close my eyes, but even doing that is scary because all I see is him. I try to take a bath, but all I smell is Brendan. I cried until I couldn't cry anymore, but my heart was all confused. Why? Why? Why? Why? Why? I'm going over our last conversation in my head, and I don't know why I didn't see that something was wrong. I feel like it's my fault in a way. Was Brendan crying out for help and I stupidly ignored him? I was supposed to be the one person he could turn to and I let him down. I called Brendan's mom and she wasn't able to come to the phone. I think I'm numb right now. I can't sleep, I can't think, and I definitely can't eat. I haven't been able to even think of calling Jasmine or Kenya because I realize I'll have to vocalize that my boyfriend, the man of my dreams, is dead. I'm going to lie down now, although I know I won't sleep. My heart feels as if everything has been ripped out and readjusted. How do I go on without him?

Lauren Washington

———

I couldn't fathom being away from Brendan for a day, let alone forever. My heart ached; it literally ached. I hurt from the crown of my head to the soles of my feet, and I needed Brendan to feel better; I needed him badly. I couldn't convince my eyes or my heart that this was *it*. I mean he was me and I was him; right? *What was I supposed to do now? What had all of our years together prepared me for except loneliness?* When I went to breathe, all I could feel was the huge lump in my throat that felt hot as fire.

I had cried so much that my breath felt like it was being

snatched from my lungs. I tried to grasp something, anything with my hands to make it feel the pain I was in. I dug my nails deeply into the carpet and wailed as my nails scraped past the carpet and hit the hard board underneath. I couldn't imagine my heart beating any faster, my eyes producing any more tears, or my body feeling any frailer. I was spent. My mind wandered to how much I loved and was dedicated to Brendan. *He took it all away?*

At that moment, I wanted to kill him. I wanted to revive him only to wrap my hands around his neck and strangle him; but not before I told him how much I hated him. But I didn't hate him; and that was the twisted part of it. *How could I wrap my mind around the thought of never hearing his voice or never seeing his face?* That beautiful face I loved to stare at for hours. *How could I explain to my heart that what was my "forever" had only been a short intermission?* As the tears blurred my vision, I realized that my breathing was heavy. I wrapped my arms around my body and rocked slowly to my own rhythm. I shut my eyes, allowing a large group of tears to fall from my eyes. I tried to remember the last time I had seen Brendan, the last time we had laughed together, the last time we had kissed, and the last time we had made love. I replayed each moment pathetically, searching for the feeling I had received when it initially happened.

A dull ache in my heart caused me to remember that our last memories would be the final chapter in the story of us. There would be no more butterfly kisses, soft touches, encouraging words, or hair-raising entrances which made my body shiver. I reached out weakly, as a vision of Brendan entered my sight.

How could this happen to Brendan, of all people? He was handsome, charismatic, had plenty of money and friends, and was envied by plenty. *Why was he gone? Why was there a huge lump in my throat that was bobbing up and down every time I thought of "What could have been?"* I was feeling a range of emotions, but pity topped them all. I thought about God and why He had chosen *me* to be the person to deal with this situation. I thought, *with the murder of my mother, haven't I already been subjected to enough grief for a lifetime?*

As I sat on the floor, allowing the reality of the situation to sink in, a rush of loneliness came over me. I knew my support system was larger than most, but yet my heart felt as lonely as the day my mother was buried. *How could he do this? How could I not know to stop it?* Brendan could easily make me smile, simply by the mention of his name, but being faced with the finality of his departure was more than I could bear. I wasn't given the option of a goodbye; nor was I given the chance at receiving closure.

How could my heart and soul let go of what had served as my heart and soul? Where was the fairness in my pain? Where was the sense in it all?

The cliché *"Everything happens for a reason"* rang in my ears as I tore myself from the ground. As much as the cliché made sense in everyone else's circumstance, I couldn't understand the reason in Brendan's suicide.

I made my way to the bathroom and stood in front of the mirror motionless. My swollen eyes, the bags underneath them, and my tears stared back at me. I watched myself as the water continued to roll down my cheeks, hitting my shirt. After minutes of crying, I inhaled and tried to pull myself together. Brendan had promised me forever, *but where was he now? How could he leave me like that?* My pain wasn't gone; but the anger inside of me was boiling over. I was pissed. My tears became damp streaks down my cheeks, and served as a simple reminder of my situation. Before I knew it, I was pulling out all of the reminders of Brendan from drawers, underneath the sink, and even on the counters. He was everywhere, and I needed him gone immediately. If he could leave me so easily, I needed his every memory out.

I pulled together pictures, soap, cologne, and a toothbrush

belonging to Brendan, and dumped it all in the trash. I didn't feel better, but it felt just like sweet revenge, only duller. As I reached underneath the sink and pulled out his overnight bag, I noticed his personal barber clippers and held them tightly. I stared at them closely, dangling them from my fingers in disgust. I didn't have anything against Brendan's passion for barbering, but I needed his memory gone. The clippers swung effortlessly from my hands as my anger took over me. I had loved his man – LOVED him, and this is what I was left with? I loved him, but I hated that I did.

Why couldn't I just let go? Why couldn't I just cross him off and be done with it?

I wanted this whole suicide "thing" to be done with. I wanted my life back. I stared at the clippers closely and cursed Brendan. As I screamed loudly, I flung the clippers at the mirror in aggravation. Just as the glass shattered, the clippers headed back toward my arm and nicked one of them. I didn't know if my loud cries were from the blood coming from my arm or from my dreams going up in smoke.

This wasn't a dream, and it definitely wasn't some twisted joke. I couldn't talk myself out of what was happening. The only thing that felt real in that moment was the warm, spreading wetness on my arm. My whole body trembled as I pressed it against my chest, the movement smearing the red across my shirt in uneven streaks.

My back hit the wall, and I slid down until I was sitting on the cold tile. The chill of the floor shot through me, sharp enough to make my breath hitch. Tears blurred my vision as I watched drops fall from my elbow and splatter onto the tile— soft, muted taps that somehow made everything feel even more surreal.

I sobbed, the sound raw and unsteady, trying to convince myself that this physical pain—this shaking, this sting, this shock—was somehow preparing me for the emotional storm I knew was coming. That maybe surviving this moment meant

I could survive the rest. When it was all over, I cleaned up my mess, tried to explain the broken glass and screams to Pop, and headed straight to my room to lay down.

I watched motionless as Martin Lawrence joked about Pam's beady beads. I thought about Brendan as I listened. *What was he doing before he killed himself? Did he think of me? Had I been the reason? What could I have done to stop him? Why hadn't I driven to his condo despite his objections?* The endless thoughts poured in and out of my mind.

The police had informed me that he had been found inside of his Escalade with the note and a .32 revolver, which he had used to put a bullet through his chest. It was all I could picture when I daydreamed.

Even though I knew he was gone, it didn't stop my hands from dialing his phone number over and over, just to hear his voice. The husky, often overpowering, voice filled my ears and gave me a little bit of comfort. In those moments, I could pretend he was still alive and things were back to normal.

I lay in my bed barely moving when I heard a knock at my door.

"Who is it?" I said softly.

"Brendan," I thought I heard the voice say. I jumped up from my bed and ran to the door, tripping over the sheets on the way, and swung it open.

It wasn't Brendan; it was Kenya. My mind was playing tricks on me. I could tell she had been crying and had heard the news. She embraced me, and we both sobbed softly. But even though tears were flowing, I still had not come to accept that my boyfriend wasn't coming back.

"How did you find out?" I asked, getting back under the sheets and looking over at Kenya who was keeping her distance from me.

"Your dad called me; I came right over," she said, wiping her nose and eyes.

I stared at Kenya, and somehow felt like I needed to

comfort her. She quietly watched me until I called her over to me.

"How are you holding up?" she asked, sniffling.

"I'm not sure, really. I just…I can't believe it."

My head was thumping a little bit and my mouth was dry. All I wanted was for Brendan to walk through my door, like he'd done so many times before, and tell me it had all been one huge joke. A cruel joke – but a joke nonetheless. Then I would punch him in the shoulder and tell him I would never talk to him again; then he would take me by the waist and kiss me until I giggled. That's the reality I wanted right now. A heavy feeling came over my chest. I just wanted my life back.

"Do you need anything?" Kenya asked, sitting softly on my bed.

I shook my head and kept my eyes on the television. I watched as Gina caressed Martin's big ears tenderly as he said some corny joke about how beautiful she was. I bit my bottom lip as I forced myself to watch someone else doing the things I would have given my life to do with Brendan again.

Here I was sitting in my pajamas, in the middle of the afternoon, with my best friend by my side, mourning the loss of my boyfriend. But regardless, I felt the need to keep going, keep busy.

"I need to go to the station," I said, removing the covers and marching over to my closet.

Anything I could do to keep my mind off of Brendan, I was game for. Kenya sat frozen on the bed watching my every move, in shock.

"Honey, you need to lay down. I think the station can do without you today," Kenya said finally.

I shook my head and proceeded to scan my closet for clothes suitable for work.

"I need to get there; I've got some things to do," I said over and over as I slipped on a shirt and jeans.

Kenya pulled me by the arm and into a tight hug; I tried my best to break free. I pushed and I pushed Kenya's petite body away from me, but she wouldn't let go.

"Just leave me alone, Kenya!" I wailed loudly as my arms flailed in the air. Kenya was fighting me all the way, and we ended up on the floor with tears streaking down both our cheeks.

"Just relax, honey," Kenya said through gasps of air. "Relax."

I was still trying to fight her grasp, but my energy was draining, and the reality of the situation was coming to the forefront.

"Why, Kenya? Why!" I screamed loudly as I kicked my legs and gripped her arm tightly. I heard my bedroom door open, but it was as if my entire body was cement. As hard as I tried, I couldn't move. Finally giving up, I continued screaming and crying. Out of nowhere, I felt another set of arms holding me down and caressing my back. *Was my mind playing tricks on me again?* My tears were preventing me from seeing exactly who it was; but before I knew it, I looked up and saw Kenya was standing over me crying into her hands, while the other set of hands were wrapped around me rocking my body slowly.

I turned around to see who was holding me and I saw the only face, besides pop, I could have wished for.

"I'm here," Jasmine said while she, too, gasped for air. "I'm here now."

My entire demeanor changed; I was finally weeping, crying, and howling the way my soul had been begging me to. I leaned back into Jasmine's hold and I cried out Brendan's name.

"Brendan! Damn, Brendan!" I screamed loudly. "Not my baby, y'all!"

My girls rallied around me, and after minutes of hoarse voice, dry-eyed, body-aching crying, I was back in my bed resting comfortably. As my eyes drifted off to sleep, I could hear Kenya and Jasmine talking over me softly.

"Lance told me that some of the guys from the shop are saying Brendan had been stressed lately. But why would he do this?" Jasmine paused before she continued. "Why would he do this to her and everyone?"

Kenya and Jasmine left me alone in my room, and I sat up on my headboard and prayed for Brendan. I prayed that his mother and brother would be okay, and that Brendan was at peace when he did what he did. But no matter how tight I closed my eyes and prayed for acceptance, as soon as I opened my eyes I was back to reality.

My heart ached, and I couldn't get it to stop. I knew Brendan had been acting strangely, but I had no idea he had been stressed enough to want to take his own life. *Why hadn't I seen what everyone else had been able to see? Had I been that consumed with my own agenda?*

"Why didn't you talk to me?" I asked as tears streamed down my face again.

And for the first time in a while, no one was there to distract me from the question only Brendan could answer, and I could not ignore.

chapter six

Dear Diary,

I go back to work today. I can't run from my life and the truth forever. My boyfriend killed himself; by now everyone else knows what's going on. A lot of my fans have been sending flowers, notes, and presents to the station to help me cope. The funeral is set for this Saturday, and I even contemplated not going. But I've got to say goodbye; even if he can't say it back. "I love you, Lauren," were his last words to me. I feel miserable, slightly depressed, and unsure of my purpose. But I'll push through. Ralph was supposed to meet me at the station today, but he called and said he needed more time. I'm glad, too. I'll have to deal with that next week.

Pop thinks I need to take a vacation and get out of town for a week or so, but I can't. I've got to keep moving to keep my mind off of the fact that eight years of my life is being buried on Saturday. Eight years of happiness is gone; eight years of togetherness, love, and a future. I still can't figure it out, and I don't know if I ever will.

I keep looking at my tattoo in the mirror; I don't know if it was a foreshadowing for the current events, or just a fitting way to say goodbye. How long had Brendan thought about killing himself? Why hadn't he talked to me about it? So many questions are running through my mind but I've got to get ready to head out the door for work.

Lauren Washington

———

When I was driving to the station, I got the eeriest feeling in the pit of my stomach. I felt like Brendan was sitting right next to me, telling me that everything would be okay.

"It'll all make sense," I said out loud, recalling the note found with his body.

I pulled into the station parking lot. I was surprised, for the first time in years, Lenny wasn't parked in my space. I knew I looked a mess. My hair was in a rough looking ponytail, and my shirt and jeans were old and ragged. It was a completely different look than any of my colleagues were used to, but I didn't care. I had no reason to focus so much energy on my looks.

As I walked into the office, everyone stopped what they were doing. Whether it was conversations or work, they paused to watch me like a science experiment gone wrong.

I ignored them all and kept my focus. Lenny stood up when he saw me and bowed his head in respect. I knew it took a lot for him to be nice to me, so I accepted it graciously.

I looked on my desk and saw a bundle of roses sitting on top of my keyboard. I picked up the card and read it to myself.

We're all here for you! Lenny & The Buzz staff.

Tears filled my eyes as I reached out and touched Lenny's hand softly.

"Thank you,"

"It's my pleasure," Lenny said softly.

I sat at my desk and gathered my news as usual. People avoided me like the plague, not knowing what to say, or how to say it. It was better that way, because all I wanted was to be left alone. Kenya and Jasmine called to check on me during the day. They were the friendly breaks I needed. As the clock ticked down to my airtime, I gathered my papers and headed into the studio. I remembered the last time I had been in the studio; I was thinking my life would be starting anew; boy was I right.

"Hey, hey, y'all. It's your girl Mystique. I've been out of the loop for a minute, but I'm back!" I said laughing loudly.

I had weighed whether or not I would speak on what had happened. *Did they want to know the things I had been fighting?* I knew I was jumping out on a limb, but I decided they deserved to know since I included them in everything else.

"I share everything with y'all, so we're basically like family; and because we're like family, I know I can keep it all the way real with y'all. I had a death in my family; the death of someone extremely close to me...my boyfriend of eight years, Brendan, committed suicide this past weekend." I paused as my producer pulled the instrumental down for the more serious vibe I was giving. I could feel myself starting to cry, and as I did I paused to gather my words.

"It's been the hardest thing I've ever had to deal with. So...just like I can talk about all the good things in my life, now I feel pain just like y'all," I said, trying to put my emotions in check.

My producer pointed to the phone line and motioned for me to take the live call.

"Buzz, what up?" I said, wiping my face off and preparing myself for the backlash.

"Hey Mystique. My name is Shemika, and I just want to say that we're all thinking about you and your boyfriend's family! Keep your head up, girl."

"Thanks Shemika!" I said as my producer pointed for me to answer another call.

"Buzz, what up?"

"Hey, is this Mystique?" the male voice asked clearly.

"Yeah, this is your girl!" I said plainly.

"Well, you don't know me, but I've been listening to you since you started at Buzz. I love your spirit, and I've got to say my prayers are with you, sister! I commend you for speaking out too!"

I was touched and couldn't believe that so many people cared about my life.

"Thanks going out to everyone out there who's reaching out and touching me in prayer and thought. I appreciate it so much, y'all! I've got to say that if anyone out there is feeling depressed, sad, or doesn't know what to do, make sure you talk to someone. Anyone," I said before introducing Tupac's "I Ain't Mad at 'Cha."

Strangely enough, this song had been one of Brendan's favorites. After my show was completed, I packed up my things and swung by my desk to pick up my purse and cell phone.

"Lauren, we've gotten so many calls from people who want to know more about your story," Lenny said, waving a stack of phone messages in his hand.

"I think we're onto something," he said, raising an eyebrow.

I smiled politely and put the phone messages on my desk. If I was going to tackle a hurdle, it would have to be one day at a time.

Instead of heading over to Kenya or Jasmine's house, I headed straight home. I was surprised to see Trey's truck in the driveway, and parked my car right next to his.

"Hey," I said looking at Trey and Pop as they sat at the kitchen table drinking beers.

I had been crying in the car, and the last thing I wanted to do was feel pity from my old crush and my father.

"Hey, Sugar Baby," Pop said, patting a seat next to him. I put my purse on the back of the chair and sat down.

"Do you want one?" Pop asked, lifting up the six-pack of Heinekens in front of him. Trey looked at me intensely while I barely made eye contact.

"No. I'm actually about to take a shower and go to bed; it's been a long day," I said as I proceeded to stretch my arms and yawn loudly.

I excused myself and made my way up to the bedroom, showered, crawled into bed, and sobbed quietly until I was numb.

The next couple of days leading up to Brendan's funeral were uneventful. I still hadn't been able to get a clear understanding as to why Brendan ended his life. Lance, who was usually full of answers, knew nothing; and no one on the street seemed to have any information either. I was stuck; and I realized if I was going to find out why Brendan killed himself, I was going to have to do it on my own.

While I dressed for the funeral, I tried to tell myself that everything would be okay. Kenya and Jasmine would be meeting me at my house so we could ride over to Brendan's mother's house, and then ride to the funeral together. I had all the support I needed.

I couldn't stop my hands from shaking as I pulled my simple black dress over my body. I had gained a little weight in the week since Brendan died, and I could see it – primarily in my face. My appearance had drastically changed, and I really didn't care how I looked.

"Let me do your makeup," Kenya said as she pulled out a small makeup bag. I didn't object, although I didn't see the reason for makeup. I was going to a church to see my boyfriend in a casket. I doubted powder and lipstick would help the situation.

I looked decent, though. My hair was pulled into a bun, my simple black dress stopped right above my knees, and my Nine West heels were as plain as they came.

As we stood inside Brendan's mother's house preparing to get in our assigned vehicles, my attention went to the absence of Brendan's older brother, Terrence. Brendan had always told me that when they were younger the two of them were glued at the hip.

"Ms. Pat, is Terrence here?" I said, looking around the house. The only difference between Brendan and Terrence was that Terrence was a certified, straight up and down… nerd; he even used to wear pocket protectors. From what I knew, he moved back to New Jersey after graduating high school, and he never looked back to Georgia or his family. The closest I had ever gotten to Terrence was the pictures Brendan showed me.

"Oh, my baby couldn't make it," she said, dabbing her eyes. She squeezed my hand tightly and I reached over and hugged her plump body.

Ms. Lewis was a short, round, dark-skinned woman with plenty of gray hair to show the years of worry caused by her boys. With the exception of her breasts and her skin tone, Brendan and his brother looked just like their mother. The grin that Brendan and his mother shared was eerily familiar. While the two of us were never at odds, we often battled for Brendan's attention. There would be plenty of times he and I would have something planned, and his mother would call five minutes before we left and demand he spend time with her. The good ole guilt trip of "I'm your mama boy; she's just a *girl*" worked earlier in our relationship; but as we both got older, her guilt trips stopped working.

There were very few, if any, mentions of Brendan's father Darrin. When we met, Brendan had told me that his parents had gotten married up North as teenagers, and they stayed together for five years. Soon after the separation, Ms. Pat and the boys relocated to Atlanta, and Darrin popped in and out of their lives until Brendan and Terrence were in their mid-teens. I didn't expect to see Darrin there, but I was curious who he was and what he looked like.

I watched as family members and close friends piled into the tiny house. Kenya and Jasmine stood closely behind me while Pop kept to himself on the front porch. It was a rainy day, and as I stood beside the window staring at the black limousines, with black mirrored tint, I quickly diverted my attention to something else. I traced my fingertips over a baby picture of Brendan that lay on a nearby table. Kenya smiled sheepishly while Jasmine shook her head in silence.

"Wasn't he a beautiful baby?" I asked. I picked up the picture and held it tightly.

My friends didn't respond, and I wasn't sure if I wanted them to. All I needed was someone to listen to me.

The only thing that had kept my attention off of Brendan's death had been the investigation into my mother's murder. In a way, the investigation had given me a purpose to keep going.

I had talked to Ralph, the private investigator, the day before the funeral, and I asked him what he had found out about mom's death. Surprisingly, he had news. He said he had learned that a neighborhood homeless man, who we all knew as "Dirty Larry", had apparently been around when mom was murdered and had seen "something." As much as I wanted to be excited about finding closure with one aspect of my life, I couldn't be.

I listened to Ralph, but my mind kept drifting to Brendan and the funeral that was still ahead of me. Ralph and I agreed to meet on the Monday after Brendan's funeral so he could give me the full run down on what "Dirty Larry" had seen. I didn't feel like now was the time to update Pop so I kept the little bit of information I had received to myself.

"Are you ready to load up?" Jasmine asked, tapping me on my shoulder.

"Yeah…I guess," I said, sighing.

Jasmine held my hand tightly as I walked toward the car. I could see Ms. Pat was having a breakdown as she ducked into the first car. As I headed toward the same car, I felt myself going in the same direction. I had intentionally stayed away from the wake because I wasn't ready to see my boyfriend – the love of my life and my best friend – cold, stiff, and in a casket. In a nutshell, I wasn't ready to say goodbye.

"It's okay to cry," Pop said, stroking my back softly as raindrops hit my forehead and trickled down.

I knew it was okay to cry, and I really wanted to. But looking at the black limo in front of me, I started to feel as if I was walking to a slow grave. It was like the Grim Reaper was in front of me, and I was walking toward the inevitable. It was closure that I didn't want.

I had done well up until that moment. I was able to function, live, and try to force a smile on my motionless face. But as I walked toward the death mobile, I felt like I was hearing the news all over again.

We found him dead.

I felt a tear on my face. My head began to swim. Just as I turned to leave, Pop was there with his arms outstretched.

In that second, I felt like I was a motherless nine-year old again; with pigtails, a Kool-Aid and pickle addiction, Cross-Color clothes, and a toothless grin. I fell into his arms and wrapped my arms around his body.

"Pop, I don't want to go," I said, keeping my head on his shoulder.

Pop tilted my chin up and stared into my eyes for a minute before speaking.

"Sugar Baby, it's your choice; but I think you'll regret it if you don't at least say goodbye," Pop said, wiping a tear from my cheek with his thumb. I thought about it as I stared at the ground. Immediately, I knew not attending the funeral wasn't an option. I bit my lip, took a few deep breaths, and barreled into the car with the rest of the family. I stared out the window as I heard people talking around me.

"Did you hear about the barbershop?" I heard one older woman, who I thought was Brendan's Aunt Cleo, say softly.

I had no idea what she was talking about, and as I turned my head to get more information, Kenya was in my face.

"Let me just touch up your nose and forehead and put on a little lip gloss," she said, reaching into her bag with excitement. I know Kenya just wanted to help in the best way she could, and since I wasn't openly talking about my feelings, her bag of magic was the next best therapy she could provide.

Even though I was in a car full of grieving people, I felt

miserably alone. It was as if I were watching everyone talk in slow motion. Their mouths and gestures were moving so slow that I had to shake my head to make sure I wasn't dreaming. I watched as Jasmine, Pop, and Kenya talked amongst themselves. I wasn't staring at anyone in particular, but I wanted to be where they were – sad, but functional. I couldn't function and I couldn't smile.

I looked out the window and kept my eyes on the trees as I thought about what I was about to face. That's when I started thinking, *What are funerals exactly?* A forced public method of saying goodbye and healing? A performance of grief with a dress code and a program and someone's aunt at the piano playing too slow? I had been to enough of them to know the shape of it; the flower arrangements that were always slightly too bright, the obituary with the photo they chose because it was recent instead of the one that actually looked like him, and the way people signed the guest book in the foyer like grief had an attendance sheet.

But in my eyes, I had already said goodbye to Brendan. I said it the moment he hung up the phone on the night he took his life. That click and the silence after it…that was my goodbye. It didn't wait for a Saturday. It didn't wait for a casket or a program or the right black dress. It happened in the dark, with no witnesses and no one handing me a tissue.

Up until this moment, funerals had made sense to me. They were for other people's losses. Now I was facing my own public goodbye to the man I loved, and I was starting to see it differently. Starting to understand what it actually asked of you.

Why did I have to say goodbye *openly*? Was it just so other people could watch me grieve and walk away quietly deciding whether I had mourned enough or too much? Whether my tears were the right kind - not too messy, not too composed, not too angry? Was this moment for me, or was it for them? And why did this have to be the expiration date, the official end, the moment the world decided my grief had been witnessed and could now be wrapped up and filed away?

I pressed my fingers against the cold glass of the window and watched the trees blur past.

As we rode the interstate, my eyes stayed fixated on the trees, which blew so beautifully in the wind. It was small things like trees that made me jealous; jealous of not being able to enjoy the things around me. I tried to make sense of everything as best as I could. Every thought led back to the infamous question: *"Why?"*

I thought about the possible answers, but none of them seemed severe enough for Brendan to end his life. None of it seemed so detrimental that suicide seemed the only way to go. I had taken the trip from Bankhead to New Birth Missionary Baptist Church plenty of times before, but this day, everything was moving sluggishly. All the cars, the talk, and the drive, were all going slower than ever, and I couldn't understand why. I wanted to grab a remote and press Fast Forward so I could skip the funeral, the mourning, and the stares…just to get in my bed and sleep.

The drive seemed so familiar; almost like muscle memory. Brendan and I had driven this route before. I wanted it to stop. I wanted thoughts of his hands in mine, and his bright smile, to vanish from my memory. Even though I was sad, I was also angry. I heard laughter in the limo and turned to see Brendan's cousins giggling about the "good times" with him. I had plenty of "good times" to add, but I could only think about the selfish act that had caused us to be there.

How could they act like he was being honored, or telling old war stories? Brendan had killed himself and they were acting like he was being given the key to the city. I shook my head and looked outside. Brendan was gone – by his own choice, and at his own hands. I wanted to tell them all how Brendan had murdered me when he had pierced his heart with the bullet. Everything I knew would be buried with him.

I tried to tune out the talk and laughter, but I picked up a story from one of his aunts who was as calm as they came about Brendan being a "good kid" and how "perfect" he was. My face felt scorching hot as I tried to hold back how I was truly feeling. The truth of the matter was, I wasn't only angry with Brendan, I was angry with myself; angry because I couldn't stop my man from killing himself. I was angry because I didn't even know suicide had been an option in his heart or mind. I was riddled with guilt as I stared into the faces of all of his loved ones. I felt as responsible for killing Brendan as the bullet itself. *Did I even deserve a seat in the limousine?*

My mixed emotions were swirling everywhere as I tried to keep them under control. I had had the responsibility of taking care of my man; and yet, the funeral would serve as confirmation that I had failed. I mean, look at my track record...I thought, *I had a dead mother and boyfriend. I wasn't exactly the angel of luck or life.*

There were hundreds of hundreds of cars parked inside the spacious parking lot of the church. The mega church, which was always packed for Bishop Eddie Long's sermons, was now packed to say farewell to my boyfriend. This was the same church I had secretly planned on walking down the aisle and becoming Mrs. Brendan Lewis in. But today, I would be walking down the aisle saying goodbye to what would never be. I sobbed softly into a tissue as the limo pulled up to the entrance of the church. The cement feeling was back, and my body was starting to feel like dead weight. With Pop's help I was standing—though not very well. My legs were shaky, my eyes were red, and my hands couldn't stop trembling.

As we all piled into the church vestibule to prepare for our entrance, I scanned the room in awe. Some people were already seated, while others were scrambling around to the bathroom; but as soon as the family entered the building, everyone took their places, as if on cue for some pre-rehearsed play.

"This turn out is wonderful," Jasmine said in my ear as I barely smiled.

It should have been comforting to know that so many people loved my boyfriend, but it wasn't. What would have been comforting…would have been Brendan walking through the door with his signature grin plastered on his face.

But when I heard his mother wail as she started making her way down the aisle, I knew the comforting moments I wished for would, in no way, be happening.

Ms. Pat had allowed me to sit right next to her and Brendan's grandmother – the same place that a spouse would sit.

With Pop by my side, gripping my hand tightly, and Jasmine and Kenya directly behind me, I knew I had nowhere to go but to the dreaded casket. The minister had told us that when we entered the church we would bypass our seats and instead circle in front of Brendan's open casket. After paying our respects we would, then, take our designated seats.

As much as I wanted to remember what I was supposed to do, I couldn't take my eyes off all the people staring back at the long line of family members ushering down the aisle.

My eyes caught a couple of people I knew from Brendan's barbershop, and they looked just as ragged as I did. I searched the crowd and smiled sweetly at a couple of them, and then I saw *her*. It was the mystery girl that Brendan was with at my birthday party. As we passed her pew, I saw her drop her head and weep into her hands quietly. I kept my focus on her even after we passed her row. I knew I needed to talk to her because maybe, just maybe, she would have some answers to the questions burning a hole in my soul.

We approached the casket just as grandma Lewis and Ms. Pat were being escorted to the front row. I turned and looked at Pop, whose eyes were bloodshot from crying, and quickly turned back to face what I had been avoiding.

Brendan.

He laid there perfectly still, like sleep had just taken him mid-thought. He looked good. One of the guys from the barbershop had come in to give him his Caesar, the one that always brought out the deep waves he was so particular about. His eyebrows were still perfectly shaped. His lashes still full and dark against his skin. I reached out and touched his face, and the cold stopped me cold — that sudden, certain cold that the living are never prepared for, no matter how many times someone warns you.

I lost it.

I heard myself scream before I understood that the sound was coming from me. My hands moved frantically across his chest, searching without knowing what they were searching for — the wound, the reason, some physical proof of what had taken him. Kenya and Pop and Jasmine closed in around me, their hands on my arms and my back, trying to hold what was coming apart. I couldn't feel them. I could only feel him — still and solid and *gone* beneath my fingers.

"Brendan." His name tore out of me over and over, my hands gripping the edge of the casket like letting go would mean something final.

People were lined up behind me, waiting their turn, and I did not care. This was my man. Nobody in that room had loved him the way I had, and I was not going to be rushed through the last moment I would ever have with him. I leaned down and pressed my lips to his. They were stiff and cold and unyielding; nothing like the lips that used to warm me from the inside out, that used to make me forget whatever I'd been worried about. I stayed there for a moment longer than was comfortable for anyone watching.

I didn't care about that either.

"Oh baby, why?!" I said, whispering in his ear "Please don't leave me. Come back!"

I knew he was gone, but I had to plead my case; maybe God could make an exception this *one* time and give him back. I wanted to believe that miracles happened. But I knew the truth. No amount of pleading, begging, or crying, would undo what had been done.

It couldn't have been his "time," I thought, as I traced my finger up and down his clean, manicured nails.

He was dressed in a clean, black and white pin-striped suit. He had bought it a year earlier to wear to a black-tie function, but when he had to cancel, he kept it hanging in his closet for a "rainy day" as he said. Strangely enough, the rainy day would be his funeral.

"Sugar Baby, let's go have a seat," Pop said kindly in my ear as I turned and looked at him like he was crazy.

How dare he rush me when I'm trying to say goodbye?

I turned back to look into the casket and I studied Brendan's face, body, and hands. I had to remember everything about him because I knew how forgetful I was. I wanted to remember those almond eyes, beautiful wide nose, luscious lips, smooth skin, and strong manly hands. I couldn't forget him…I just couldn't. With hesitance, I stepped away from the casket, and turned to face all the mourners who were either staring at me or crying.

As I made my way to my seat, I looked over the crowd and tried to think about how excited Brendan would have been at all the people who had come to see him off.

"Brendan!" I heard a woman scream at the back of the church. I turned, and looked over my shoulder, trying to find her. But with the ever-growing number of people in the church, it was pointless. Just as I turned my attention back to the front of the church, my eyes connected with Trey's.

He was sitting in the pew across from mine, staring at me

with a concerned look on his face. Next to him was a cute little girl who couldn't have been more than five years old. I smiled modestly at him, and returned my attention to the pastor and prepared for the service of my life.

Brendan's funeral was filled with tears, memories, laughter, and love. I couldn't get over how many people had such beautiful stories to tell about him. During some of the stories, I would forget where I was and the occasion, and thought I felt Brendan sitting next to me. But as I stared up at the now closed casket, I shivered at the reality. After the casket was carried out and put into the hearse, I stared at my feet while I walked toward the car.

We all jumped into the limo as the rain hit the windshield roughly, and headed to the burial site. It was a long ride to the cemetery, and I used it to rest my eyes.

"We're going to have food back at the house for anyone who wants to join," I heard Ms. Pat say softly to the silent car.

There was no more laughter and joking about Brendan's "good days." We were all just barely looking into one another's eyes, as we started coming to terms with the ultimate ending in the next part of the service, the burial.

I kept my eyes closed, hoping that someone would let me be and not make me go to the cemetery. I hoped that maybe they would forget I was there, and just skip over me. But just as I thought, when the car stopped, I felt hands poking my stomach and shoulder.

"Sugar Baby, it's time to get out." Pop said as he cleared his throat.

Kenya and Jasmine were already outside of the limo when I got out, and we gathered underneath the green tent that was set up for us. I felt dead. I found it easier to ignore the situation rather than deal with it. I knew I could scream and cry as much as I wanted, but none of it would get me the answers I desperately wanted.

I stared off into the distance while friends and family cried quietly. We all realized the cemetery was the end scene to the entire play. There were no more wails, there was no more shouting, and there was no fainting. By then, everyone understood that it didn't matter. Brendan was going six feet under, and we had no other choice but to deal with it.

I looked over at Ms. Pat who looked more dazed than anything. Her hair was standing on top of her head, her dress had makeup stains on it, and her hands shook uncontrollably. But even still, she sat there, like me, waiting for it to be over.

After they lowered the casket into the ground and people started walking away, I picked one of the white roses off of the top of a bundle of flowers and held it tightly in my hand. I played with the silver band which still sat on my left hand, while I contemplated what I needed to say to let go. Jasmine, Kenya, and Pop hugged one another while they stood behind me and watched without a sound.

"I wish I knew what to say to you right now, but I don't. I don't understand how, after all this time, I could feel like I know nothing about who you were. I love you more than anything in this entire world, and nothing anyone can do can change that," I sighed as a puddle of tears formed on my cheeks.

"You told me that you would always be here, but what now?" I cried.

I looked up at the sky and stared at a gray cloud forming above. The rain had let up, slightly, but it looked like it would be coming back in no time.

After dropping the rose into the casket, I tried to rack my brain of other things to say, but all I kept coming up with was the obvious.

"I love you," I said, watching the flower gently hit the top of the casket.

I wiped my eyes and looked up at the hill where the limousine was. There was a line of people around the car and they all looked like fans I had seen before.

"You okay?" Jasmine asked, putting her arm around my neck.

I nodded and started the trek toward the vehicle that would return me to the world without Brendan.

Up until the day of the funeral, I was able to act like my boyfriend had just been on a long vacation where he was denied phone and e-mail; but seeing the casket lowered into the ground, and feeling his cold body, let me know it was as real as my pain.

"H-hey…Mmmstique," I heard a young man's voice say softly while I walked toward the limousine.

Great, I thought, *a fan.*

Jasmine played her role as bodyguard, telling fans to give me space before I could even turn around myself and ask for a moment of privacy. It touched me that my fans cared so much about me that they would come out to show me support; but I needed a moment for Lauren…not Mystique.

"Hey, she's really not in the mood for talking right now," Jasmine said politely. I could tell she wanted to snap on the kid, but she kept her cool. I turned around to flash a quick smile and saw a familiar face and eyes staring back at me.

"Oh…mmmmy bad," the kid stuttered as he dropped his shoulders and head.

"Oh no…I know you. It's Dee, right?" I said, turning and walking toward him. It was Dee, the kid I had met at the station.

"Yeah. Yyooou remember mmme?" Dee stuttered as he ran his hands over his rough looking hair. He seemed like he hadn't had a decent haircut in at least three months. Nevertheless, he was a cute kid. He was wearing a simple, white button-down shirt with a pair of black church pants.

"Of course I remember. How are things going with you?" I asked kindly.

"The other cat in the group, Lamont, he's tttrrripin," he said, talking quickly.

Before I could tell him to slow down and gather his words, he was closing his eyes and doing it himself.

"Lamont, that's my boy...he went and got himself locked up a couple of days ago," he said, rolling his eyes.

I turned around to let Kenya, Jasmine, and Pop know everything was cool. I knew this kid was genuinely interested.

"I told you these streets aren't a game," I said, nodding in his direction.

"Yeah. I hhheear that," he said, trying to laugh.

"So, how's school? You got back in, right?" I asked.

"Yeah...I...I'm ggooood!" he replied grinning excitedly. I could tell Dee was thrilled to know that someone, even someone like me, cared what he was doing.

"Well, you make sure you remember me when you blow up, and when you get that degree in your hands," I said, winking at him.

Then it struck me. Had Dee come to the funeral just to show his support for me? If so, the least I could do was thank him.

"Did you come out for me?" I asked, raising an eyebrow curiously.

"Not entirely," he said, sucking his teeth and looking over his shoulder at a distraught looking older woman who I assumed was his mother.

She looked like she was thirty to thirty-five years old with a serious overbite, long blonde weave, golden skin, and hazel contacts. Her body was flabby, and her beer belly couldn't be contained in the tight black and red dress she was sporting. If it wasn't for the red eyes and nose she was sporting, I would have thought she was going to the club instead of a funeral.

I returned my stare back at Dee who was crossing his arms.

"My ddddad's funeral was tttoday, and since wwwweee

missed the fuuunneeeral, moms made me ccccooommee to the burial," he said, hurrying to get the last of the words out.

I looked around the cemetery for any other funerals that were taking place at the same time; I couldn't see any...but I thought this cemetery was the biggest one in Atlanta. His father's service could have been taking place anywhere.

"Well, I'm really sorry to hear about your loss," I said, wanting to escape the rain that was beginning to trickle.

Dee stared at me like he wanted to say more but couldn't.

"Dee, bring your ass on!" his mother yelled loudly as she jogged off toward a beat up old Chevy sitting on some dusty-looking rims.

"I'm sorry about your loss too," he said matter-of-factly.

"I heard about it when you said it on air."

I nodded my head and reached out to hug him. For some reason, I felt the need to hold him, hug him, and let him know that everything would get better for him. I knew what it was like to lose a parent at a young age, and I hoped that Dee's mother would comfort him the way Pop had comforted me.

As I let go, I stared into Dee's eyes and a certain sense of familiarity fell over me; one that I hadn't felt before.

"What was your father's name?" I asked quickly.

Dee smirked and started to jog toward the direction of his mother.

"I wouldn't even call that nigga a father," he said, running backwards.

"He was a daddy. But the bastard's name was Brendan Llleeeewwwis," he said nonchalantly.

Kenya, Jasmine, and Pop all stopped what they were doing and focused their attention on Dee.

"W-what did you say?" I said, almost marching toward Dee who, sensing my aggravation and disbelief, stopped in his tracks.

"I said my dad's name was Brendan Lewis...why?" he said with an attitude and no stuttering.

I felt my legs getting ready to give out, and before I had a chance to extend my arms and break my fall, my body hit the ground with a loud thud.

If what Dee was saying was true, the man I thought I knew everything about was slowly starting to become someone I knew *nothing* about.

chapter seven

Dear Diary,

Isn't it strange how you can think you know a person and rudely be proven wrong? Less than five minutes after he was in the ground, I found out that Brendan had been keeping a huge secret from me. He has a thirteen-year-old son named Dee! It's the same kid from the rap group "The Rhymesters." As numb as I was when they put the casket in the ground, I think I'm more frozen now that I know Brendan was keeping secrets. Of course this could all be one big misunderstanding and this kid and his mother could be way off. Kenya and Jasmine are in disbelief too. Lance says he heard a rumor about Brendan having a kid, but he never saw a kid, so he never thought anything else of it. This has definitely solidified my decision to look into Brendan's lifestyle and death. A part of me is exhausted and literally drained. I can't bear to deal with any of this until I have some concrete information.

I'm supposed to meet with Ralph, but this situation with Dee can't wait any longer. Lance may have only heard rumors about a child, and might not have ever actually seen one, but he had known Brendan long enough to know the family. He knew where Dee's mother stayed. If Dee was Brendan's child, then she's the place to start. That was the only lead we had, and right now it was enough. Me and Jasmine are going to go over there and get some answers. Nothing at all is making sense, but I can only hope that soon it will. Trey is at the door and I'm not sure what for, but I need to go.

Lauren Washington

————

"Hey, I thought maybe you were asleep," Trey said, looking like he had been caught in the act of doing something he wasn't supposed to be doing.

I was aggravated. Not necessarily at him, but more or less at the situation. I was looking at him and hearing him, but my mind wasn't connecting the dots.

"Hello! Earth to Skeeter," Trey said, laughing with his hands behind his back.

I snapped out of my daydream of Brendan and focused my attention on Trey.

"I'm sorry, Trey. I've just got a lot on my mind right now," I said, opening the door wider so he could come in.

I was wearing a tight vintage t-shirt and a pair of Capri leggings that hugged my body like they were too small for me. I had every intention of going out and exercising that morning, but the closer I got to the door, the more nervous I felt about seeing someone I knew. They, of course, would ask how I was and I would have to lie and say "okay" or "I'm coping." Both answers were untrue. I wasn't okay, and I wasn't coping. I was sad as hell, and starting to get angrier by the day.

"I just wanted to...uh...I wanted to bring you these," he said, pulling a bundle of daisies from behind his back.

For as long as I could remember, daisies have always been my favorite flower. They signified the innocence of my childhood and the carefree days I had spent doing nothing. It was also the flower we had placed in mom's hair when she was buried.

"Daisies!" I said, trying my best to smile widely. "How'd you know?" I asked, taking the flowers and walking into the kitchen to find a vase. Trey took a seat at the kitchen table.

"I've got a good memory, I guess," he smirked.

After I put the flowers in water and had prepared them neatly, I spun around to him and narrowed my eyes.

"Good memory...from what? I've never told you I liked daisies," I said, joining him at the table.

I was getting used to Trey's presence in my house, and as

much as I wanted my own space and time, he was a really good listener. It had only been a week since he started work, and I was already seeing improvements in certain areas of the house.

"Think back to Ms. Buzzett's "Flower Power" play we had to put on," he said, fidgeting with a piece of paper on the table.

My jaw dropped. Ms. Buzzett, our fourth grade teacher, had the entire class put on a play called "Flower Power." It was about the importance of plant life, and we all had to dress up as our favorite flower. I remembered it vividly as Pop sewed my white and yellow suit together the night before the play. I stood proudly on stage, the next day, wishing my mom was there to see me shine.

Trey, with his goofy self, went as a weed because, as he put it, *"even weeds were flowers to someone."*

"That was almost twenty years ago, how did you remember that?" I asked, not knowing if Trey was flirting with me or not.

He chuckled and crossed his arms.

"How could I forget your stick legs and huge feet?" he asked, laughing loudly.

I rolled my eyes and sucked my teeth as I got up from the table. If there was any thought in my mind that Trey was flirting it had just flown out of the window, right along with my patience.

"I'm kidding, I'm kidding," he said, trying to catch his breath as I stood with my arms folded.

"What did you need, anyway?" I asked, cutting his apology in half.

"I was coming by to see if your dad was here; we were supposed to be going to look at some tile for the kitchen," he said, sitting back in the chair with a grin still plastered on his face.

"Oh, well...he should be back in about ten minutes; he just went to the corner store for some jerky."

The two of us stood silently in the kitchen not knowing what to say to each other, but soon enough Trey was filling the silence, as he always did.

"I'm so sorry about Brendan..." he said, not looking into my eyes.

I had this urge to laugh, because it was the one time Trey had ever been serious with me, and yet, I was biting my lip out of nervousness.

"Thank you. I really appreciate you coming to the funeral," I said, hoping the awkward silence would end.

"Who was the pretty little girl with you?" I asked, smiling as I thought about the butterscotch-colored little girl with braids and beads in her hair.

Trey started smiling at the mention of the little girl and put his hand over his heart.

"That's my baby girl, Shawntae," he sighed with his eyes closed. "She's my world."

I stared at Trey with an envious look. I wanted a child, and I wanted the love I had somehow lost with a bullet and a note.

"That's wonderful."

"Her mother and I are in court for custody. She's living the single life now, and Shawntae is the one suffering. So, let's just hope she gets to stay with her dad full-time. She's a perfect little girl."

"And she's beautiful," I managed to say when I returned to the kitchen table with Trey.

"I've got to say she's got all of my looks, thank God!" he joked.

I laughed quietly.

"I don't know if that's a good thing," I said, finally getting my one jab in.

Trey grabbed his side in fake pain and winced. "Ow! That hurt, Skeeter!"

I slapped his arm playfully and jumped up from the table, trying to escape the return slap I knew was coming.

Trey reached out and tried his best to get me, but was unlucky. We ran throughout the house like kids playing tag. I ran up the stairs with Trey close behind me. Laughter rang throughout my house as I hid behind a wall. After Trey passed by the wall without seeing me, I ran back toward the kitchen.

I thought I had outsmarted him, but when I turned to check my back, he was standing right behind me with a smirk on his face and his hand in the air ready to slap me back.

I grabbed his hand and tried my best to keep it away from me.

"You can't even slap me!" I teased as he tried to break free.

By this time, unbeknownst to me, we were close enough to kiss; as Trey placed one arm around my waist in an attempt to grab my other arm, I got chills. I slowed down, and soon my smile disappeared. Trey was still playing, but almost immediately, he was staring intensely into my eyes. I wasn't sure how long we were standing in that position, with his hand wrapped around my waist and one of my arms wrapped around the back of his neck, but as much as I was telling my body to break away, I couldn't. His hands lightly traced my back and ran delicately down my spine and onto my butt. I didn't know what to do; because as much as I wanted to touch him…I couldn't. I was putty in his arms.

Trey went in for a kiss. I pulled away, just as Jasmine walked into the kitchen with one twin on her hip and the other one holding her hand.

The three of us stared at each other, and it was then I knew that what I was doing was wrong. I had, after all, just buried my boyfriend; and here I was gallivanting around like I had no cares in the world.

I pushed Trey away and darted past Jasmine and the children toward my bedroom in embarrassment.

"Move," I said, not making eye contact with my best friend.

In minutes, Jasmine was at my door with the children in tow. She had a look of concern, surprise, and anger on her face.

"What the hell was that?" she said in a whisper.

I brushed her question off. I slipped on a pair of jeans and pulled my hair into a ponytail.

"You do realize you just buried your boyfriend, the love of your life, right?" she said, sitting Michelle on the floor and placing Mikayla on my bed.

I loved Jasmine, but the last thing I needed was her judgmental words.

"Don't you think I know that, Jas?" I said, spinning around with my hands on my hips. *How dare she challenge whether or not I was grieving?*

The only excuse I could come up with, for my close encounter with Trey, was grief. I was grieving, and I wanted to be close to someone who could make me feel half the way Brendan did.

Yeah, I told myself, *that was the reason*; it was a damn good one.

"I'm just saying," she said, sitting on the bed and dropping her head.

"Are you ready?" I inquired with one eyebrow raised.

Jasmine struggled with her children as I hurried down the steps and past Trey who was waiting with a fretful look.

"Hey, wait…" he said, grabbing my arm lightly. I turned to look at him and couldn't connect my eyes with his. I was ashamed that I had even allowed myself to get caught up in emotions from the past. I didn't care about Trey; hell, I barely tolerated him, *so why hadn't I been able to pull away?*

"I'm sorry. I was wrong for that," he said nervously.

I nodded my head and stared out the window as he spoke. It wasn't that I was ignoring him, or even angry with him, I just didn't want to risk staring into his eyes and getting that tingling feeling all over again. Staring out to the street gave me the perfect distraction.

"It's okay, Trey," I said, exhaling as soon as Pop opened the front door. I slid my arm out of his grasp and exited after kissing Pop on the cheek.

I turned to look back, and Trey was still standing in the same spot, with the same fretful look on his face, staring into my eyes.

I got into my car, laid my head on the steering wheel and waited for Jasmine.

"Thanks for the help," she said sarcastically as she strapped the children into the car seats.

I ignored her smart comment and started the car.

"Not another word about what you saw, okay? It was a mistake, and I would appreciate it if it stayed between us," I said, not taking my eyes off of the road.

Jasmine nodded slowly once and that was enough. I knew she had me.

We had what we called the "friend vault," and it had been holding secrets since I could remember. Every mistake, every embarrassment, every thing we'd done that we weren't proud of and couldn't tell another soul; it went in the vault and it stayed there. No receipts, no reruns, no bringing it up at the wrong moment with the wrong people around. Jasmine had deposited plenty of her own over the years, and I had never breathed a word of any of it. She knew I wouldn't. That was the whole point. I didn't doubt for a second that mine was already locked away.

As we pulled up to Dee's house, which was incidentally close to Ms. Pat's house, I cringed. It was a ragged house… and when I say 'ragged,' I mean it. *You know the house on the block with the mold on the siding, torn screen door, dirty toys in the yard, and beat down cars in the driveway?* Dee's house was the one that made that house look like a mansion. It was *that* bad.

"Are you sure this is it?" Jasmine asked curiously as she looked back at Michelle and Mikayla.

I checked the directions again and nodded my head.

"Yup. This is it," I said, opening my door and signaling for her to do the same.

Each of us grabbed a twin and prepared for our journey. I stepped over dog crap, mud puddles, and trash as I made my way to the front door. The house looked like it had been built in the sixties and hadn't been properly cared for. There were trees hovering over the patched roof and dead plants at the entrance. It could have been a cute house if only someone would paint it and keep it clean.

Jasmine knocked on the door as I switched Michelle to my other hip. I played with one of her thick twists. She smiled at me just as Dee opened the door. He looked like he had seen a ghost and quickly stepped outside the torn screen door and closed it behind him.

"Mmmyyystiqqque, wwwwhat yoooouuu dddddooooi-innng hhhere?" he said as he straightened out his dirty white t-shirt and denim shorts.

Jasmine stared at Dee and I assumed she was looking for a hint of Brendan in him. I could see it, but only in fractions. Dee stuttered like Brendan did when he was nervous, he had his skin tone, his cuteness, and his tiny bow-legged stance. It was all there.

"I came over to talk to your mom; is she here?"

Dee stood silent for a second before opening the door and allowing us in. I could tell he was embarrassed. But I wasn't judging him, I just wanted to know the truth.

"Ma!" he screamed as he cleared newspapers from the dirty living room couch, making room for Jasmine and I to sit. As soon as our butts hit the couch, we sank into it. It was made with that itchy material that seventies outfits were made of; and as much as I wanted to scratch, I knew it would have been rude.

"What boy?" Dee's mother appeared in the living room doorway with a blunt in her hand and wearing a pair of tights and an oversized t-shirt.

Her blonde hair was now pulled back away from her face, and I could tell she was a halfway decent looking lady. Her hazel eyes were missing that day, but her bad body was still very much there.

"Ma, this is Mystique…reemmeeemmmbeerr I was tttelling you about hhheer, from 104.5?" Dee said, smiling widely.

I saw his mother roll her eyes and then scream at the top of her lungs at Dee.

"What the hell do I tell you about that damn stuttering? Get that shit under control!" she said harshly as she settled into the loveseat across from us.

Dee stood against the wall with his head hung, and an aura of disgust and hate lingering over him.

"Y'all wanted something?" she said, focusing her attitude toward me and Jasmine.

"Hey, I'm Lauren, and this is my friend Jasmine. I was talking to Dee yesterday, and he was telling me about his father who died…" I said swallowing, hoping the lady would stop me and tell me Dee had been lying.

"Yeah, so what?" she said, taking a drag from the blunt in between her dirty fingers.

"I'm sorry. What's your name?" Jasmine asked loudly as she challenged the woman with her own attitude.

"Tanya," she said as she blew the smoke from her blunt into our faces. If I wasn't holding Michelle, and Jasmine holding Mikayla, I might have gone Bankhead on her; but with Dee staring at me, I wanted to keep it professional.

"My boyfriend was Brendan Lewis and…" I started as I let my hands move freely.

"Oh, so you're the uppity bitch, huh?" Tanya said, sitting the blunt down in a nearby ashtray and leaning back into the love seat. "Yeah, I've heard about you."

I cleared my throat and smiled at her comment. For as long as I could recall, I had been called uppity and bourgeoisie; but I knew it only derived from the fact that I kept to myself. But, to be clear, just because I didn't wild out every second of the day didn't mean it wasn't in me.

"Look, Tanya…we're just trying to find out if Brendan is Dee's father," Jasmine said, cutting in with her hand in the air. She sat Michelle on my lap and leaned forward a little bit, letting Tanya know she could act crazy too.

"Hell yeah, that's his daddy! Look at them damn eyes and lips and tell me that ain't his son!" Both Jasmine and I looked over to Dee and stared at his features. I knew deep inside that Dee was Brendan's son. My only question, though, was did Brendan *know* he was a father. Before I could finish asking the question, Tanya was already blowing up at me.

"What do you mean *'did he know*?' Was the nigga there when he went up in me raw? Was he in the damn delivery room when I pushed this mutherfucka out?" she said, pointing toward Dee who stood back with his arms crossed and his head down. He looked like he was in deep thought, but I couldn't tell; Tanya kept talking.

"He had been sending us payments up until about five months ago; and when I threatened to put his ass on child support, that nigga just got ghost on us," she said with a hint of sadness in her voice.

I sighed and tried to hold back the tears I desperately wanted to let out.

"Can we see his birth certificate?" Jasmine asked as she patted my leg softly and continued with the interrogation.

"What the hell are y'all all up in *our* business for?" Tanya shot back with her eyebrows burrowed into her forehead.

"Brendan, Ms. Pat, Terrence, and everybody in their

family knows about me and Dee, and they don't even give us the time of day," she said, rolling her eyes again and clutching the seat in anger.

Based on what I was seeing, I understood why no one wanted to be around Tanya. She was rude, loud, mean, and just plain foul. I tried to catch my breath and keep my composure as I looked around the room for a distraction. My eyes met a picture of Dee as a baby. While Jasmine and Tanya talked amongst themselves, often getting close to a screaming match, I reached over and grabbed the picture. If the baby in the picture wasn't wearing Jordan tennis shoes and a small chunk chain, I would have sworn this was a picture of Brendan. My hands shook while I traced my hands up and down the picture.

"Look, if you won't show us the damn birth certificate then why should we believe this is even Brendan's kid?" Jasmine said, forgetting Dee was in the room.

"And who the hell are you supposed to be? Why the hell do I need to prove anything to you and this trick?" she said, nodding in my direction.

She and Jasmine stood up from their seats and stood nose to nose; ready to throw down. It took everything in Dee and me to get between the two of them and break it up.

"You don't know me, bitch!" Tanya yelled loudly as a man came rushing from the back of the house with a gun in his hand.

"Whatever…you doing all that talking, shake something!" Jasmine started to reply, just as I shoved her to shut up.

The man stood in the doorway wearing a wife-beater, a pair of boxers, and a do-rag. I wasn't as scared of him as I was of the heat in his hands. All I had done was come down to see what the truth was, and now I had a gun pointed at me.

"Put that down!" Dee said, stepping in front of the ashy, dark-skinned man with the confused look on his face. I could tell he had been asleep and our loud conversation probably frightened him.

"What the hell is going on in here?" he said, slowly bringing the gun down and staring at me and then Jasmine and the babies.

Jasmine's leg was tapping a mile a minute as she and Tanya stared at each other as if they were challenging each other to make a move.

"Go back to the room, man-man," Tanya said, not taking her eyes off of Jasmine.

As soon as the man left, I threw both of my hands in the air and shut both of them up before they could even get anything out.

"This *is* Brendan's son, Jas; it's true."

"How do you know?" she said, looking defeated.

"What do you mean, how the hell does she know? I just told your stupid ass he was the father." Tanya said, plopping onto the couch with a sly grin.

"This *is* Brendan's son," I repeated as I ignored Tanya's comment.

"Look at this baby picture of Dee; it looks exactly like the one Ms. Pat has of Brendan," I said, handing the photograph to Jasmine who looked at it with wide eyes.

I inhaled and quickly blew out the air. This was a lot to handle; and as much as I wanted to take it all in, my head was swimming and I felt like I had been hit with a sledgehammer. Saying "Brendan's son" out loud had more of an impact on me than I thought it would.

Before I could turn and tell Jas not to respond, she was already in Tanya's face spewing off at the mouth.

"Looks like you need to do a better job of being a mother; look at this pigsty, and look at *you*. Dee would have been better off with his father than in this mess," she said, backing up as Tanya geared herself up for a reply.

"Brendan could have taken that mutherfucka from me a

long time ago, but he didn't want to. Hell, I'm still young, and I don't need a fucking child holding me down. Ms. Pat was supposed to take Dee years ago, but her flaky ass backed out on me. And if you think I'm such a pig, then get your sorry ass outta my pigsty," she said, sucking her teeth and opening the screen door to let us out.

Dee had already left the room and gone to the back of the house. I wanted to say goodbye to him, but the last thing I wanted was for "man-man" to bring his crazy self back out with his gun in hand.

"And let me catch that ass out in the streets, it's over!" she said, pointing to Jasmine.

Flicking her off with a polite bird, Jasmine loaded both of her children up in the car and then got in.

"I can't believe you just showed your ass like that. You know Lance is going to go off on you when those babies start talking like that."

My best friend was a *great* mother, but her temper often got the best of her; and when it did, every mothering trick she had learned went out the door.

Just as I put my car in reverse, I saw Dee running out of the house flagging me down.

"Mystique...I nneeeed tooo ggggiiivvee yoooouuu sssooommmething," he said as he pulled out a piece of paper and pen from his pocket and looked at me for my address.

Normally I would have shot Dee down; especially giving out my home address, but this *was* Brendan's son, wasn't it? I took his paper and pen and scribbled my address on it.

After he got my information and I pulled out of the driveway, Jasmine laid her head on the headrest and exhaled.

"Looks like we've opened up Pandora's Box."

They say when you open Pandora's Box, everything bad happens. I was wondering if I could handle it anymore.

———

I'VE ALWAYS BEEN TOLD that food is one of the best ways to cure heartache. With that in mind, I headed to the grocery store to pick up some food for dinner. I had invited everyone close to me, maybe as a means of keeping them within arm's reach.

Pop didn't want me keeping so busy that I couldn't express my pain; but after I reassured him that I was dealing with things in my own way, he allowed me to have the dinner party.

I was making collard greens, yams, ribs, cornbread, potato salad, macaroni and cheese, and a nice, moist red velvet cake to top everything off. Jasmine was bringing her legendary Peach Iced Tea, and Kenya was stopping to get fresh rolls. I eventually picked up all the items I needed.

I stood in the baking aisle trying to figure out whether or not the new cocoa powder would be okay in my Red Velvet recipe. I glanced up and my eyes followed a figure that looked exactly like Brendan. It wasn't that he was dressed like him, resembled him, or even kind of walked like him. This guy was Brendan, *but how?* I dropped the powder on the ground and pushed my buggy toward Brendan. I was behind him and everything about him was pointing toward it actually being Brendan. He walked like him, his head was shaped just like his, his skin tone was identical, and he was dressed like him.

This couldn't have been happening, I thought as I pinched myself. *Brendan was alive!* I started thinking of things I would say to him when I snuck up on him and yelled, "Surprise!" I continued to follow him until he turned down the beer aisle, and as I opened my mouth to call out his name, he turned to face me. It wasn't Brendan. When I blinked, it was like the man standing before me looked nothing like I thought. He was darker, bigger, and uglier; and he didn't have any of the qualities of Brendan. I sheepishly bowed my head and pretended I was picking up a bottle of Red Stripe beer and scooted my way out of the aisle to get the rest of my things.

After paying for and loading my bags of groceries in the car, I sat with my head in my hands. *Why was my mind playing such horrible tricks on me?* It had convinced me that Brendan was alive and well, and shopping for groceries. Go figure.

"Get yourself together," I said as I put the car in drive and turned on the radio.

I rode with the radio blasting, while my thoughts were in other places. So much was going on in my life that I hadn't even taken a moment to breathe. I hoped that I would be able to smile without putting on a front. I wanted so badly to pick up the phone and dial Brendan's number, but I knew it would only cause me more emotional trauma.

I lugged each one of the bags into the house and began preparing the food for my guests. Normally I would let my collard greens soak overnight in turkey, but with a time crunch...I did my best to work things out. Whenever I stress about anything, cooking or listening to the radio would always guarantee to get me out of my funk. But my situation with Brendan's death wasn't a funk; even cooking couldn't get my mind off of it. But, as usual, a friendly distraction came to take my mind off things.

"Yum. It smells good in here, girl!" Kenya said, walking through the kitchen door with a Publix grocery bag in one hand and her Balenciaga purse in the other.

It was true. The aroma in the kitchen was outstanding; after hours of slaving in front of the stove, I was ready to take a break.

"Whew!" I said, taking the bag from her hand and sitting it on the kitchen table.

"Busy day?" Kenya asked, raising one eyebrow. I had purposely not invited Kenya to Dee's house because I figured the less people the better. Looking back, I wished she had gone instead of Jasmine.

"Yeah, I guess you can say that," I said, massaging my neck with my eyes closed.

"How did everything go at Dee's house?" she asked, standing up and taking my neck into her hands and applying pressure. I moaned a little bit before shutting my eyes and allowing Kenya, my multi-talented best friend, to do her thing.

"Stressful is all I can say," I managed to say while she moved her hands up and down my tense neck.

"What happened?"

"You know the usual with Jas. She got there and got in a screaming match with Dee's mother over whether or not Brendan was the father."

"What's new?" Kenya laughed lightly.

"And then Dee's mom's boyfriend came out with a gun in his hand after they were almost to the point of things getting physical," I said, exhaling.

Kenya stopped. I opened my eyes and looked up at her face.

"A gun?"

I gestured for Kenya to sit in the chair across from me; when she did I finished my story.

"So here I am trying to get some answers and this lunatic, looking like he was on something, comes out waving this gun," I laughed while Kenya stared at me in shock.

"It's okay, Kenya. We all made it out in one piece; but Tanya did promise to rough Jasmine up if she saw her in the streets," I said chuckling.

Kenya chuckled, like I knew she would, and she put one of her hands on the table beside mine and looked into my eyes.

"Is it his son?"

"I think so. I really do," I said, biting my lip and staring back at Kenya.

By this time, I had grown used to saying, "Brendan's son"

and it flowed well. It hurt like hell knowing he had been keeping a secret like that from me, but I had accepted it. I think Kenya thought I was going to be a big ball of mess, which I was when no one was around, but at that moment I was okay. I was able to pretend, if only for that moment, that Brendan was in the next room and none of this was happening.

"How old is that boy? He looks a little old to be Brendan's son," Kenya said, rubbing my hand sympathetically.

I had figured it all out while I stood over the hot stove with greens and potatoes boiling; it came like an epiphany.

Dee was thirteen years old, possibly turning fourteen that year, and Brendan was twenty-nine. That would have made him around the same age as his son was now when Tanya gave birth. Unbelievable, but it didn't shock me.

Growing up, it seemed like everyone in our neighborhood was having babies before they could even drive. The first one of my classmates to get pregnant was a girl named Táchira; she was, even in the fifth grade, what adults always called "a fast little girl". She wasn't an especially pretty girl, but she could dress her ass off and she knew it. She came to school almost daily with a new outfit and hairdo. She and Trey had been boyfriend and girlfriend during some of the fourth and fifth grade, and I often wondered what he saw in her. She was curvaceous as hell, had a raspy voice, was rude, had huge breasts, and had the boy of my daydreams. In elementary school, the only drama that goes on is "who is going with whom" and Táchira's list of boyfriends read like an elementary celebrity list. On the first day of the sixth grade, I heard the teacher call her name, but didn't see the fashionista anywhere in sight. Two weeks later, when she finally showed up for class, I noticed an eleven-year old Táchira sporting not only the latest duds, but also a huge baby bump. She was pregnant. Our teachers tried to ask Táchira and her parents to cover her up, but they saw nothing unnatural about the state their daughter was in and refused. I watched in awe one day, during gym, as the other little girls clamored around her and rubbed her stomach like she was the Queen of the pack. She was ahead of all of us, obviously, and Jasmine and I couldn't believe someone our age was about to be a mother. Some of the boys teased Trey, saying he was the father; but I had heard that it was an older boy in the neighborhood named Andy that had knocked Táchira up. Three months after the first day of school, Táchira's best friend, Portia, came around telling everyone that Táchira had given birth to a baby girl. As exciting as it was, I still couldn't believe that at eleven years old, Táchira was now a mother. Táchira never did come back to school after having her daughter. Jasmine said she saw her about a year ago working at Pizza Hut in the Airport.

I broke out of my daydream and looked at Kenya who was waiting for an answer.

"Brendan would have gotten Tanya pregnant when they were about thirteen or fourteen. It is possible," I replied.

"How do you feel about it?" she inquired carefully.

"I mean…I feel like…I feel like he was keeping something from me. He obviously didn't want me to know about his son, and it makes me wonder what else he was hiding," I said as I stood up and went to the stove to stir my pots.

"For thirteen years, he and Ms. Pat have been paying her child support and doing what he has had to do as a father," I said, shaking my head in disbelief.

"And you know what gets me? How no one knew Brendan had a son. How is that possible?" I asked, not wanting any feedback.

I took a deep breath. I sensed a migraine coming on and calmed myself down.

"That's crazy," Kenya said, looking off in a daze.

She looked pretty that day with her full, curly afro pulled back effortlessly at the top of her head. I put the tops back on the pots and exhaled. I knew Kenya didn't want to sit and talk, day in and day out, about Brendan's death. It seemed to take a lot out of her; especially since she had never known anyone close to her who had died.

Standing in front of my friend, I grinned. I wasn't sure where I would be, in the wild state of affairs, if she and Jas hadn't been there to provide me company. At times, though, I wished I could just crawl up to my bed and hide underneath the covers while crying. I wanted to feel sorry for myself; I mean, hell, I *had* lost my boyfriend. But they were keeping my spirits high and my distraction level even higher. I thought about what was going to happen after we all returned to our normal routines. It was those times I feared most.

"Don't you look cute?" I said, pulling at Kenya's gray ruffled button-down shirt.

She was wearing a fabulous pair of skin tight jeans and open-toe stilettos. I looked at her and she giggled. She knew exactly why I was looking at her. We were about to have Sunday dinner and here she was looking like she was going to walk the red carpet.

"Shut up," she said, pushing me lightly. "I just wanted to get dressed up, that's all."

"Umm hmm," I said, narrowing my eyes as I studied her behavior.

I knew when she was lying, and I knew when she was trying to hide something from me; that day her actions were telling me it was both.

Nervously, Kenya checked her phone and typed a couple of messages to someone before finally looking up at me. I had my hands on my hips, a grin on my face, and I wanted answers.

"Fine! Pull it out of me, why don't you!" Kenya squealed excitedly.

I raised an eyebrow and listened closely.

"Do you mind if I invite Lorenzo over for dinner?"

"Lorenzo who?" I asked, puzzled.

"Lorenzo Black, girl," she said, rolling her eyes into the back of her head as she giddily laughed.

"Lorenzo Black?! Why would you be inviting him to dinner?"

"We've been talking every day since the club, and he was saying this morning how he wanted some good, old fashioned, home-cooked food," she said, looking at me sympathetically, hoping for a yes. But I wasn't giving in that easily.

"So what? That's your boyfriend now?" I joked.

Kenya just blushed. I couldn't believe it. The one type of man she vowed to stay away from had, somehow, turned my girl completely out.

"You've been holding out on me…" I said, hitting her with the towel.

"He's a really good guy, Lauren. I *really* like him."

"So now you want to invite that man to my unfinished house to eat up all my food?"

Kenya snapped out of her daydream and tilted her head to the side like she was looking for a little compassion. I had to admit; the mere fact that Lorenzo had Kenya whipped was kind of frightening. Kenya was the one who didn't take much BS, which resulted in a number of guys getting the cold shoulder from her. For the longest time, Jasmine and I were thinking Kenya would never find someone who met her criteria, who spoke proper English, dressed as well as she could, held at least a Bachelor's degree, and wanted kids. Of course, that was the tip of the iceberg; Kenya had other specifics that even I thought were crazy.

"It's fine with me, girl," I said, shaking my head.

"Thank you!" she smiled as she jumped up from her seat and embraced me. "Just be careful with him; you know how those actors are," I said.

But Kenya wasn't listening to me; she was already on the phone with Lorenzo giving him directions to my house.

I didn't care about him being in my house; after all, I

wasn't fazed by his fame, but I had been looking forward to relaxing with all my friends and family…and he wasn't one of them.

I checked the clock and finished up some things in the kitchen. After giving Kenya instructions on how long to cook the rolls, along with what time dinner would be served, I scurried up the stairs to take a quick shower. Now that I knew someone else would be in the house, other than family and friends, I needed to make sure I looked decent. I knew Lorenzo had heard about Brendan because he was a regular at Brendan's shop. I wanted him to take a look at me and think I was doing okay, even though I wasn't. I wanted to look bold and fearless, but I knew that as soon as the clothes were stripped off I was back to being the shivering cold, scared, nervous and downright gloomy woman.

As I got in the shower, I heard Pop downstairs talking to someone…Lorenzo I assumed. I pulled my hair into a ponytail on top of my head, and I leaned into the warm shower water. I sighed with contentment as I lathered my body and noticed that extra weight was starting to show.

"Got to start exercising," I said.

The water fell in welcomed drops and trickled down my back and breasts, and it felt alarmingly great; like no other shower I had ever taken. I wanted to stay there and relax. I closed my eyes and I saw Brendan's face again.

"I love you, baby!" I heard his voice say.

I jumped and flopped against the wall as I gripped the shower curtain for support.

I knew I looked crazy, but as I turned off the water and sat motionless in the bathtub, I broke down again and thought about what Brendan's death was doing to me. I couldn't do anything without seeing his face, I couldn't talk without wanting to hear his voice, and I couldn't think without wanting to know why. I crumpled in the tub and cried. It was when I was away from the distractions, the people, and the laughter, that I allowed myself to show my true feelings. When I couldn't hear anything else but Brendan's voice ringing in my head, telling me "I love you," I didn't fight it; I couldn't. So I just sat there. While I clung to the shower curtain, my naked, damp body laid out in my bathtub waiting for the strength to get up. I replayed memories of my relationship in my head – the good and bad times, and the more I cried, the weaker I got.

I'm not sure how long I was lying in there, but when a knock at the door came, it took everything in me to say,

"Help." I couldn't move.

It was like an out-of-body experience, and I was standing over a shell of myself who was trying, extremely hard, not to break down. But the breakdown was inevitable.

My whisper for help wasn't heard; and seconds later, I heard footsteps leaving. I closed my eyes again and inhaled deeply, trying to get my energy together. If this person was going to hear me, I needed to be louder.

"Help!" I managed to shout, though this time it wasn't much louder.

"Lauren, are you in there?" I heard Jasmine ask me from behind the door.

Before I could answer, Jasmine was swinging the door open and staring at my naked body in the tub. Immediately, she could tell something was wrong.

I didn't care about Jas seeing me naked; hell, she had seen me nude plenty of times before and in more awkward situations. She rushed over to me and the look in her eyes told me she was scared.

"Lauren, what's wrong?!" she screamed loudly as she tugged at my arm, which flopped like a fish out of water.

All I could do to respond to her screams was turn my head to the side and look at her with a silent cry for aid.

"Let's get you up from here," she said, finally realizing I wasn't going to be talking or moving on my own.

She lifted my body, and wrapped her arms around my waist. My limbs flailed wildly as she pulled me from the tub and onto the tile in the bathroom. I heard footsteps racing up the stairs, and I knew everyone had probably heard Jasmine's horrified screams, and was trying to see what was wrong.

"Cccclose the door," I said, breathing heavily. The last thing I needed was for Pop, Kenya, and Lorenzo to run in on me with my ass in the air.

Jasmine did as she was told, and as we lay on the floor, she wrapped a towel over my body and rocked me slowly. Pop pounded on the door and was growing antsy, even after Jasmine told him I was okay.

After Jasmine shooed everyone from upstairs, I finally stood up and wobbled to my bed. Jasmine dressed me silently, not mentioning the breakdown she had witnessed. I scurried under the covers comfortably.

"Are you okay?" Jasmine asked, finally sitting on the side of my bed. I was sipping on some hot tea, and remarkably, I did feel a lot better; but I was not okay.

"He's *gone*," I sighed as I looked into the dark liquid. I couldn't cry anymore. They say when you're all cried out, you know. That much was true that evening.

"I wish I could say I understand what you're going through, but I don't. But just know that regardless of anything, I'm here for you," Jasmine said, rubbing my hand softly.

Jasmine was the closest thing I had to a mother since I lost mine. She had been there when I got my period, and she showed me how to wear a pad and tampon. She was the first person I called when I lost my virginity to Brendan and when we had a pregnancy scare. She was the comforter I needed.

"I have something I need to give you..." she said, taking a deep breath. I raised my eyebrows and braced myself.

"Lance got a bunch of things from Brendan's mom. One of them was a folder and it had a letter inside."

"Okay," I said, sitting up on my elbows.

"The letter was from Brendan…to you."

I almost lost my breath trying to make sense of what she was saying.

"Here," she sighed, pushing it my way. "You can read it, or you can burn it. Nobody will be mad at you either way."

My hands shook as I took the envelope from her.

"Close your eyes and rest, I'll clear everyone out of the house," she said, standing up. I sat my tea on the nightstand and turned to Jasmine with my eyes widened.

"No. I slaved over that food for hours; hell, I'm coming down to eat," I said, forcing a laugh.

Jasmine raised an eyebrow and cocked her head to the side.

"Are you sure, girl? You need to rest," she said.

I nodded my head and watched as she closed the door behind her. I ran my hands over the white envelope and took a deep breath. *What was the worst that could happen?* I had already lost the love of my life.

My hands shook as I turned the envelope over.

Brendan's handwriting stared back at me.

Lauren,

If you're reading this, then I finally ran out of strength pretending everything was okay.

I've started this letter more times than I can count. Every time I tried to write it, I convinced myself I didn't need to. I told myself tomorrow would be different. Tomorrow

I would find the words to tell you what was going on inside my head.

Tomorrow never came.

You loved the version of me that smiled, made plans, and talked about the future like it was something we could touch. The truth is I loved being that man for you. You made me want to be better than I knew how to be. But there was another side of me that I kept buried so deep that even I stopped understanding it.

I know you're probably asking yourself a thousand questions right now. Why didn't I tell you? Why didn't I let you help me? Why would I leave you like this? The truth is I didn't know how to explain something I couldn't control.

You were the best thing in my life, Lauren. And that's the part that makes this even harder to write. Loving you meant showing up as someone strong, dependable, someone who had everything under control. I didn't want you to see the parts of me that felt broken.

So I hid them.

Every time you asked if I was okay, I told you I was. Every time you tried to look a little deeper, I changed the subject or pushed you away. Not because I didn't trust you, but because I didn't know how to let you see the parts of me that scared even me.

You were never the problem. I need you to believe that.

You loved me the best way anyone ever has. The laughs we shared, the plans we made, the nights we spent talking about the life we were going to build together...those were the best moments of my life.

If I could be that man all the time, I would have stayed. But somewhere along the way I lost the ability to carry the weight I was pretending didn't exist.

I know you're going to be angry with me. You have every right to be. I wish I could take away the pain this is going to cause you. I wish I could rewind time and do things differently. But I couldn't keep pretending I was okay when I wasn't.

I want you to do something for me, though. Don't let my ending become the thing that defines your life. You have too much light in you for that. Too much strength. Too much love.

One day you're going to wake up and realize that surviving something like this doesn't mean you stop living. It means you find a way to keep going even when you don't understand why things happened the way they did.

And when that day comes, I hope you remember the good parts of us. Not this. Just the love.

I will always be grateful that I got to share my life with you for as long as I did.

Be happy, Lauren. You deserve that.

Love always, Brendan

BRENDAN'S WORDS on the page had done something to me that I was not prepared for. It was not his voice, not really, but reading his handwriting felt close enough to undo me. The loops and slants of his letters, the way he pressed hard on certain words; it was all so distinctly *him* that for a moment the room felt too small to hold both me and my grief at the same time.

I sat with the letter in my lap for a long time after I finished reading it.

I had told Jasmine I was coming down to eat. I had meant it when I said it. But somewhere between that promise and this moment, my body made a different decision entirely. The weight of everything, the funeral, the letter, the revelation about Dee, all of it pressed down on me at once, and I simply had nothing left. I set the envelope carefully on the nightstand, pulled my knees to my chest, and was asleep before I could think better of it.

I woke up some time later to the smell of food still drifting up from downstairs. I lay there for a moment getting my bearings, then pulled myself upright and reached for something to wear. I threw on a pretty red and white shirt with a pair of jeans and flip-flops and stood in front of the mirror applying a little eye shadow, going through the motions of putting myself together. I stepped back and took stock of what I was working with. My eyes had bags underneath them, my hair had gone frizzy at the edges, and my skin was breaking out around my mouth. I told myself I looked cute anyway. Sometimes that is the most you can do.

"Damn," I said, rubbing one of the pimples that was appearing. I headed downstairs slowly, trying not to think about what the letter said. Pop was the first to speak as he dropped his fork and walked toward me.

"Are you okay?" he whispered in my ear as we hugged. I looked up to him and shook my head before kissing his cheek.

"I'm fine, Pop," I said, looking around the living room at

the gathering of people who were looking at me with worried looks on their faces as well.

Kenya and Lorenzo were seated on one end of the long mahogany table, while Jasmine, Lance, and the babies were across from them. Pop pulled out my seat next to him, and I looked next to my chair at another plate that was full of food but missing a person.

"Remind me to fix the…" I heard Trey say nonchalantly.

He looked fine as usual. My eyes met with his, and I was drawn in; but before I knew it, Jasmine was clearing her throat, snapping me out of my daydream.

"Sit down, Sugar Baby," Pop said, pointing to the chair.

They had already fixed me a plate and poured me a tall glass of Jasmine's iced tea—the kind I loved, sweet enough to calm my nerves. I eased into my seat, feeling every pair of eyes flick toward me and then away, like they were afraid to stare but too worried not to. The whole table was quiet, the kind of quiet that presses against your skin.

I glanced around, offering a small smile I didn't fully feel. I could sense them studying my every move, waiting to see if I would break again, if I was fragile, if I was okay. And the truth was, I wasn't unraveling or losing my mind. I had simply loved deeply…and lost in a way that rearranged something inside me.

Sitting there, surrounded by people who cared but didn't know what to say, I felt the weight of that truth settle in my chest. It seemed as though, right when I sat down everyone grew silent; it was irking me. Trey, however, rubbed my leg and picked up the conversation.

"So, Lorenzo…you were telling us about that project you're working on with Tyler Perry…"

Lorenzo smiled, exposing his perfect teeth, and started talking about his new movie role. I pretty much kept my eyes on my food, often getting a tingling feeling inside as Trey brushed my arm or my leg accidentally.

"You know the last movie of his I saw was better than I thought it would be," Jasmine said with a mouthful of food.

Kenya and Lorenzo seemed to be really in tune with one another as they both leaned into each other and laughed.

"That's the same thing I was telling him last night," Kenya said, poking Lorenzo's side.

"We interviewed him at the station," I said, smiling widely, and returning to my normal behavior.

"And he was saying how he's going to start focusing on television and stuff."

From then on, everything was good. I was eating, I was socializing, and I was distracted. Trey looked over to me and grinned.

"What?" I asked, turning up my nose.

"I hope it's okay that your dad invited me," he said, wiping his mouth.

"No, it's cool. I mean…I wasn't expecting you, but it's cool," I said nervously.

The Lauren that was sick of Trey and aggravated by him was slowly disappearing. Trey made me nervous now.

I kept my eyes on Jasmine, who was watching me and Trey like hawks. I excused myself from the table and carried my plate into the kitchen sink. Trey followed me.

I stood over the sink and rinsed off the residue. Trey grabbed me by the waist and slid me out of the way.

"Let me get that," he said, winking.

I watched him clean the dishes and dry his hands with a paper towel.

"We need to talk," he said, low enough for only me to hear. His head was titled and I had mine hung down.

"I know," I said, finally looking into his eyes.

He was so close I could smell the food on his breath; so close I could see exactly how many fillings he had. My mind started racing as I finally brought my eyes to meet his. Immediately, I stepped back.

"Do you want to go outside?" he asked as he moved his hand closer to mine.

I shook my head and allowed him to hold my hand. *Us touching shouldn't be a problem, right?* When we got to the front door, the doorbell rang, interrupting everything I had been thinking about. A startled Trey jumped and dropped my hand.

Standing in my doorway, shivering, with two backpacks on his back, and a look of desperation, was my boyfriend's son, Dee.

Dee, Trey, and I stood in our places for what seemed like ten minutes before he finally spoke up. I was pretty sure my face looked screwed up, so Dee made the first move.

"I wanted to bring you this, I'm leaving town," he said, handing me an envelope.

"Wait, you're leaving? Where to?" I said, bothered by the information. Dee looked at Trey, and then to me, and then he put his head down in shame.

"IIIII cccaaan't live wittth them no more," he said, breathing heavily. I could tell he was trying to be tough, but didn't know how to handle his emotions; very much like myself.

Staring into his eyes, I knew I needed to do my best to help this kid out. I watched him as he looked around my house in amazement.

"Tell me what's going on," I said as Dee put his bag down by the front door and stood frozen.

"IIIII jjjjust gotta go," he said, pointing to the envelope in my hand. "But I wanted you toooo hhhaaavvee that."

I had remembered him handing it to me, but it didn't hit me that it was actually in my hands. I tore the envelope open and stared at the piece of paper. It was Dee's birth certificate, the original at that, with both Tanya and Brendan's signature. My heart sank as I felt my face get hot out of embarrassment. I wasn't angry at Dee, or even Tanya, I was mad at the man who was turning out to be a stranger. I scanned the certificate and learned Dee's real name was DeAndre Brian Lewis. This *was* Brendan's son.

"Thank you for this," I said, holding the paper up before stuffing it back in the envelope and handing it to Dee.

Dee held up his hands and blocked me from giving it back to him.

"You keep that," he said. "I've got a copy."

Pop, Trey, Kenya, and Jasmine were crowded around us, staring at Brendan's little boy.

"I've got to go, the bus stops running in a little bit," he said, checking the *Sponge Bob* watch on his wrist.

I tugged on his jacket and looked at him deeply for some sort of answer to my earlier question.

"Where are you going?"

"I've got to get out of Atlanta," he said, speaking like a grown man.

I was impressed by Dee; although he was only thirteen, he acted much older.

"What about your mom? You can't just leave her."

"You heard her, Mystique...ssshhhee don't even want me."

I couldn't even challenge what he was saying; his mom had made it perfectly clear that she didn't want him, and would be better off without him, *but was she serious?*

"All my life I've been hearing how I won't ever be sh... anything...and how I'm nothing, and how she hates me; so I'm leaving."

"To go where?" I asked curiously.

"Anywhere is better than here," he replied, picking up his bags and slinging them over his shoulder.

"Young man, why don't you come in and have something to eat, we've got plenty for you; maybe you can take some on the road," Pop said graciously.

Dee looked at Pop for a moment, then gave a small nod.

Something about the way Pop said it — the quiet authority of an older man who means exactly what he says and expects you to know — left no real room for argument.

We filed back inside, the screen door swinging shut behind us. The noise of the street gave way to the warm smell of food and the low hum of conversation picking back up in the other room. Dee followed behind Pop with his hands in his pockets, taking in the house like he was trying not to look like he was looking. I fell into step behind them and guided him gently toward the dining room where the spread was still laid out, barely touched.

Someone handed him a plate without making a production of it and he settled into a chair at the edge of the table. Dee didn't hesitate. He piled food on top of his plate in a way that told me he hadn't had a real meal in a while. Something about that made my chest ache in a way I wasn't ready to examine.

I moved quietly to the kitchen and packed him a bag of food to take with him. I didn't know where he was going, but standing there folding the top of that bag over, I felt like I needed to stop him.

But what was I going to do? Who was I to step in? Yes, he was Brendan's son, but was it my responsibility to intervene?

"That boy acts like he hasn't eaten in days," Jasmine said with Kenya close behind her.

"I bet he hasn't," I said, putting the top on some Tupperware and putting it in a grocery bag for Dee.

"You saw the way that house looked," I replied to Jasmine.

"So you're really going to send him out there by himself?" Kenya said, biting her nail fretfully.

"He's just a baby."

She was watching Dee as he ate. All Kenya wanted was for everyone to get along, and to be happy and content. But this wasn't the *Cosby Show*, I reminded her, and life doesn't always end perfectly.

"What else am I supposed to do?" I asked, not looking at her as I put two Powerades in his bag.

Jasmine sucked her teeth and rolled her eyes.

"You want her to take that little bad ass into her house or something, Kenya?"

I spun around and looked at Jasmine with disgust; *how dare she say he was a bad ass?* She didn't know anything about Dee and what he had gone through in life. It wasn't like I did either, but at least I wasn't judging.

"Chill out with that," I said sternly as Kenya blew Jasmine's comment off and went back into the living room to join Lorenzo.

After Dee had finished two plates, he gathered his belongings, said goodbye to everyone, and made his way out the door.

He turned around to hug me, and as we embraced, I gripped him tightly; I didn't want to let him go. Just like his father, this kid had some kind of hold on me.

I had already lost Brendan, and now that a piece of him was back in my life I didn't know if I was ready to lose that too. Dee definitely couldn't go back to living with his mother; that was a fact, *but what was I going to do? Raise a thirteen year old? I could barely wake up on time, how could I be responsible for someone else?*

"You make sure you call me when you get to wherever you're going," I said as I let him go and watched him back up.

"I'll do that," Dee said, waving at everyone as he walked down the driveway.

I followed him as far as my eyes could see, and soon I couldn't spot him anymore. I closed the front door and stood with my back to it. I felt bad, like I had done the wrong thing, and in the pit of my stomach I knew my conscience was right. Dee was a bright kid, with a bright future, and I needed to step in and be the parent he never had. I had to do this, not only for him, but for Brendan. I was, in essence, righting Brendan's wrongs.

I raced upstairs, grabbed my keys off the nightstand, and ran out the door while everyone watched me with their mouths open.

I found Dee sitting on the bus stop with all of his bags surrounding him.

"Hey, get in," I said as Dee's eye lit up with excitement; I watched him as he rushed toward my car and got in.

"You're going to stay with me until we get things straightened out, okay?" I said, not leaving him room to answer.

"But we've got to get some things straight; we will have order…it *is* my house and you will listen to me." Dee leaped forward and wrapped his arms around my neck; I felt good.

"I swear I will," he said excitedly. "I'll do whatever you say."

When the two of us walked back into the house, me carrying one bag in my hand and Dee carrying the other two, I could tell by the look on some of their faces that they were astonished at my decision. I showed Dee the guest room and told him to take a shower and join us downstairs for a movie.

"Are you sure you want to do this? Are you ready for this?" Jasmine said, rushing up to me as Pop and Kenya smiled in approval.

"I might not be ready, but it's what I'm doing," I said.

I knew she didn't agree with me taking Dee in, and I knew she didn't see my reasoning behind it, but I didn't care.

Whatever I needed to do to help Dee out, I was going to do it.

chapter eight

Dear Diary,

I don't think I've been up this early since I was an undergrad and had those 7:00 A.M. classes. Yuck. I had to get up this morning and drive Dee to his school on the other side of town. Being that I sleep in on most mornings (every morning!), I had forgotten how bad the morning traffic was. We didn't get him to school until close to 9:30. So, let's just say...I'm already bad at this parenting thing. I signed Dee in and came back home to catch a couple more hours of sleep. I've asked Trey if he can keep an eye on Dee when he gets home from school, since Trey will be working on the house anyway. Pissed wouldn't even be the word to describe how I feel when I glance at the pictures of me and Brendan that once made me tingle. If I could only talk to him, I would probably scream till I didn't have a voice, and then I would kiss him until my lips hurt. I miss him so much. But I figure the busier I am, the less time I'll have to think about this. I'm supposed to meet with Ralph this morning to discuss some of the things he found out. Lenny made a smart comment about me using the company conference room for personal use, so I'll try to do everything here. And then there's the question of Trey. Jasmine gave me an earful last night when everyone left. She kept asking me over and over what I think I'm doing with Trey so soon after Brendan's death. I wish I had an answer for her, but I don't. It's not like I'm planning to say, "Oh forget Brendan! I hate him!" It's just when I look into Trey's eyes, there's something that's slowly pulling me in. Last night, Trey asked me out on a date, and when I hesitated, he told me to think about it. I don't know, though, that does look a little off, right? Every time I look at Trey, it's like I feel Brendan right over my shoul-

der; it feels wrong. Well, I need to get showered and dressed to meet Ralph in a half
hour. I'm not sure I'm looking forward to
this meeting, though. What did he find out?
The suspense is killing me.

Lauren Washington

––––––

As I showered, I thought about my journal entry and decided now wasn't the time for me to start getting involved with anyone; if Trey wanted me that badly, as his touches and body language suggested, he'd wait, *right?* But the question was…*how long should he have to wait?*

I was a big ball of confusion, and I really didn't know which way I should be going. On one hand, I wasn't ready to let go of my relationship with Brendan, even though he was dead; on the other hand, I didn't want to live in the past. *I had time to decide*, I thought, as I stepped out of the shower and ran to my room to get dressed.

"Skeeter! Someone's here for you!" I heard Trey yell from downstairs. I hung my head over the railing.

"Can you stop yelling in my house? Tell Ralph I'll be right down," I said, shaking my head as I wrapped the towel tighter around my body. Trey winked his eye and chuckled before heading into the living room where I could see Ralph's feet at the table.

I threw on a pair of jeans and a t-shirt. I pulled my hair back into a loose bun before darting down the steps.

"I'm *so* sorry, Ralph," I said, extending my hand and shaking his graciously.

"Would you like anything to drink?" I asked, raising an

eyebrow. I needed to be as nice as I possibly could to the man who, possibly, held the answer to my mother's death.

"I'm okay," Ralph smiled.

I took a seat across from him, clasped my hands together, and sighed as I prepared myself for the worst. *Maybe it was just as simple as a hit and run and the person just got scared and left*, I thought. But no, someone had shot my mother.

"First let me say, I'm sorry about your boyfriend's su..." he started to say.

"Thank you," I said, cutting him off. I was here to handle one tragedy, and he was throwing me off with the other one.

"Now, about what you found," I continued, clearing my throat.

Taking my cue, Ralph opened a folder and placed it in front of me to see. I couldn't make out what I was seeing, but it looked like portions of police reports.

"I don't understand," I said, looking up at him perplexed.

"It seems that between November 1988 and July 1989, there were about fifteen domestic abuse police reports filed by your mother," Ralph said as my eyes shot open.

Domestic abuse reports? I had never even seen my father yell at my mother, let alone put his hands on her.

"What does this mean?" I asked, wanting to cry. This couldn't be a good sign and I knew it.

"Well, when I went in to pull the files for the reports, all of them were gone," Ralph said, sucking his teeth. "So, I'll have to dig a little deeper on that one." He moved the stack of papers out of my way and dug in his bag for more folders and papers.

"Domestic abuse? I don't understand."

"Why don't you talk with your father and find out as much as you can about any arguments he and your mother might have had. Nine times out of ten, the reports would have been filed regarding a significant other."

My head started hurting as I thought about what Pop

could have known about these reports, and how they tied into mom's death.

"And you think these reports have something to do with her murder?" I inquired as Ralph shifted his lips from left to right.

"They could. I just found it really unusual that *all* of the reports are gone."

I agreed with him, if mom had filed fifteen domestic abuse reports against Pop and they were all missing, *what could my father possibly have been hiding?*

I tried to focus on the rest of the information Ralph was giving me, but I kept thinking back to all the times Pop had begged and pleaded with me not to get a private detective. I couldn't help but wonder, *had he been trying to keep me from finding all of this out?*

"Now, do you remember I told you I spoke with a local man who said he was there the night your mom was killed?" Ralph said in his thick Hispanic accent. I nodded and took a deep breath.

"It turns out he saw something, but not everything," Ralph said, pulling out a piece of paper. "It seems like he saw your mother and her killer arguing loudly with one another. He said your mother was apologizing profusely, and the next thing he knew…he heard gunshots." I covered my face as I tried not to visualize my mother being shot, but it was useless.

"So, she knew her killer?" I asked, pulling my head up at the realization.

"More than likely," Ralph said as he adjusted his reading glasses. "He didn't report anything because he was high that night, and he wasn't sure if anyone would believe him."

I listened closely with a kid-like stare. I wanted to run away and forget about anything I had ever wondered about mom's death. It all was becoming more than I had imagined.

"He says it was a late eighties model, brown, tan or black Chevy."

I exhaled loudly. I knew Pop wasn't capable of doing any type of harm to his wife, but my Uncle Rico, my father's brother, did have a dark brown '88 Chevy throughout my childhood. I hoped and prayed that my assumptions were way off; that Pop had a good explanation for all the coincidences.

"I'm going to talk to a couple more people and find out some things. I'll call you when I have something new," he said to me as I stared off into the kitchen.

I thanked him for his help, and made my way to the TV room to take a break. I tried to process everything, but I was on information overload. Mom knew her killer; she was arguing with the person, and she had even filed some domestic abuse reports. *Why hadn't the police been able to uncover any of this?* My blood was boiling, my mind was racing, and tears were slowly trickling down my cheeks when Trey walked in.

"Skeeter, do you know where..." Trey started before seeing me.

I was balled up on the couch and wasn't paying attention to anything he was saying. I was a mess. I had done a really good job of keeping myself together when Trey was around, but with him and his workers mulling around my house, I had no choice but to let it out.

"Are you...are you okay, Lauren?" Trey asked.

I glanced up at him and saw the look of concern on his face, and I returned my head to my hands and wept silently. Trey took a seat on the couch and placed an arm around my shoulders and pulled me into a bear hug. I didn't resist, as I cried into his chest.

"It's okay," he said over and over as I thought about mom, Brendan, and Pop. *Why was I the last to find out everything?*

The two of us sat intertwined on the couch in each other's

arms. I couldn't let go of him; and yet, I couldn't shake the feeling that he was Brendan. He was comforting, holding and staring deeply into my eyes the way that Brendan used to.

"I'm sorry," I said, finally realizing I was crying on the shoulder of the man I should have been avoiding.

I wiped my eyes and pulled away from him in a hurry. I didn't need Trey getting the wrong idea about our closeness.

"Why are you apologizing? Are you okay?" Trey said, allowing me to pull away from him.

He looked like he wanted to say something to comfort me, but as I stood up and continued wiping my face, I saw he was struggling.

"I'm okay," I repeated.

It didn't work, and as I straightened my clothes and pushed some pieces of my hair behind my ear, he was still sitting in the same spot staring at me.

"Are you sure you're okay?" he asked again, further agitating me. I couldn't understand why he wasn't getting the hint that I wanted to be left alone. Sure...I looked a mess, and I had just cried in his arms, *but didn't he realize that I was over it?*

"I *said* I was okay, Trey," I replied, rolling my eyes as I crossed my arms across my chest. He stood up and approached me. As I saw his hand coming closer to my shoulder, I pulled back.

"What's the matter with you?"

"Nothing."

"Okay, so *nothing* makes you act crazy then," Trey said, laughing at his own joke.

I didn't smile.

"Okay, well...I guess I'll just get back to my work," Trey said uncomfortably.

His hand had barely grazed my arm, and already, my body was responding in ways my pride had absolutely no say in.

I took a small step back and pretended to busy myself with something, anything, because I needed a moment that Trey could not see or read. The truth was that I was tired. Not just the kind of tired that sleep fixes, but the kind that settles into your bones when you have been running on grief and adrenaline for too long, holding yourself together by sheer will, going through the motions of being okay for everyone around you. And somewhere in the middle of all of that, I had forgotten that I was still a woman with a body that had needs, that grief did not suspend just because life had gotten complicated.

It had been weeks. Longer than I had gone in years, and I felt every single day of it.

I had not wanted Trey here. I had told myself that more times than I could count. He complicated things. He showed up uninvited and took up space in rooms and in my thoughts. I resented him for how easy he made it look, just existing, unbothered in my vicinity like that.

But then there were his arms.

I did not mean to notice them. I noticed them anyway. The way his biceps pressed against the fabric of his shirt, a slow bead of sweat tracing the curve of muscle in the afternoon heat. He smelled clean underneath it; warm and familiar.

I exhaled slowly through my nose and looked away.

This was inconvenient. This was the absolute last thing I had time or energy or emotional real estate for. I was not going to give Trey the satisfaction of knowing that his presence alone was doing something to me that I had not given him permission to do. I had too much dignity for that and too much sense; or at least I was going to keep telling myself both of those things until they felt true again.

I turned around, needing the conversation to be over, needing distance between us before my body completely overruled my better judgment. That was when I caught him.

He had not walked away yet. He was still standing there,

and he was watching me with an expression I recognized and immediately wished I didn't. Not a smirk, not anything arrogant or presumptuous. Just a knowing glance that confirmed I was seen.

I held his gaze for exactly one second longer than I should have.

"What?" I asked with plenty of attitude in my voice.

"I was just wondering if you had a chance to think about me taking you out; I really think it would be good for you," Trey said, fidgeting with his tool belt.

I sucked my teeth and rolled my neck as I tried to push Trey away. He was one complication I didn't need.

"It's too soon, and it just feels *weird*," I lied, knowing that being with Trey gave me a sense of normalcy and calmness. I wasn't supposed to like or lust after someone else so quickly after Brendan's death, *was I?* My heart still ached to feel Brendan's hands around my waist and his breath upon my neck; but here I was yearning for something from Trey.

Trey nodded like he understood and was okay with my decision, but I could tell he was a little disappointed. His shoulders slumped and he exhaled before turning to walk away. I laid my head on the wall and blew out some air. It was already shaping up to be one of *those* weeks.

When I left for work, Dee had just gotten home and was about to do his homework. Pop was working late. I had left him a message telling him there were some things that Ralph told me about mom's death that I needed him to clarify. I waited as long as I could before I had to leave for work, and still no Pop. He was normally pretty good at getting home every day at the same time, but today was different and that made me nervous. I wondered if he knew more than he was letting on.

After I made sure dinner was ready for Dee and Pop, I made my way to the radio station. My show started in less than an hour and I was in no way prepared for my entertainment news. I rushed in, quickly looked up some news, and made my way to the studio with less than five minutes to spare. This was the first time I had ever cut it so close. When my producer, Dave, looked up from his clip board, I could tell the news would make it to Lenny.

"Sorry I'm late," I said, plugging my headphones into the board and starting my intro. I barely skated by. My entertainment news was just enough to get me through, but I knew I couldn't afford any more close calls.

And just as I suspected, Lenny was on the office phone before I had a chance to log off my computer and leave for the night.

"Dave told me about your tardiness. Consider this your first warning. Don't let it happen again," Lenny said.

"Right," I replied hastily. *Damn that Dave; he had already sold me out.* I checked my watch and yawned; I was tired.

I stopped by McDonald's and picked up a burger and fries and headed home. I thought about my hectic schedule for the upcoming week, and was weirdly happy about the recent chaotic events. Later in the week, I was hosting a fashion show for one of the upscale black modeling troupes in Atlanta, and on Friday and Saturday I had club appearances to make. I hoped that Dee could adjust to my fast life and, even more, that I could adjust to having him there.

When I got home Pop was fast asleep on the couch with the television watching him. I kissed his forehead. I watched as he breathed. I knew this man well; almost too well. He had dried almost every tear I had cried from the time I was nine until I met Brendan. He was there for every big event in my life and he seemed to feel my pain. But with all the new information surfacing, I needed to find out everything I didn't know about Pop.

I cleaned up the kitchen, put away some dishes, and started a load of laundry before I stuck my head in on Dee. I saw the flicker of the television hitting the tan and blue twin comforter. I didn't see the head or the body of the little boy I was looking for.

"Dee?" I said quietly, hoping he was playing hide and seek with me. I knew he was too old for that game, but I wanted to believe he could still be playing.

I pulled the covers back and was met with rustled bed sheets. It looked like he had been there, but was now gone. I briskly walked throughout the halls of my house calling Dee's name, and as I reached the living room where Pop was, I turned and faced him.

"Have you seen Dee?" I said, wiping sweat from my brow. Pop ran his hands over his hair and exhaled.

"Nope. He was here when I fell asleep."

My hands began to shake as I felt for something to hold me up. I had only been Dee's guardian for a day and had "lost" him. I sucked at being a parent. It was almost one in the morning; *where in the hell could he be?*

Pop and I got in my car and drove the streets of Bankhead trying to think of somewhere that a thirteen year old would go. I was praying that he would show up. I tried to think of a way I was going to explain this to the police.

Yes, I lost my dead boyfriend's son.

I racked my brain for friends he might have in Bankhead, but I kept drawing a blank.

"Where is this boy?" Pop said, extending his neck out the window and looking around.

The city was far from dead, but there weren't many people walking up and down the streets. Some of the dope boys were making their rounds on the corner, and as a black Chevy slowed down to make an exchange, I remembered what Ralph told me. There was dampness on the streets and a peaceful silence that accompanied my two-party search.

"Pop, I talked to the private detective today about mom's death."

I had to find the appropriate way to introduce the information to Pop; I didn't want to come off like I was already accusing him of something.

"Yeah..." Pop said nonchalantly as he continued looking away from me.

"And, well, he said...something about some domestic abuse reports that were missing," I blurted out. He shook his head from side to side.

"Your mother filed some reports, Lauren, but it wasn't anything."

What did he mean it wasn't "anything?" This was news to me; after eighteen years of wondering, *now Pop was admitting that there had been some abuse in their relationship?*

"So...she filed them against you?" I asked for clarification.

Pop shook his head. "This is something you'll never understand."

I must've looked crazy, because even though he was stuttering and looking nervous, Pop continued.

"We weren't perfect, but we loved each other," he managed to say as he ran his hand up and down the seatbelt. "We both made a lot of mistakes, and I regret some of them."

It was the first time I had ever seen fear and guilt on my father's face.

"You...you *beat* mom?" I struggled to say the words. Growing up, I didn't receive beatings like all my other friends. Pop didn't think it was the right way to discipline; so that's why it perplexed me that he could have hurt my mother.

My father's eyes shot toward me and I swore I saw flames spitting from them. Immediately, I knew he was hurt by my finger pointing. Before I could apologize, he was changing the subject.

"Did you check with Trey to see if he had seen Dee?" he asked coldly.

I wanted to reach out and touch Pop's face and apologize, but I knew what had been done was already set in stone; I couldn't take it back. I slowed the car down and looked over at Pop.

"Did you have something to do with mom's death?"

Pop didn't reply, he just posed his question again.

"I asked you if you checked with Trey about Dee?"

I pulled out my cell phone and Trey's business card, and called him.

"Hello?" Trey said groggily. I could tell he had been asleep, but I pushed on with my question.

"Hey, Trey. It's Lauren. Have you seen Dee? He's missing," I said, blowing through my question.

Trey sounded like he was trying to catch his breath and scrambling. "Oh damn! What time is it?"

"It's almost two in the morning," I said, checking my watch. I was panicking as Trey yawned in my ear.

"I'm sorry, Lauren, he's over here at my house," Trey said. "I was going to have him back before you got home, but we fell asleep."

I rolled my eyes and blew out air angrily. *Who the hell did Trey think he was taking Dee to his house?* It was one thing for him to invade my privacy, but now he was crossing the line. After I got directions to Trey's house, I told him I would be right over there.

"What right does he think he has to just *up* and take him?" I said to myself in the car as Pop stared out of the window, visibly more relaxed.

"Calm yourself down, Lauren; the man was doing you a favor by watching that little boy," Pop reminded me.

It was one of the few times when he called me Lauren, where his tone alone made me realize that he wasn't in the mood for my bitching and complaining.

"I guess so," I said, turning the volume up in the car.

When we arrived at Trey's house, I couldn't believe what I was seeing. Trey was doing well; I mean really, really well. His traditional, yet contemporary, brick home was two stories, and had the cutest wrap around driveway with a three-car garage. His lawn looked like those from a gardening magazine; I was impressed. I knew Kenya told me he was doing it big, but I didn't know it was *that* big.

When I got to the front door, I was fuming. I spent twenty minutes thinking about what I was going to say to Trey; but when the door opened, and I saw him wearing an undershirt and sweat pants, I lost my train of thought. Before I could yell or scream I saw Dee wiping his eyes sleepily.

"Get in the car, Dee. Pop is in there."

With my arms crossed, I watched as Dee did just as I said.

"See you later, man," Trey said to Dee.

"What the hell were you thinking?" I said irritably. "Do you know how worried we were?"

"I'm sorry. Dee and I were talking about him wanting to be a rapper, and I told him I had some old school rap tapes I thought he should listen to," Trey said.

"We were just supposed to run in and out; get the tapes. But we started watching television and we both fell asleep."

"Anything could have happened to him," I countered.

Trey continued to apologize as I looked up and down his sculpted body; I was listening, but not closely.

"Come inside for just a second," he pleaded.

I wanted to say no, but my legs said yes.

"Pop is in the car and I really need to get Dee home."

"It'll just be a second," Trey responded as he grabbed my hand and led me into the foyer.

If I thought the outside of Trey's house was impressive, the inside was a designer's dream. Hardwood floors caught the light from above and threw it back warm and golden. Glass tables sat clean and deliberate against walls that were dressed just right — not overdone, not sparse, but considered. Beautiful elegant carpet anchored the living space, and granite countertops stretched across the kitchen in a long, cool sweep. The layout was open and spacious in a way that made the whole place feel like it was breathing. I stood in the middle of it and turned slowly, taking it all in.

Trey had come a long way from Bankhead.

"This is beautiful," I said, my eyes traveling up to the high ceiling where recessed lighting hummed soft and low over-head. I kept my gaze up there, genuinely caught by it, my neck tilted back, and my guard temporarily somewhere else entirely.

I felt him before I heard him.

Trey had moved without me noticing. He had a habit of doing that. Before I knew it, he spoke again and his voice was no longer across the room. It was close. Right at my ear, low and in his typical carefree tone.

"Thanks," he said softly. "I hope I can do something like this to your crib one day." And then he blew the softest stream of warm air against my ear.

My entire body responded before my brain had a single thing to say about it. Chills moved down my neck and across my shoulders in a wave I could not stop and did not see coming. My feet stayed planted, but every-thing else went soft. I could not move. I could not speak. I could not fully decipher what was happening inside me, or sort out what any of it meant. All I knew, standing in the middle of Trey's beautiful house with my eyes still pointed at the ceiling and my heart beating somewhere in my throat, was that whatever this was, it felt amazing.

"I...I should be going," I said, snapping out of my momentary fit of insanity. Jasmine and Brendan's faces popped into my head as I imagined Trey undressing me.

"I'm really sorry, again. Hopefully you'll let me make it up to you." Trey said slyly.

I grinned at his humor and quickly retreated to the door. Trey stood on his doorstep and looked at me. It was strange to me — both the timing of his return into my life and the way it made me feel — and as I looked in the backseat at Dee sleeping soundly, I exhaled.

I knew Pop was still livid with me but was covering it up well.

"This here is a nice house," he said, admiring the house from the car.

"Yeah, Pop...maybe one day you'll let me buy you one like this," I joked, knowing my father didn't want to be anywhere but Bankhead.

"No, not me; this is your life," he joked as he reclined his seat and closed his eyes.

I pondered things on the way home. I missed Brendan so much I couldn't think or see straight; yet I felt something strong for Trey.

I had devoted every waking moment to Brendan and his pleasure; now it was time for me to figure out what *I* liked and needed.

It wasn't going to be easy.

chapter nine

Dear Diary,

It's been a couple of days since I jotted down my thoughts, and things still aren't back to normal yet; at least in my eyes they aren't. I still wake up in the morning waiting for Brendan's call. I still sit at my desk, hoping that flowers will come my way; but they never do. I woke up last night with tears streaming down my face. I didn't even know I had been crying. I've been trying to get in touch with Ms. Pat to find out everything I can about Dee and Tanya. How could she not tell me that Brendan had a son? Better yet, how could Brendan, the man I thought loved me, fail to tell me something so major? It makes me want to say forget him, and forget everything I ever thought we were...but I can't. My heart won't let me forget, and my mind has a tendency to hold on to good memories despite the bad.

Ever since I asked Pop about the domestic abuse reports, he has been acting strangely. I've apologized in more ways than one, and still nothing. I don't know what to do other than hope he comes around.

Dee is transitioning well, I believe. He has a girlfriend, and from what Trey tells me, she's a nice little girl. I completed one of my hosting gigs last night, and it was pretty cool. Anyway, this morning I'm taking Dee down to the barbershop so we can cut off that wild hair that's been growing! Plus I need to find out from Michael, the assistant manager, if he remembers anything about the week Brendan died. Maybe he has some answers. I sure hope so, because all of this is running me ragged.

I've got to jet.

Lauren Washington

———

I've never been a frequenter of "Cutterz" barbershop & salon; not because it wasn't the best barbershop/salon in Atlanta, but because I'm so picky about the people I let touch my hair. Since we met, Kenya has been the only person that's been my regular hairstylist, and I'm more than happy to keep it that way.

"I don't want to cut my hair," Dee whined as we got in the front seat of the car and buckled in. I glanced over at him sternly. Whining wasn't going to get him out of a trip to the barber.

I didn't let Mike know I was coming, but I figured he would be cool with seeing me. It was the first time I had stepped in there since Brendan died. I wasn't looking forward to seeing Brendan's chair, or seeing the front desk where he would take care of business, and I definitely wasn't looking forward to the empty parking spot marked "Owner only."

It had actually been a couple of months since I had been able to make it down to the shop and the visit felt long overdue.

"I want you to see, first-hand, the blood, sweat, and tears your father put into his barbershop and salon, okay?" I said, not wanting a reply from Dee who rolled his eyes and sat back in the seat with his hands across his chest.

I knew he was sick of me forcing lectures on him, but he needed it. He needed to know that deep down, although he had only seen one side, his father was a good man with a good heart.

I had tried to give Tanya a call a couple of times throughout the week, just to let her know that Dee was okay, but the phone was cut off. After our last visit, I definitely wasn't going anywhere near her house.

As I pulled up to the business, I noticed a big gray Chevy Suburban parked in Brendan's usual spot.

That's strange, I thought as Dee and I got out of the car and headed toward the door.

When my foot hit the black and white tiled floor of "Cut-terz," all eyes were on me. It was like everyone was waiting on me to show up. Some of the girls gathered in a corner and whispered amongst themselves, while the guys all gave me their "wassup" nods. It wasn't the welcome I had been hoping for, but I hoped after seeing Michael that things would pan out.

"Hey!" I said when Michael came from the back of the shop with two cardboard boxes in his hands.

He stopped walking the moment he saw me. The boxes stayed in his grip, but he went still, his expression shifting through something I couldn't quite name. Surprise first, then something softer underneath it. He set the boxes down on the nearest surface and stood up straight, looking at me with the infamous tilted head of sympathy.

"Hey there," he said finally.

He crossed the floor and pulled me into a hug before either of us said another word. It was the sympathy hug I had grown used to: no pat on the back, just a real hold that lasted a few seconds longer than a casual greeting. When he pulled back he kept his hands on my shoulders and looked at me directly.

"Lauren, I am so sorry about Brendan," he said, his voice dropping low and sincere. "I mean that. He was a good man and..."

He shook his head slowly like words were no longer adequate.

"How are you holding up?"

I opened my mouth and closed it once before answering.

It wasn't that I didn't have words. It was that nobody had asked me that question like they actually wanted the answer. For weeks I had been swimming in condolences — *so sorry for your loss, praying for you, let me know if you need anything* — all of it warm and well-meaning and none of it requiring me to actually respond. People said those things the way you held a door open for someone. A reflex. A kindness that asked nothing in return.

But Michael had gone still when he asked. Like whatever I said next actually mattered to him. I wasn't prepared for that.

"I'm…okay. Every day is a different roller coaster."

Everyone else fell in line to share their condolences. I smiled bravely as I pointed out Dee and introduced him as Brendan's son; everyone gasped at the resemblance the two shared.

"I didn't even know he had a son," Michael said rubbing his goatee. "Join the club," I said low enough that Dee couldn't hear.

I could tell by looking at Dee that he was relishing in the attention he was getting from being the "boss man's" son. A grin came over his adorable face that I hadn't seen up until that time.

"What can I do for you today?" Michael said, looking Dee and I over again before sitting in his seat.

"We need a haircut," I said sarcastically as I pointed to the pile of mangled hair atop Dee's dome.

"You sure do," Michael joked as he went and checked the stylist's calendars.

"Looks like everyone is booked but my appointment is late so I can cut him," he said, pulling out his black cape and showing Dee where to sit.

On Saturdays, barber and beauty shops were like a totally different world. The smell hit you before you even got through the door — hot curling irons and that sweet chemical bite of relaxer, "Pump It Up" hairspray thick in the air, and if you were lucky, somebody had run next door or down the street and come back with a foam container of barbecue that had the whole shop smelling like a cookout. You learned early not to wear anything white on a Saturday.

Inside, it was organized chaos in the best way. Clippers buzzing, blow dryers roaring, somebody's gospel or old school R&B floating underneath all of it...because the music was always on, always loud enough to feel but not so loud it drowned out the conversation. If we're real, the conversation was the whole point. The walls were covered in laminated style charts, women with french rolls so sharp they looked sculpted, Halle Berry cuts, wrap sets, spiral curls, finger waves laid so clean they looked painted on. You'd stare at those pictures as a little girl and decide who you were going to be when you grew up.

I could remember sitting in the beauty salon with my mother as a child, legs swinging off the edge of the chair because they didn't reach the floor yet, just taking it all in. The women in that shop had a particular kind of elegance; the way they talked with their hands while someone worked on their hair, the way they laughed from somewhere deep, the way they passed information around the room like a relay race. Who was cheating, who had gotten their car repossessed, whose daughter was fast, whose son had finally gotten himself together. Nothing was off limits and everything was delivered with authority. Those women knew things. And they were never not well-dressed, even sitting under a dryer with a plastic cap on their head.

On any given Saturday you could get your hair done, pick up a bootleg mix CD someone's cousin had burned, grab a plate of barbecue delivered straight to your chair, and leave knowing everything that had happened in the neighborhood for the past two weeks. It was a mini flea market, a therapy session, and a community bulletin board all in one.

I walked in and felt that familiar warmth settle over me: the noise, the movement, the smell of it all. People were moving through the shop with purpose, tending to clients and walk-ins, as they packed into the shop, trying to get right before the weekend really started. I watched with a quiet grin, proud in a way that surprised me. This was Brendan's legacy.

He had built something that actually meant something to people.

I took a seat in the lounge and picked up an old copy of Ebony with Beyoncé on the cover, naturally, and flipped a few pages before putting it back down. Then I looked around and really took in what had changed in the month since his death. The old Coke machines were gone. Complimentary beverages now came to you on a tray. The tiny speakers that used to blast whatever the loudest stylist wanted to hear had been replaced with an overhead system that was currently working through some of the best old school hip-hop and R&B I'd heard outside of my own booth. Brendan had taste, and whoever was carrying his vision forward had clearly been paying attention.

It seemed like an hour passed before Dee was ready. When he stood in front of me with his fresh low haircut, I saw Brendan. My eyes filled with tears and as he rushed to my side, I wiped them away.

"Are you okay?" Dee asked concerned.

"I'm fine, honey," I said, catching my breath. "I'm fine."

Michael came over and hugged me again before sending me away with a free haircut; but he didn't know I had come for more than that.

"Mike, can we talk in the back for a second?"

When I got to the back office, where Brendan and I had made love so many times I lost count, it felt strange; like an entirely new place.

"What's going on?" Mike said casually as he cleared the desk of a couple of papers and motioned for me to sit down.

"It's about Brendan," I started as I closed my eyes. "I just don't understand why he ki…why he did it."

Mike watched me with little emotion, and blinked a couple of times as I continued.

"Was he acting strange the week of his death?" I inquired, hoping I wouldn't have to say anymore.

He seemed deep in thought. "I couldn't say."

"What do you mean, you 'couldn't say?'"

"Just what I said, Lauren, I don't know what state B was in when he did that shit," he said angrily. Mike was a relatively calm guy with an emotionless face, droopy eyes, and the business sense that few college graduates had; I understood why Brendan had chosen him as the assistant manager.

I took my time before responding; I looked around the room at the plaques and trophies on the walls.

"The last time you saw him, what did he say; how was he feeling?" I asked.

Mike looked at his desk and ran his hands through his bushy, thick afro, and moaned loudly. It was like it was painful for him to fill me in on the little things I needed to know.

"The last time I saw him was about four months ago," he said, inhaling and holding his breath. He was looking at my reaction; trying to gauge how far he would have to go.

"Four months?!" I screamed loudly before catching myself.

"What the hell are you talking about? Brendan's only been dead a few weeks," I reminded him.

"I don't think I should be the one to break this news to you like this."

"What news? What are you talking about?" I said, leaning forward. I could feel it in my veins and in my heart…another secret.

"Look, you need to talk to his mother or something; not me. It's not my place," Mike said firmly.

I refused to leave. I was fed up with crying and feeling sorry for myself; someone was going to tell me the truth, even if I had to drag it out of them.

"No, Mike…you're going to tell me *exactly* what the hell is going on!" I said, grabbing him by the shoulder.

"How could you have not seen Brendan in four months

before he died? This *is* his shop and you *do* work here, right?"
I said, putting my hands on my hips.

He turned around and looked into my eyes, the same eyes
that were pleading for an answer, and shook his head.

"B sold me the shop about five months ago," he said,
dropping his shoulders.

My mouth dropped open as I continued listening.

"I was letting him cut hair here, though…but he hadn't
been here in like four months."

"W-what?" I stuttered.

"He said he wasn't going to tell you because you would
just try to talk him out of it. But then I heard he got involved
with Quito, and…he stopped coming in."

As I stood motionless in the office, I could feel my breakfast coming up, so I ran to the restroom with my hand over
my mouth. Luckily, though, nothing came out.

I sat on the cold tiled bathroom floor, and I gripped the
toilet tightly with my hands. *How in the hell could all of this
have been happening right underneath my nose?*

Brendan had kept his child from me, and the sale of his
shop – his most prized possession. And as soon as I heard the
name Quito, my skin crawled. Quito, or Marquise Jonsen, was
one of Brendan's friends who rubbed me the wrong way. He
didn't have a job, had plenty of trashy women around him,
lived deep in the hood, and yet he sported the latest fashions
and the hottest rides. It didn't take a genius to know what
Quito did for a living. Knowing that Brendan had been
involved with Quito and his low-life thugs made my head
and stomach hurt.

*Who had I loved? Who was Brendan? And most of all, where
had the man I knew gone?*

I hung my head over the toilet bowl and sobbed silently.
My heart was thumping uncontrollably and I was sweating.
All the times Brendan called me and said he was at the shop,
had been a lie. When I would offer to come by and bring him

lunch, he would quickly rush me off the phone. It had all been a lie. *One big lie.*

I straightened up and flushed the toilet. As I was leaving, I ran into the mystery woman from the club and Brendan's funeral. I knew it was her by the look she gave me when our eyes met. Her hair was still in a short, texturized do, and I could see a little pouch sticking out of the t-shirt she was wearing. She was short, too; really short. She had dimples that I could see, even though she wasn't smiling. She spun around after she saw my face.

"What's your name?" I said forcefully with tears staining my cheeks.

"Brandy," she said nervously. She was a cute girl, but because of the situation, I hated her. She had come in between me and my man; and for that, she was on my bad list.

"I'm sure you already know who I am," I said, rolling my eyes.

Brandy shook her head while she dried off her hands and looked at me.

"I'm not looking for trouble," she said, reaching for the doorknob of the bathroom. I blocked her hand and stood with my hands on my hips.

"You're going to tell me everything," I said.

Brandy looked like she was about to pee all over herself. I could understand her fear.

"How did you know Brendan?"

"We met here. He hired me to work at the shop as a shampooer about two and a half years ago," she revealed.

I racked my brain; *why hadn't I ever seen this girl before?*

"Uh huh," I said signaling with my hands for her to continue. I knew there was more, and I knew she was holding out on me.

"And..." she said, looking at the ceiling as she tried to keep the tears from falling. I felt bad for the girl, but not bad enough to stop the interrogation.

"Were you sleeping with my boyfriend?" I asked bluntly, not expecting an honest reply.

"Yes." Brandy looked at me defiantly; she wasn't backing down. As I recovered from the blow my heart was dealt, I gasped for air.

"We started fooling around about two years ago; I swear I didn't know he was with you, but by the time I found out I was already in love with him," she said.

It felt like someone picked me up, pulled my hair, and slammed me into a concrete wall. As I listened in, I felt everything in front of me spinning. *How could Brendan have been cheating on me? What wasn't I giving him that he felt the need to go out and get elsewhere?* My eyes filled with more tears as I fought to hold everything in; I bit my bottom lip.

I held up one hand for her to stop and took a deep breath before responding.

"You were…in love with him?"

"*We* were in love," she corrected. "He loved me too."

I felt like I couldn't breathe, like someone was literally knocking the wind out of me. Maybe this little girl had Brendan confused with someone else, so I silently prayed.

"I've been with Brendan for eight years. Did you know that?" I asked curiously.

For some odd reason I couldn't cry. I wanted to scream, but I couldn't cry. I was more pissed off than anything.

I felt like I was on an episode of *Maury Povich* and someone was about to come out and tell me some outrageous, drama-filled secret. It felt that surreal; and as I listened to Brandy talking, my eyes met with an unusual shine on her left hand.

"What's this?" I asked, annoyed.

"My engagement ring," she said, smiling widely. "Brendan proposed right after he sold the shop."

I stumbled backwards against one of the stall doors and clutched my stomach in my hands.

Brandy reached out, kindly, to help me stand. I smacked her hand away and covered my head in my hands in embarrassment. Now I knew why everyone was so shocked to see me in the place where Brendan and his mistress had decided to call home. I wailed loudly, partially in physical pain and partially because I was emotionally wounded. I stared up at Brandy who had tears in her eyes as well.

"What the hell is going on?" I screamed.

I tried to think back to a time when Brendan and I *weren't* happy. He always told me he loved me, and his moans were always genuine during love-making. I slumped to the ground and ran my hands through my hair. I wrapped my arms around my body and sat on the ground rocking slowly. Brandy joined me and it looked like she wasn't going anywhere. I brought my knees into my chest and laid my head down on them.

"I *loved* that man, and he did *this* to me," I said, pointing to her.

I wasn't trying to be rude, but it was definitely a hell of a way to find out that the man I had been committed to had loved and lived for someone else. My heart ached as Brandy rested her hand on my shoulder.

"I'm sorry. I told Brendan a long time ago that he needed to straighten things out," she said softly.

I wanted to hate her, and I wanted to hit her...but it wouldn't do anything. She was still sporting the rock I had dreamed about.

Brendan had obviously loved her a little bit more than me, I thought as the canary yellow diamond shined in my face.

"And I swear I was going to end things, but then..." she said, trailing off as she dropped her head.

My eyes were filled with tears; and as I looked over to her, I could tell that her hand was on her stomach and she was caressing it slowly.

"But then what?" I asked, trying to regain some sort of composure.

"I got…*we* got pregnant."

At this point, Brandy could have told me anything and I wouldn't have been shocked. Brendan was engaged to – and having a baby with – another woman, *AND* he had a thirteen-year-old son I was now raising; *how much more shocking could things get?*

My mouth trembled uncontrollably as I banged my fists against my head. *How stupid could I have been to think Brendan, the man with more numbers in his phone than a celebrity, could be with me and only me?* Brandy continued talking before I could ask any more questions.

"But when he found out, he flipped on me. He stopped returning my calls, he wouldn't answer his phone, and he said he wasn't ready for all of that," she said, wincing as she relived the day.

I stood up and splashed water on my face over and over. I had to get out of the bathroom because it was driving me crazy. Brandy followed closely behind me, and as I turned around, we ran into each other. I hesitantly reached out and rubbed her small bump of a stomach.

"How far along are you?" I asked.

"Three months," she said beaming. "I'm so sorry you had to find out like this," she said, looking back up at me.

I wasn't sure why I was conversing with my boyfriend's mistress, but one thing was for sure, I had all the answers I had come for and I hoped there wouldn't be anymore.

"Mike told me that Brendan had gotten involved with Quito, what was that about?" I asked, hoping she could shed some light on the situation.

Brandy rolled her eyes and crossed her arms. I was guessing that Quito had that type of effect on a lot of people.

"He was making drop offs for Quito so he could stay

afloat and keep the condo and the Escalade," she sighed. "I told him he didn't need all of that stuff but…"

"Why did he sell the business?"

"Money; he said he was going broke."

It was sad and almost humorous that another woman knew my man and his secrets better than I did. Brandy looked like she was young, almost too young for Brendan; she was pretty, too. The thought of Brendan cheating on me had crossed my mind a time or two, but I never thought he would actually do it; yet, I had a pregnant, in love and engaged girl showing me that it was true. He *was* cheating.

"Was Brendan acting strange the night he killed himself?" I asked.

"The last time I talked to Brendan was when we came to your birthday party," she said, sucking her teeth and continuing.

"He called me out of the blue, told me to get dressed, and said it was a surprise. I was so happy because I figured he was coming around about the baby," she smiled before sadness poured over her face.

"But he was only using me to get you jealous," she revealed as the knife in my heart went deeper. I loved this man, *why would he want to intentionally hurt me?*

I had heard enough; and as much as I wanted to continue to hear all the juicy details of the secret affair, I had to leave. I had to get out of there. I was clamoring for breath as Dee jumped up and opened the front door.

"Are you okay?" he said, patting my back gently.

"No," I said out of breath. "I'm not."

But I looked up in the sky and prayed that I would be.

———

I CALLED Trey and asked him if he would watch Dee that night, while I hosted my gig at Compound; so after I dropped

Dee off, I headed home. My routine of hiding my emotions was starting to wreak havoc on my sanity.

As soon as Dee exited my car, I couldn't think or see straight, so I cursed Brendan the entire way home. I was over feeling sorry for him or the situation; although I was pissed, I didn't want Dee to have a negative opinion of the father he never knew. Kind of like the pot calling the kettle black.

I didn't feel like hosting the party that night, but it was what I had scheduled and I wasn't about to back out. Being in a club full of people who were dancing and having a good time wasn't the way I wanted to spend my weekend, *but what choice did I have?*

My body was hurting, and as I looked at myself in the mirror, all I saw was pain; when I tried forcing a smile, I grimaced. Kenya and Jasmine were on a three-way call with me when I updated them about what I had found out; like me, the wind was knocked out of them.

"My goodness; this is like one of those damn soap operas," Jasmine said as she sighed heavily.

"I know, right," Kenya chimed.

"So now what?" Jasmine asked curiously. My best friend was always thinking about the next move, even when I was still stuck on the current one.

"I don't know; maybe I'll call her to get more information."

"About what?" Jasmine said with plenty of attitude.

"About Brendan's death."

"Haven't you already found out enough of his skeletons? What else is there to know?"

Kenya exhaled. "Why *wouldn't* she want to know why her boyfriend killed himself, Jas?"

I was through with going back and forth with the two of them; and while I understood Jasmine's hesitance with me continuing with the investigation, I had already made my mind up. I had come this far so I might as well finish the race.

"Hey guys, I'm getting ready to go. I've got to get ready for tonight," I said, cutting into their argument.

"Do you want me to come over and help you get ready?" Kenya asked sympathetically.

"No, I got it. Thanks though."

After I hung up, I sat in the tub and took a nice, long, relaxing bath. The suds from the bubble bath surrounded me and soon I felt like I was in heaven. I closed my eyes and wondered what Brendan was thinking when he pulled the gun out, when he put it to his chest, and when he pulled the trigger. I wondered if he was nervous, and if he was thinking of me or Brandy. I slid lower into the tub, allowing the bubbles to cover my closed mouth; before I could rise up, I thought about what it would be like to drown right there in my bathtub. *Would I be taken away and not have to deal with any more drama?* Maybe I could sleep forever without any interruptions. *Would anyone miss me the way I missed Brendan?*

I slid lower and lower until the water was at my forehead and I couldn't see anymore. I was over the pain and I was through with the secrets. All I wanted was to die and have it all be over. But before I knew it, I felt hands. Manly, callous-filled, strong hands, gripping my backside and gently pulling me up; yet, when I looked around the room, I was the only one there.

"Hello?" I called out, my voice bouncing off the bathroom tiles and coming back to me empty.

I sat up in the water and looked around the spacious bathroom, wiping the bubble residue from my face with the back of my hand. The room was exactly as I had left it. Candles still burning. No one at the door. Nothing out of place. But I knew what I had felt, and I was not crazy, no matter how much the silence was trying to convince me otherwise.

I stayed still for a moment, listening.

Then it hit me, just how far my mind had drifted. How dark the water had gotten in my thoughts before whatever I felt pulled me back. I had let the idea creep in like it does when you are exhausted and hollowed out and running out of reasons to keep pushing. I had entertained it, if only for a moment, and that frightened me more than the empty bathroom or the feeling that something had been in the room with me.

I cursed myself for even allowing my mind to go there.

I pulled myself up out of the warm water quickly, suddenly needing to be out of it, needing to be on my feet and present and somewhere other than alone with my own thoughts in the quiet of a bathroom that felt too big for just one person.

The pain I felt from being alone, driving alone, and sleeping alone was something I prayed I could deal with one day; I couldn't imagine making Pop, Jasmine, and Kenya go through the same thing I was. It wasn't an option.

I had no idea what I was going to wear for the club, but as I rummaged through the closet I started feeling sorry for myself. I didn't have the right to feel sorry for myself. If anything, I felt sorry for Brendan. Sorry that he had to be such a wimp that he couldn't end things with me so he could be with the one he loved. The angrier I grew, the shorter and tighter the clothes got. When I normally did club events, I would always wear tight jeans and a cute, trendy t-shirt. But tonight, I was stepping out, and I was going to show any and every one that I wasn't mourning, even though I was. *Brendan didn't give a damn about me so why should I care about why he had done all the things he did to me?*

I stepped into a skin-tight, metallic blue dress and inhaled as I pulled it over my stomach. It didn't look bad. I turned from side to side and examined my get-up. My butt looked perfect, my legs were freshly shaved, and my hips were undeniably thick – just what the dress called for. The top of the dress crisscrossed around my neck and gave my perky breasts the support they needed.

I remembered when Kenya had purchased the dress for herself only to find that "blue wasn't her color." I knew I would never wear the dress, so I tossed it in my Goodwill box to give away; but, luckily, it never made it.

As I turned and checked myself out, I smiled. I applied some bronzer on my legs and shoulder blades for a glowing look, and made sure I wasn't ashy. Since my hair was wet from my underwater adventure in the bathtub, it was perfectly crinkled and curly. I smoothed the edges down and fluffed it up. I normally didn't wear my hair curly, but tonight I wasn't going for the ordinary, plain, safe Lauren; I was going for "Wow!"

I applied my deodorant, makeup, and perfume perfectly; and then grabbed my silver stilettos and matching clutch purse and headed downstairs. My thighs rubbed together as the dress pressed them closer and closer. It wasn't a sluttish dress; but rather a seductive one that left something to the imagination.

When I entered the kitchen and found Pop watching television at the bar, I raised my eyebrows as if to ask how I looked. Pop's mouth dropped open, and the fork he was holding fell from his hand while his eyes grew large.

"Sugar baby?" Pop said, looking at me. I spun around in a circle with my hands to my side, and threw my leg up in the back like I had always seen those sexy models do.

"How do I look?"

"You look...you *look* like a woman," Pop said.

I laughed to myself as Pop stood up beside me and pulled the dress down a little bit.

"I've always been a woman," I said matter-of-factly.

"But you've always been my Sugar Baby; now you're *Lauren*," he said, tugging at the material again.

I shooed his hands away as I adjusted the top.

"I've got to get out of here," I said as I twisted off toward the front door.

Pop rushed around me and raised his eyebrows like the concerned parent he had always been.

"Where are you going?"

"I have to host a party tonight, remember?"

"Um…okay. Do you think you'll be home late?"

I cocked my head to the side as I replayed the question in my head. Pop had always trusted me and never questioned my whereabouts. *Where was all this coming from?* Pop must have seen the confused look on my face as he relaxed and exhaled.

"It's just you're dressed so…*differently*," he said, pointing to the dress.

My father knew me…almost too well. He knew when I was in trouble, when I was scared, and when I was running from something; that night it was all of the above.

"Lauren, don't change who you are because of what's going on. You are who you are for a reason," Pop reminded me.

I tried to ignore his comments. But he was right, and I knew it. The only reason I was in disguise that night was to prove something to myself. I didn't need Brendan, and I didn't need to be who he wanted me to be.

I kissed Pop on the cheek.

"I'll be back later tonight."

As I got in my car, I watched Pop hang his head, and finally retreat into the house. I felt bad, but I couldn't change my course now. There were things that had to be done, and I had to do them. I scoped out Compound from the parking lot across the street. As I strapped my shoes on, I bobbed my head to the music that flowed from my speakers. I must have been really into the song because I didn't notice the line getting longer.

I jumped out of my car and headed toward the club as I adjusted my dress. Guys were whistling out of their cars while some girls rolled their eyes at me.

At that moment, I wanted to run home, throw on my sweats and t-shirt, and curl up on the couch while watching "Living Single." Hell, I thought as I strutted across the street, I still could if I wanted to. The appearances I made paid well, but they were minimal in the grand scheme of things. I was different from the other on-air personalities and DJs in the business because as much as I loved my fans, I only did club events once in a blue moon.

As I approached the club entrance, the club promoter Drew, walked out talking on his cell-phone. One look at me, and Drew was obviously impressed with how I cleaned up.

"Damn, you look good tonight, L," he said winking.

I hated when people called me L, L.A., or even Ren. It takes two syllables to say Lauren, so what's the use in shortening it?

"You ready?" he asked as I stopped to speak to fans.

Drew was a cute guy with newly-started dreadlocks. He was high yellow and had a booming deep voice that sent chills down my spine. If it wasn't for his enormous ego, I might have thought he was the kind of guy to take home to Pop. I finished my conversations and hustled past Drew and into the club. I headed toward the DJ booth and chilled out there watching the crowd slowly pile in as sounds from Atlanta R&B singer, Johnta Austin, blasted from the speakers. Girls in short dresses, and fellas in white Ts and jeans were making their way to the dance floor.

It wasn't hard to host a party; all I had to do was show my face, say a couple of words, and make sure people had a good time.

Drew appeared in the DJ booth and shoved a microphone in my hand and whispered in my ear all the things he wanted me to say. I honestly never saw the sense in hiring someone to host a club night. People didn't pay attention to me for longer than five minutes; but this was what I was paid to do, so I was going to make the best of it.

"Hey y'all! It's your girl Mystique from 104.5 The Buzz. The most talked about DJ in all of Atlanta. We got a lot of people stopping through tonight! Are y'all ready to have a good time?" I screamed into the mic. The crowd screamed back at me with their drinks in the air.

"Then DJ run that joint!" I said, pointing to the DJ who winked at me as he started the record. I stepped off of the stage and headed toward V.I.P. where I was ready to do some live cut-ins, and took a seat in one of the plush couches. I had done this club so many times before that I had the routine down. But this night, it seemed like the girls were cautiously eyeing me while the guys' smirks were growing wider and wider as my dress rode up higher and higher.

"Hey there, I'm Rome," a dark-skinned guy said as he slid next to me on the couch. I tried not to laugh as his ten gold teeth shined in my face, but the giggles were hard to contain.

"Hey," I said, not taking my eye off of the dance floor.

"You know you're looking sexy as hell in here tonight, right?" he asked, rubbing his ashy hands together.

I smiled and nodded my head.

"Thanks, sweetie," I said as I started to get up from the couch and make my way somewhere else; anywhere else.

"I'm going to *let* you have my number because, see, girl…I can tell that you are *the one* for me," he said, winking his eye like he was doing me a favor. I swear I could have choked on my own tongue if I wasn't careful.

What did he mean he was going to "let" me have his number? This guy in dirty pimp's clothing had to be kidding. What would give him the idea that I was even remotely interested in dating a man with teeth shinier than the sun? I laughed to myself as I got up and ignored his comment.

"Baby, I paid $100 to get in this V.I.P. to get next to you. You're going to talk to me!" He shouted as he got up to chase me. He grabbed me by the waist and pulled my body into him. I could feel his manhood on my stomach. As much as I wanted to say I wasn't turned on by his force…I was. Hell, it had been weeks since I had had sex, and frankly, I was horny.

"You like that don't you?" he asked as he whispered in my ear. I backed up as his funky breath hit my nose.

I stepped back and looked at him like he was a loon before turning to walk away. Rome mumbled something to one of his friends before turning to pick up a bottle of liquor and sloshing it around. I rolled my eyes. *This is why I should have stayed home*, I thought.

I did my cut-ins and kept to myself in the DJ booth as everyone had a good time. As much as I wanted to prove to myself and everybody else that I had moved on and was ready to be happy…I wasn't. I sat quietly with my legs crossed, listening to music.

Saturday nights in Compound can go one of two ways: either it will be a festive night with great music, people, and dancing; or it will end in a huge fight. I prayed that this night it wouldn't be the latter.

But as I eyed Rome from V.I.P. talking to another girl by the bar, I knew that *he* was going to be the reason for any issues we had that night. And, as if on cue, I saw the thick girl push Rome away violently. I could see Rome's eyes, even from the booth, and it wasn't about to end in a good way.

"Do you see that guy? You might want to get him out of here; I think there's some trouble over there," I said to the bouncer standing beside me. I pointed out Rome just as he looked in my direction. I dropped my hand and hoped he hadn't seen me rat him out.

Teddy, the bouncer, jumped down within minutes. All I could see were fists, arms, and legs swinging. I couldn't tell what was going on; so I decided to make my way out of the club. The DJ tried to calm people down; but, after a few minutes, even he was packing his things and leaving. I had stayed around one too many fights turned into gun shoot outs. No amount of money Drew was paying me would make me risk my safety.

I grabbed my purse, began the dangerous trip through the club, and managed to duck and weave all punches being thrown in my direction. But as I looked up and saw Teddy kneeling at the bar in pain; I couldn't just leave him there.

"Are you okay?" I asked, putting my hand on his back and kneeling down to his face.

A shoe whizzed by my face, and I heard the rumbling and arguing getting closer.

"Yeah…you get out of here," he said as he saw other women running toward the exit.

"No, let me help you."

I put my arm around Teddy's shoulder and tried to help him up. But when I lifted my head I saw Rome.

With plenty of malice and anger in his eyes, he walked toward me, smirked, and pulled his big, black, ashy fist back.

"Duck, Lauren!" Teddy said as he tried to pull me down.

The last thing I remember seeing is Rome's fist colliding with my face. I felt my body hit the ground, and I heard a scuffle ensue as I blacked out.

———

"MYSTIQUE, ARE YOU OKAY?" I heard Drew ask pathetically as I opened one eye and stared at him.

"What happened?"

My head was hurting like never before, and I could taste a little blood in my mouth.

"That crazy mother punched you," he said, sighing.

It was then that I remembered Rome and his sucker punch that had landed me right on my ass.

"Is it bad?" I asked, rubbing my slightly swollen cheek.

Drew blew out air while gently stroking my cheek.

"It's not *that* bad, but I hope you don't have any photo shoots coming up."

I closed my eyes and exhaled as I stood up. I could see that the club was completely cleared out; and me, Drew, Teddy, and two police officers were the only people still there.

"We were hoping you would wake up so you could give the police your statement," Drew said, rubbing my back.

My cheek was throbbing like I had been fighting Mike Tyson and Muhammad Ali at the same time. From the look on Drew's face, I could tell Rome had done a number on my face.

"Where's my purse?" I asked as I sat on the couch and pulled my dress down.

Teddy scrambled to me and handed me my clutch.

"I'm sorry about all of this," he said, sounding like he was feeling guilty. I knew it was only Rome's fault that half of my face was swollen.

"It's not your fault," I said, taking the purse from him and cracking it open.

The police were approaching me, and all I was concerned about was how I was going to explain the black and blue swelling to Pop. I pulled out my compact mirror so I could see the damage.

"Wow," I said, running my hands softly over the bruise. It wasn't as bad as I was thinking, but it was enough to upset me.

The swollen area, which was about the size of a small plum, was growing by the minute. I knew I needed to get some ice on it as soon as possible.

"Ms. Washington, do you mind answering a couple of questions about what happened?" the White officer said as I closed the compact and looked up at him.

"Fine."

The officer went through question after question as I answered them all to the best of my ability. I didn't know who

Rome was, we weren't having a domestic dispute, and no...I hadn't put my hands on him first.

"Okay, this is good. Let me get you a copy of the police report, and I'm sure you'll be hearing from us again," the officer said as he scribbled something down on a piece of paper.

I sat back in the chair and exhaled.

"I'm sorry about your night being ruined, Drew," I said. Drew blew me off and shook his head.

"Never mind," he said smiling.

None of us could have predicted the night going the way it had. I placed my hand over the sore spot and took a deep breath.

"Here you go," the policeman said as he ripped a piece of paper off and handed a copy to me and Teddy.

"Is this all?" I said, standing up and yanking on my dress...again.

What had I been thinking of wearing something like this to the club? What kind of attention had I been asking for when I advertised myself the way I did?

Drew and Teddy both saw me wobbling, and ran to catch me before I fell.

"I'm fine," I said agitated.

"You are *not* fine. Let me take you home," Drew said, moving Teddy's hands off of my back.

"I'm okay, Drew...really I am," I said as I opened my eyes widely. I wasn't drunk, high, or even out of it. I was just a little bruised and a lot embarrassed.

"I'm taking you home," Drew said, grabbing my purse from the couch, and then putting my hand in his. I looked down at our hands and quickly slipped mine out of his.

"I don't need you to take me home, I'm fine," I said as I took my purse from him.

Drew looked like I had taken my hands and punched him

in his gut; like I had taken the wind out of his sail. I felt bad, but not bad enough to let him take me home.

I had to get out of there.

Whatever composure I had managed to hold together inside those walls was running out fast. I said nothing to anyone. I grabbed my purse, kept my head down, and moved toward the exit with quiet urgency.

The night air hit me the moment I pushed through the door, warm and heavy, carrying the muffled thump of the music behind me. I kept moving, cutting through the small clusters of people with my eyes forward, heading toward the parking lot where I had left my car.

I was almost there when I heard it. "Mystique, are you okay?!"

The voice came from somewhere in the crowd behind me. I did not stop. I did not turn around. I just walked faster, my heels clicking against the pavement in a rhythm that I needed to stay even and controlled.

Then I saw the flash.

A camera. Someone had a camera pointed in my direction and I dropped my head instinctively, angling my face away as I picked up my pace.

"Tell us your side of the story!" another voice called out from across the street.

I reached my car and yanked the door open, sliding into the leather seat and pulling the door shut behind me. I sank lower, dropping beneath the sight line of the window, my pulse loud in my ears.

I needed to go. Right now. I needed to just go.

I reached for my keys and turned the ignition. Nothing.

I tried again.

Nothing.

"Dammit!" The word came out before I could catch it.

The interior lights. I had left them on the entire time I was inside, and now my battery was completely dead, sitting in a parking lot with cameras across the street and people starting to drift in my direction, drawn by the commotion the way people always are.

I sat there for a moment, gripping the steering wheel with both hands, trying to think. I tried dialing everyone I could think of, with no luck. Finally, I called the only person I could think of who would be ready, willing, and able to get me home: Drew.

"So you changed your mind?" he laughed as I sulked in his seat.

"My car wouldn't start; I didn't have a choice," I sighed.

"I hope this shit doesn't get back to The Buzz. That's the last thing I need."

Drew turned up the volume on his stereo. I sat back in the seat and thought about my night.

"Crazy night, huh?" Drew asked as he looked over to me from my legs to my face.

"Right," I replied, just wanting to be left alone.

"How's your face feeling?" he asked sympathetically as we slowed down at a light.

I smiled as much as I could before cracking a joke.

"It could have been worse; he could have punched you in the face," I said playfully as I thought about how Drew would have reacted to someone messing with his pretty boy face.

Drew chuckled as he revved up the car and started driving.

"I would have whooped his ass!" Drew said loudly. I could tell he was trying to impress me.

"Right," I said, trying to hide my disbelief. I didn't doubt that Drew, who was athletic in his own right, couldn't have handled Rome. But something told me he was all talk.

"Girl, you don't know about me!" Drew snickered.

I nodded my head. I knew getting in a ride with Drew was going to be a mistake. I wasn't into Drew; and regardless of how cute he was or how much money he flaunted, there was nothing between us. With Brendan, the fireworks, butterflies, and desire had always been there; I always wanted him. The only thing I wanted from Drew was for him to shut up.

"You know I don't blame him for getting all uptight over you," Drew said, lowering his voice as he looked over at me. He looked like he was trying to pucker his lips seductively. But it ended up looking like he had sucked on a big, fat lemon.

"Why is that?" I said, unsure of where this was going.

"If I had your fine ass next to me I would have been fighting anybody I could to keep you near too," he said as he started to whistle.

The cat was out of the bag and Drew let it be known that he was feeling me. I was about to be sick. It wasn't that Drew was repulsive, or even ugly…but he wasn't the guy for me. If he wasn't going so fast, I would have jumped out of the car as quickly as possible; but as I stared out at the street, I decided one bruise was enough for the night.

"I know you're going through a rough time right now, and I want to be here for you. I think I can make you feel better. Trust me," he said, grabbing my chin lightly and pulling my face closer to his.

I jerked back and crossed my arms. There was no amount of smooth talking from Drew that was going to convince me that being with him was a good idea.

"Hey, can you get off on this exit?" I asked.

"I thought you lived in Bankhead not Buckhead?" Drew said, turning off the interstate.

"My friend lives over here and I would much rather go there tonight," I said, smiling as I rubbed my sore face.

"You could always stay at my crib."

I raised one eyebrow and kept my attention on Drew's face. I was trying to figure out how serious he was.

"I don't think that's a good idea, Drew…"

I gave Drew the directions, and he drove in silence, with a

salty attitude brewing in the air. When we pulled up to the house, I sat back in the leather seats and put my hand on top of Drew's.

"Thanks for the ride."

"Yeah, sure," he said, not looking at me.

I hesitated before getting out of the car. I realized if I lingered any longer, I would be giving Drew all the ammunition he needed.

I walked up the perfectly manicured grass and rang the doorbell. Drew screeched off down the street as the door opened.

"Lauren? W-what are you doing here?" Trey asked, rubbing his eyes.

The darkness must have initially covered my bruise because when Trey finally did see it, he pulled me into his house.

"Sit down," he demanded as he rushed to the freezer and grabbed some ice. "What the hell happened?"

"I'm okay, just a little fight at the club."

"*You* got into a fight?" he said, fishing for answers.

"Something like that."

"Lauren, either you're going to start talking now or we have a problem."

I told him the entire story. It wasn't until we both sat on the living room couch, that he saw my outfit.

"You went to Compound dressed like *that*?" he interrupted.

I nodded, pleased at the reaction Trey was giving me, and continued with the story.

"Are you okay?" he asked.

I was sure I looked disfigured, deformed, and a mess; but despite all of that, Trey wasn't backing up.

"I am," I said softly as I closed my eyes and continued to enjoy his soft hands around my face.

"You're a bionic woman, now…huh, Skeeter?" Trey joked as he flexed his muscles.

"No, I'm not," I replied, rolling my eyes.

It seemed like every time Trey would make an intimate gesture, he would screw it up with some corny joke.

"Remember that time in school when you broke your leg and hopped around all day looking like a one-legged deer?" he laughed as he hopped around the room playfully.

Trey sat down on the couch.

"That's not funny to you?" he asked, poking my side.

"No, it's not," I said, getting bold. "And, in fact, it's never been funny. You know all throughout elementary school I put up with you making fun of me, even when I was at my lowest; I will not do that now!" I said, crossing my arms.

Trey quietly sat back in the chair.

"Wow, that's what you thought I was doing? Making fun of you?" he said, turning to face me.

I shook my head. *What else was I supposed to think he was doing?*

"The only reason I ever *joked* with you was because I saw how sad you came to school, day in and day out, and I figured if I joked I would make you smile. After your mom died, I made it my mission to see you smile at least once a day; I always met that quota. But I am sorry if you thought I was making fun of you," Trey said, dropping his head.

I had never looked at it that way. After all those years I thought Trey didn't even notice me, I now knew his true intention. I remembered that Trey *had* made me laugh every day in school. I felt bad for coming down on him the way I did.

"Where's your car?"

"It wouldn't start; I left it at the club."

"I see."

"Please take me to get my car. I'll need a jump."

"Go upstairs, the second door on the left is the bathroom.

There are plenty of towels and wash rags up there. Go take a shower and I'll bring you something to change into." Trey said forcefully. "You're staying the night and we'll take care of your car in the morning."

Something about the way he took charge turned me on. I didn't fight his orders, and as I undressed in the spacious bathroom, I looked at myself in the mirror. My hair was a mess, my bruise was a solid dark blue, and I still had some remnants of blood below the swollen spot.

"Yuck," I said to myself as I stepped under the warm water and allowed it to cover my body. It felt relaxing as I allowed the jet shower head to hit all the aching spots. My back, my butt, and my neck were killing me, and as I allowed the water to do its job, I thought about Brendan.

What would he have done if this happened when he was alive? Would he have been there for me like Trey was?

I grunted as I remembered my pact to forget about Brendan Deondre Lewis for one night; here I was showering, relaxing, and still stressing about the man with a million secrets.

I hadn't heard the door open, but when I stepped out of the shower there was a beautiful silky nightgown sitting on the toilet. I had never seen anything as elegant and beautiful in my life. But what was Trey doing with something this gorgeous and feminine just floating around his house? Maybe I had misconstrued everything and there *was* a woman in his life.

The nightgown fell to my ankles and hugged my body perfectly.

I walked past the bedroom where Dee was fast asleep, and I stuck my head in.

"That boy even sleeps hard like his daddy," I said to myself as I leaned against the wall and watched Dee snore loudly. The more I looked at Brendan's son, the more I was starting to love him like he was my own.

"Hey," Trey said, eyeing me.

"Hey," I repeated as I spun around to fully see his face.

"You look amazing in that," he replied.

"This is beautiful. Where did you get it?" I asked, biting my bottom lip.

"My ex-wife…"

"Wait a minute. I'm *wearing* your ex-wife's nightgown? Trey that's…"

Trey was laughing hysterically as he pulled me away from Dee's bedroom door.

"You've *got* to stop interrupting me," he said as I walked with him back downstairs to the living room. "I was saying… I bought this for my ex-wife the day before she left me."

I could have knocked myself upside the head for jumping to conclusions.

"Oh," I said with my head hung.

"So are you hungry? I can cook something for you," he said eagerly as he walked over to the marbled kitchen and flipped on the light.

Trey's kitchen was, by far, the classiest I had ever seen; I was impressed. Stainless steel appliances, beautiful dark cabinets, and a rack full of expensive wine.

"I'm not hungry."

I felt stunning in the gown. I watched Trey closely.

His body was amazing, and his swagger was undeniable. He walked like he had all the confidence in the world. This man was beyond fine. My body began to throb as I watched him bend over and pick things up in the kitchen. I could feel myself getting damp from his presence alone.

As Trey threw something in the microwave, I watched with satisfaction as his muscles bulged from underneath his white wife beater. I wondered what his manhood looked like. It made me horny.

After the food was cooked, he plopped next to me and began eating a hot dog slowly. I leaned into him and inhaled, taking in his manly fragrance. I could feel myself going to a place I had promised I wouldn't; I had to stop.

"What room can I sleep in?" I asked, standing up.

I turned to find Trey staring at me; finally our eyes met.

"I'm sorry," he said, blinking nervously. "It's the first room on the right." I smiled and thanked him for taking me in and headed toward the steps.

"Are you sure you're ready for bed?"

"Yeah. I'm a little worn out," I lied. I was wide awake, and the only thing that kept me from pouncing on him was Jasmine's voice in my head. I wanted him; and my body was begging for me to make the move. I wanted to know what his hands felt like as they rubbed up and down my thighs, and what his breath felt like as he breathed heavily over every inch of my body. *Did his lips taste like cinnamon?* I wanted to know it all.

As I tucked myself into the cute little guest bedroom with boat sails hung all around the room, I sighed.

"Dammit," I said as I thought about Trey naked.

I tried to think of something, anything, to keep my mind off of the fact that my body was pleading for pleasure. A couple of thoughts of Brendan popped into my head, but I quickly dismissed them and tried to fall asleep.

I closed my eyes and pictured myself in Trey's bed, laid out wearing the fabulous gown he had given me. I wondered what it would feel like to have him inside of me, kissing me, holding me, and making me feel loved; my body began to quiver.

I tossed a pillow between my legs and clamped down tightly.

"No!" I said to myself as I thought about walking back to the living room.

"Good night!" Trey said as he stuck his head in the dark room and looked around for any sign of movement. Even though I was awake, I feigned sleep and listened as he walked down the hallway toward the master suite.

I heard his bedroom door close, and soon the house was as still and silent as it was before I had banged on the door earlier that night. I started breathing heavily and thought about what Kenya would tell me to do. *Sure this was her cousin, but what piece of advice would she give if it wasn't?*

"Do it girl!" I heard her say to me. I could visualize Jasmine telling me not to do anything, but I was already heading to his bedroom door. I waited outside for minutes until I saw the light go out. He was alone, it was dark, and I hoped I wasn't about to embarrass myself. I turned the door knob and entered. It was huge; bigger than any bedroom I had ever seen. My feet hit the cold hardwood floors and I moved slowly toward the bed. Since the door didn't squeak, Trey didn't hear me coming, and as I tip-toed, I looked around the room at all the fancy things he had. There were paintings, statues and beautiful plants everywhere. It looked like one of those bedrooms you see on "Cribs." The King sized bed sat in the middle of the floor. I reached halfway before I thought, *was I ready for this? What would people say?* I decided there was no way to know if my body would be satisfied by another man other than to do it. The moon was shining into his huge bedroom window and hit his beautiful toffee-colored skin perfectly.

I crept up behind him and glided underneath the covers and onto the foam mattress that swallowed my body comfortably. I slid close to him and within seconds my hands were around his waist.

"What the…"

I put my finger to his mouth and I slid my hands up and down his leg until I got to the spot I had dreamed about for weeks. For once, I wasn't feeling guilty. I wanted Trey and I wanted all of him.

My hands met with his manhood and as I looked in his

eyes I could tell he was confused; but that didn't stop me. I stroked him gently and felt him getting bigger by the moment. I grabbed him and began to jerk him seductively. He leaned in and kissed me roughly; it was all the validation I needed that he wanted this.

His hands crept up and down my nightgown and before I knew it, it was over my head and on the floor. I lay on my back and covered my breasts with my arms. He removed them slowly.

"Let me see them," he said sternly.

I moved my arms away from my breasts and allowed them to peek out. Trey stared at my breasts with adoration in his eyes and began to slowly lick and suck each mound while he caressed the other. My body tingled everywhere as his warm tongue went around my clean body; although no words were spoken, he knew I was satisfied. I grabbed his neck tightly and pulled him from my stomach to my face and looked at him for direction.

"Are you sure?" he asked as he watched a single tear fall.

I *was* ready and I was sure. I leaned in and kissed him. Our tongues collided and I tried to keep myself off him, but I couldn't. I felt irresistible as he grabbed my hips and pushed my legs open.

Without hesitation, he dove into me with his tongue. I shivered at the perfect ways he dibbled and dabbled. With every lick and suck, my body was closer and closer to being his. I lifted my hips higher and watched as he continued devouring me.

"Oh my gosh!" I screamed as I neared a climax. I had never cum so quickly. I was shaking and felt sensations throughout my body.

Trey looked at me with a sly grin, like he had conquered something, and licked his lips.

"Delicious."

"Do you have protection?" I asked.

"Yeah," he said, reaching into his nightstand and pulling out a box of condoms. He slipped one on and looked at me closely.

I watched as he guided himself into me. We exhaled out of satisfaction. I knew Brendan fit me like a glove, but the fit between Trey and I was on another level. It was like every groove in me was being perfectly filled. He slowly pumped in and out of me; and after building momentum, we got our rhythm down. Our wet bodies clapped together as we held onto one another. I couldn't keep quiet as we connected.

He opened my legs up wider so he could see himself going in and out, and see the grip I was having on his manhood. I clinched tighter as he whimpered in satisfaction. He rubbed his hands delicately over my clit as he continued making love to me. I wanted to scream, but didn't want to wake Dee.

He then flipped me onto my stomach and entered me from the back. He smacked my butt powerfully, and grabbed my waist for a better grip.

Trey was grabbing some of my hair and pulling it back, which made me go wild. It was like he knew everything I liked, disliked, and even had thought about trying.

As his thrusts got deeper and harder, I knew the time was coming and my body was gearing up to cum with him.

He leaned down into my ear, until I couldn't take it anymore.

"Cum like a good girl."

"Oh my gosh, I'm cumming!" I screamed loudly as Trey continued stroking me. Within seconds of me climaxing, Trey was reaching his own peak and shaking ferociously.

We lay still for a moment trying to catch our breaths. Trey then made his way to the bathroom.

"Damn!" he said loudly from the bathroom as I giggled in the bed. I got underneath the covers and rolled around in the moist sheets, still not believing I had slept with Trey.

When he returned to the bed, I wanted to go for round two; but as he yawned, I could tell I had worn him out.

"I can't believe that just happened," Trey said, scooting closer to me underneath the covers.

I felt his penis rub against my arm as he pulled me into him. I looked up at him and I smiled widely.

"Me either," I said, grinning.

We kissed. I couldn't keep my hands off of his perfectly chiseled chest as I swirled my tongue in and out of his mouth.

I lay my head on his chest and exhaled. I finally felt close to someone again, and I had Trey to thank for that.

"Thank you," I said, smiling.

"For..."

I looked up, and for a second, saw Brendan. Shaking myself, I crawled on top of him and kissed his lips softly.

"For just being *you* and being there," I said softly as I lay my head on his chest. Trey didn't say anything.

I didn't know it, but I had complicated my life more than I could have ever imagined. But for that moment, I wasn't concerned about complications.

As I curled up against Trey, I finally felt a piece of normalcy returning. *Or did I?*

chapter ten

Dear Diary,

Okay...I'll admit it; it's been a week since I last wrote. I've been out of commission. I got in a fight and got my ass whooped at Compound the other night by some dude named Rome. Crazy! But it's okay; the police told me this was his third strike and homeboy is going to be spending A LOT of time trying to not drop the soap. I can't say I'm glad he's going to jail for so long, but if you do the crime you do the time!

After that night, I went to Trey's house to unwind and relax. Well, relax I did. Trey and I had THE best sex I've ever had. But then again, the only other man has been Brendan! I've seen Trey every day since, and it's been something I look forward to. Our conversations are getting deeper. It's like Trey's my drug, and he's filling those cravings I get at night. But I don't know how far I want to go with him. He's a good guy, and he's established, successful, and handsome; but my heart is still with Brendan (I know it shouldn't be, right?). Maybe this is just some sort of rebound? I've been trying to block out all the thoughts I'm having about Brendan and his deceit, and as much as I try...I can't. I think about him when I wake up, when I go to sleep, and while making love to Trey. I don't know what I'm doing, really.

Lenny has been out of town for a week on business, and he returns today. Great! So I have to make sure I'm there on time because he's called some sort of staff meeting. We'll see what that's about.

I'm supposed to meet with Ralph in a week or two; hopefully he has some new information. Ms. Pat called yesterday to ask if I would help her clean out Brendan's condo this weekend; I said yes. I'll be sure to take Dee with me!

I've got to get up from here; I think
I hear Trey bumping around downstairs.

Lauren Washington

———

"Hey there," I said, pulling my hair into a ponytail and smiling as I leaned up against the oven and looked over at Trey. He nodded his head and finished what he was doing before turning to face me.

"Hey, yourself!" he smiled as he wiped his hands on his jeans and moved in for a hug.

I fell into Trey's familiar body with eagerness, and quickly inhaled his scent. I wasn't sure what was going on, but I gripped his back tightly. I knew exactly what Terry McMillian was writing about when she penned "Waiting to Exhale." Not the drama, not the men; the *exhale* itself. That specific release that only happens when your body finds somewhere it recognizes as safe. I had been holding my breath for months without realizing it, wound so tight that I had forgotten what it felt like to just *be* somewhere without bracing for what came next.

Pulling away slowly, Trey backed up and put his hands in his back pocket.

"So what's new?" he said slowly as I regained my composure.

I shook my head, still a little gone from our hug, and exhaled.

"You were going somewhere?" Trey inquired as he picked up some tools and started placing them neatly in a toolbox.

I grabbed a plum from the refrigerator and returned to my spot so I could watch him closely.

"I have a meeting at work this afternoon."

"Cool," he replied.

I watched as he moved and worked in the kitchen. I wasn't sure what I was looking at, but my eyes wouldn't leave his body, his eyes, or him.

"Wanna get something to eat later on?" I said, taking a deep bite into the plum.

"I…I can't," he stuttered, sounding a lot like Brendan and Dee wrapped into one.

"Okay," I said, embarrassed.

Up until then our conversations had occurred while watching television or over dinner, with Pop and Dee sitting close by.

Trey wiped his hands and walked toward me. "I've got another big client that I've got to take care of tonight," he said, placing his hand on top of mine gently.

Something changed. It was as if the spark, the fireworks, and the interest was gone. I nodded my head as I continued biting into the plum; stuffing all of it into my mouth so I wouldn't have to respond.

"I'm actually going to be pulling an all-nighter, which is why I showed up so early today."

"It's fine. I understand," I said, trying to force a smile.

Trey silently watched me as I brushed past him and retrieved some items from the kitchen before heading for the front door.

"I'll see you later," I said nonchalantly as I turned to face him in the kitchen.

I was so glad that Dee had opted to stay home that day instead of hanging out on the corner. Growing up where he did, the corner was never just a place to pass time. It was where trouble found you even when you were not looking for it; where the wrong moment, the wrong words, the wrong person walking by could change the entire trajectory of your life in ways you never saw coming. I had seen it happen too many times to count – good kids with real potential who just happened to be standing in the wrong spot when everything went sideways. Some of them never recovered from it. Some of them did not get the chance to. The streets had a way of collecting people who were not careful, and Dee was still young enough, hungry enough, and unprotected enough to be vulnerable to all of it. So the fact that he had chosen four walls and a roof over that corner on this particular day, whether by instinct or exhaustion or something else entirely, felt like more than just a small thing to me. It felt like grace. It felt like a window that was still open, just barely, and I was not going to waste it.

Dee was starting to grow on me. He did what he was told, he was always respectful, and most of all, he loved Pop and Trey, which I was thankful for. Since I was off that day, I had planned on catching up with Jasmine and Kenya before heading back to the house to get Dee and then heading to Brendan's condo to help Ms. Pat.

Every time I mention Brendan's condo, I get this weird feeling in the pit of my stomach. I was hesitant about setting foot in Brendan's home. *Was I ready for this?* According to Ms. Pat, she had the majority of the things packed and shipped to Terrence, but she wanted me to go through some things as well. I wanted to tell her how devious I had found out Brendan had been to me, but I knew she was grieving like I was, and she didn't need the additional stress.

I checked my watch and gasped. I hadn't realized I was running five minutes late for the staff meeting. In Lenny's e-mail he asked that everyone "Be prompt and on time."

"Dammit," I said as I weaved in and out of traffic toward the exit. When I reached the station, I was ten minutes late. When I entered the conference room, everyone turned and looked at me silently.

"I'm sorry I'm late,"

Everyone turned back to Lenny, as though waiting to hear his response.

"Do you know how many people would have been fired because they were late today, Lauren?" Lenny shot at me with fire in his eyes.

"A lot, I'm sure."

"You better be glad these sponsors are paying for you to..." Lenny started. I sat next to Gina "GiGi" Teesly, the station's promotions director who looked at me with sympathy.

My face got hot as Lenny turned back to the dry erase board where he had written a message about team work in purple marker.

"Did I miss anything?" I whispered to GiGi who shook her head while keeping her eyes on Lenny.

After Lenny had given us an update on the ratings, listener feedback, and upcoming promotions, he pulled a paper off his clipboard and smiled widely. Lenny's smiling was such a rarity that everyone in the room had to catch their breath as the yellowish teeth became exposed.

"And speaking of promotions, we've got one of the biggest names in radio, Steve Harvey, stopping by *exclusively* with The Buzz this coming Monday. He's promoting his movie "*Steve Harvey Exposed*," and he's going to be doing one of the biggest giveaways in 104.5's history," Lenny said with excitement.

I leaned forward and placed my hands close together.

"104.5 and Steve Harvey are teaming up to give away a 2008, fully-loaded Range Rover courtesy of his new movie!" Lenny said, looking around the room at the stunned faces.

We had given away vacations, Ford Escorts, and even cash prizes…but a fully-loaded Range Rover *was* a big deal.

As all of us whispered amongst ourselves, Lenny's serious face returned, and he raised his hands high, exposing his pit stains, and hushed everyone.

"But this is a quick promotion. We're going to start running spots today, and the winner will be picked *live* on

Monday during Lauren's show, right after the interview," Lenny said.

I was excited as I thought about the questions I would ask my favorite comedian. I would ask about the movie, his syndicated radio show (which we carried), and of course, his marriages and divorces.

As I snapped out of my daydream, I smiled at the possibilities. People in Atlanta loved Steve Harvey; and this promotion would, no doubt, be the talk of the weekend.

After everyone cleared out of the conference room, I stayed so I could talk to Lenny about my tardiness. After Lenny and GiGi finished up their conversation, I leapt from my chair and walked toward him.

"Lenny, look…I'm really sorry about being late; that's completely my bad," I said as he gathered some of his papers together without acknowledging me.

"And I really appreciate you choosing my show for the Steve Harvey promotion. I think…"

He quickly looked at me, and within seconds he tossed his papers onto the desk as he glared at me. I couldn't be sure if he was joking or if he was seriously upset about me being late.

"You should be *glad* corporate told me I *had* to put him on your show. You think I would have recommended him to be on *your* show?!" Lenny shouted.

I backed up from Lenny and listened in confusion. *What was he talking about?* My show was the highest rated show on the station, and I was one of the most recognized faces in all of Atlanta.

"What are you talking about?"

"The way you've been parading around here…you're lucky you even have a damn job,"

Lenny said, turning his back to me and digging in a pile of papers.

"Wait a minute, you're going to need to slow down and explain to me what the hell you're talking about!" I shouted.

"This!" he shouted as he tossed a picture at me.

I bent down to pick it up, and before I could place my hands on it, I knew what it was. I saw my blue club dress before I saw anything else, and then there was the huge, black and blue shiner on my face. There I was laid out on Compound floor with my dress hiked up and my hair mangled.

I slowly picked up the picture and gripped it tightly in my hands.

"Where did you get…?" I said, looking down at the piece of paper. Without finishing my sentence, I knew who had planted the picture. I recalled that Drew had shown the police officers pictures of me from his camera phone.

"Damn, Drew," I said as I rolled my eyes.

Lenny shook his head as we both stood silent, breathing like angry bulls, looking at each other.

"This is the second time in two months you've been in the news about stuff like this." I couldn't say anything as flashbacks of me arguing with Brendan surfaced.

"Yeah. You're speechless now, right?" Lenny said, sounding as if he had some sort of power over me.

I cleared my throat and allowed him to finish his rant.

"First off, I was assaulted that night by a club patron. I can bring the police report in for you if that's necessary," I said as my blood started boiling. "Secondly, you act as though I wanted to be photographed after I got my ass kicked by a fucking man!" I screamed while people stuck their heads in the conference room.

But Lenny and I were nowhere near letting up. Lenny started laughing as I carried on with my explanation.

"And lastly, what kind of man are you to automatically worry about your precious reputation and not the safety and well-being of your staff?" I said, turning my back to march out of the conference room.

Lenny quickly grabbed his things and chased behind me.

"I don't give a damn about your safety. What I do care about is the way people view this station," he finally admitted as everyone gasped. It stung, but I kept it moving toward the exit.

"I've been at this station for more years than you've been living, little girl…and I'll be damned if you just come in here and throw away the reputation we've built! If it was up to me… you'd be out on your ass!" Lenny said as I impatiently waited on the elevator.

I was tapping my foot nervously as he stood close behind me. It was taking everything in me not to call Lenny a name or hit him; but I knew that's what he wanted so he could fire me.

Just as I was turning to say something, the elevator opened, and I hopped in quickly.

"Bastard!" I said as I stared directly in Lenny's eyes. I wanted him to know how much I hated him.

"You need to have your ass here on time and ready to work on Monday, okay?!" Lenny said, ignoring my comment.

When I got in my car, I put my head in my hands and screamed. I wasn't sad about my behavior and I wasn't nervous about losing my job; but I was frustrated. It was going to take a miracle to lift my spirits.

———

DEE SEEMED like he was in a shitty mood. I watched him sulk all the way to the car. I had decided to reschedule my lunch with the girls so I could get the condo cleaning over and done with.

"What's wrong with you?" I said, irritated. I thought that maybe the two of us should have been relaxing versus spending an hour helping Ms. Pat go through the belongings of my ex and his father.

"Nothing," Dee said, looking out the window.

I wasn't in the mood to prod Dee for any information; I was dealing with my own stress.

The two of us rode in silence to the condo, and the closer we got, the more upset Dee was getting. He threw his arms across his chest and huffed loudly. I wasn't in the mood for his attitude. He suddenly kicked my dashboard.

"What is your problem, Dee?"

He took a second before responding. He seemed to be thinking over what he wanted to say.

"I don't see why the hell...excuse me...why I have to help *her* out with cleaning *his* condo. He killed himself, and that's *her* son. Shouldn't *she* be the one to do it?" Dee yelled.

I looked over at him and all I could see was anger.

I was mad at Brendan for the lies. Not just the big ones, which I was still untangling, but the small quiet ones too. The ones that had stacked up so neatly over the years that I had mistaken them for a foundation. I was mad because I had given him my best years, the years when a woman is still figuring out who she is and what she deserves, and I had spent them building my entire world around a man who was standing in the middle of secrets I knew nothing about. I had turned down opportunities because of him. I had made myself smaller in certain rooms so he could feel bigger. I had measured my own future against the future he kept promising me – the house, the ring, the life – and I had been patient with a patience that I now understood had been taken advantage of. Those were years I could not get back. He had not just lied to me. He had borrowed time from me under false pretenses and spent it on a life I had not been invited into.

And yet I still loved him.

I felt an obligation to him that my anger could not seem to

touch no matter how hard I pushed. In some crazy way, I felt in debt to him for what he had provided me with: security; the kind that had let me stop looking over my shoulder and just breathe for a while. Regardless of the pain I was feeling, the deception I knew he had taken part in, or how upset I was over everything I was still learning…my heart would not allow me to be anything but loyal. I did not fully understand it. I just knew it was true.

"*She* is your grandmother, and *he* was your father."

"She's the mother of my daddy; big difference," Dee shot back. "He ain't never done a damn thing for me other than send those small ass child support checks. He never taught me nothing; he never came to see me…hell, he never even sent a damn birthday card. Why should I care what happens to his shit…excuse me…his stuff?"

I completely understood and agreed with Dee's argument; but we were still going, and he was going to meet his grandmother.

"Listen, your father was a great man, and I just want you to see sides of him that you probably never would have known about," I said, keeping my eyes on the road as we exited the interstate. My stomach began to do nervous flops as I got closer and closer to the spot Brendan had called home.

"If he was such a great man then why do you cry every night about him?"

I looked over at Dee and tried to figure out the best answer. Our rooms were so close, I knew he had probably hear the moans, cries, and shrieks that emitted from my room almost every night. I didn't respond to his question. Instead, I turned on my blinker and drove into the community of Buck-head Grand.

Buckhead Grand was one of the most elite condo communities in all of Atlanta. The luxurious thirty-six floor building looked like something out of the pages of an upscale magazine. With its funky glass designed ledges and trendy tenants, Brendan always fit in perfectly. I parked my car and played with my keys as Dee slowly got out of the car. We didn't say anything to each other as we boarded the elevator in the lobby.

"This is nice," Dee said under his breath as he played with the stainless steel railing in the elevator. I had to admit that every time I had been to Brendan's place I was always impressed at how upscale the place was. The building had a wine cellar and tasting room, massage services, and even a full-service juice bar and lounge. It was nice, but I had always felt completely out of place.

As we got off of the elevator, my mind wandered everywhere as I thought about the many times I had come to Brendan's place ready to see his face, hold his hand, and kiss his lips. If I closed my eyes and breathed in slowly enough, I could almost smell his cologne. This was almost more permanent and real than the funeral. I prepared to part with all his possessions. *Was I ready?*

I took a deep breath as I rang the doorbell and waited for someone to answer. Dee stood behind me with his hands crossed and sporting a defiant look.

"Hey there," Ms. Pat said as she wiped her nose with wrinkled tissue. Her nose was red and her eyes looked as though she had smeared her mascara crying.

I leaned in to hug Ms. Pat lightly, exposing Dee who was staring wide-eyed at his grandmother.

"Hey Ms. Pat," I said, letting myself in.

Dee trailed behind me and looked around in awe. There were tons and tons of boxes packed against a wall while all of Brendan's sports
memorabilia lay on his red leather couch. I looked around the almost bare room.

Dee headed straight to the kitchen and ran his fingers over the cold dark brown and black granite countertops. I watched him loosen up as he opened the huge, stainless steel refrigerator.

Ms. Pat stood back looking like she wanted to scream or cry at the curious child. I couldn't tell if she knew who Dee was.

"Can I see you in the bedroom?" she said coldly as she wiped her nose.

I looked over at Dee who was going through one of the boxes and looking at the football jerseys that were strewn over them.

"Dee, I'll be right back. I need to help Ms. Pat with something," I said without giving him a chance to respond. He shooed me away.

I stepped into the empty bedroom and almost lost my balance. Everything that had once filled the room was gone. My heart dropped as I looked at the pale white walls. I swallowed to keep from screaming.

"Who is that?" Ms. Pat said as she crossed her arms and stared at me for an answer.

"That's DeAndre; *your* grandson. You know…the son that Brendan had, but everyone mysteriously forgot to tell me about?" I said, putting my hands on my hips and jerking my neck.

If I couldn't take things out on Brendan, Ms. Pat was the next best thing. She nervously began wiping her forehead and pacing.

"I don't have any grandchildren, chile," she said sweetly as she spun around to see if I believed her.

I rolled my eyes and started to lay the evidence out when Ms. Pat cut me off.

"I *said*…I don't have any grandchildren. That boy ain't Brendan's. I've never even seen him." I couldn't believe that after everything…Ms. Pat was lying to me.

"This is your son's son; your grandson. I have the birth certificate, and *your* child support payments to prove it."

Ms. Pat looked as though she wanted to reach across the room and slap the living daylights out of me. I, however, wasn't backing down. I needed answers; and I needed her to start cranking them out.

"You can take the three boxes by the door; all of those seem to be things I'm sure you'd like to see," Ms. Pat said as she ignored my comments and pushed past me to get back to the living room and kitchen.

I followed closely behind her and watched as she stared at Dee. The mini-Brendan was sitting on the red couch reading a school yearbook belonging to Brendan.

"Give this back to me!" Ms. Pat said as she rushed up to her grandson and snatched the book away from him.

Dee looked shocked, and a little hurt, by the cruel tone coming from Ms. Pat's voice. It was as if he had spit in her face, or killed her best friend, or even stomped on her prized flower bed.

Ms. Pat held the yearbook tightly to her chest, then inhaled and exhaled loudly.

"I think you need to leave," she said, looking at me as tears formed.

"This is *your* grandson, the last link to your son…and you're just going to send him off?"

Who did she think she was to treat her own flesh and blood that way?

"I told you I don't have no grandchildren!" Ms. Pat said, screaming. "Get out of here, now!"

Dee stood up from the couch and walked slowly toward me; we both watched as Ms. Pat flew into hysterics. Her body was shaking, tears flowed down her plump cheeks, and her hands were trembling. I became worried when I saw Ms. Pat wobble toward the couch and fall flat on her face. She was still shaking and trembling.

"Ms. Pat?!" I said, trying my best to turn her over. Dee

stood back with his hands crossed and watched as I struggled to turn her over.

With Ms. Pat's history of diabetes and high blood pressure, I was scared that I had just killed my dead boyfriend's mother. *Great,* I thought, *isn't this exactly what I need today?*

Dee took a second, but eventually came around and helped me roll her over.

"Get me a glass of water," I said, directing Dee.

I heard him fumbling around in the kitchen, and he quickly returned with water. I lifted Ms. Pat's head and put it in my lap. Slowly, I poured the water into her mouth. She wasn't swallowing, and the water poured over the sides of her mouth.

"You've got to swallow this water, Ms. Pat. Please swallow it," I pleaded as I stroked her hair. We had had our problems; but now I just wanted her to get up and get better. Sure enough she started swallowing the water.

"Is she okay?" Dee said.

I knew that every time I gave Dee a chance to prove he was a good kid, he always impressed me. He might have seemed wise beyond his years, but as I looked into those big brown eyes, I knew he was nothing more than a scared child.

"Yeah, she'll be fine," I said as I lay my head back on the couch and took deep breaths. We sat on the beautiful hardwood floors for half an hour watching Ms. Pat slowly improve.

She was eventually hoisting herself up from the floor.

"I'm…I'm really sorry about all of this," she said, smoothing out her wrinkled shirt. Her salt and pepper hair was matted to her head, and her eyes were bloodshot.

Dee and I hopped up from our seats and looked at Ms. Pat as she tried to resume the things she had been doing before her breakdown.

"Like I said, you can take these three boxes," she said, trying to avoid eye contact with me and Dee.

"Ms. Pat, we need to talk…"

She looked up at me and pursed her lips like she was trying to hold a whimper from coming out, then she quickly dropped her head; I took that as my cue to continue with the questions.

"This is your grandson, DeAndre. I think you already know about him," I said as I continued. "DeAndre, this is your grandmother Ms. Pat," I smiled, looking over at Dee who was staring at her.

"I told you I don't have any…" Ms. Pat started as her voice began to quiver.

"Lauren, can I go to the car?" Dee asked.

I had to rectify the situation. I had taken Dee from a mother who didn't want him, only to bring him to meet someone else who wasn't claiming or acting like she wanted any parts of him either.

"Ms. Pat, look at me!" I said sternly "Look at me!"

Slowly, Ms. Pat brought her eyes to mine and I marched up to her.

"This *is* your grandson; and regardless of what you want to say, Brendan fathered a son. I know you paid child support. I can send Dee away, and you'll never have to worry about seeing him or me again," I said confidently as I took a deep breath.

"But do you know the young man that you are passing up on getting to know? He's smart, he's funny, and he is *exactly* like his father. I wanted to expose him to the people who knew his dad best; so he could see that Brendan wasn't a low-life, non-supportive, dead-beat father."

Ms. Pat's eyes lit up as she turned to Dee.

"Brendan wasn't a dead-beat," she said softly.

Dee crossed his arms and looked up at me.

"Dee's never known the man you and I have known. All he knows is he has a father who sends a little bit of money each month but wants nothing to do with him," I said.

"Is that the man you want Dee, and even me, to remember?"

Ms. Pat took a deep breath and began talking; this time her voice was clear.

"When Brendan came to me and told me he had gotten that girl pregnant, I was devastated. I've had Brendan and Terrence's lives planned out from the day I came home from the hospital with them," Ms. Pat said with a reminiscent smile on her face.

"Brendan was going to be an engineer; and Terrence, well, he had made it clear that he wanted to be a doctor. My boys were going to be the saviors of my life. So when Brendan told me he was going to be a father to some heifer's baby, I did the best thing I knew how to do," she said, looking away from Dee and instead looking at a picture of Brendan.

"I took care of the situation for him. I paid child support for his...*son* until he was financially able to do so. When he got some money he *did* pay a huge lump sum of it to the child's mother; then he heard that she squandered it on some foolishness, so he just sent a little money every month."

My mouth dropped as Dee shook his head...not in disbelief, but in shame.

"My son was fourteen when he got that girl pregnant, and I thought it would be best if she just took the money and lived her life with that baby. I didn't want my son involved with that mess," she said. "Brendan had his entire life in front of him, and everything I had planned for him was flushed down the toilet the moment that girl came home pregnant."

"She didn't get pregnant on her own. Brendan played his part too," I said, reminding her of how babies are made.

"It was my decision to keep that child away from my son and our family. So if you're going to hate anyone, hate me," she said, pointing to her chest as she stared into Dee's eyes.

I looked over at Dee and nodded my head at him to speak.

"I don't hate either one of y'all," he said, like the words

were coming to him as he spoke. "I just feel sorry for you. Lauren…can I go sit in the car?" he asked as I nodded my head.

"Yeah, here…take these two boxes down with you," I said, tossing him the keys and pointing at the boxes.

I watched as Dee left the apartment with his head high. As soon as the door slammed, Ms. Pat was on me like white on rice.

"Why'd you do that? Why'd you bring that child here? My son didn't want anything to do with him when he was alive, and now that he's dead, you want him to be father of the year?" Ms. Pat rambled on.

I put my hand in her face to block her from getting any closer.

"You don't see the idiotic way of thinking you created in Brendan, do you?" I asked with a sad laugh.

"What are you talking about?"

"Your son learned how to skip out on responsibilities and do what *he* wanted, not what he was supposed to do, and he missed out on being the father that he never had."

Ms. Pat's eyes got watery as she looked at me.

"Thank God ignorance and irresponsibility doesn't trickle down throughout generations. Truth be told, Dee's life will probably turn out better than the ones you had planned for your sons," I said, picking up the box and heading toward the exit.

Ms. Pat scrambled behind me shouting.

"Get out!" she said over and over as I smirked.

"When you realize how wrong you were about the decisions you've made, and lives you've screwed with, let's hope it's not too late," I said before leaving.

"I'm fine with my decisions, little girl! You remember that!"

———

THE AFTERNOON HADN'T EXACTLY PANNED out the way I was hoping; but after dinner and drinks with my girls, I hoped for some sort of light at the end of the tunnel. The truth was, however, I had just entered the tunnel...and the light seemed extremely distant.

"I'm looking for a party of two, Kenya Green and Jasmine Wilkes," I said, peering over the hostesses' podium to see if I could locate my girls.

"Right this way, madam," the White male hostess said as he picked up a menu and led me toward the booth.

I exhaled when I sat down with them, and quickly ordered a drink.

"What's wrong with you?" Kenya said smiling as she looked over the menu.

"Stressful, stressful day!" I said as I massaged my temples.

I had somehow managed to calm Dee when we got back to the house, and I left him in Pop's care. I understood his frustrations, and I echoed them; but I couldn't imagine what he was feeling. A child's biggest fear is rejection, and Dee had been rejected twice, both by people who should have been protecting him.

"We've already ordered. Do you know what you want?" Jasmine asked, tapping my menu.

The waiter appeared with my apple martini. I gave him my order before taking a sip of my martini.

"What happened with the condo cleanup?" Jasmine asked as she crossed her legs and picked up her glass of water.

I tried to explain everything; capturing every heartbreaking, shocking, and cold moment I experienced.

"Damn!" Jasmine said, sitting the glass down.

"She's at least admitting that Dee is her grandson, right?" Kenya said, jumping in.

"She's admitting Brendan had a son and Dee is him; but she doesn't consider him her grandson or herself a grandmother," I said.

"I think you're putting way too much stress on yourself when *you* should be the one grieving, not taking care of everyone else's grief," Jasmine said.

Kenya looked over at Jasmine and nodded her head in agreement.

"Listen, Lauren…you just lost the love of your life…"

Jasmine interjected and put one finger in the air. "The man she *thought* was the love of her life."

I picked up my drink and took another swig before looking at Kenya.

"It's just…we don't think you're allowing yourself the time it takes to properly grieve."

I was listening to them; but all I could think about was Brendan and Trey standing side by side. On one hand I had Brendan, the man who made every part of my body quiver with excitement, the man who held every piece of my heart in the palm of his hands. Then, on the other hand, I had Trey who made me laugh beyond words, and was one of the most handsome and successful men I had ever met. I knew I didn't have a choice at this point because obviously Brendan was out of the running, but comparing the pros and cons was becoming a daily escape for me.

"I really do appreciate the two of you thinking of me. I guess I could do a better job of taking care of myself, huh?" I said, smiling sheepishly.

My girls sat back in their chairs smirking, and then started laughing.

"Girl, you would take care of the devil before you took care of yourself!" Jasmine joked while Kenya covered her mouth and laughed.

We laughed, talked, and drank, until our meals arrived. I wanted to share with them my situation at work.

"So, I heard on the news that the guy who hit you in the club, Rome something-or-another, was being charged with aggravated assault. Have the police made contact with you for anything?" Kenya said, digging into her chicken salad.

I shook my head as I cut into my steak, "They told me he admitted guilt for everything and it wasn't going to trial; he pleaded guilty."

"Well, thank the Lord because I was going to have to go down there and show them that they had messed with the wrong chick!" Jasmine said, smiling widely.

I had ordered my fourth apple martini, and somehow, convinced Jasmine and Kenya to have a drink. I knew Kenya had a barbecue to attend with one of her clients, and Jasmine had to get home to her babies; I wasn't trying to get them drunk, just trying to loosen them up.

"Oh yeah, I forgot to tell the both of you..." Kenya said, finishing off her third Cosmopolitan.

"Oh boy, what now?" Jasmine asked as she dabbed her mouth.

"It's nothing bad; calm down," Kenya joked as she continued with her news.

"Lorenzo has asked me to move in with him...and I said yes!" Kenya said enthusiastically. I set my fork and my napkin down on the plate and watched as Kenya called the waiter over for another drink.

"One more round! It's a celebration!" she said after she placed the orders and shooed the guy away.

"Wait, are you kidding? Kenya you've known Lorenzo for all of what...a month or two?"

She had always been the sensible one, but I was sure Kenya could see that her decision wasn't a smart one.

"No, I'm not kidding, girl; aren't y'all happy for me?"

"Happy? About what? You moving in with somebody you barely even know? What's the rush, anyway?" Jasmine said with an attitude.

Kenya rolled her eyes and looked in my direction, like my words were going to be much different.

"I'm with Jas, honey. Why are you in such a rush to move in with Lorenzo? I know you said you like him a lot, but… moving in? That's kind of a big step," I said, rubbing her hand on top of the table.

"It's not like I'm marrying the guy y'all, damn. I just spend all of my time over his house, and he does the same over mine. So we thought it would save time and money."

"There have been plenty of times I've accepted news y'all have shared with a smile. I voice my opinion, and if you still want to make *your* decision and it does not agree with mine, I respect that and have your back. Why is it so different now that I want to take a chance at something?" she shot back while looking at the both of us.

The way she had laid it out…I had to totally agree with her. We always expected her to be the safe friend; the one who never made bad decisions, always helped us with ours, and never moved too fast with a guy. But Kenya was her own woman, and I respected her for standing up for what she believed in and wanted; obviously Lorenzo was just that.

"I love that man, okay?" she said after she slammed the glass down.

Love? Wait, I thought, *when had it escalated from moving in, to love?* But I didn't bat an eye as I watched my friend move uncomfortably in her seat.

"Kenya, if you decide to move in with Lorenzo, I've got your back. Hell, you've had mine through everything," I said, hoping she wasn't too mad at me.

"Thanks," Kenya said, staring into her pink drink.

Jasmine wasn't budging, though; and I knew she wasn't about to give Kenya her blessings –although they weren't offi-cially needed. I glanced over at Jasmine and slightly kicked her underneath the table until she spoke.

"I think it's a bad idea, honestly I do; but if it's what you want, then it is what it is."

Kenya cracked a smile and nodded her head. "I appreciate that," she said, winking at Jasmine.

I sat back and finished my meal and my last drink. I was, officially, feeling right. I wasn't stressing, I wasn't thinking about Trey, Brendan, Dee, Pops or even my job being in jeopardy.

"When do you move in?" I said, breaking the silence.

"Probably next weekend, girl," she said with excitement.

It felt great knowing that my best friend was happy and in love. And, yet, I was a tad bit envious. I wanted a man to sweep me off of my feet, offer to let me move in with him and change my life around. But the more I thought about it, the more impossible it seemed.

"Damn," I heard Jasmine say as she sipped her drink through a straw.

Kenya ignored the comment.

"Do the two of you want to go to this barbecue with me tonight? It should be fun!" Kenya said, nudging me. "And we know who could use a little fun."

I rolled my eyes playfully, "I'm game."

Jasmine chimed in and said she was down for crashing the party as well. "Y'all know I'm going wherever the party, people, and drinks are!"

"Where is it?" I asked as I checked my makeup in my compact mirror.

"I think it's somewhere in Roswell."

"Damn, are you putting it on him or what?" Jasmine asked as we left the restaurant and stood face to face with Lorenzo's silver, fully loaded Mercedes Benz 745i.

Kenya laughed while she clicked the alarm and slid into the leather seats. I had to admit, this car was beyond perfect, it was *the* car of the moment, and my best friend looked fabulous driving it. I got in the passenger seat, and Jasmine climbed in the back.

"Lorenzo has a nice car!" I said, letting the window down and sticking my arm out as the wind whipped it.

"It's mine, actually," Kenya said, not taking her eyes off the road.

Jasmine and I sat up quickly and looked over at Kenya who was cracking a smile.

"Yours?!" We both screamed in disbelief.

In seconds, Kenya was giggling like a school child and was giving us all the juicy details we were dying to hear.

"He surprised me with this last night, and then asked me to move in with him!" she said, grinning.

"Wow!" I said, running my hands up and down the black leather seats. This was impressive, and as much as I knew about Lorenzo, I couldn't have predicted this by a long shot.

"I know, right?" Kenya said, looking at Jasmine and I as we exchanged glances.

"What about your car?" Jasmine asked curiously as she settled into the seat and the idea that Kenya was smitten.

"Lorenzo said I really didn't need that old thing anymore so he's going to give it to his nephew for his birthday."

"That *old thing*?" I said confused. "Kenya, you drove two-year old Acura SUV and it was in perfect condition."

"Yeah," Jasmine agreed.

"Just trust me," she begged pathetically.

I sat back in the seat and thought about Kenya's situation. *Why was she allowing Lorenzo to walk into her life and completely turn it upside down? Who was she becoming?* I considered various scenarios for the outcome and immediately settled on the calmest one. Kenya and Lorenzo, matched up with Jasmine and Lance, along with me and Trey, could become the new "it" couples. I imagined us taking trips to beaches, exotic islands, and faraway countries. Trey and I would get married in a quiet little ceremony with only the couples and Pop invited; then we would all celebrate over fabulous dinners. I smiled as I thought about the possibilities.

"Hand me those directions, girl," Kenya said, pointing to her Louis Vuitton purse. I reached in and pulled out the MapQuest directions and handed them to her.

Jasmine seemed restless in her seat as she wiggled, moved, and sighed.

"What is wrong with you back there?" I said, turning around to find her with a frown on her face.

"I keep sliding out of this damn seat! Tell your man he needs some seat covers or something," Jasmine said playfully as she sat up.

Kenya gripped the directions and quickly turned left at the light.

"So what about you and Mr. Trey?" Kenya said, smiling slyly toward me.

I sunk lower into my seat as I felt Jasmine's eyes burning the back of my head.

"What do you mean? We're friends," I said, not making eye contact with either of them.

"Um hmm...I'm sure," Kenya said, slapping my leg.

If I could have given Kenya the signal to shut her mouth, I would have. *The only problem?* I hadn't been prepared for her sudden interest in her cousin and me. *Had Trey opened his mouth? Did he tell her about our night out?* Embarrassed, I looked out the window while biting my bottom lip.

"Seriously, we're only friends."

"Friends with *benefits*," Kenya snickered.

She didn't realize how red my face was getting from the mention of our "special" relationship. I had opted not to tell them about the night Trey and I had together, because I was sure they would both jump down my throat; I didn't need it.

"Whatever," I managed to say as I crossed my legs and looked out the window.

"Let's say...hypothetically, if you were kicking it with Trey, would you tell us?" Jasmine said.

I took my time answering this question and thought about it long and hard.

"Probably not."

"Why not?!" Kenya screamed with a smile on her face. I could see out of the corner of my eye that Jasmine wasn't smiling.

"Because…hypothetically, it would be *my* business, and I know how judgmental *some* of us can be."

"You're talking about me, right?" Jasmine asked as she slid closer. "Just say it."

"So what if I was?"

Jasmine was quiet for a while.

"So, now you're mad?" I quizzed playfully.

"No, I'm not mad," she said softly. "But it's funny when you mistake being judgmental for caring about someone. I'm sorry if during our friendship I've looked out for you when you couldn't do it for yourself," Jasmine said.

"Jasmine…" I started.

"No, hear me out, L," she cut in. I could see Kenya focusing on us. "Go ahead," I replied.

"I see you looking at Trey, and I see you thinking that you can automatically jump back into this fairytale relationship; it can't happen like that. You've got to give your heart time to heal. You were with one man for a long time," she said passionately. "You need to know that not all men are good guys. Look at all the secrets Brendan was keeping," she said.

I took a deep breath and silently nodded. "Thank you."

It wasn't that I wasn't appreciative of the things Jasmine was saying; I was. But I also knew that I had to trust my heart. *If I felt like I wanted to jump into another relationship why couldn't I?* Brendan had lied, hurt, and screwed me up…and if another man was willing to come along and heal my heart, I was ready for him.

We pulled up to a marvelous mansion that looked like it had been on *The Sopranos*. It had huge ceramic statues of nude men in front, and there were lantern lights strung around all the perfectly maintained hedges. The driveway, which was in the shape of a horseshoe, had tons of cars packed in; and Kenya's new ride, surprisingly, didn't come close to the rest.

"Damn!" Jasmine said as she climbed out and stared in amazement at the beautiful blue water that was spraying from the fountain.

I had to admit that while Jasmine and I were doing well, we still reverted back to our childhood days and would flip through the pages of *Ebony* and *Jet,* and stare at the beautiful homes that graced the pages.

When we stepped into the party, it didn't look like any kind of barbecue I had ever been to. There were naked women and men prancing around the house, music blasting, and people – who I assumed were drunk, dancing to their own beat.

The house was beautiful. Tiled floors ran throughout the house with ketchup and mustard splattered all over it. I could smell the scent of burnt coals in the air as Jasmine and I looked around the room in astonishment.

"Y'all go outside; I need to find my client," Kenya said as she continued looking around the house.

Jasmine and I clung to each other, amidst the cat calls and aggressive grabs, and headed out toward the pool. It was a little bit calmer outside so Jasmine and I took a seat at a table and watched the fireworks unfolding. Women were kissing on women, and men were watching close by – egging them on. I wanted Kenya to bring her narrow ass back outside and take me back to my car so I could go home.

Jasmine laughed loudly as one girl got thrown into the pool.

"You know I'm not judging you, girl," she said. "I'm just looking out for you. I love you."

"I know."

"I just want you to take it slow with this guy, if you two are *actually* kicking it like that," she said, raising an eyebrow.

I didn't have the courage to tell Jasmine that I had slept with Trey. "We've been talking and getting to know each other better, that's all."

Jasmine nodded, like she understood what I was saying but was still searching for something.

"And you like him?"

"I do."

"Just be careful," Jasmine said.

"I will."

The two of us continued watching as a drunk older man came toward our table. His stench, which was a mixture of Black & Milds, beer, and weed, was too much for us. We went back into the house looking for Kenya.

As soon as I stepped foot inside, instead of finding Kenya, I saw Trey.

My mouth dropped wide as I replayed the conversation the two of us had the morning before, when he told me he couldn't go out because he had an all-night project to finish.

I looked around the room. I didn't see any projects that needed to be finished. Jasmine, sensing my anger boiling and seeing Trey approaching with a pitiful look on his face, tugged on my arm.

"Come on, let's go this way," she said before I could yank my arm from her. Trey walked right in front of me and stood silent for a couple of seconds.

"So *this* is your project, huh?" I said, getting an attitude.

"Wait..."

"So...next I suppose you're going to tell me that she's your assistant, and the two of you just happened to come by this party," I said, pointing to the woman who had tagged along as he walked toward me. She wasn't cute at all; that pissed me off even more.

What was it with all of the men in my life picking other women?

"Lauren…" Trey said, trying to get some control. Jasmine had her arms crossed and was staring the woman up and down, daring her to make a move.

"Shut up, Trey! I thought you were different!" I said, trying to fight back the tears that were on the brink of falling. "But then you *lie* about this?"

Trey's head was in his hands, and he was breathing heavily.

"Let me explain; come with me," Trey said, pulling my hand. Before I knew it, Jasmine was intervening, and stepped in between us.

"She's going home…now!" she said as she pulled me away. I was moving toward the door, but my eyes never left Trey's.

When we got outside, Kenya was sitting on the front steps with her cell phone glued to her ear, and in a, seemingly, deep conversation.

"Kenya, we need to go!" I said, pulling her by the arm.

"Baby, I'll call you back," Kenya said quickly as she looked over at Jasmine and I concerned.

"I've been trying to call you two; I didn't know where you were," she said, pulling out the car keys. "My client must've gone home early; I can't find her anywhere."

Jasmine and I walked to the car, and I was trying not to fall apart, but I couldn't help it. I felt like I was reliving the night of my birthday party all over again. *How could Trey, the person I had grown to trust and care about, do this to me?*

"What's wrong?" Kenya said when she climbed in the car and glanced over at me. I had my head on the window, and tears were slowly rolling down my face. I thought I was over being hurt, lied to, and jerked around…but Trey had proven me wrong.

"I hate him!" I screamed as I looked out of the front windshield and saw Trey sprinting down the steps toward the car. I wanted Kenya to speed out of there, but my body took over;

before I knew it I was swinging the door open and rushing toward him.

"Listen to me!" he screamed.

"You know what? You don't even deserve me listening to you. After all that we've been through...you do *this* to me? You lie to me about this stupid stuff?" I wailed as my girls sat glued in their seats.

"I can't believe you would do something like this to hurt me. Why? Why would you do this? Why?" I screamed as I stared into Trey's confused eyes. "I loved you! Did you know that? I loved you!"

My eyes were closed and I was having the conversation I had been dreaming about having for weeks, but it was with the wrong man.

"Lauren..."

"I hate you! I hate you! I'm glad you're dead..." I said.

I covered my mouth. My anger toward Trey had, somehow, boiled into the on-going anger and frustration I had toward Brendan. I was unconsciously using Trey to say all the things I would never be able to tell Brendan. I thought I was ready for a relationship with Trey; but apparently, I wasn't.

"I'm not him," Trey said. "I'm sorry I lied...but I'm not him."

Jasmine hopped out of the car as Kenya sat dumbfounded in the front seat. I was a broke-down, snotty-nosed, fool...and I couldn't stop myself.

"Come on, girl," Jasmine said, placing her arms around my shoulders and pulling me into her chest. I sobbed like a baby as all the different emotions hit me. First it was shame, then embarrassment, and finally shock. *Who was I fooling? Why did I think I was ready to move on from Brendan?* I was still angry about his lies.

Trey walked up to me and wiped one of my tears.

"I got off early from one of my projects and called you at the house, but Dee said you were out with your girls; I decided to go out with my cousin," he said, pointing to the girl.

I felt like an idiot, and I just knew Trey saw me as one.

"I'm sorry," I said, looking up at him. "I can't do this anymore with you."

Trey looked like I had sucker punched him as he backed up and looked me over. I wasn't making sense, and I didn't know where the words were coming from; but I knew it was what I needed to say.

"But I said I was..."

"I'm a mess, and I need to get *myself* straight first," I said.

I laid my head on the car window and watched as Trey stuffed his hands in his pocket and glanced over at me. I couldn't tell if he was pissed, or if he was just stunned by my revelation. I watched him closely as the car pulled out of the driveway; it was as if we were moving in slow motion. Before we had pulled completely out, Trey was taking a seat on the steps, watching our every movement.

"Lauren..." Kenya said after a few minutes of riding in silence.

"I really don't want to hear either of you saying, "*I told you so*," I said, trying to catch my breath between words.

Jasmine reached forward and massaged my shoulder, "We wouldn't do that!"

I sighed deeply and wanted the pain to go away.

"I just thought...I thought...I could just walk away from the pain," I said, inhaling as tears continued to fall.

Jasmine leaned forward in the seat and wrapped her arms around the back of the seat all the way to the front of my chest.

"Honey, you did what's best for you," she said sympathetically.

"Your boyfriend died a month ago; and already, you're trying to find someone else to distract you from that pain? That's not fair, and it's not right, Lauren."

"But…" I started. I wanted to let Jasmine know I hadn't set out to find Trey; rather, he had surprisingly come to me.

"Think about it, Lauren. All your life you've had one distraction after another. When your mom died, your dad bought you every toy imaginable and gave you whatever you wanted whenever you wanted. Then when you met Brendan, he took over. Then when Brendan passed, you jumped on Trey, hoping he would keep you from experiencing the one thing you can never *truly* escape – pain," she said tenderly.

"But a man can't help you get over something like this; this is up to you. Only you can forgive Brendan – if you choose – and move on. Only you can find peace, and only you can choose to be happy without someone distracting you."

My eyes filled with tears as the truthful words stung me deeply. I had never realized how many people I relied on to "distract" me from the obvious things I didn't want to deal with.

"I think it's time for *you* to see what life is like on your terms. Cry, scream, yell, and let things out, honey."

Kenya nodded her head as she slowed the car down at a yellow light. "You can't make someone else happy if you aren't happy. I think for so long you told yourself you were happy and content with Brendan; when in actuality, when you weren't. You were dependent on him for your happiness; and it shouldn't be like that," Kenya said as the light turned green.

I wanted to be happy; but it was going to be a journey only I could take.

chapter eleven

Dear Diary,

I've been asleep all day, and when I woke up this afternoon, my house was silent. Pop left a note saying he and Dee had gone to church. I know I need to be in there with them, but I needed to rest and collect my thoughts while plotting my next move. Tomorrow is the Steve Harvey interview, and Lenny has already called twice today, telling me that I need to get up to the station today to cut some promos for the promotion and the interview. I don't feel like it; but it's part of the j-o-b. Last night was such an eye opener that I'm not sure I'll ever be able to look at Trey the same again. I'm ashamed of myself for letting my emotions, and the situation, get the best of me. I woke up this afternoon and found three messages from Trey asking if we could talk; I can't, though. I've officially decided to drop out of the race. I've got to stop running from my problems; and after my three-hour long conversation with Jasmine and Kenya, I realized that my life has been one big distraction. But if I continue down this road I'm going to self-destruct. And as much as I think I've done an okay job, things have to change. I'm going down to the station so I can prepare for the show.

Lauren Washington

When I got to the station, no one else was there. I was able to crank out all the promos and spots that Lenny had left on my desk. I jotted down all my questions and placed them in my chair. I was prepared in every way possible, and I prayed that tomorrow went off without a hitch. After I was finished with the preparation for the interview, I headed down to Centennial Park for a jog. This was the first time that I had jogged without being angry about something; it felt good.

I slipped my headphones over my ears, and my iPod around my arm, and began stretching. With each bend and extension of my arms, my muscles began to slowly loosen up. I watched as couples ran by me, and I smiled. I was still envious; but I was more focused on figuring out my own way to happiness rather than standing back and hoping it would find me. When I completed my workout, I was sweaty and content. Brandy was blasting in my ears as I did my post-workout stretching beside my car. A dark blue Mustang pulled up beside me.

"Excuse me," I heard a lady say as I looked up and removed my headphones.

"Yes," I said kindly.

"Are you Mystique? You look so much like her," the girl said.

"Yeah, I am."

"Well, I'm sorry for interrupting your workout, but I had to come over and thank you for telling the story of your boyfriend's suicide on-air."

"Uh…okay…you're welcome?" I said as I wiped the sweat off my forehead.

Of all things, Brendan's death never registered with me as one of the things I thought people would be appreciative of me talking about.

"I'm sorry, my name is Lina," she said, extending her arm.

She was wearing a pair of jogging shorts and a sports bra, and I could tell she was definitely one of those chicks who could run five or ten miles without missing a beat.

"I'm a faithful listener," she commented as I shook her hand.

"And I'm a crisis counselor for the Georgia Suicide & Crisis hotline."

"Oh okay," I said, nodding my head. Now it made sense. I listened as the woman continued.

"When you told your story, and then I read about it in the paper, my heart went out to you and your boyfriend's fami-ly," she said, dropping her head to the ground.

"Thank you."

"There are a lot of brothers and sisters who are losing their battle to suicide, and…well, for someone like Brendan to have committed suicide…I think it opened a lot of people's eyes to the reality of it. It doesn't just hit White communities; African-Americans are prone to it as well."

"Yeah, that's true."

"If we had more suicide awareness in *our* community, we could save so many more lives," Lina smiled. "So, I was wondering if maybe we could do something with you. You know, like shoot a commercial or do a radio spot or something." she said cautiously.

My eyebrows raised; and while it was something I was definitely interested in, I didn't know if I was ready to be an advocate for suicide. After all, I was still mad at the *term* and could barely even speak the word. *How would I look standing in front of a crowd speaking out on one of my daily struggles?*

"Well…"

She turned and went to her car and pulled out a brochure and a business card.

"Just think about it. Here's my information. Please think about it and the lives you could save," she said, handing the documents over.

I took the colorful brochure and looked it over.

"I've got to get to my personal training session, girl," she said, looking over her shoulder at the buff guy who stood with his arms crossed; I assumed he was the reason she looked so damned fit.

"Yeah, okay."

I looked the information over and wondered if *I* could really do this. There were a lot of helpful things inside, including tips for coping with the loss of a loved one. I flipped the pamphlet open to the tab and read.

"Step 1: Allow yourself to go through your feelings about the death." I, obviously, had skipped this step.

"Step 2: Let go of any self-blame." My entire mantra after Brendan died was that *I* could have single-handily saved him. As I sat in the car, I knew that wasn't true.

"Step 3: Join a support group."

"Step 4: Nurture yourself."

"Step 5: Take any pressures or expectations off of yourself to "get over it" quickly."

"Step 6: Talk to a doctor if you start having trouble with sleeping or eating."

I stared at the words over and over. Soon, I began to comprehended the fact that I had skipped over each and every one of the steps listed. I had my own plan, and it evidently hadn't worked out very well.

I headed toward the house in silence. I thought about advocating suicide awareness, and told myself I wasn't ready. I was taking baby steps at handling all of this, and while I knew it was a good cause, I needed to do it on my own terms.

As I pulled up to the house, I saw Trey and Dee standing in the driveway. Trey had his hands on his hips, and Dee's shoulders were hunched over and his eyes on the ground.

I took my time getting out of the car; but when I did, Dee scurried off into the house.

"Hey," Trey said as the anger on his face disappeared and was replaced with worry.

"What was that about?"

"Nothing, I handled it."

"What do you mean *you* handled it? He's my responsibility, Trey. What was that about?" I said firmly, this time letting him know I was serious.

"When I got here to finish up some things in the backyard, your father was on his way out the door for a meeting. So he asked if I would watch Dee; of course I said yes. When I finished, I went up to Dee's room to see if he wanted to grab a bite to eat. I opened the door and he and little girlfriend were on the bed; in an…uh…compromising position."

My eyes shot open just as my mouth dropped.

"Are you sure?" I asked as Trey clenched his jaw and nodded his head.

"It wasn't sex, but it was definitely getting there."

I couldn't believe what I was hearing. Before I knew it, I was pushing past Trey and rushing into the house. *Everything I had done for Dee, and he had the nerve to come into my house and blatantly disrespect it?* I was twenty-seven years old, and even I hesitated about bringing Brendan to my house for a little action. Yet, this thirteen-year-old boy was trying to get some action in my house.

As I got to the stairs, skipping every other one, I thought about how I was going to handle Dee. I knew his hormones were getting the best of him, but I would be damned if I started raising my ex-boyfriend's secret son's child. It wasn't happening.

"What the hell were you thinking?" I said as I flung his door open. He didn't respond.

"I *said*…what the hell were you thinking? You brought a little girl up in my house so you could sleep with her? Do you know how disrespectful that is?" I said as Dee zoned out.

Realizing I wasn't getting the attention I needed or deserved, I grabbed him by the shirt and pulled him up.

"Do you hear me talking to you? What were you think-ing?" I said as Dee looked up at me with his lips pursed.

"I wasn't."

"Exactly, boy!" I said, pushing him away. Dee looked at me like he wanted to push me back and cry, all in the same breath.

"Talk to me, tell me something," I said, frustrated. Dee paced his room and finally plopped back on his messy bed.

"I just brought her up here so we could *talk,* but then one thing led to another and…"

"First, you don't just invite anyone in my *damn* house

without permission; and secondly, y'all could have talked outside."

Dee looked away from me, crossed his arms, and acted like he wasn't listening to me. I knew he was, though.

"So, you don't care about my rules?"

Dee stared at me quietly.

"If I would have known you were going to deliberately disobey me and the rules I had laid out, I wouldn't have taken you in, Dee."

He looked down at the ground; and then, as if the words finally registered, he snapped his head up toward me.

"I knew you didn't want me here to begin with. You didn't have to take me in just because of that nigga," he said, standing up to face me.

For a split second, I thought he was going to hit me. I watched him closely. He then went back to the bed and dropped his shoulders.

"I didn't only take you in because of your *father*," I said. "I did it because I see a lot of potential in you and what you can do."

Dee seemed to be shocked by my response, and looked up at me skeptically.

"But if you can't follow my simple ass rules, then I don't know."

"I'm sorry," he said reluctantly.

"Do you want to end up a father at a young age?"

"Well, they do say like father like son, right?" Dee joked.

I leaned against a wall and put my head back. *What had I gotten myself into by taking on Brendan's son?* This was stuff his father needed to be taking care of, not me.

"Did you have sex with her?"

Dee looked at me seemingly embarrassed.

"Did you or didn't you?"

"No. Today was going to be our first time."

I exhaled and thanked God Trey walked in when he did.

There was no telling what I would have done had it been me who opened the door.

"If you want to stay here, you'll keep your hormones in check and respect my rules. If not…"

"Fine," Dee said quickly before falling onto the bed with his hands behind his head.

I left his room and headed downstairs. Trey was sitting on the loveseat with his hands clasped together.

"He's going to hate me tomorrow," Trey laughed as he stood up and smoothed out his pants.

I tried not to look into his eyes; instead, I headed to the kitchen. Trey followed me.

"He'll be *okay*," I said, opening the fridge. "By tomorrow, all that anger will be gone."

"What about you?" Trey said, draping his smooth arm over the open refrigerator door and looking down at me as I looked up at him.

I was speechless. I heard the hum of the fridge filling the silence in the room. I closed the door and took a seat at the kitchen table. Trey looked at me and waited for a response.

"I think we should keep it strictly platonic. You can finish the house; and when it's done, I'll pay you, and that will be that," I said, not making eye contact. I was afraid that if I looked into his eyes he would be able to see how much I didn't want my words to come true.

"What? Why? I thought we had a connection and…"

"It's just not going to work out, Trey. I've got too much baggage I need to work out; and if I'm with you…I can't," I said confidently. I knew what I was saying was true, but it hurt like a bitch.

"I'll deal with your baggage," he said, sounding as if he had no choice but to beg.

"It's not about you, it's about me…"

"I can help you deal with the issues; don't shut me out."

"I don't have a choice."

"Yes, you do, Lauren. You have a choice, and it's standing right here," he said, pointing to himself.

When I looked up at him I could see his stress. I wanted to take him into my arms, like I had done Brendan so many times before, and make everything right. But *my* issue would still be there. By being with Trey, I was denying myself the full right to properly grieve. I deserved that, at least.

"I can't."

Trey stood motionless for a minute before reaching into his pocket for his car keys. He hesitated before turning and heading to the door without a word. I heard the door slam, and my heart felt heavy. Everything was telling me to chase him and beg him to help me with this pain, but I knew this was something I had to do alone.

That night, I tossed and turned in my bed and heard when Pop returned. Although I was wide awake, I stayed in my bed staring at the ceiling. When thoughts of Brendan entered my mind, I didn't fight them; instead, I allowed them to flow in and out. During some points I cried, and others I laughed; the memories are what put me to sleep. Gripping the empty pillow beside me, I smiled and thought about where my life was headed.

The next morning, I was refreshed and ready for the day. Announcing the winner for the promotion with Steve Harvey was said to be one of the biggest events in The Buzz history. As I prepared breakfast, I silently hoped that Dee wasn't salty over our conversation; either way, I needed him to hurry up and eat so I could drop him off at school.

"Dee! Let's go! Breakfast is ready!" I screamed loudly as I stirred the pot of grits.

Pop emerged from his bedroom and grabbed a plate and sat at the table.

"Trey told me what happened with Dee and that little girl," he said, yawning into his food.

"Yeah…"

"What'd you do, other than scream?"

"I told him he needed to follow my rules if he wants to stay here because I didn't take him in so he could continue to be disobedient. If he can't follow my rules, then maybe he needs to go back to his mom..."

Pop looked up at me and shook his head slowly. "You didn't say that last part to him, did you?"

I opened my mouth and then closed it again. The truth was that I had not said those exact words out loud. The thought had been sitting right there at the edge of everything I did say, heavy and sharp, and maybe it had shown on my face or come through in my tone, but I had stopped myself just short of actually saying it. At least I thought I had.

"I didn't say it exactly like that," I admitted. "But Pop, he knew what I meant. I could tell by the way he looked at me."

Pop set down whatever he was holding and gave me the kind of look that did not need any words behind it to make its point.

"Lauren, that child has already lost his father. Whether he knew Brendan well or not, that loss is real. And his mother..." He paused and chose his next words carefully. "Sending him back there is not a threat you want to be making, even between the lines. That boy heard you. Trust me on that."

"He knows I want him here, but he has to understand that he's a child," I said as I went to the entrance of the kitchen.

"Dee! Let's go!"

After five or ten minutes of no response, I headed to his room to yell at him for ignoring me.

"Don't you think you need to come on, boy?" I said, opening the door to find his room empty. I glanced around the room and realized that it was exactly how I had left it before he had moved in. Gone were the stacks of clothes, the PlayStation 2, and countless hip-hop CDs that had been strewn across the room.

"Dee?!" I wondered if he was hiding in the closet trying to

scare me. But as I opened the closet door, I grasped the reality that Dee wasn't there. I checked underneath the bed where we kept his bags, and saw that they were also gone.

As I rushed down the steps to Pop, I kept thinking about what I had said to him the night before. *Had he confused my disappointment to mean I didn't want him around?*

"Pop, he's gone!" I said out of breath "He's gone! All of his stuff is gone!" I repeated as Pop sprung up from the table.

While Pop searched the rest of the house and outside, I scrambled to the phone and called Trey, who answered on the first ring.

"Trey, have you seen Dee? He's missing," I said, hoping he had run to his mentor.

"No. I haven't seen him since yesterday," he said, sounding frightened.

This time it wasn't a joke or a misunderstanding. Dee was gone.

————

IT WAS four in the afternoon, and my show was starting in three hours. Pop had no choice but to go into work. Trey and I sat in his car trying to decide where else we could look. We had gone to his mother's house, his girlfriend's house, his school, his friends' houses, and even the malls; all with no luck. I was becoming desperate and running out of places he could be.

"Do you think we should check the bus stations?" Trey said, sounding exhausted.

I nodded and sat back in the seat.

"I did this to him. I made him think he wasn't wanted," I said.

"No...it's not your fault, Lauren; stop blaming yourself. Dee is confused about his place in the world; with everything he's dealt with, I can't blame him. But it's not your fault."

I cringed as it got closer to show time.

"Have you all seen this young man?" Trey said, holding up a picture of Dee to the attendant at a bus station.

"Naw, try the other bus station," the young girl told us as she slid the picture back.

Bus station after bus station that we visited, had the same answer for us; none of them had seen Dee.

"Don't you have that big interview today?" Trey asked as he checked the time and realized my show had started forty-five minutes earlier. I checked my phone, which had been on silent, and saw that I had missed twenty phone calls; all from the station. I contemplated calling back after I noticed how late it was, but I knew, by that time, the damage had been done. I was better off facing the music on the following day. I knew I was in trouble, but it didn't matter one bit; Dee did.

"I *did...*"

"Where could this boy be?" Trey said, hitting the steering wheel.

For the first time, I could see that Trey wasn't doing this for me. He actually cared about Dee's well-being. I glanced down at my phone and saw that yet another call had been missed. I didn't recognize the number and listened closely to the message.

"Lauren...this is...uh...Ms. Pat, and I need you to come by my house. My grand...DeAndre is over here and I don't know why."

I dropped the phone and quickly directed Trey on how to get there. *What the hell was Dee doing at Ms. Pat's house?* I imagined Dee had completely lost his mind and was trying to hurt his grandmother. I prayed that wasn't the case though.

"Ms. Pat! It's Lauren, open the door!" I said as I banged on the screen door.

Trey stood behind me rubbing his hands together. We had been running all over Atlanta looking for Dee. It was nearing 8:30 P.M.

Ms. Pat slowly opened the door and had a horrified look on her face.

"What have I done?" she said, falling into my arms and hugging me tightly. I looked over her shoulder and saw Dee sitting at the kitchen table.

Trey let himself in and stood over Dee. I pulled away from Ms. Pat and rushed into the house toward Dee. I pulled him up by his shirt and held him close to me.

"I'm sorry," he said, hugging me back.

I felt the tears falling down my cheeks. "I'm so glad you're okay," I said as relief set in.

Ms. Pat came into the kitchen and clutched a picture of Brendan close to her stomach. She was swaying back and forth and humming a song.

"What is going on here?" I said, looking at an ashamed-looking Dee and a mellow Ms. Pat.

Neither of them spoke so I sat down. I wanted some type of response as to why Dee was there.

"He just showed up on my doorstep," Ms. Pat said as she slowed her rocking. I looked over to Dee who was staring at me and Trey; finally he spoke up.

"I just wanted to find out what it was about me that made her not want anything to do with me. I just had to know," he said, breaking down. Dee's shoulders shook uncontrollably as he cried into his hands.

"As much as I like staying with you, Lauren, I want to be accepted by people who are supposed to be my family," he said between gasps for air.

Ms. Pat stood back and wiped a few tears from her face.

"I didn't know the situation. I didn't know he was living with you. I had no idea a relationship with me meant so much to him."

I lowered my head; I hadn't either.

"So, I wanted to tell her everything about me; everything

I've been through, every dream I've ever wanted…and tell her why she would like me; that's when she called you."

I looked over to Ms. Pat, who was back to rocking from side to side and humming a song.

"So what does this mean?" I asked slowly.

"I don't know…" Dee replied, looking at his grandmother.

"I want him to stay here with me, if that's okay with you," she said, nodding her head at Dee and then to me.

Dee's eyes lit up with excitement, the same way they did when I told him I wanted him to move in with me, and he looked over to me with wide eyes.

"Really?" he said, looking at a grinning Ms. Pat.

"Really. Lauren, is it okay with you?"

"Of course it is…this is wonderful!" I said, trying to hide the twinge of sadness in my voice.

I was glad that Ms. Pat had come to her senses and realized that this little boy *was* partially her responsibility now that Brendan was dead. Trey and I got up from the table and looked over at Dee and Ms. Pat, who were in a tight embrace.

"I'm sorry, baby," she said as she cried. "I'm so sorry."

"Well, I guess we'll be going now," I said softly as I headed toward the door. Ms. Pat and Dee hurried to the door before we could and stared at us.

I wanted to cry. *How was I letting Dee go so easily?* I wanted him to come back and continue living with me.

"Dee, I guess I'll see you around?" I said, leaning in for a hug.

"I'll still come around."

"Do that, please."

I don't know why we were acting like the distance between my house and Ms. Pat's house was thousands of miles, when in fact, Dee could easily walk between the two.

"Actually, I would appreciate it if Dee spent a couple of hours a day at your house. We wouldn't be here if it wasn't for you," she said, putting her arm around Dee's shoulders.

Dee smiled at his grandmother and looked back at me. It was then I knew that just as quickly as I had assumed the responsibility for Dee, I had to let go. This made more sense, anyway.

"Are you okay?" Trey asked as we drove back to my house.

"I'm getting there."

chapter twelve

Dear Diary,

I woke up early this morning for no reason at all. I don't have Dee here to take to school, and I don't have to be to work until this evening. Pop was really sad when he found out Dee wasn't returning; but he understood. Since I'm up, I think I'll go into the station early and try to do damage control. I know I messed up by not showing up; especially when we had a huge promotion. Ralph called me late last night saying he needed to see me as soon as possible. I'm going to tell him to meet me at home. Pop still hasn't given me any more answers about the domestic abuse reports other than saying, "I'll never understand." Hopefully Ralph will be able to shed some light on this. Just like I'm no closer to finding out what happened to mom, I'm not closer to solving the "Why did Brendan kill himself?" case, either. But, on the good side I am doing much better with taking care of myself. I don't have any distractions, and I can really see the difference. Jasmine and Kenya were supposed to come over last night so we could watch "Girlfriends" on TiVo...but Kenya never showed up. Jasmine came, and we called her. Kenya said she would have to bail because she had "stuff to do." I wonder what that's about. I've got to make a mental note to give her a call today. I just got back from working out, and now I'm going to jump in the shower and get ready for an early day at the office.

Hopefully the day will continue in the direction it's headed.

Lauren Washington

———

"What are you doing, girl?" I said as Kenya answered the phone groggily.

"Nothing," she said quietly and quickly.

"What happened to you last night?"

"I told you I had some things to take care of, Lauren," she snapped.

I looked at the phone for a second.

"*Excuse* me for being concerned."

"I'm sorry, girl. I just…hold on, okay?" she said.

She returned obviously more relaxed.

"I'm back."

"Okay…what was that about?"

"Lorenzo and I had a fight last night and…"

"Are you at home?"

"Yeah, why?"

"I'm on my way," I said, hanging up before she could object.

The truth was I was less than five minutes from her house, and I had every intention of stopping by there anyway. As I pulled into the driveway I saw Lorenzo's SUV parked in the driveway behind Kenya's brand new one.

"Hey," I said as Kenya opened the door before I could ring the doorbell.

Kenya looked disheveled, like she had been making love all night, and possibly all morning. She was wrapped in a tight silk robe. My best friend couldn't hide much from me. But I still couldn't put my finger on why she was acting so withdrawn.

"What's going on?" I said, lifting her chin, exposing her red eyes.

She seemed to be thinking about whether or not she was going to share things with me. She then quickly pulled me toward my car. We both jumped in and Kenya played with a couple of the window buttons before looking over at me.

"I did something yesterday that I'm not sure I thought through."

My mind immediately thought about Kenya and her strong feelings for Lorenzo; *had she gotten married?* I sat back in my seat, waiting on the revelation.

"I…got an abortion."

I felt like my heart was being ripped out, piece by piece. She was pregnant and had an abortion without telling me. I knew she didn't need to ask my permission, but I thought she would have at least told me.

"You were…pregnant?"

"We found out Sunday."

"Why'd you get an abortion? You've always talked about wanting a child."

Kenya bit her bottom lip and covered her face with her hands. It was as if my words were the reality check.

"I know; I did…I mean I do."

"But…"

"Lorenzo says he's not ready for that kind of commitment."

I dropped my head and thought about Brendan telling Brandy that exact same thing. Yet she was still madly in love with him. *Was Kenya still holding onto hope that Lorenzo could be the "man of her dreams?"*

"It's *your* body, though."

"We'll have kids someday when his career is a little more stable; you know he got let go from the Tyler Perry film because of contract problems."

I had heard that rumor; but I had heard he got let go because of a rumor of sexual harassment from one of the film's lead actresses. I knew Kenya was holding back, but I let her continue.

"Don't turn into me, girl," I said respectfully.

She looked at me as though looking for clarity.

"My life was Brendan; and anything he wanted, he got. Whatever he said was final, and that's not the way it should be in a relationship. Now look at me…I'm trying to figure out how to find *Lauren* at twenty-seven years old!" I said, trying to smile.

"But it's different…"

"It's exactly the same. The only difference is that you have a chance to get pause before it consumes you."

After we were done talking and I had told Kenya I had her back, she headed back toward the house.

"I love you!" I said with the window down as I tried to tell myself that everyone was going to have to handle their *own* problems. I wanted to trust that Kenya would make the right decision.

When I got to the station, I noticed that someone else, other than Lenny, was parked in my assigned space. When I went to swipe my badge, it wasn't working.

"What the hell?" I said, trying to swipe it repeatedly.

Luckily, the secretary, Abigail, was walking to the front door just as I was having my difficulties.

"Hey girl, my badge isn't working," I said, holding it up to her.

She nervously swiped hers and opened the door for me.

"What's going on?" I said as we got in the elevator.

"You need to talk to Lenny; he should be up there," she said.

Abigail and I had always been pretty cordial, so it was a surprise that she was treating me like an outcast.

"Lenny, why the hell is my badge not working and who's parked in my spot?" I said, rushing toward his desk.

Lenny slowly raised his head from the computer and looked at me for a second before returning his attention to the computer screen.

"You need to get your things and be out of here before I call the police," he said with little emotion.

"What? Where am I taking my stuff?"

"You're fired."

"Fired? Yeah, right...look, I'm sorry about yesterday; but I had a family emergency," I said playfully, slapping Lenny's desk.

"And you couldn't call? Do you know what we had riding on yesterday?" Lenny said, finally raising his voice.

"I didn't have access to a phone, Lenny," I lied as I got nervous. If I was reading him right, this *wasn't* a joke.

"Bullshit."

"Look, I'll do some extra commercials or something, anything…I know I messed up, but…"

"There are no more buts, no more excuses, and no more "Mystique. Now, get your stuff and get the hell out of here!"

I stood motionless in the middle of the office and looked around at people as they slowly trickled in. As embarrassed as I'm sure I should have felt, I was more pissed than anything.

"What do you mean I'm fired? Huh? Talk to me!" I screamed as I knocked over a coffee mug on Lenny's desk and got his attention.

When he didn't say anything, I continued my rant.

"Do you know how much money I've made for this damned radio station? How many times I've done all the shit no one else wanted to do? And now you're telling me, because I messed up one time, that I'm *fired*?" I screamed in disbelief.

Lenny looked up at me and smirked, "It's actually been three times, and corporate has officially given me the green light to let you go; but don't worry, we'll buy out your contract."

The money was the last thing I was worried about. As I turned to start screaming, I saw Crystal Bright, the intern I had praised and encouraged to apply for full-time positions, sitting at my desk.

"What are *you* doing?" I said, turning my attention to her.

"Crystal is your replacement," Lenny said, seeming satisfied at the egg on my face.

"Crystal?" I said, looking at her, not understanding how she could have betrayed me.

"I'm sorry," she said.

I looked beside my desk and there was a brown box filled to the brim with all of my things. I understood, as I looked at that box, that my time at The Buzz was over; no amount of yelling or screaming was going to get my job back.

"Fine," I said, snatching the box off of the ground as I headed toward the elevator. "You'll be sorry!"

I felt heat on my face as I passed all the sales reps and other on-air personalities as they eyed my box. They all knew what it meant. Without a "goodbye" or "see-you-later," I pulled out of the radio station parking lot. Mystique was dead.

———

I LAID on the couch and tried to figure out a couple of safety nets I had lined up. I had enough money saved for a year, so I wasn't that stressed about losing my job.

I could call V104, but I didn't want to go crawling so early; I could call a couple of promoter friends and try to host parties, but that seemed desperate too. While I kept running down my list of ideas, the doorbell rang. Anxiously, I got off the couch and answered the door. Ralph was on the other side of the door.

"I'm sorry I'm running so late," he said as he rushed into the door and toward the living room table.

When I got to the table, Ralph had already laid out the documents and was standing with his hands on top of his head.

"I found some things out, Lauren; you may want to sit down for this."

I doubted anything that he was going to tell me could shock me at this point.

"I was able to get my hands on the *official* police report

from your mother's murder; there seems to be a suspect that was never interviewed, although I'm not sure why."

"Do they live in Atlanta?"

"Not anymore. From what I've found out, he lives up north. Here's his work address." He handed me a piece of paper.

"I don't know why the police didn't follow up. They had enough probable cause; enough to create a file on him."

"Why did they think he did it?"

"I'm still checking into that. I was going to catch a flight to New York later this week and see if I could ask around his neighborhood for anything."

I went through the paperwork and tried to grasp it all. I possibly had my mother's killer in front of me; the last question was why. I hoped with all the work Ralph had done, that he could handle my concerns.

"What's his name?" I said, looking up from the papers. I felt like I needed to know his name.

"Taariq Mohammad."

"And you think this is our guy?"

"I'm 95% sure it is."

I took a deep breath and decided now was the time to stop living life from the passenger's side. I was taking the steering wheel into my hands.

"I'm going to New York; I want to see him."

"Lauren...this isn't ethically right, nor is it completely safe."

"I don't care. I'm going," I said.

"I can't let you go by yourself; let me go with you."

I thought about it and realized I needed to do this by myself. Ralph had gotten me this far, and was sure this was the guy who murdered my mother. I knew that as soon as I laid eyes on him, I would know. I felt like my mom would give me an indication, a signal, or a sign that *this* was the man. I didn't want to approach the person or even get them to confess to the crime. My eyes just needed to see the person responsible for my pain. I needed to know who…and maybe then I could understand the why in my equation.

"I'm going Ralph," I said, closing the folder and looking up at him.

I glanced down at the address and the name Ralph had scribbled down; then I said the name aloud.

"Taariq Mohammad, here I come."

Now that the words were spoken, I had no choice but to book my flight and sit back and wait for my time to come.

chapter thirteen

Dear Diary,

It's amazing how flying at thirty something thousand feet in the air can make you feel like you're escaping everything. I can't believe I'm heading to New York to find out if this guy, Taariq Mohammad, is mom's killer. Ralph keeps stressing that I need to be careful, because if he is in fact the murderer, then we already know what he's capable of. It's like God works things out in ways we don't think He will. If I were employed with The Buzz, I wouldn't have been able to make this trip. I don't know what this guy looks like or anything; all I have is an address. I've booked a hotel for four days; I hope that's enough time. Pop freaked out when he found out I was going by myself; Jasmine and Kenya...well, they agreed with Pop that I was crazy. I'm not sure if I'm crazy, but I know this is very much out of my character. I realized that this could actually be my mom's killer. I wondered if she would be proud of me and how I'm taking this by the horns! Ooh! We're having a little turbulence on the plane, so I'm going to take a nap.

Lauren Washington

———

I arrived at my hotel, suitcase in hand. I had been to New York before, but only on business, and rarely longer than one night. By the time I had checked in and headed to my room, I was exhausted. But no matter how tired I was, it couldn't hold me back from making a pit stop at the work address that Ralph had given me.

New York was loud; way too loud. People hustled and bustled around me. I stood on the corner and hailed a cab. I handed the cab driver the address and sat back quietly in the seat.

"You don't look like you from around here," he said in a thick New York accent.

I smiled. "No, I'm not."

"You visiting someone special?" he asked.

I pretended I didn't hear him. When the cab stopped, I paid the driver, grabbed the address, and stood in front of the fifties-like diner. As the cars whizzed by, and the horns beeped loudly, I darted in and out of traffic and made my way inside of the eatery.

"Is it just you?" the hostess asked as she picked up a menu and held it to her chest.

"Yes, just me," I said looking around. "Are there any tables close to this window?" I asked, pointing to a window that faced the sidewalk.

"Sure."

I ordered my food and sat with a notebook in front of me. I watched the comings and goings of the neighborhood. It seemed to be a pretty upscale and diverse community. I wondered where Taariq was, and what he would do when I finally showed my face and announced who I was.

"Here you go," the waitress said, sitting my BLT and orange soda down in front of me. She handed me a straw and napkin, then she smiled sweetly before asking,

"Anything else I can get you?"

"No, I'm good ...but wait," I said, remembering I needed to ask questions.

"Do you know Taariq Mohammad?"

"*Know* him? He's the manager here," she said, raising an eyebrow suspiciously.

"Oh."

"Why? Do you need me to call him down for you?"

I shook my head and started stuffing my mouth with food.

"No, I'll catch up with him later," I managed to say.

I swallowed the huge lump of food and watched the woman saunter away to a co-worker and pointing me out. They were gathered in a close circle, which broke apart when a customer entered the shop. My cell phone rang and startled me, causing me to spill my soda.

"I'm sorry," I said, attempting to blot the orange liquid up with the thin napkin that was sitting in my lap.

"It's okay, girl! What do you think all these napkins are for?" the waitress said, smiling widely.

"Hello?" I said.

"Hey there…" the familiar male voice said over the phone.

"Trey?"

"The one and only."

"Is everything okay?" I said as visions of my house in flames ran through my mind. *I mean, why else was Trey calling me?*

"Everything's fine, relax," he said, laughing a little bit. "I just wanted to call and check on you. I know you said to give you space, but…"

"No, it's cool," I said, relieved he had called.

"So, have you met the guy yet? I mean is this going to be like a sit down interview where you ask him if he *did* it? Or…"

I laughed at Trey's silliness. Even in the most intense moments, he made me smile.

"No, not yet; no, I'm not going to interview him," I said, laughing. "I'm just going to ask him if he lived in Atlanta around the time mom was killed."

Trey listened in as I rambled about nothing in particular.

"How will you know it's him?"

"I think I'll just *know*."

"Okay. I saw Dee today; he came by to see you."

"How was he?"

"Good…really good. I think him moving in with his grandmother was a great idea."

I played with the lettuce and pickle that had come off of the sandwich.

"Me too."

"So, do you know when you'll be back, or is this just a play-it-by-ear kind of trip?"

I was touched that despite me trying to push him away, Trey was still being a good friend. I loved that.

"I think I'll be back on Monday."

"Cool."

"You know it's so loud up here I couldn't hear myself…" I said stopping mid-sentence as I saw a man enter the restaurant.

"Trey, let me call you right back," I said, hanging up before I had a chance to hear his response.

I knew this face; it was familiar. I stood up from my table, and without hesitation walked toward him. It was as if my legs were guiding my body. He was standing by a coat rack at the entrance fooling with something in his pocket.

"Excuse me…" I said as I tapped him on the shoulder.

"Yes," he said, turning abruptly.

As soon as our eyes met, my heart melted, my skin crawled, and my body reacted. This wasn't the killer, but it was a familiar face to another mystery.

"Terrence?" I said, remembering all the pictures I had seen and studied of Brendan's older brother.

"Do I know you?"

I stumbled over my words as I giddily extended my hand to him.

"I'm Lauren…Lauren Washington, your brother Brendan's girl…ex-girlfriend," I said, grabbing his hand. I knew it was him by the way he was dressed. He looked just like his pictures.

"W-what are you doing up here?" he asked, smiling.

"I…" I started as my mind studied the characteristics of the "other" brother.

He had Brendan's mouth. The same slight fullness to the bottom lip that I had always craved. I felt the grief before I could name it, rising up quiet and sudden, throwing me off a bit. He was a reminder of everything that was gone.

"You look just like him," I said softly, before I could stop myself.

He didn't flinch. Didn't offer the usual sorry-for-your-loss face people gave me when Brendan came up. He just looked at me like my words had landed somewhere familiar.

"I know who you are, Lauren," he said. His voice was even. Gentle, even. But there was something underneath it, something that told me this moment wasn't as accidental as it felt.

"Brendan talked about you."

The way he said it didn't close anything. It opened something.

But before I could continue, my waitress appeared with her hands on her hips, and cut in.

"I see you found Taariq, huh?"

"What?" I said, looking at her with confusion.

"You said you were looking for Taariq Mohammad, right? Here he is," she said, pointing to an edgy-looking Terrence.

"*You're* Taariq?" I asked.

"My name is Taariq Mohammad now. I changed it a couple of years ago when I converted to Islam."

My heart stopped as I stared at Taariq for an answer. Taariq or Terrence - whatever he was calling himself - sat across from me as I fidgeted with my fork and spoon. He didn't seem to know why I was there, or why I was acting so strange. I couldn't get Ralph's voice out of my head that he was "95% sure" Taariq Mohammad was my mom's killer. I looked into his eyes and quickly dropped my head. As much as I told myself I was ready to confront someone, this…I wasn't ready for.

"What are you doing here, Lauren?" Taariq asked.

"Huh?" I stumbled before swallowing and forcing myself to look into Taariq's eyes.

"Is everything okay?" he inquired as he clasped his hands together.

"Everything's fine. I was just in town visiting uh…a… friend."

Taariq nodded his head. I must've been gawking because

when Taariq cleared his throat, I saw a strange look spread across on his face.

"What?" he asked, rubbing his face.

"You just look so much like...*him*," I said, unable to think about my reason for the trip or the questions I was going to eventually ask him. I looked at his hands in amazement. They looked just like Brendan's.

"We used to get that a lot when we lived in..." he said, trailing off as he stared into the distance.

"Bankhead?" I quizzed.

"Yeah."

"Why did you move anyway? Brendan always said you just needed a change of scenery, but you've never even gone back, right?"

Taariq squirmed a little in his seat and eventually nodded his head.

"Atlanta isn't for me, sister. I'm a totally different person."

"Aren't we all?" I smiled apprehensively.

"So, how long are you in town?"

"Until Monday."

"Well, we'll have to catch up for lunch or something. Are you staying near?"

"I'm at the Four Seasons."

"Okay...well, I wish I could sit and chat with you all day, but there is work to be done and people to manage," he said respectfully as he bowed his head and stood up from the table.

I knew if I didn't do it now, it wouldn't get done. I had to ask Taariq what he knew about mom's death.

"Terrence...I mean Taariq, can I ask you a question?" I motioned for him to take a seat.

"Go ahead," he said.

I had rehearsed the way I would ask the person all of the questions Ralph had equipped me with, but suddenly, I couldn't get it out. My hands were shaking as I played with the napkin and finally looked into his eyes.

"What do you know about my mother's death?" I blurted out.

Taariq didn't bat an eye; he didn't look shaken by the inquiry. It was as if the question didn't faze him in the least bit. He leaned back and crossed his arms over his chest.

"Nothing," he said finally. "I don't know anything about that."

He sat still in the chair for a minute, maybe to see if I was going to challenge his statement. When I didn't, he exhaled.

"Why?" he asked.

"I *know* that you know something."

"I just told you I didn't know anything about that, sister."

I had been nervous about asking the questions, but the more Taariq denied knowing anything, the angrier I felt.

"Your name is all over the police report as being a suspect; you mean to tell me you don't want to tell me *anything*?" I asked again, this time leaning forward in my chair.

"I've got to get to work, Lauren. Like I said…we can get together for lunch or something before you leave," he said uneasily.

This time I knew he didn't mean it. He wasn't going to have lunch, dinner, or anything in between with me.

"One more question," I said, holding my finger up. "Brendan left a note at the scene, and I was wondering if you knew anything about why he did what he did?"

I still couldn't speak the word "suicide."

"You mean why did he kill himself, sister?" Taariq asked. "I'm not sure what my brother was going through then," he said, pushing his chair back from the table and standing up.

"Now, if you'll excuse me," he said. He walked toward the "Employees Only" sign at the back of the restaurant.

I stayed at the restaurant for another hour, hoping I would

see Taariq and ask him more questions; but to my surprise, he never came back out.

As I hailed a cab, I could feel myself getting stronger. I didn't know what was going on or why people were intent on keeping secrets, but I was about to do the unthinkable and *find out* the secrets myself.

———

MY NEXT TWO days in New York were pretty boring. I went to the diner every day, ordered the same meal, and sat in the same chair. The same waitress, who was so helpful to me when I had been there earlier, was tight lipped about when and if Taariq would be returning.

I wasn't ready to go to his house. I wanted that to be my final destination and my last resort.

"Your name is Christa, right?" I said, wiping my mouth as I pulled out a twenty from my purse.

"Yes," she said as she started picking up the plates. Obviously, Taariq had told her not to talk to me or tell me anything; but I knew what color would always have people talking: green.

"Would you know where Taariq is today?" I said, waving the twenty around so only she could see. Christa thought about it and shook her head *no*.

"I haven't seen or heard from him in a few days," she said, biting her lip.

Reaching into my purse, I pulled out two more twenties and placed them on the table.

"Still don't know?"

Christa looked at me and quickly snatched up the sixty dollars.

"Look, he's only been coming in really late at night, like eleven or twelve, around closing time. Other than that, you can probably find him at his apartment in Harlem," she said as she pretended to wipe the table down as she continued talking.

"Here's the address," she said as she scribbled something down on a piece of paper.

Just as quickly as our conversation began, it was over and I was out of cab fare.

I left the diner and headed to a Rite-Aid and waited in line for the ATM. I looked behind me and saw that the line was only getting longer. Finally the guy in front of me got out of line with his money.

I pulled $200 out of the machine and stuffed it into my jeans. I turned to walk away, and ran smack dab into a gentleman who was talking on his cell phone.

"I'm sorry," I said, picking myself up from the ground.

The guy looked at me for a second then ended his call. He then started pointing at me.

"Your name is Lauren, right?"

I was used to attention like that in Atlanta, but I was miles away from anything and anyone familiar. *How did this guy know me?*

He was in his forties, sported a bald head, and had dark moles all over his face. I could tell he was someone in high authority because of the Prada coat and shoes he was wearing.

"And you are…"

"Sorry, the name's Troy Gaines," he chuckled as he stuck his hand out.

"Nice to meet you, Troy Gaines; do I know you?"

"Not really, but I'm a huge fan. I'm the new general manager of Hot 99."

I had heard of Troy. He was a Georgia boy, which might have explained why he recognized my face.

"Oh okay, it's really nice to meet you," I smiled.

"You know, I used to listen to you when I was home on vacation; you're really good. Ever thought about leaving The

Buzz behind and relocating to New York?" he inquired seriously.

I actually hadn't thought about making the jump. The on-air personalities in New York were deep and heavy into the game, and some of them had waited ten years, sometimes interning at a station before being considered as a DJ.

"I actually am no longer with The Buzz, but I'm only here on… vacation."

"Wow. Well then, I guess it's a good thing that we ran into each other, huh?"

"I guess so."

"Why don't you take my card and give me a call before you leave. We should have lunch and discuss some possible opportunities for you up here. I think you're just what we're looking for."

I grabbed the card and watched as Troy walked away. I couldn't believe the way things were shaping up. New York really wasn't my cup of tea; and the thought of leaving Pop, Jasmine, Kenya, Dee, and even Trey, kind of frightened me. But maybe it was just what I needed in order to break free, I thought. I had plenty of time to think about what I wanted.

"Please God, don't let anything go wrong in here, and please let Taariq tell me something," I prayed as I crossed the street to the apartment.

When I got to the thirteenth floor, I slowly stepped off and looked to my left and right. The apartment building was nice…really nice. Almost too nice for a diner manager to afford. Apartment 1312 was on my right. I placed my finger over the peep hole and knocked on the door heavily.

"Who is it?" I heard Taariq say. I could tell he was placing his face to the door and trying to see who it was, but I wasn't moving my hand, and I wasn't saying who it was.

"If you don't move your hand, I'm not letting you in," he said.

Slowly, I pulled my hand away, and I heard Taariq say

something under his breath before moving the chain and opening the door.

"Lauren? Why are you here?"

"I needed to see you. We need to talk."

"About what?"

"You know about what..."

"I'm afraid I don't, sister."

I wanted to smack the smug smile off of his face, but he held the key to the answers I so desperately needed. I stepped inside without waiting for an invitation.

The apartment gave me nothing.

No photographs on the walls, no mail on the counter, no coffee cup left out by habit. Whatever sense of a person usually leaked into the spaces they lived in, Taariq had either never let it happen or had already cleaned it up. The furniture was fine but forgettable; the kind that didn't suggest taste so much as a decision not to have any. Even the light felt neutral, coming in flat through blinds cracked just enough to see by but not enough to see much.

Boxes were stacked along the walls, some open, some sealed and labeled; straight up organized chaos. He hadn't volunteered a story, but I was already creating one in my head.

"Going somewhere?"

He spun around and saw the evidence that were the boxes, and turned back to me with sweat already forming on his brow.

"I'm actually just redecorating, that's all."

I looked around the room slowly and then back at him, letting him know without saying a word that I was not buying a single syllable of that.

"Taariq, don't you think you at least owe me a discussion? I was with your brother for years. Don't you think we should sit down and talk, even just about him?"

Taariq studied me for a long moment, something moving

behind his eyes that he was working hard to keep off his face. Then his shoulders dropped just slightly, barely enough to notice, and the smug smile softened into something harder to read.

"Would you like some water?" he said calmly, already moving toward the kitchen.

"Actually, I'm okay," I replied, my gaze snagging on the one thing in the room that didn't match: a photograph sitting loose on top of an open box, like it hadn't been packed so much as displaced. Brendan, Taariq, and Ms. Pat, sometime in the early eighties. Brendan couldn't have been more than nine or ten, squinting into the camera with both front teeth missing, Ms. Pat's arm wrapped around him from behind. Taariq stood just slightly apart from them, already practicing something.

I picked it up without asking.

There was a whole version of Brendan in that photo I would never get to ask about. A childhood I had heard pieces of but never held. I had loved him for years and this picture was proof of how much of him existed before me, outside of me, in rooms I was never in and moments nobody thought to save for me.

I set it back down gently.

We sat on the couch and looked at each other until I broke the silence.

"Taariq, I just need to know what happened, that's all. I'm not looking to put you in jail if you had something to do with this. I just need to know for my sake."

"Sister, I can't tell you something I don't know."

"Please," I begged, looking into his eyes. "Anything you can tell me would be helpful."

Taariq dropped his head and then looked away from me.

"You seem like a good man, and it *was* eighteen years ago; and if it wasn't your fault, I'll understand."

I did have every intention of turning the killer's name into the police, regardless of what I promised Taariq.

"I'm sorry," he started. "I'm going to have to ask you to leave."

I couldn't believe my ears. I had gotten *this* close to getting some answers, and I could see Taariq breaking down. Now he was kicking me out. I needed to work some magic, and I needed to work it *now.*

"When I was nine years old, I was awakened from my sleep by a phone call from the Atlanta Police Department telling my father that life, as we knew it, was over; my mother was dead. And ever since then, my heart has stopped when the phone rings at night. Then, eighteen years later, I got a phone call from the same police department telling me my boyfriend, the man I loved more than anything, was dead. Do you have any idea what that feels like? I just want some answers. I want to live my life Taariq," I said, allowing a tear to fall.

He looked almost emotionless.

"I didn't ask for *any* of this; yet, I'm the one that has to deal with it all. I'm trying to move on, but until I have answers, I feel like I'm stuck in the same place - the same nine year old with the same insecurities and worries. I want to live!" I screamed.

"I just want to live!"

Taariq reached out and rubbed my back lightly as I continued with my impromptu speech.

"I'm not asking for you to understand where I'm coming from, because you can't; but I'm asking for you to see that I'm only trying to find out the truth about everything. But if you need me to leave, I will…" I said as I smoothed my jeans and wiped my tears.

Taariq pulled on my jean leg. I stumbled to the couch and looked at him.

"We just wanted our father, that's all!" Taariq screamed

with his head toward the ceiling. I sat back and watched as he poured his story out to me.

"When we left Jersey for Atlanta, mom and dad had separated and were taking a break; then some years later, after we were settled in our new life, they decided to give their marriage another try. You don't understand how much that meant to me and Brendan. All we wanted was to have the "Cosby Show" family. You know the mom, the dad, and the well-behaved kids," he smiled, not paying attention to me as I pressed record on the tape recorder I had in my purse.

"So, everything was going great. Mom and dad were finally back on track, and it looked like he was going to be permanently moving his things to Atlanta to live with us. But then *she* came along. For a second time, a woman with big hips, a pretty face and long hair, took our father away from our mom. He was sneaking out to bars with her, taking her on dates, and Brendan and I were listening every night when mom would go to bed and cry herself to sleep. We hated *her*," he said with anger in his voice. His eyes were fixed on something, but I couldn't tell what.

"I mean it was like she had some sort of hold on him mentally; he would do anything for her, but nothing for us. And it started to eat away at us. So one night, we randomly hit the streets looking for her. We had a plan to kill her, and we hoped that dad would find his way back into mom's bed and arms," Taariq said, dropping his head.

"We stole my dad's car and headed out into Bankhead looking for the home wrecker. When we found her, there was no turning back; she had to go."

I was trying to follow, but I didn't know who "she" was, so I interrupted.

"Who is she?" I said, knowing I needed to have all the questions answered before I could understand.

"Your mother," he said, looking at me.

I heard the words. I just couldn't find anywhere to put them.

"Excuse me? My mother was not having an affair with your father."

"Yeah…she was."

"This can't be true." I shook my head and looked around the room, as if the walls might offer something - a reason, a contradiction, anything.

Ignoring my comments, Taariq continued.

"So when she pulled us over for the stolen car, she told us to get home and she wouldn't file a police report. But the more we argued with her, the more she realized we weren't going anywhere, so she started calling my dad. I knew that if my dad knew we were with her, and that we killed her, he would put the puzzle together and definitely leave."

I listened with my eyes closed, trying to envision it all as it was happening. Part of me was still back at *your mother*, turning it over, pressing on it, waiting for it to fall apart. The other part of me was already running ahead, already dreading whatever came next.

"And it was you and your friend, or…"

"It was me and Brendan. Brendan and I were the only ones in the car."

The disbelief cracked first. Just enough to let everything else in.

I felt like I couldn't breathe, and like little pins were sticking me all over my body. Tears slowly fell as I realized what Taariq was telling me. But before I could sort it all out, Taariq continued.

"I pulled out my dad's gun and told her I was going to shoot her. But then I got scared. I couldn't do it. I couldn't just kill her like that. So, Brendan picked up the gun and fired. She lay on the ground shaking while we argued about what to do. We wanted her dead; but I never actually thought it would happen," Taariq said as tears stung his eyes. He wiped them away and continued with his story.

I couldn't keep tears out of my eyes and air in my lungs. The grief hit me like something physical. And underneath it, quieter but just as real, something that felt like rage. At Taariq for saying it so plainly. At my mother for a secret she took with her. At Brendan - *Brendan* - for a thing I had loved him through without ever knowing I was doing it.

I couldn't hold all three at once. So I just sat there and let them take turns.

Brendan had killed my mother.

"I knew she wasn't dead when we shot her because she was still moaning and crying, so I did the only thing I knew how to do. I ran her over with the car. I'm sorry! I'm sorry, sister!" he screamed as he came to terms with what he had done.

I stared at a stain on the carpet and tried to remember all the times Brendan had told me that hiring a P.I. was a bad idea, or that he thought I should just leave it alone. Now I know why. I couldn't think or see straight. All I heard was Taariq screaming.

My boyfriend killed my mother.

"And your dad…did he know anything?"

"He suspected things, which was why he left us and never came back. He said he couldn't stand the sight of us knowing that we had done something horrible," Taariq wailed.

"I didn't *really* think I would kill her, you know? But the next day when I woke up, it was all over the news, and I knew this was bigger than what either one of us could imagine."

"Did you know she had a husband and daughter to go home to? Did you know that you took that away from me and my father?" I screamed.

"With all due respect, sister…I was fifteen years old when this happened. Brendan was eleven. We were only thinking about our family. Your mother complicated *our* happiness."

I walked to the window and placed my hands on the cool glass. I wanted to pinch myself and say this had all been one big, bad, dream; but it wasn't. *How was this happening? Why was this happening?*

"Why me? Why did Brendan date me and love me all this time if he had done this awful thing?" I cried, hoping Taariq would tell me it had been a cruel joke.

"He loved you, sister. He did. But he always told me he wanted to right the wrong of killing your mother. So he loved, protected, and showered you with affection. But every day he looked at you and saw you falling deeper in love, he realized he was seeing your mother; he had to pull away…"

"Is *that* why he killed himself? Because of all of this?" I said, waving my hands in the air.

What was Taariq telling me? That he and Brendan had killed my mom and Brendan had begun dating me out of pity turned to love?

"I really don't know what was going on with Brendan when he took his life; that's the truth. He was supporting me for a while, but when he sold the shop, the money stopped coming; eventually he stopped calling, writing, or sending anything. I found out about everything from mom, and I couldn't bring myself to come home for the funeral."

I could feel myself getting lightheaded, so I turned and grabbed my purse and clutched it tightly to my chest.

"Please, don't leave," Taariq said, lightly blocking the door. But I couldn't breathe and I needed to get out immediately.

"Please forgive me," Taariq said, dropping to his knees and wrapping his arms around me. I could feel his sobs getting heavier and heavier; and soon, we were both crying loudly. I howled at the thought of all the years I had invested in a man that had committed the ultimate betrayal –killing my mother.

"I've got to go," I said, pushing Taariq off me and opening the door. I darted down the hallway, turning only when I reached the elevator.

Taariq dropped his head as I stepped onto the elevator.

I listened as he screamed, "I'm sorry!"

––––––––

WHEN I WOKE up the next morning, I didn't feel better. I just felt done.

Done crying, done replaying it, done waiting for the version of events that made more sense. There wasn't one. My mother had kept a secret that rewrote everything I thought I knew about her life, and the man I had loved had carried the reason for her death in his chest every single day he looked at me. That was the truth. It wasn't going to get softer with more sleep.

I lay there for a few minutes staring at the ceiling, taking inventory of what I had left. My heart. My tribe. My name. My own reflection, which at least belonged to me and no one else's story.

I got up.

My plane didn't leave until four, so I called Troy Gaines and set up an early afternoon brunch. I didn't have answers yet, and I wasn't sure I ever would, but I was done letting other people's secrets decide what I did with my day.

I walked over to the hotel window in my bare feet and pulled the curtain back. The city was already moving below me, unhurried and indifferent, just like cities are in the morning. It was going about its business without any knowledge of, or interest in, the week I had just survived. I stood there for a moment just breathing it in.

Everyone I had ever loved had lived their life in secret. Quietly. Carefully. Behind closed doors and sealed boxes and unsent confessions. I had spent years loving people who were protecting me from the truth, and what it had cost me was a grief I hadn't even known to prepare for.

I was done living like that. Whatever came next, I wanted it loud. I wanted it mine.

I was just settling into that thought when my eyes drifted upward and landed on a sign across the street, glowing soft and pink against the morning light. A beauty salon, already open, already busy, the silhouette of a woman in a chair visible through the wide front window. I stared at it for a moment and then laughed quietly to myself, the first real laugh I had managed in days. If that was not the universe being obvious about something, I did not know what was.

I grabbed my phone off the nightstand and looked up the number.

"Something short," I told the woman who answered. "Like Halle Berry or something."

"Are you sure?" the lady asked.

Not about a single thing in my life. "Positive," I said.

When I walked in twenty minutes later, the salon was already in full session. The smell hit me first — that specific mix of heat and grease and something faintly sweet underneath, the smell that had meant Saturday mornings and patient hands and being still long enough to be taken care of for as long as I could remember. A woman under the dryer had her eyes closed and her head moving just slightly to whatever was playing through the speakers. Two stylists were talking across their clients the way stylists do... not ignoring them, just comfortable, deep in the shorthand of women who have shared the same floor for years.

Nobody looked up when I walked in. Nobody needed to. I was already accounted for.

My stylist's name was on a laminated card at her station — *Neese* — and she had the kind of presence that settled the room around her without trying. She ran her fingers through my hair once, assessed it and said, "Okay, sis. I see you. What are we doing today?"

I told her. Short. Clean. Done with the weight of it.

She didn't ask why. Didn't tilt her head and search my face for a story. Just nodded once like she'd heard everything she needed to and reached for her shears. There is a particular gift in a stylist who can read what a woman actually needs when she sits down in that chair; who knows the difference between the one who needs to talk it all out and the one who just needs to be handled with care and left to breathe. Neese knew. She kept things easy, laughed softly at something her neighbor said, handed me a water without me asking, and went to work.

I watched in the mirror as the length came off in sections. With every pass I felt something release; not healed, not resolved, but lighter. Like I was setting down weight I had been carrying on behalf of people who were never going to carry it themselves. My mother's secret. Brendan's guilt. Years of being loved by someone who was also, quietly, every single day, trying to repay a debt I didn't know existed.

I let it fall to the floor with everything else.

When Neese turned me to face the mirror full-on, I went still.

It was tapered and clean, close at the sides, exactly what I'd asked for — but somehow it was more than that. I looked like a woman who had arrived at a decision. I looked like someone who had stopped apologizing for taking up space.

"It looks fabulous on you," Neese said, standing beside me and adjusting one small piece near my temple; that last unhurried touch at the end, the one that says *I'm not finished caring about this until you walk out satisfied.*

I ran my hand slowly down the back of my neck and turned side to side.

The woman in the mirror was not who I had been before all of this. She was someone who had learned things she couldn't unlearn and gotten up anyway. Someone who had decided that if the people she loved most had spent their whole lives hiding, she was going to spend the rest of hers doing the opposite.

I tipped Neese more than the cut cost. She had done more than she would ever know.

I met Troy over lunch. He walked past me a couple of times without recognizing me.

"I'm over here!" I smiled sweetly.

"Wow! New look, huh?" he said, looking over my new cut.

"That really fits you!"

"Thanks."

"This lunch is going to be quick, but I just wanted to let you know that we really want to work something out to get you to Hot 99. If you're interested, I can fly you back out in a few weeks for a meeting."

"Do you need an air check tape or anything?"

"The big guys are taking my word on you. They know you sound great and have that '*umph*' factor."

"I never really thought about moving to New York."

"Well, start thinking about it now; because, if I can help it, we would like to have you on-air in less than two months."

Everything was happening faster than I expected.

"Do you have a card?" he asked me.

I took one out of my purse and passed it over to him.

"We'll be in touch," he said, embracing me and then racing out of the restaurant.

My eyes widened as I screamed. I couldn't contain it. *Was I really about to be on-air at the hottest radio station in the United States?* I ate my food and relaxed my legs and watched as people walked around. It amazed me how wonderful it felt not to worry about things.

I thought about Trey and the places I had told myself I wasn't going with him, and then I thought about Pop and the news I was going to have to break to him. I wondered if Kenya had handled her situation with Lorenzo, and whether or not Dee was happy with his new living arrangement. My mind wandered about Lina, the suicide counselor I had met in Piedmont Park. I questioned why I had been so scared to record the PSA or commercial she had told me about.

I walked back to the hotel and studied faces; a couple of times I could have sworn I was seeing Brendan. I would look at someone only to be disappointed when he got closer. I don't know why I was allowing my mind to play tricks on me, to think that he was actually going to be alive and walking toward me on a New York street. I hurried and got my things together and got ready to check out.

"This was dropped off for you," the hotel clerk said as she checked me out and swiped my credit card. She had slid an envelope, which was addressed to me, right in front of me.

"From who?"

"I'm not sure, ma'am. He was a thin guy with a thick black beard."

Taariq, I thought to myself.

I jumped in a cab and got myself settled before opening the unexpected letter. It was from Brendan.

Lauren,

I'm sorry. Let me just say this...if you are receiving this, then I know you've figured out my secret. I'm sorry. I don't think I can say that shit enough. I'm writing this letter and listening to you on the radio at the same time; your voice is so beautiful, baby. Tonight, I'm going to do something that I know you'll never forgive me for; but I can't take this anymore. I'm mailing this letter to my brother Terrence; I hope it finds its way to you. I was eleven years old when the incident with your mom happened. I was young, I was stupid, and I really just wanted my life back; instead, I took your mother's. I'm sorry. Damn, I'm sorry. If I could take it back, I would. But I can't. I've struggled with telling you the truth; but every time I saw you drop a tear because you missed your mom I knew I couldn't do it.

In a perfect world, though, you would have been my wife. But then I met Brandy, the girl I brought to the club at your birthday party, and she was a safe outlet. I never loved her the way I loved you...but I did love her. I didn't realize how in over my head I was until she told me she was pregnant. I wasn't ready for that. I have a son. His name is DeAndre Lewis and he should be about fourteen now. I never meant to be a bad father, but I didn't know anything about being a father at such a young age...and so I just left it to his mother, which was a mistake. I would have made a great dad. It's too late now, though. Also, I sold my shop to Mike. I'm sorry I didn't tell you. I needed to know that when I left this Earth, my shop would be taken care of.

Lauren, you have been there for me and I appreciate it and I love you. I'm sorry for the pain that you'll endure because of my actions, but know I never meant you any harm. The moment I laid eyes on you I knew I was through; but I had to remind myself that I was the reason for your pain; I couldn't live with myself knowing that. Please try to look out for my son and my mother if you can. I hope that one day you can forgive me and move on. Life is too short not to be happy...I promise I won't be mad. I really, really do love you, baby; but I can't do this thing called life anymore...it's much too painful and I want out.

Until we meet again...

Brendan Deondre Lewis

I held his letter tightly. The only thing I had to do was face reality back home.

chapter fourteen

Dear Diary,

I got on an earlier flight and am due back in Atlanta early. This will be perfect. No one will see it coming when I come home with my new hairdo! I feel like a weight has been lifted off me. I have the tape to hand over to Ralph, and I've decided I do want to press charges for the murder of my mother. I don't know what I'm going to do with all of the information I have, but I hope it answers some questions for Pop. The plane just landed, so I'm going to get off and catch a cab to the house!

Lauren Washington

———

"Hello?" I yelled throughout the house. I knew people were there because I saw Jasmine, Kenya, and Trey's cars in the driveway.

"Is anybody here?"

I set my bags down by the front door and headed toward the music. I watched as Trey, Pop, Jasmine, Kenya, and Dee all played Monopoly. Laughter rang throughout my house; I hadn't heard that in years.

"What time does Lauren's plane get in?" I heard Trey ask as Jasmine rolled the dice.

"I think it's at 6:30 or something," Pop said, clearing his throat.

I sprung around the corner and threw my hands in the air.

"I leave for a couple of days and y'all forget all about me!" I said loudly.

"Lauren!" Pop said, getting up and rushing toward me.

Kenya and Jasmine sat dumbfounded at the table at my new look. I wasn't sure if that meant they didn't like it, or that they liked it so much they were in shock. Trey and Dee were next to get up and hug me.

"I missed you, L-llllauren," Dee said, wrapping his arms around me.

I smiled; it felt good to be missed.

"I missed you too, you little knucklehead."

Trey and I looked at each other, trying to decide how to handle our embrace; finally I stepped forward and wrapped my arms around his neck tightly.

"You look stunning," he said, whispering in my ear.

"Thank you."

"Honey, that hairstyle is you!" Jasmine said, pushing Trey out of the way so she could get her hug in.

I held my best friend tightly and didn't want to let go. I wanted to grab her hand and tell her everything I had discovered, but I couldn't. Kenya walked toward me with a huge grin.

"I *told* you that hairstyles like that would be cute on you," she said, running her hands through my short hair.

I felt rejuvenated, and if I needed any type of booster, seeing my family and loved ones was all I desired.

"Pop, when you have a moment, we need to talk," I said as he passed by me.

I headed to my room and crashed on the bed. All around the room were reminders of my life with Brendan. Some people might have thought I was crazy and irrational, but if I was going to start with a clean slate, I needed it completely cleared. I stood up and began tossing everything that reminded me of Brendan into a box. I didn't stop until my room looked like I had just moved in.

"Perfect," I said out loud.

After searching and researching, I was able to find Lina's number. I placed a call to her telling her that I would be more than glad to record a PSA or commercial for her, free of charge. She was ecstatic. I was moving myself out of my own way and it felt great. I then called Ralph and told him I had a taped confession from Taariq. Just as I hung the phone up and sat back on the bed, my door opened and Pop was standing there like a deer in headlights.

"Hey, Sugar Baby…" Pop said cautiously.

"Pop, I found out some things I think you should know," I said, patting my bed.

My father sat with his shoulders raised.

"I found out who killed mom."

Pop's eyes grew large as he squeezed my hand tightly.

"You did?" he said, astonished.

"Yes."

"Who was it? Was it anyone from around here?"

"Pop…it was Brendan and his brother Terrence."

I could see the disbelief wash over his face quicker than a forest fire; and still, Pop was squeezing my hand tightly.

"W-what?"

"Terrence admitted it all to me yesterday," I said delicately while I stroked Pop's hand.

"W-why?" he said as a tear hit his cheek.

This was the part I had been dreading and I hoped that Pop didn't flip out when he heard the news of mom's affair.

"He claims that mom was having an...affair with their dad."

I didn't get the reaction I had hoped for as Pop asked me, "What was his name?"

"Darrin....Darrin Lewis," I said as I tried to recall his name.

"That was Brendan's father?!" Pop yelled, jumping up from the bed as if a thought popped into his mind.

"You knew about this, Pop? You knew mom was cheating on you?"

"Sugar Baby, your mom and I had our ups and downs, but we were young; I did a lot of stupid things that pushed her to have an affair with Darrin. I had no idea that Darrin was Brendan's father," Pop said, rubbing his mustache as he paced my room.

"So, the domestic abuse reports..." I said, trailing off.

"Were from her relationship with Darrin; they had this passionate, abusive relationship that sometimes got out of hand."

"And you were okay with your wife being with another man who beat her?"

"Of course not, Sugar Baby; but there was only so much that I could do to make your mother see that enough was enough. I also knew that neither one of us was going to say goodbye to each other. We were each other's everything. We were just young and confused, and we thought life would be here for us forever," Pop said, stopping to shake his head.

"I had your mother's partner pull the domestic abuse reports because I didn't want any of this to ever get back to you and make you think differently about your mother. She was a good woman; but we were young and dumb…Did he say why?"

"They wanted their mother and father back together, and killing mom seemed to be the only way to do that," I said.

Pop shook his head. "Umph! I just can't believe this. How are you?" he said.

"I'm fine. Well…I'm surprised and hurt, of course; but my mind is clear, and I'm ready to live life," I smiled. This time, though, I wasn't forcing it.

Pop and I joined hands and walked down the stairs toward the rest of the party. Someone had ordered pizzas and the Monopoly game was getting intense.

"I bought Boardwalk, pay up!" I heard Dee laugh as Jasmine forked over her play money.

I took a seat and watched them. When the game ended, everyone broke for something to eat.

"Do you want me to fix you something?" Trey asked, pointing to the paper plate.

"I'm okay," I smiled.

Kenya plopped down next to me and laid her head on my shoulder. Without a word from her, I could sense she had made the right decision for herself.

"I decided to stay with Lorenzo," she said, wincing as she tried to gauge my response.

"Okay," I said, waiting to hear more.

"After I explained my side of things, he understood where I was coming from and we're going to work on things," she said, smiling widely.

"Well, as long as you take it slow. Isn't that what y'all told me?"

Kenya giggled and covered her mouth.

"I'm not moving in with him, and I gave the car back. I don't want to become *that* chick; you know the one who is so dependent on a man that she can't function or deal without him," she said quickly.

Of course I knew that chick; she used to be deeply embedded in my soul.

"You're my girl, so whatever you do...I've got your back," I said, reaching over and hugging her tightly.

I was sure Kenya had expected me to blow up about her decision, but this was *her* life and like Brendan said, *"Life's too short not to be happy."* If Kenya thought her relationship with Lorenzo was worth working out, I backed her 110%.

Everyone joined around the glass dining room table and stuffed their faces with pepperoni and cheese pizza. Trey took a seat next to me on the couch and smiled.

"What?"

"Nothing, I just really like that cut on you."

"Well, I'm glad you do."

"I was thinking...I know you said that we're only friends, but I would like to ask you out on a date, *strictly* as friends," he said, winking his eye.

I had had the time to think over the Trey situation and I knew the moves I was going to make with it.

"Yeah okay...but only if you let me pick the place."

"Cool, you name it," he grinned.

"Jamaica."

Trey scooted closer and draped his arm over my shoulder.

"Then Jamaica it is, Mon!"

I stared into his eyes and allowed myself, for once, to acknowledge how I truly felt about him. He was everything that I was looking for. I appreciated that. I had allowed myself to think that there was some sort of flaw in my personality because I had thought about Trey in *that* way; but in hindsight, there wasn't. Life was moving on, and I had no choice but to move with it. I just wondered if Trey was game for the changes.

"How do you feel about New York?"

chair and stretched my arms, with the phone cradled in my shoulder.

Shawntae. Trey's daughter. She was seven years old and had her father's same easy smile and his same habit of tilting her head to one side when she was thinking hard about something. Trey had been awarded full custody, and he made it clear that their relationship and time was sacred. I had noticed early on, everything else adjusted around her. Plans got rearranged. Phones got put down. She was the exception to every rule he had about his time; watching that told me more about who Trey really was than anything he had ever said about himself. She had taken to me slowly and carefully, like she was smart enough to know that not everyone who shows up in a parent's life is worth attaching themselves to. But somewhere over the past few months, without either of us making a big deal of it, we had found our footing with each other. Hearing her name on the other end of a conversation still caught me a little off guard sometimes, in the best possible way.

My relationship with Trey, after I returned from New York, was a strange one. I was stuck between trying to figure out how to evolve from his friend to his woman, and of course, the drama surrounding that. Jasmine still didn't agree with our relationship, but Kenya told me to go for it. Pop was thrilled that I was moving on.

We did take that trip to Jamaica, and let's just say, that erased all of my worries. I had felt Trey's warm hands all over my body and it felt great; but I knew it was more to us than that. When I cried, the first person I called was Trey; when I was confused I called Trey. I had slowed myself down enough to where I knew relationships were more than giving and more giving. There had to be some sort of reciprocation in order for everyone to feel appreciated; with Trey I always did.

So, four months after I moved to New York, I bought a pretty little brownstone, and Trey and Shawntae moved up here. It never, once, crossed my mind that I was moving too fast because I was following my heart, this time, and not my fears.

In a lot of ways, I'm grateful to Brendan for what he did.

I went on a gut-wrenching, eye-opening, and at times, hurtful experience; but I made it out with the best prize of all – a renewed sense of my self-worth. I never thought I would get to a place, in my life, where I felt comfortable enough to appreciate anyone else like I had Brendan; but it's true what they say, *You never forget, but you grow to adapt.* I'll never forget Brendan, or the great times we shared together, but my past is behind me; I can't change it. The future, however, is still within arm's reach.

Ralph had taken the tape to the police and by the time they had surrounded Taariq's building and job, he was long gone. I figured that he would skip town; so it was no surprise to me.

Dee is doing great and about to start the ninth grade and I can't believe it. *Boy how time flies when you're living life, huh?*

Just as I started thinking about the bright future Dee had ahead of him, my producer knocked on the window to tell me it was air time.

"Hey, what it do y'all? It's yah girl Georgia Peach, and I'm going to be holding you down all the way until 4:00 with the best in Hip-Hop and R&B."

I took a couple of requests and phone calls and then went back on-air.

"So, my question of the day is this: "What do you do when an ex just won't leave you alone?" I'm going to open up my HOT lines right now!" I said, pointing to the producer who pressed a button and cued me to speak.

"Caller, wassup. What's your name?" I said, leaning back.

"This is Lorraine, and I say if a cat won't leave me alone I'll just change my number!"

I laughed into the microphone with Lorraine, "Man, that's ruthless!"

After a couple of callers, my producer signaled that this was the last call for the segment.

"A'ight, caller what's your name?"

"My name is Travon, and I know you guys are asking about exes and whatnot, but I want to take this time to ask *you* a question, Georgia Peach."

I swallowed a heavy lump as I wondered what the hell Trey was doing on my airwaves.

"Go ahead, boo."

"Right now, there should be about seven dozen daisies being ushered into the studio," he said as I turned and looked at some of the interns carrying the bundles and placing them on a table next to me.

"Okay…." I said, getting excited.

"I've never really met anyone like you, Lauren…I mean Georgia Peach; I wanted to know if you would do me the honor of being my wife," he said as his voice cracked.

By this time, everyone in the station was in the control room waiting on my answer.

I couldn't speak, though and my mind – briefly – flashed flashed back to Brendan and the expectations I had for that relationship. I was in a totally different place, and in less than one year, I was fully ready to move on.

"Yes! Yes!" I squealed as one of the interns, Josh, walked up with a black velvet box and opened it up.

It was the ring that I had dreamed of and it was all mine.

"It's Hot 99; we got to go to a break!" I said, rushing to pick up the phone as the producer went to break.

"Are you serious?" I said, admiring the ring on my finger.

"As a heart attack."

I had never felt so fully accepted and wanted by anyone, other than my father and mother, as I felt from Trey. Although we both knew a wedding was far away, our commitment to each other was sign enough for me that happiness was back in my life; and in my case, it's only getting better. Neither my pain, nor my story, will ever be over; but for now, I'm content with moving on.

I guess this is what happens after the three dots in the statement "Life goes on…"

epilogue

I kept every diary I ever wrote.

Not because they captured the best years of my life.

But because they proved something I didn't understand back then.

I survived.

I slowed my car and parked, looking up at the street sign for Kori Washington Way. I sat there for a moment with the engine idling, just looking at it, taking it in.

Kori Washington Way.

My mother's name had been Kori Bordeaux-Washington. She had been gone long enough now that some days the sound of her name felt like something I had to reach for, something stored carefully in a place I didn't visit too casually. But then it would show up somewhere unexpected — it always did — and the reaching would stop being necessary because there it was. Right in front of me. Pressed into a street sign in the neighborhood where so much of my story had unfolded.

And then there was Jasmine's daughter, Kori.

Whether she knew the full weight of what she was passing forward, or whether she had simply loved the name, the result was the same. My mother's name was going to belong to the next generation. It was going to belong to the daughter of one of the women who had held me together when I had nothing left to hold myself with.

I turned the engine off and sat in the quiet.

It was eerily quiet today. Unlike any other day on this street, there was nothing moving, no children, no music drifting from open windows, no distant conversation. Just stillness and a street sign and a name that had followed me through more chapters of my life than I had ever planned for it to.

I thought about what it means when a name refuses to die. When it keeps showing up. When it attaches itself to people and places and moments that matter, as if it is trying to tell you something about continuity, about the invisible thread that runs beneath the surface of a life connecting everything you thought was separate.

My mother would have loved Jasmine's daughter. She would have loved that her name was going to be spoken in a whole new voice, by a whole new person, in a whole new life still being written.

I smiled at the sign one more time before I got out of the car.

I glanced around at how much had changed, and how much had stayed the same. It wasn't the same place where I had grown up; but it still smelled and felt like home. Some of the houses had been renovated. Others were gone. A few stood exactly as they had when I was a little girl.

I finally stepped out of the car after sitting in silence for a while.

The familiar Atlanta heat hit me square in the face; like an unwelcome, but loving reminder of where I was. Kids laughed somewhere down the street as a breeze moved through the trees.

I was home.

I was with my mom.

I closed my eyes and exhaled, remembering the times we drove down this same street blasting music and laughing together. The times she held my hand while we walked to the corner store.

It was strange. I had never felt her presence here as strongly as I did that day. I hadn't expected the memories to come rushing back the way they did. But they did.

A police car whizzed past and I instinctively gripped the turquoise necklace Pop had restored for me. I hadn't touched it, or even come back to this street, in years.

I remembered being a little girl and how much that necklace meant to me.

"You know one day this is going to be yours, right?" Mom told me once while getting ready for a date night with Pop.

I wished I could hug that little girl. The one staring at her mother wide-eyed and excited for a future she didn't know would break her heart.

Now the necklace was mine. And I was the one wearing it.

I wished I had known then how little time we would have. I wished that "one day" had been so far away that we could both laugh about it.

But here I was getting older. And she never did.

For so long I believed my life had been defined by loss. My mother's murder. Brendan's death. The truth about everything that had happened in between.

But standing there that day, I realized that wasn't the whole story.

A little girl with sandy brown hair ran past me with a jump rope, laughing the biggest laugh I had ever heard.

"Scuse me!" she shouted.

For a moment she reminded me of myself.

Music blasted from a passing car. The smell of barbecue drifted through the air. An older couple stood on the corner laughing together.

That's when it hit me. Life had kept moving. And somehow, so had I.

I had lost a lot. I had grieved harder than I ever thought I could. But so much had survived.

My father's love. My friendships. My voice.

My career. My ability to love.

And a strength I didn't even know I had. My mother's story didn't end with tragedy. Neither did Brendan's.

Their bodies might have been laid to rest, but their lives continued through the people they left behind. Through the people who were survived by their love.

When someone dies, obituaries say they are survived by their family. But I realized something standing on that street. Being survived by someone doesn't mean you were left behind. It means your influence lives on. Your love continues. Your story is carried forward.

I looked up at the street sign again and smiled softly.

"I hope I'm making you proud, Ma."

For years, I thought my story began the night my mother died. But I was wrong. My story began the moment I decided to keep living. Some people leave this world quietly.

Others leave pieces of themselves behind in the people who loved them. In their own ways, my mother and Brendan both left strength.

They left courage.

They left someone who refused to disappear.

And in the end, that may be the greatest legacy anyone can have. To be survived by.

about the author

Ebonee Monique has always believed in the power of a good story.

A Tampa, Florida native, and proud alumna of Florida A&M University, Ebonee began writing at an early age, drawn to stories that explored love, ambition, friendship, and the complicated choices that shape our lives. Inspired by literary greats such as the late BeBe Moore Campbell, and guided by the mentorship of Bestselling Author Sheneska Jackson, Ebonee Monique developed a voice that speaks honestly about the highs, lows, and lessons of life.

Through her writing, she invites readers into worlds that feel familiar, emotional, and deeply human. Her stories celebrate resilience, growth, and the moments that define who we become.

Ebonee Monique lives in Atlanta with her family.

Visit her online at **www.EboneeMonique.com**

www.RoanokeAndKin.com